BABY, BABY

To my mother, a woman of humour and common sense,
and with love and thanks to Edmund, Ben, James & Nicky

Baby, Baby

Mari Howard

Wendy,
Enjoy!
all best & love
from
Mari H.

"It's the great ACW
Reading Challenge,
2017!"

HODGE PUBLISHING

I look forward to the
Dagger's Curse!"

Published by Hodge Publishing,
10 Bainton Road, Oxford, OX2 7AF

ISBN 978-0-9564769-0-6

Design and typesetting: Reading Type
Cover design: Kim Vousden

ACKNOWLEDGMENTS

No writer is an island: writing although a solitary occupation draws on many human resources. I owe thanks to the following people:

At the very beginning, to Dr Beth Knight for directing me to read Ian Wilmut, Keith Campbell and Colin Tudge: *The Second Creation* (Headline, 2000) to get my head around cell science. And then enormous thanks to Dr David Shotton, Dr Chris Graham, and Dr Bas Hassan, of Oxford University Department of Zoology, for showing me around and talking to me about their work. To the staff of the John Radcliffe Hospital, Oxford, Fertility Unit, for showing me around and explaining what goes on there.

To various friends who read the manuscript at different stages, especially Penny Silva who read and commented on early drafts, and Tommie Smith Dunavent who thoroughly supported the enterprise. To Dr Liz Williams for advice on medical details, the loan of textbooks of the time (especially that heavy volume, *Nelson's Paediatrics*) and also supplying and sharing the necessary retail therapy breaks. To Professor Marsha Fowler for sharing extensively both her knowledge of Presbyterianism, from growing up in a Presbyterian family and as a minister, and of medical ethics. And Dr Lianne Davis for looking over and clarifying the Hox genes references. Any remaining scientific errors overlooked are my own.

To Anne Borrowdale, life coach/literary consultant/editor, for all her work reading and advising as a longer manuscript was thoroughly weeded and tweaked. And to Fay Sampson who read professionally and commented on the first 'final draft', especially for pointing out an error of emphasis, which means that now this story is told far better.

And to everyone who has worked on typesetting, copy editing, listening to ideas, computer support, believing I was not wasting my time and theirs, and in many other ways been hugely supportive.

All characters are fictional, as is the 'Northumberland Market Town' location of the Manse and First Truly Reformed church with attached school, which are not based on any church or school. The Drey Clinic is likewise imaginary. Uncle Euan and his practice in Hexham have no factual counterparts. I chose to base Jenny in Clare College because it's small college, centrally placed, and has a beautiful garden.

ABOUT THE AUTHOR

Mari Howard is a writer, painter and sometimes a poet, with a lifelong interest in the natural world. She studied in the North East and now lives in Oxford.

Cambridge

'Here's looking at you, babe!'

A folded piece of A4, a lecture handout from four years ago, flutters to the floor. And I, leaning down to retrieve it, am overtaken by all the gnawing regret of an old love affair I'd intended Cambridge would help me forget.

The cartoon occupies the bottom third of the page. It's drawn in ball pen, and it's ridiculous: under a dinner table, a pair of bony male knees (below a kilt), equipped with human eyes, regard a pair of shapely female legs, ending in elegant feet in high heeled shoes. Max always liked to do daft things, even as he was also absorbing the scientific information. I can see it now: him passing me the drawing while maintaining that serious expression and looking straight ahead at the slide the lecturer had on the screen.

The lecture, early January 1984, was by one of my father's contacts from Caltech. It was held in London, and I took Max as my guest.

The subject was *Hox* genes, a family of 'super genes', each member of which recruits its own unique set of 'worker' genes. These Hox master switches, thrown at their appropriate points during development, help sculpt the complex shapes of a mature animal from a simple ball of cells. The lecturer was talking about Pax-6—the 'super gene' that coordinates the making of an eye—and an experiment where the mouse version of Pax-6 was artificially inserted into a fruit fly. Remarkably, extra eyes are produced all over the fruit fly, on its body, wings and antennae, and these are not mouse eyes, but compound insect eyes; the mouse Pax-6 had hijacked the fruit fly's own worker genes. I've since seen pictures. I've seen the real thing.

And now, I've just finished my final exams and I'm clearing up my undergraduate textbooks and stuffing two weeks' dirty washing into a bag for the launderette, having a peaceful, relaxing day—until I see that reminder.

Disturbed by the strength of my reaction, breathlessness, heart thumping, anger rising, I can't stay here. Grabbing what books I've sorted, and the washing, I set out. Taking with me Dad's present for my twenty-first last year, a Sony CCD-V90 camcorder. Will try to capture Cambridge, like sunshine in a bottle!

At the market, my eye to the viewfinder, is that Daze? My stepsister? Browsing the market stalls? Small and wiry, so unlike me and Hat, great galloping blondes! Daze should be thousands of miles away in Colombia! Why's she here? Lowering the camera, moving closer, I tap her on the shoulder.

'Hey—Daisy! You're back: was it amazing? Not here just to visit me, are you?'

'Four-Eyes—gosh, yeah I was gonna come by your place later ...'

'Nearly gone already,' I say, ignoring her use of my insulting school nickname, indicating my bag, and noticing something new about Daze. An aggressive, Celtic-style, red and gold dragon undulates over the bump under her black T-shirt. Her straight, black, well-worn jeans must be fastened under that with a whopping great pin. 'Undergraduate stuff,' I say anyway, 'for sale to the next generation. So, was Colombia—'

She smiles her distinct, crooked smile. 'Yeah, it was. Gold Museum: you should see it. Ancient, weird, amazing stuff.' I'm amazed by her belly. 'So what?' Daze says.

'You're preggers: when did that happen?'

Daze glances downwards. 'So I am,' she says, like she'd never noticed the bulge before.

'And?' I say. I can't simply rudely ask, *Who's the father?* Or even, *Are you in a relationship?*

Daze tries to move on.

I reach for her: a person can't just get pregnant and have a baby without telling their family anything.

'Hang on,' I say, hand on her shoulder. 'Nobody knew did they? At home?'

'Jen, you look tired.' Daisy picks my hand off herself. 'Go and sleep off your exams. And when do you stop being the big sister to everyone?' She turns away, picks up an orange.

'I just ...' I say, standing between her and the stall.

'Just? Just nothing: my body, my baby, huh?' Her fingers pump the orange like she wants to squeeze it then and there.

'Odd you didn't tell anyone and don't want to talk about it.'

Her eyes blaze: 'Odd that you should care so much.'

And stressed, sleep-deprived, and this morning hung-over, after Finals, besides being upset by that concrete reminder of Max, I go further. She's really riled me. 'Daze, you are being mysterious, you know. You've been working at a fertility clinic. Now you're pregnant.'

'Give it a rest, Jen,' she says, flinging the orange back onto the pile on the fruit stall. 'I was going to ask you to film the birth but ...'

'I don't mean to imply anything. I'm just concerned for you.'

'No need, I've got my own friends. Even discovered a long lost cousin out there. Lost when Mum ran off. She didn't just deprive me of a mum, she took away a whole half of my family!'

'So Daze, he's not—'

'Jen, did I say a male cousin?'

'Good, okay: not that wise for cousins.' She gives me a look: I deserve it. 'Daze, come over if you like, we'll have a coffee—or a herbal tea—or something?'

'You're such a lady bountiful,' she says. 'Like Mum. Like *your* mum.'

So then, I totally lose it: 'Mum took you in and looked after you and brought you up! Is that the thanks she gets?' Both of us forget about the shoppers and the browsers at the stripy-awninged stalls as I shout, 'The thanks I get for being a sister to the new girl on the block?'

'You fucking loved doing it, didn't you?' Daze yells. 'You fucking enjoyed doing your caring act.'

It's not a caring act: it's genuine. But Daze is one of the few people I know who, when you try to be nice to her, bites your head off.

And now, the promising day's turned chilly. I am so ashamed. I walk home with the words we'd flung at each other ringing in my ears. The fight was everything bad. Immature. Degrading. I'm a Cambridge graduate (almost), I'm just twenty-two, I'm about to launch myself on the scientific world and hope to do research, but I screamed like a fishwife at my stepsister.

*

Later, I'm eating supper alone—tinned tomato soup, housemates both out—when my father turns up.

'Jenny,' he grins when I open the front door, 'last days in Cambridge? But you'll be back, won't you? Can I take you to the best restaurant this side of the border?'

'Which border?' I ask.

'Any border. County boundary, anyway.'

'I've just downed most of a tin of cream of tomato.'

'Aw, baby, and alone? I've brought you something. Very exciting. Bring a friend.' And he hands me tickets for his latest venture: an academic forum, *Towards a Baby for Every Infertile Couple?*

'Tomorrow?'

'Yeah—you busy?'

'Not really ...'

'Come then—things to learn, people to meet.'

'Dad, did you know Daze is pregnant?'

He hardly misses a beat. 'Well I'll be—' he says. 'Daisy.' Laughing, he adds, 'Does it suit her?'

'Be serious. I don't think Des or Mum know. Did she—did she have anyone? In Colombia?'

'She ran around with one of the technicians a bit: he was keen on animal rights. English. Everyone else there is American or local.'

'So maybe?'

Dad shrugs. 'Maybe,' he says.

Maybe sharing a house with a genetic researcher is not the wisest move I've made. But I needed short-term accommodation. And there was the advert on the med student bulletin board: *House share, large airy room available March–September. Contact Wil du Plessis.*

Sometimes, I feel as much a refugee as Wil. South African politics drove Wil here: his skills as a researcher and teacher in the expanding biotech area are keeping him here. And back in Cambridge after four years, I am so relieved to be escaping First Truly Reformed Presbyterian, and family ties. Newcastle had no places for prospective GPs to take the necessary paediatric rotation.

But Wil turns out to be teaching Jenny Guthrie—with the big specs and strawberry blond hair! Do I or do I not want to make contact again? She's not only sweet, and amusing, she's a sharp inquisitive mind. She was a perfect foil for Dad's views on science, religion, and women. Jenny represents the evil which lurks within all three. Together we once attended a lecture on the newly discovered Hox genes.

Forget that: I'm wrestling with a reply to a letter from my Uncle Euan in Hexham, coffee and a cigarette as aids to this. The front door bangs and Wil appears, making appropriate remarks about the willing and conscious destruction of my cells.

I get up, stretching. 'Aye, and my Uncle Euan expects a good Christian guy to join him in his practice once I'm qualified. As my father says, "*if you havena' a Call then medicine's a grand second-best*".'

'How about this?' Wil slaps a flyer down on the kitchen table. The blurb describes a day forum on fertility, open to post-doc research students and others in the field, at the prestigious Drey Clinic. Medical Director Dr John Guthrie will speak about new developments in this rapidly expanding biotech area.

If I were to attend this day-long academic meeting, would Jenny be there?

Wil reaches into the fridge, and brings out two cans of lager. He pulls the ring on one and hands me the other.

'Guthrie's rumoured to be into cloning: in certain quarters, people are concerned. We—the academic geneticists and embryologists—should know more about what is being done on our doorstep. Even you generalists should.'

'I'm concerned we've an empty fridge tonight. Why's it always me who buys the provisions, man?'

'Family eldest: exaggerated sense of responsibility for others. Shall I buy the take-away?'

I chuck my empty ciggie pack at him, and tell him I have an older sister. He says, 'So introduce me sometime. And scratch that itch.'

'What itch?'

'Did you not tell me you used to date Miss Guthrie? I discern there's a remaining interest—or do I?'

How far does Jenny go along with her father? Do I want to meet her again? Last chance, before she graduates and moves on.

JENNY. SATURDAY 11 JUNE: THE DREY CLINIC, CAMBRIDGE

In my four years at University here, I've learned that impressive as I thought he was, my father—dynamic practitioner and researcher at a privately funded clinic—is regarded by the brotherhood of the academic community with a slightly jaundiced eye. Since Carter, American Presidents have been less keen on some kinds of scientific investigations. So after years across the pond, Dad returned to England, financed by some huge biotech organisation who appointed him Medical Director of their labs and attached clinic. Where? Down the road from where I was studying!

I'd not connected him with Daze until she mentioned her plans for after graduation. A few months admin working for my Dad. At a clinic in an out-of-the-way South American country where he's giving some of his time to an experimental programme. It really was weird: why'd she want to go there?

The Drey clinic has its own lecture theatre for conferences and symposiums, the auditorium—windowless, air-conditioned, fluorescently illuminated by concealed lights—slopes downwards to the usual long desk, podium and blackboard.

And it's filling up. Today, the university scientific establishment's jumped at the chance to view and critique Dad's private setup. Dad sent me three complimentary invites: I'm here with my housemates. Laura, who's writing a thesis on Immortality. And Maeve, a just-finished Nat Sci like me. Maeve's a real eye-opener. My first week in Cambridge, October, 1984, this Irish girl knocked on my door, smiling, 'I'm College Rep for the Christian Union and I'm here to invite you to our Freshers' Squash.'

'No, thank you. I'm not religious.'

A few weeks later, in lonely first-year mode, I went to M and S, to buy a nightshirt. Retail therapy. I learned it at Mum's knee when Dad left: it remains her, and my, medicine of choice.

There's Maeve by the racks of glam knickers!

'Sure it's for my bottom drawer, Jenny!' Nudging me and grinning. 'Sure you imagined being a believer would mean I wear white cotton cross-your-heart bras and full briefs? When the work gets me down I come away to add to my outrageous underwear collection. Wouldn't you feel better, wrestling with that complicated maths they dish us biologists, knowing underneath it all you're clad in red lace with hearts and bows?'

Well, how'd I know? Raised on the Bible, given to offering her work to God in prayer, Maeve's also generous, warm, and intelligent. Of course I didn't join the Christian Union. But I did join the college choir, and so did Maeve.

I kind of hope nobody will link me up with Dad, especially as, turning, I see that Wilhem du Plessis, a golden pin-up rugby-type post-doc in the genetics department (who has taught me a fair amount this past year) is moving crabwise down an already-crowded row, two or three behind us. Followed by a friend ...

Max Mullins. Heart stops. Have to look away. Don't want to know. Max dropped out of my world as suddenly as he'd entered it.

Can't not glance back again. Taking slow, deep breaths. The others don't notice, but I'm going hot and cold and sweaty. Max, here for the Forum? Or here as in, back in Cambridge?

Concentrate: *don't give in to the feelings.* My father's on the podium, introductions are over. He ruffles his notes, requests someone to pull the blinds, and switches on the overhead. I focus, deliberately, on the subject of the lecture. Try to immerse myself in the forward march of biological science.

'Pre-implantation Genetic Diagnosis' Dad says, 'is a logical consequence of IVF.' Yes, I think: and Max even toyed with the temptation to move into research because he believed so passionately in this. He mentioned PGD the very first day we met.

'IVF is becoming normal practice. Fertility clinics such as ours have been set up with the express purpose of combining clinical excellence in terms of pregnancy outcomes, with clinical excellence in terms of ongoing research.'

Dad's naturally into the now vocabulary—*excellence.*

'We are proud to announce that we are in the forefront of offering pre-implantation genetic diagnosis to our patients. Our scientific predecessors,'—Julian Huxley, J. B. S. Haldane, scientists I was raised by him to admire—'predicted PGD would come about in the second half of this century, and they were not wrong.'

As Dad speaks, slides of children affected with the diseases and deformities he mentions appear on the screen in rapid sequence. Thick scaly skin, twisted limbs, distorted features ... Making the tragedy of these diseases far more real. As he tells his audience that 'the key to the elimination of those diseases which we see in paediatric wards and clinics—and those other diseases—hidden silently, symptomlessly away within the genes of young apparently healthy children to appear in later life, lies in the development of PGD.'

So did Max finally defy or persuade his father, and find funding to re-train?

'Pre-implantation diagnosis—what does this phrase imply? In the natural course of events, a fertilised ovum tumbles downwards on its secret journey towards the safe, nurturing home—the womb—where it expects to spend the next forty weeks or thereabouts, growing into a human baby.' Dad has superb podium presence. He presents his stuff compellingly. His slides, the tone of his voice, the pace, all work together.

'In cases of infertility, we may now introduce the ovum and the sperm to one another ...' (*Introduce*. I know my Dad, he chooses his words, he speaks not of the *uterus*, but of the *safe, nurturing womb*, and although it's perfectly scientific and might have no double meaning, here we have an anthropomorphic interpretation for those who want to smile and even titter. The sperm and ovum are dating.) '... within the relative safety, but under the bright and penetrating lighting, of a laboratory. In a sterile environment. And in a suitable medium. But still we take care to honour that human conceptus—the fertilized ovum—and to replace it as gently as possible into the environment which best suits its needs, the body of its mother.'

Oh boy, Dad, don't you just understand crowd appeal!

Then, he switches modes. Confidently outspoken against the pro-life lobby, he argues, 'Why, then, should there be any constraints put on the necessary research? When we look at the costs in terms of finances, as well as in suffering, these are surely worth the setting-aside of concerns as to whether, at the blastocyst stage, a few cells bundled together should be granted human dignity.'

Max mayn't like that. And after all that sentiment about honouring the human conceptus. Replacing it gently into the body of its mother. Stuff which sounded almost like Mills and Boon. And, better not catch Maeve's eye.

There's a certainly a little ripple across the audience: Dad has touched some sensibilities even among academic researchers who'd you expect to share his views.

Has Max noticed me? If so, what's he thinking?

'You may feel the PGD process puts an unnecessary burden on the embryo. It is at this point in time a somewhat invasive process: but, a life-enhancing, life-affirming process.' Yeah, buzzwords. Is Dad really concerned about being life-enhancing, life-affirming: isn't it perhaps the power of the science that seduces him?

'And,' (as he begins drawing to a close), 'for all fertility doctors, PGD—and a related technique called aneuploidy screening—brings in a new and fertile class of patient—genetic disease carriers—and offers a new service to infertility patients who have failed with lesser therapies.'

Well, there we have it: an increased field of patients. Several murmurous exchanges take place behind conference papers. Though, has to be said, aneuploidy screening seems a great idea.

'One final word: I would predict a future in which every embryo produced in the course of IVF cycles will be tested—is that not the way of clinical excellence, of putting our patients' interests first?' Dad makes some additional remarks and concludes to a standing ovation. The vast majority here must be his supporters: at least in terms of attitudes. And Max? Is he amongst the predictable few who don't stand or clap?

I can't see where he's gone. My father's surrounded by hordes wanting to ask questions but he works his way through the crowd, shaking hands until he reaches me.

Where he introduces Maeve and Laura to a few people and dispatches them towards the food. While I'm swept up to have to lunch with his party. Find myself sparkling more than necessary, gulping too much Chardonnay with the buffet of salmon, quiche, mange-tout salad with a fromage frais dressing. Still surreptitiously running my eyes around the room: do I want to see Max or avoid him? I make rather unsteadily for the table—stiff white cloth, porcelain army of tiny white cups and saucers—where delicately boned girls are serving real coffee from wide-bottomed Pyrex jugs.

'Jenny?'

'Hi,' I say. This is it, then. 'You—came down for the conference?'

I should've walked away. I know immediately I sound inane, and that those quizzical grey eyes still captivate me.

He smiles. 'I'm back in Cambridge. Can I fetch you a coffee?'

'Please. "Back"?'

Max somehow corralling me, we carry our scalding coffee out onto the terrace, stand staring at the green Draylon lawns of the clinic and lab complex, all glistening in dazzling midsummer sun. There's even a staff tennis court: *puck-puck* of tennis balls, and white figures leap and run and yelp. I try to sip my coffee elegantly and stop the shaking of my insides.

'Yes. Back. And you?' Max smiles, clinking his cup back onto its saucer. 'Just finished Tripos part two?'

We are *being adults*, making brittle cocktail-party conversation over bone china. I can't do this. Turning away, 'I have to go,' I say.

'Jenny—' Max has me by my arm. Everyone else has returned to the lecture room: we're alone out here: *puck-puck*, tennis balls.

'Don't,' I say. 'I'm—with—' Max lets me go.

'I didn't want to scare you—I just—' He stops. Our eyes lock: but I can't read his expression: intense, but what else? 'Jenny—all that—it was me, not you ...'

'Thanks,' I say.

'Could we maybe—' Max shuffles his feet.

'What?'

'Have a coffee some time?' he says.

'We're having one now!' I retort. My legs are buckling, but my brain's re-activated.

Max looks wary. I'm sorry I tried to score off him. A bell tinkles. 'Seems we're needed for the afternoon programme,' he says.

Relieved, 'See you in there,' I say, and make for the Ladies'. The Men's turns out to be right next to it, and we bump into each other exiting the bathrooms. 'Sorry—oh sorry.'

'Sorry.' I swallow.

I kick myself for not walking away.

*

Of course, I've not found out why Max's here. I remember only too well the time he was in my life before.

December 1983, my college interview weekend. Raw from a West Cornwall comprehensive, I was so immature! Did I really let him pick me up, as I walked through the college gates, where he was locking up his bike?

'Hi, up for interview?' Our eyes met.

'Ever hopeful!'

'Subject?'

'Nat Sci.' He gave me a look. 'Okay, I can do it, you know!' Tottering a bit in my tight new heels.

'I'm not doubting you. Tough course though.'

'You?'

'I've been here a while: medicine.' Slight, soft regional accent: encouraging, seeing I'd arrived with my own West Cornwall voice intact. I lingered a moment.

'I'd hurry if I were you: groups to tour the University leading off already. You can leave your stuff at the Porters' Lodge.'

'Yes, thanks.'

A horde of interviewees swarmed towards us: I dodged around the edge of the group, stepped onto the cobbled edge of the paved path, and tumbled into the lavender hedge. The interviewees hurried, chattering, past. Wafted with newly-crushed essential oil, stared at and stepped over by twenty-odd bright eighteen year olds, how stupid can a person feel?

'Och, what happened to you?' Same guy: Scots accent. Dad carefully lost his while working in America.

I glanced past my grazed knee and saw the problem. Held up my bereft left shoe. Met eyes with that guy again: his grey, and mischievous. We laughed.

'I did the heel trick, didn't I? Okay, it's a classic. But they're new shoes! That shouldn't have sheared off!'

'Can you stand: you've not hurt yourself?'

'Only my dignity.' I brushed my behind, looking over my shoulder. 'My granny's word!' We laughed again. 'I'll have to find a shoe mender's.'

'If you're sure you're all right, and you've a spare pair of shoes, why don't I take you to find one and then we'll do the tour? I know all the places you'll need to see. Max Mullins—and you're?'

'Jenny Guthrie.' Okay: he seemed okay, laughed with me not at me. Nice looking: dark hair, slim, tall but not too tall. Love those eyes! 'Thanks.' We moved off, me having left my luggage at the Lodge and hurriedly changed into trainers, carrying my high heeled patent pumps.

'Jenny. If this college accepts you, you'll end up well placed. The labs are in Tennis Court Road, just around the corner.'

'And the shoe shop's—?'

'We'll find it as we go.'

Trinity Lane, Gonville & Caius, Kings Parade, Trumpington Street. The wind catching at my hair, blowing through my coat. 'Which branch of Nat Sci, Jenny?'

'Genetics? Embryos?'

'Perfect timing—I'm about to—I should be—writing an essay on human aneuploidies this evening.'

So Max was studying the very subject, growth and development and why it can go wrong, which had caught my imagination. For him, just a small corner of his training.

Time flew by: Max obviously knew a fair bit about genetics. Then, 'Diversion: shoe menders!'

We waited while they worked on my shoe. 'See here: never should've used that glue,' the shoe mender demonstrated gleefully. 'You brought the other one?'

Max grinned at me.

'Look, you've work to do, I shouldn't be keeping you here!'

'No—it's okay—I can manage, we haven't finished what I want you to see. And hear.'

So as dusk fell, and as we passed another college, 'Listen!'

Carols or something very like them seemed woven into the air. 'You like music? You have to experience this. After all, if you don't get in— well, you won't have heard the best choir in the world, will you?'

'How d'you know it's the best choir?'

'Cambridge Singers? They know they're the best.' Max, grinning, seized my hand and hauled me inside the chapel.

'This isn't still the tour?'

'What else?' Dimly lit, warmed by the light of a thousand candles, a tall Christmas tree with twinkling lights and an amazing choir. We lurked at the back: by now I was on such a high! Like, maybe they're human or maybe they're angels, just here for us? Did I believe in angels? No.

'Amazing. What Christmas is about.'

'Some of what it's about.'

And then, we let go hands: it wasn't the cinema, and I wasn't required to pay for it. Like guys at school who soon wanted to get something from you for anything they gave you: a snog, a fondle. Watch them play footie, or pound, sweating, around the athletics track. With Max, I'd had a serious discussion on embryology. I'd glimpsed so much already, I had to pass the interview!

'Are you hungry?'

'Now this is really not the tour, is it?'

'We all have to eat! Or don't you?'

'If you're certain …'

So had I picked him up, or had he asked me out? We ended up in a vegetarian eating place, neither scruffy café nor formal restaurant.

'Thinking about tomorrow?' Max asked over our pizza, like he could read my mind.

'About how it'll be if I don't get in.'

'When's the interview? You can come and find me—afterwards. We could—'

'Yes?'

'We'll see: we have a child with what appears to be Patau's on the ward just now.'

'Which means?'

'I can't tell you more than that she has certain dysmorphic features—you know the term?'

'Yes. I've read a bit. Don't most babies like that just not make it to birth? And with amniocentesis, shouldn't all—most—be, like, weeded out, today?'

'Jenny, a lot of people believe abortion, painless infanticide and euthanasia is justified in the case of severely disabled infants. They argue the lives of others—parents and carers—are ruined. As well as the suffering of the child itself. I'm not convinced by those philosophers … and I do see these children. Some worse than Serafina—than this one.'

Why did this fantastic guy have to sound like he was religious? Avoiding why, I quoted Dad, 'If we could see the genetic problem in the embryo, we could simply offer the parents IVF, and throw away the duds.'

'Yes—we could—if we were certain about them.'

'They're only embryos.'

'Human ones.'

'Okay: Serafina, the child you talked about. A worse one—what kind of worse?'

'You want to know? Maybe you've seen pictures. Skeletal deformities, thick scaly skin, maybe unable to communicate, with a desire to self-harm—yes.'

'And the embryos should be—'

'What I want, maybe, is to get into research on the genetics—the diagnosis—' Max shook his head as if clearing the thought away.

'So why don't you?'

Silence. Both of us stymied by developments.

'You finished?' Max asked. 'I'll get this.' Waving away my offer to pay my half.

Outside, 'It's cold: I'd better take you back, then? To college?'

'Yes—yes I'd better go ...'

After his initial confidence, he seemed more diffident, hesitant and quiet. Such a perfect afternoon: how frustrating to stumble over something difficult. 'You're not, like, a pro-lifer, are you?'

A dry laugh. 'My father's a big-shot minister!'

'Government? Oh my God ...'

A grin. 'No. Presbyterian. Extreme.'

'Like—church? Ouch.'

'Like church.'

Embarrassed, I tried to sound nonchalant. 'We live in a church: an ex-church. It was built as a Methodist chapel.'

'But you—?'

'No, not religious.'

'Medicine is respectable, you see. And Cambridge is good: the pursuit of excellence.'

'My mother's a doctor. General practice.' I wanted to maintain our links. So I didn't mention Dad. Strangely, Max didn't ask. I shoved my hands in my pockets and must've hunched over, because what he asked was, 'You're not cold? You want this?' Offering his scarf.

Gratefully, I took it: though it tickled my neck.

And we walked on in silence: I thought about his ironic comments on his studies here. We reached my staircase. 'It was nice of you to do this.'

'All part of the service,' Max bowed, quietly mocking his use of that phrase.

'And the pursuit of excellence?' I countered, matching his irony.

'You could add that,' he said, laughing.

Next day was my interview. Then I went to the children's ward, where Max loaned me someone's white coat and introduced me to the Patau's child, Serafina. Mosaic Patau's, a survivor now eighteen months old.

And I went home.

*

We phoned, we wrote. Were a Creator God and a scientific outlook incompatible? We had to argue for and against the existence, relevance, importance, of God. I pulled out some reading matter Dad had supplied, and realised my atheism was simply second-hand. Max did the same with his faith.

Dad arrived back from the States, announcing he'd be working in Cambridge too—or at least very near by. And gave us tickets to that exciting lecture in London: Hox Genes.

But although Max dreamed about genetic research, his family wanted him in general practice with an uncle. Mum's turn: part of the clinical course was a six-week GP placement, and experience in a rural practice in West Cornwall—my home—looked like a good contrast to Cambridge. Despite the evident rural poverty, past and present, Cornwall's seductively beautiful. And wild. As he worked with my mother, Max and me kind of slipped from being close friends to being much more.

*

It was late May, pink ragged robin, blue scabious and yellow trefoil flowering everywhere. The last week, on Max's afternoon off, we walked the family dog across the cliff tops to Land's End. I took stacks of photos. Then, pausing to sit amongst the heather, we silently shared a bar of chocolate. The sea was a misty indigo, gathering clouds touched the horizon. I didn't want the afternoon to end: soon we'd part, Max would be gone. First on a visit home, and then, back to Cambridge.

'Last square,' Max said. 'Open, Jenny ...'

He placed it in my mouth, and as we kissed, I let him gather me up and lay me on my back. I pointed out a tiny speck high above. 'Look, that's a lark: *The Lark Ascending*?'

We both knew that music.

Max leaned over me, blocking out the sky. Kissing my throat, my breasts, my belly. I lay trembling, hardly breathing, as the lark sang.

I undid my thin cheesecloth shirt so I could better feel his mouth on my skin. It was me who undid the top button of my jeans. Max who slid his hands inside like an expert, and me who thought, 'Hmm, the minister's son's done this before.'

And then without thought I flopped my thighs open as he explored me, I let my specs fall off, and probably made a stupid groaning sound: though when I felt how hard he was, I tensed up because, whatever, things were going further ... And at that point, a huge raindrop fell into my eye. Max rolled off me, cursed as I'd never heard him do, and said roughly, 'We can't do this.'

'Why?' Though part of me was relieved.

'It's wrong. You're eighteen, you're off to college.'

My world was fuzzy, I groped for my specs. And, as he rearranged his clothes, and straightened up, Max cursed again.

'What?' I said.

'Your glasses,' he said. Handing them over. 'Not as they were.'

'It's just an earpiece gone.'

'I'm sorry.'

'I can balance them.' Grabbing them from him. Calling the dog to heel.

Max marched ahead, kicking the heather. I marched behind, holding my jacket over my head as the rain slammed down, my camera swinging from its strap against my chest. It took maybe five minutes for Max to stop, wait for me, and take my by then icy-cold hand. 'I'm sorry.'

I said nothing. Max tucked his arm round me, and we marched on. 'Jenny: wrong time, wrong place. If we're soulmates, that's more important. Isn't it?'

'Soulmates? Do you have to be religious, for that?'

'What do you think?'

'Describes the feeling.'

The feeling I thought we shared: that we couldn't part.

And whether or not we have souls. Max hadn't made a lot of his religion while he stayed in Cornwall. Then after he left, he wrote the most awful, cold, distant, letter. *'Something's come up, I'm leaving Cambridge.'*

No Max when I arrived to start my studies?

I should've thought, *'This is your mother's clinical rotation student you've got here, Jenny, he's only here for six weeks' GP experience. You're going to mess up things for him as well as you.'*

I should've known religious people have a strange guilt about sex.

But that couldn't be the real reason.

Still hurts when I think about it.

I'm astonished by his appearance at Dad's Forum. Amazed he'd the audacity to walk up and casually suggest we had a coffee. Devastated I'm still reacting to his presence.

For me, the afternoon programme's all but destroyed.

'No guy's worth breaking your heart over, twice,' Laura wisely counsels. 'Didn't he drop you just before you arrived here? Isn't that the most heartless thing to do to somebody?'

'Did he apologise yet?' Maeve adds.

Laura's an example to follow, enjoying Cambridge while keeping the guys at arm's length. I develop a running mantra, pounding the early morning streets: *no guy's worth it.*

MAX

Phew! Walked right into her: pretended that was cool. What did she think, what did I really think?

Stupid, inane conversation we had.

Back come all the memories, and after them, back comes the old temptation, to go delving into the science of human imperfections, physical ones, mental ones, and their prevention. Work leading to what my father describes as having murder built into it. A conversation with Dad in which I dared broach the subject of developments in pre-implantation genetic diagnosis ended *that* ambition!

Mum was in the kitchen with two Down's syndrome kiddies she childminds. 'Max, we gonna make fairy cakes today!' they'd told me.

'When they're ready, can I have one?'

I went out into the hallway: Dad's study door opened a crack. As I entered, he was tossing a file into a drawer, his back turned. 'Would you all learn to knock first—the Congregation doesna' pay for a secretary in my home—' he snapped.

'Dad—d'you want to be left or can we share that dram you promised?'

'Max—come in, come in—how is Cambridge? What can I do for you—you had something to discuss?' Yes, a smile for me, his expensively educated medical student son. 'Sorry, I thought it was another twin tumult falling across my threshold. *Children are a gift from the Lord ...*' he quoted dry-humouredly, scratching his head.

Dad circumnavigated the desk and closed the door, very quietly. Took out glasses and golden Glenmorangie. We sat: he on his swivel chair beside the desk, me on the pink Draylon-covered loveseat he keeps for couples come for counselling. Sipping a dram with my father. Laddish stuff which gives me the heebie-jeebies: *beware Greeks bearing gifts*. 'Well, Max?' he said. 'How was your term?'

First I asked about his plans to expand the Christian school attached to First Truly Reformed. 'Indeed!' Dad glowed, rubbing his hands, then seizing the file he had just put away and thrusting it into my lap. 'Building plans. We'll need to be asking the Lord for funding. A large number of parents are very keen. I've been interviewing for a headmaster experienced with an older age group: d'you recall Colin Eccles?'

'Colin's applied? I thought he was happy at the Grammar?'

'The Lord's timing, Max.'

The phone interrupted us. His demeanour changed as he talked: someone's problem or tragedy took over. After that, Dad seemed to have forgotten about Colin.

'Max, what was it you came for?'

Referring to Mum's growing conviction that children with disabilities are not being catered for in the church, I appealed to his belief in God's love for his whole creation. 'Dad, I want to be where I can make a difference, reduce suffering—and the difference we medics can make is changing.'

'Yes, I believe you do, I believe it is,' he said dryly. 'You discerned God guiding you towards being a doctor; I hope you're no' going to change now?'

My father dislikes bad planning as much as he dislikes imperfections. He suspects any hint that his God's guidance can be in any way flawed. A change of heart is in his eyes merely a message from the human mind—a corrupt entity if ever there was. Every perfect gift arrives from the holy and unchanging God's perfect, inscrutable-to-the-fallen-human, mind. With God's perfect timing.

'Och, just listen: I see desperately sick or defective kiddies on the wards, their short lives filled with pain. I think of First Truly-type families for whom termination's not an option. Termination of pregnancy is vile. But, without it, we doctors must care for these infants destined for almost immediate death. We should also try to use science to prevent these terrible tragedies.'

Dad looked dubious.

'Listen,' I tried coaxing him, speaking as abstractedly as possible. 'Pre-implantation diagnosis—once we reach the clinical stage—would give IVF patients a safeguard against the most common genetic disorders. And guarantee genetic abnormalities are not transmitted into the next generation. Conditions like cystic fibrosis?'

Silently Dad surveyed the Oriental rug for answers. Its amazing regularity of pattern just might have a fault: I hunted one out, and drew his attention to the squashed pattern in one corner, 'D'you see there how that's not quite right? If a fetus were to have that—imperfect patterning—d'you know what it might do to the overall phenotype? D'you also realise the pre-natal tests we have at present increase the risk of miscarriage—they actually pose a threat to the possibly normally developing fetus?'

Dad's eyebrows drew together as he gazed into the future in that crystal tumbler, 'And would you not think—as your mother does—of those children as equal in the sight of God?' he asked. 'And there is the touchstone of ethics, is there not? There is taking science too far—'

'Can that be done?'

'Do you imagine when they split the atom—' Dad said.

Did he have to open up that classic? 'Do you not think that if the parents could choose—however they love the kids—they'd have chosen—do you not feel that—even given equality in the sight of God—it is preferable in this world for a child to be born as near a perfect image of Him as possible?'

My father held up his right hand, STOP-sign-style. 'I'll not hear more of this, James Maxwell—you're away down there having thoughts unworthy of you put in your head. A lassie, engaged in investigations tending to interfere with the Almighty's ordering of things, has bent your ear. God's image is marred by human sinfulness, not by disease or defects.'

'Disease and defects enter into the world as a consequence of sin. You taught me this.' I realized that I was crossing a line here: arguing with him around scripture, which he won't tolerate, seeing himself as the expert in the mind of God. So I hurriedly backed off. 'Dad—can we be a little less emotional? I am as compassionate as you—Jenny—'

A real slip there!

He seized upon it. 'Who is this, that you listen to her? A lassie has bent your ear and—'

'Och, Dad! Jenny's concerned as I am to relieve human suffering.' The look on his face was hard to read. Then, 'Humph,' my father responded. 'She doesna' ken the Lord, does she?'

And then he was just looking at me, silent. Waiting for more?

This looking can be very effective—I got the feeling of condemning myself by every extra word I said. My words bounced back into my own ears to make me reconsider. 'I—I'll leave you to think about it,' I said. 'It's maybe a lot to take in?'

'It is a lot to take in from you.'

I walked quietly to the door, opened it, and passed through: hoping I had made a dignified exit, leaving Dad to consider my point.

Mum called me into the kitchen. At the table, two small aproned figures, plump, smiling, hair tied back in ponytails, were very carefully spooning frosting from a bowl onto individual sponge fairy-cakes, and spreading it with blunt knives.

'Not ready yet!' they called, scattering on bright-coloured hundreds and thousands.

'How was he?' Mum asked softly. As always seeing her task as gathering up the shattered pieces of her children's hopes and gluing them back together in a different, acceptable pattern.

'I'm fine,' I lied, 'just waiting for my fairy cake, hey?'

'Never forget—he loves you, Max,' she said. (She means Dad—or God?) *'I lift my eyes to the hills, from whence cometh my strength? Even from the Lord, who made heaven and earth ...'* she quotes.

Research? Making a difference? Impractical student dream.

So—and ignoring Dad's remarks about Jenny—off to her mother's workplace for clinical experience in a rural practice. Shameful, really, the way you can deceive yourself. Until God appears to be providing the way out.

Shameful how we all jump to Dad's command.

JENNY. 17 JUNE 1988

For the next week, I try to forget who I met at Dad's forum, and what that person had done to me. With an effort, I throw away that cartoon, the last I want to see of Max.

Then, I rescue the torn pieces from the wastepaper basket and stick it back together. Last reminder. I know, Daze: you lose someone, you want to keep something of them. You kept the baby. I suppose. Seeing you wouldn't be drawn and spill about the father, I can only guess you broke up.

I'm off to face reading my results from the lists they pin up, when I open the front door and there's a person on the step. Three people: a woman who looks more Daze's type than mine, baby on her hip. Clutching her trouser leg, peering shyly around, a tousle-haired, crumby-faced toddler. 'Jenny Guthrie?'

'Yes?'

'Your sister's in labour. I'm Lily—we're neighbours. Our bus is next to Daze's on the Site.'

'Site?'

'Traveller's site—she didn't tell you?'

'Oh my God, she wasn't due was she? Where?'

'Addenbrooke's. Probably early or a false alarm, but they took her in.'

I manage not to say, *I really don't want to get involved.* Even if since seeing Max again, I imagine I understand how bad Daze is feeling about her baby's father.

'Listen,' Lily says, 'she's okay, but she said maybe you'd come over with your—' (gesturing with her free hand) '—she wants it filmed. I can take you up: we've got the car today. Would you?'

The baby clutches her breast, bare under her T-shirt.

17

'Okay,' I say slowly. Daze must be desperate to get this filmed, to ask me. So, maybe I can make up for our row at the Market?

Typical, Mum had said when I rang and said, 'Did you know Daze is expecting?' And Des, her Dad, acted the totally hands-off parent: *this is Daze's life, she's an adult making her own choices.* But keep him informed, and he'd come over once term ends. Meanwhile, he's busy directing the end of year production of West Side Story at the sixth form college.

And Daze absolutely wouldn't want the parents there, filming her in labour!

Lily's car's a 2cv equipped with a tangle of kiddies' toys and books and crocheted blankets. We rattle up to Addenbrooke's and she leaves me to cautiously find my way to the maternity department.

The obstetrics team seem totally unfazed by Daze's idea, supply a gown, and before I know it I'm both labour partner and, primarily, film producer for the first appearance of my step-dad's grandchild.

'So Lils found you, then?' is Daze's greeting.

'Yeah: ready to record the celebrity entrance!' I say. Hoping Daze's request and my response signify apologies all around.

I pan the room, while Daze leans over the disposable vomit-basin. Then the midwife takes a look up her butt: I can almost feel it myself, that opening-up. Why do people get themselves into this? Some of them even endure painful treatment up at Dad's clinic first.

'You okay—the sister okay?' they say as if I'm not there.

'C'mon—she's about to deliver—' The midwife looks again at Daze's dilation, shoving the junior registrar aside. They glare at one another, poised to pull rank: he's an inexperienced doctor, she's an old hand.

I'm an unwilling film-director. Unused to the clinical setting.

'Right—she's fully dilated, the head is crowning—I need that paediatrician!'

The midwife looks at the registrar: *I told you so.* Daze's on the delivery bed.

The midwife stops her commanding 'Hold on!' and says, 'Push! Push! Now, pant like a dog!'

'I know, I know!' Daze gasps.

Through my lens I watch, waiting for a first sight of my step niece or nephew. Out between her thighs pops the head—but should it look like that? It's tiny, purply-coloured, and strangely shaped. Its eyes minute, malformed, its nose what a textbook might describe as a proboscis, its mouth—hare-lipped.

On the next push, the trunk and limbs appear. I almost stop breathing: internal organs in a sac outside its abdomen. Should I stop filming? But part of me's curious to have a recording of this. A picture from one of Mum's textbooks. The ones I illicitly gaped at when I was a kid.

The midwife has the thing now: lying limp in her hands. Its spindly legs have very strange feet, the underneath curved, the toes webbed. Its hands are clenched, the five webbed fingers holding down the thumbs. Can it, will it, live?

First time I've seen human birth. My hand on the camcorder wobbles. I focus on anything, anywhere, as boing!—the door swings open. Next frame's another shock for me: 'Paediatrician on call!'

I'm back in Cambridge. Can I fetch you a coffee?

'So where's the baby—what have we got?' he asks.

I let the camera fall onto the delivery bed.

MAX. ADDENBROOKE'S MATERNITY DEPARTMENT, SAME TIME

'So what do we … have?'

I glance at the silent medical team grouped in a huddle. Then for a moment, I don't believe it.

Suspend your personal feelings.

One week after that Forum where I had re-encountered Jenny, here she is, gowned up but recognisable. And the new mum's—*Daze Potter.*

I cross the room, tap the senior midwife's shoulder. 'Paediatrician on call. So where's the baby—what have we got?' I quietly repeat.

A beat passes. Then, 'Better you take this.' Midwife dumps a warm, softly limp, blood-streaked humanoid into my hands. I'm used to babies, but here we have a tiny, severely dysmorphic child. As I take one quick overall look, it opens its mouth, gasps, and that's it: gone.

The obs team are back with Daisy.

'Nice and smoothly—' someone says. 'Can you just push for me?'

But rightly picking up on the atmosphere, Daze stretches out her arms for the infant. 'Give me my baby! Aren't newborns meant to cry?' She turns to me, accusing. 'The kid's not crying! Shouldn't you put it on my tummy?'

I hold it in my arms, deciding. What can we do? What shall we say?

'Oh that's normal, very little babies usually—' someone interjects.

'Placenta when you have it,' I say.

'—need help with breathing—' someone adds helpfully. We're all used to suppressing our natural shock and empathy.

'I'll see if—' Jenny's voice, trembly, breathless. I blank it out.

In every textbook they tell you: *experience the widest range you can in a big teaching hospital.* There was a hint this bairn might have problems. Professor Nicholson, the paediatric neonatologist, would've sent me, if I hadn't been already on call. The rarer chromosome changes flit through my mind, but mainly I think drugs, I think environment—*young girl from a travellers' site,* they said?

They have the placenta now—but it's not complete. I continue cradling the dead baby; they cut the cord. I double-check there's no sign of life, and place it not on the heat-pad, not wired up and linked to a battery of helpful machinery, but alone, naked, in the Perspex cot.

Jenny peers in. 'No—oh *God,*' she breathes, biting on her knuckles.

I take her shoulder, gently turn her away. She gives a sharp intake of breath. 'You don't have to look—why don't you—'

'Max,' she says. 'How ironic is this?' Our eyes meet a second, hold.

At least we both know it's no time to talk. A couple of paeds nurses who've arrived to take the baby to SCBU cluster over the cot while I make a more detailed check. A baby about nine inches long, grossly dysmorphic in ways which don't indicate any known syndrome—a pathetic little scrap, born into a family I know personally. Quite a challenge.

'What's happening? Why's he—?' Daisy asks.

'The paediatrician? It's quite normal. Your baby's very early,' someone responds before I can explain anything. Normal—*normal?*

'Yes—I expect they'll need to—' someone's saying. 'Need to what? Dr Mullins? Max?'

'Yes—yes I'll consult Professor Nicholson—take the usual samples— he's not here at the moment—'

We're all keeping our voices down. The retained pieces of placenta are what worry the others. Jenny goes back to trying to soothe Daisy: Daisy's fully aware there's mystery and trouble. They're both pale, tense. Jenny, I think, is close to tears.

Daze rounds on me, 'Look, just stop lying—what's wrong? Let me see—or tell me! You're Max, who dumped Jenny, aren't you?'

I'm hit in the stomach by her words, but try to keep a cool professional attitude.

'We're just thinking about you—Dr Mullins will explain the baby later—' says the obstetric registrar.

It'd be easiest for me to leave the room taking the baby along in the cot. Jenny's knowledge of early embryos won't help her or me. I could try to ignore and avoid her from now on. But life is suddenly throwing us together repeatedly. I'm exhausted by the whole scenario. As Daze starts up again wanting her child, I snap at Jenny. 'See to your sister.'

She touches Daze's arm, then holds her and looks in her eyes.

'I don't think your baby made it, Daze. I am so, so sorry.'

So Daisy's suspicions are confirmed, and she yells out in grief. Or something. And then someone shouts 'That placenta—we have a bleed!' They bash open the doors to the interconnecting theatre and the whole shebang—all of us—shove Daisy through on her bed. 'Sorry, the sister can't come through!' The doors swing shut.

JENNY

Shuddering a bit, I touch it. Gingerly, I pick it up. Tiny, fragile, warm and blood-smeared.

Vexed to nightmare by a rocking cradle? And what rough beast, its hour come round at last, Slouches towards Bethlehem to be born? Horrible poem—O-level? Hadn't known what Yeats meant. Know now.

Oh the poor creature, the poor thing! Can't believe myself: tears try to come: it's a kind of a baby. What'll Daze do, think, feel? What'm I feeling, shivering with shock?

That Max was the paediatrician. That we can't avoid each other.

Snuffling, try to calm myself with science. This is big teaching hospital where there are people who'd be interested. Where we can access all kinds of research facilities. So what went wrong with you, baby? However did this happen?

I'd really like to know.

Even before O-level, my developing interests were moving towards Dad's. Though he lived and worked on the other side of the world. Being in cutting-edge fertility research, he was thrilled when I won the fifth form essay prize for arguing that Louise Brown's birth had more long-term significance than the moon landings.

Daze's response to my success was a weird piece of art work, featuring a battery powered, print fabric, beating heart. A creepy animated *installation* which sent the school into a tail spin. Daze out-did me with a big, big scandal then, and now with a horrific tragedy.

I'm rooted to the spot, rocking this scrap of screwed-up humanity, as if it's alive, going over the last I knew about Daze, before that row at the market. It's easier than wondering about me and Max.

Me and my housemates went to view her final year exhibition last summer. 'Next stop Colombia!' Daze announced.

'University—to grad school?' American Laura asked politely.

'Grad school?' Laughing. 'Not *Columbia*! The country. Latin American place where they had a volcano erupt? Help rebuild some lives?'

'You can't be serious!'

'Building Bridges is a new international youth project—'

'Does Mum know—?' I began, but Laura interrupted. 'You can't build bridges in Colombia, Daze. Nobody should. It's crawling with guerrillas. Haven't you heard of abduction?'

'By apes?' Daze said. 'Hmm—could be interesting—'

'Why, Daze? And are Mum and your dad okay with it?' Daze's obsession's always been her development as an artist. Since forever. Focus is what she and I have in common. So why take a whole load of time off, to work in the Amazon rainforest?

'I said, *possibly*. It's not, like, fixed,' Daze said. 'Your father's lab, Jen, is helping a clinic there financially—his company is ploughing in resources as they call it.'

'Dad?' I said cynically. 'Would you believe it, Dad's company. Why'd he invite you?'

'Plenty of art—or rather, archaeology.'

Of course I was curious. And jealous! Each long vacation, Dad would arrange me a summer job that paid and gave me experience. I'd stay with some rather sedate hardworking American academic family. But Daze (a non-scientist!) goes to work for him in this exotic place, where there's all kinds of excitement and adventure!

'I get to travel in the company jet apparently—wasted on me, but the attention'll be nice,' said Daze.

So, what went on out there? And Max? Would he still be interested in dysmorphic kids, in the causes of stuff like this? Could we ... look, it's all weird ... I'll show him I've grown up since his beastly letter—I'll show him I don't care. Shivering, I smudge a tear away with the back of my hand.

MAX

In theatre: 'Max—why're you here? You can go now,' they say.

'Go on, man—go—'

I don't need telling twice. But turning, I walk into Jenny in the corridor outside the delivery room.

Jenny cradling the weird child in her arms, her head bent close over its malformed face. It's bizarre: like Mary on a Christmas card.

'You picked it up,' I stumble on the words.

'Sorry—aren't I allowed?'

We look at each other. They always say junior doctors aren't well prepared enough to give bad news.

Or for bizarre events. My very first experience of paediatrics was the same term I met Jenny the aspiring embryologist. For now, by silent agreement we stick to the subject of the baby. 'Could you—could you hand that to me?' I say awkwardly.

'She'll ask the usual questions,' Jenny says. Keeping the baby held close. 'Boy or girl? Did it have hair, and the right number of toes? What d'you think's gone wrong?'

'I—I don't know. I don't know. I am so sorry.' I grab onto half of a professional attitude, force down my own jangled-up mood and try to think of her as I would anyone else in this situation. Cautiously, I put my arm just enough around her shoulders to scoop her along. Towards the sluice room, still carrying the infant. 'C'mon—walk with me. There's nothing we recognise.' Basic ideas first: 'Is your stepsister a pro-lifer? Some mothers who don't agree with abortion refuse the maternal serum alpha-fetoprotein test.'

'Maybe. Daze believes in doing things alongside of nature.'

'Well, obviously she avoided initial testing. AFP would've been leaking into the amniotic fluid. With ultrasound, we could've saved her this experience.'

'It would've been a baby by then. I think she'd have wanted—you know—not to kill it?'

'I understand.'

'I only just knew she was pregnant like last week. Baby's tiny. For how far on she looked, I mean.'

'Polyhydramnios—extra liquor often occurs with neural tube defects.' I let go of Jenny, and hold out my hands, palms up. She lays the baby carefully on them. Very gently, I turn it over, so we can see its back. 'As you know, the damage would've happened before she knew. But she refused ante-natal care?'

'She's alternative, but she's not daft. I don't know anything for definite.'

She hesitates. I wait. She regains composure. 'I'd like to do some tests—could I have it? The baby?'

I doubt they'd let her work on it. So, it's crazy, but I find myself offering to help here. 'I'll be submitting something to Professor Nicholson, the consultant paediatric neonatologist. Would you like me to request you remain involved?' She's hesitant. 'No strings,' I say. 'Professional involvement. I may have a few advantages to offer. I could at least help ease the process—if you were to apply to research, and they wondered how you knew about the child—and then discovered that it's your sister's baby.'

'Not a blood relative though. Anyhow, yeah. So. I can take photos? Get some of that cord blood? I'd have to—we'd have to—do it soon.'

'Biopsies, probably. Right. Refrigerator,' I say. 'Got a pen? No? Take this,' I hand her the baby, 'I have.'

Property of paeds/neonatology—do not remove, I write, on a green paper towel from the dispenser. Then I drape that over the baby, which she hands back to me. 'We can't just start straight away—need permission. Today, Daze will need you. Will you call your family? We leave this in the delivery suite refrigerator, come back for it—' She looks at me, lips a bit quivery. 'You've had a bit of a shock,' I say, 'could do with something hot and sweet? I have had one long night. Was going to grab some breakfast in the canteen—It's all been—'

'Pretty awesome,' Jenny interrupts. We're through to the changing room where she can get rid of that gowned-up look. And I remove my scrubs. 'I'm very sorry,' I say.

'Yeah. And you know what it's like, me and Daze. God, why did I agree to be here?'

'Because she's your sister.'

'Thanks. Yep.' She takes a breath. Smiles. 'Thanks. Thanks, Max.' Pulling off the disposable hair covering, so that her blonde mane—still shoulder-length, flecked with gold, and gorgeous—falls around her face. And then, suddenly, 'God—Max—she's got my camera! Video camcorder—I dropped it on the bed!'

MAX. THE HOSPITAL CANTEEN

Ten minutes later, Jenny loads two white coffees and two chocolate ring doughnuts onto the tray and pushes it towards the checkout clerk. By now it's midday, the scent of lamb stew drifts over the queue, and two first year clinical med students behind us—clad in white coats despite the notice to remove them before entering the canteen—are anxious to pay for their lunch. Embarrassment one: I feel in my pocket and there's not enough change. Two, my wallet's empty of all but cards and receipts.

Jenny pays for both of us. Walks ahead towards a table: I'm very discomfited by being caught out unable to treat her. 'But what I can do I will do: make sure your property's restored to you. The camcorder—'

'Got your pen? Thanks.' Jenny turns over the tiny till ticket, and writes. 'My address. To restore it. And thank you.'

'So ...' I say, not wanting to get into discussing our relationship or lack of one, 'does Daisy do drugs? Do you know anything?'

'About Daze? Not much. She was in South America, Dad's got a clinic in Colombia.'

'Colombia?' I'm taken aback—only for a moment, I have met Daze, I can imagine her there. 'Guerrillas? Drug barons? Didn't a volcano erupt recently?'

A smile from Jenny, a moment of understanding we can share. Not doing too badly, then. 'Yeah, Dad's kind of place,' she says, almost conspiratorial. 'His parent organisation's a—a rather murkily defined conglomerate. They finance cutting-edge medical research and dabble in helping the development, would you believe, of underdeveloped countries.'

'Aye, by developing new fertility solutions. Inside the Ring of Fire,' I say with irony.

'Called the enterprise culture,' Jenny says, equally ironic. 'They're helping a clinic there financially—*ploughing in resources*—the resources include my Dad's expertise, part time!'

We're both silent. Professional attitude is trying to desert me. Jenny re-focuses on why we're here.

'Anyway, Daze was doing admin and having an adventure out there— maybe drawing the rainforest flora, if she managed to get to the rainforest. Next Georgia O'Keefe?'

'Who?'

'Painted huge, bright flowers and stuff like that.'

'Right.' Jenny's stepfather, Des Potter, is an artist. She knows all kinds of cultural stuff I don't.

'Whatever, she hasn't been living at home since she graduated last summer. Can we ... talk about something else?'

Again, I fear discussing our relationship. We're both in shock. From meeting like that, over Daze's tragedy. 'Wonderful anthem on Sunday. Saw you in college chapel.'

'I joined the choir to sing the music,' Jenny says carefully. Presumably indicating that in four years, and even with evangelical Maeve as a friend, she hasn't acquired additional faith in God. 'I've—never seen *you* there.'

I drop the apparent God-subject. 'You aren't applying for research here?'

'I'm not expecting to've got the marks it takes.'

'But you always wanted—'

'Teenage arrogance!' She laughs, irony maybe. 'Four years of real life down the line. Of course, if I do I'd still love to work in human embryology. Dr Woods suggested cancer research will often fund you to do growth stuff. Or there's Roslin research station: you know, near Edinburgh? They're ministry of agriculture I think, but the work's in my area. But ... we all mature don't we?'

As we fall silent, around us the chatter and clatter hems us in. I begin to know I can't manage this. Everything's so delicately poised. It made me feel good initially, her apparent warmth and gratitude: now I don't want to do or say what I might regret. And I'm going hot and cold, my skin tingly and my throat dry. Should've told her *no, you cannot have this body for research*: been harsh, and distant, and quite within the rules.

Jenny begins again. 'Laura's thesis on immortality includes extracting philosophy and ethics out of nature's weirdest mistakes and asking why to be human—well, actually to be anything alive—means to be mortal.'

'Well, some people have an easy answer to that.' I say, meaning Dad.

'Social anthropology is full of myths and assumptions. You can't prove them.'

'Life just handed you some hard fact scientific research.' Striving to retain appearing cool, I smile ironically. 'Physiological and biochemical answers to the whys of life.'

'Yes. Actually, it's awful. You know, Daze and me. I should remain objective ...' Jenny's hands cover her face, her glasses are dumped onto the table. Which makes me feel mean, and even more embarrassed, worse in every way.

'Jenny, I shouldn't have—we—'

'Colombia! I was so jealous of her!' The words dissolve. I wait. She takes out a tissue, blows her nose, wipes her specs and puts them back on. Recovers herself.

'Max—no, it was decent of you. I needed the energy-shot, the blood sugar was low. Yes, it's a bad business but, ironic, isn't it? You're—still interested in the human development issues, aren't you?'

'I think it'll be general practice. Lower the sights, same as you.'

'So, why were you at the forum on PGD and the afternoon stuff—new solutions to male infertility? I hoped it meant you'd managed to follow your dreams.'

'Meant?'

'Okay, my real question, and don't be cryptic. Your letter was cruel: I hadn't expected you'd be capable of that.'

Ouch. And such a poised barbed sentence: no more tears.

I recall Dad: *'You have begun something which you knew could lead nowhere. Never start when you cannot follow through.'*

'Jenny, I was, as you described yourself over research, another person. My father's a very powerful—' (I'm about to say influence, but stop myself), 'person. It was—all me, none of it was you. I made the running, I made the mistakes. You did nothing wrong. I was—I was—wrongly influenced. I made a stupid decision.'

She stares at me. Over a doughnut cut into several pieces, and half a cup of cold coffee. Picks up the spoon, stirs the coffee. Carefully, she says coldly, 'Doesn't that make it worse? Casting me as a victim?' Eyes fixed on me. 'I had no say, and was given no chance to respond.'

JENNY

I'm so mixed up, fighting for air when he looks at me like that. My skin tingling with desire to touch him. Once, I thought Max was the person who understood me without having to ask, whose interests mirrored mine. But he let his father come between us.

In the maternity department, we turned shock and dismay into cool clinical behaviour.

But I'm not too clinical to be human. And hurt. Work together? Excuse! Stupid decision!

I could love Max without any of the physical things. But the physical things are still there as well. The way he looks. And moves. The way he looked at me. The way he touched me. Gentle, cautious, the passion just below the surface.

I've hurt him with my words now. I can't and mustn't trust him.

But I want to show him what a valuable person he's cast aside.

'Jen? Jenny?' Max asks.

Can't speak: memories and intentions fight.

I'd torn his awful letter to pieces. *Dear Jenny, It seems I shan't be in Cambridge when you begin your studies after all: something's come up and I shall have to transfer to Newcastle for the remainder of my clinical course …* Flung the bits down the loo. Flushed and flushed, but they wouldn't go away! They floated: drifting in the pan, exposed to prying family eyes.

Mum came to ask why I was in there so long, flushing so often. I cried.

She tried to touch me. I yelled, 'Don't!'

She realised. She knew. More angry with him than me. *Scottish religious guilt*, she said. *Forget him.*

Finally I let her slide that comforting arm around me.

'Jenny,' Max says softly, now. 'Dad was taken ill. He'd already had a hint he'd maybe develop multiple sclerosis. But it was a shock to arrive home to that. I'd been happy in Cornwall, they'd not told me. Wheelchair in the hall. Trappings of illness … I only saw I'd not been there for him—for my family … and that he'd disapprove of our relationship.'

Why? Why give in to your father? I think. People don't do that today—do they? 'But …' I manage. Max just looks helpless.

'I …' he shrugs.

'I'm sorry. That he's so ill.'

'He's in remission … working hard again.'

'You—with anyone now?' I hardly want to know the answer.

'There was someone. It didn't work out. You?'

'A few—tries. But no, nobody special.'

Thoughts spin. 'I should call my parents.' Safe, sensible action. 'They'll need to know, about Daze.' I swallow the rest of my coffee, stand to go, pushing back my chair, and picking up my shoulder bag.

'What about—?' Max asks, still seated. His eyes are red, I feel guilty for keeping him up talking.

'About?' I ask, as he hesitates.

'The research?' He stands up and hunts in his pockets. Pulls out his pack of Marlboros.

'I thought you'd have changed your mind by now,' I say.

'No—I still want—'

Somehow, we walk towards the exit, and when we're outside, Max is still there with me. He lights up, and offers me one. I hesitate. I've given up.

But, then I reach out my hand, 'Thanks. I could use that.'

Max flicks his lighter, cupping his hand around mine. I want to touch it, touch him. Not to do this silly ritual that avoids eye contact.

And then, as I draw in the smoke, I notice we're part of a little group huddled furtively around the doorway. What a foul habit this is—which used to be mine. We all stand around, addicts—doctors, nurses, care assistants, medical students—destroying our own cells. Crazy.

The spin on my present situation is the simultaneous appearance of Max—as his professional, efficient, in-charge self—and the Thing: either would've been enough.

It shot out of Daze—*the head's crowning, you can see the hair!* Its distorted face shocked me right back to being a sneaky inquisitive kid browsing Mum's medical textbooks behind the sofa. The Thing which had grown in the secret darkness of Daze's distended belly, which had been present as we fought at the Market last week.

How come Max was there at the birth? Is life really random?

Max returns to practical issues. 'Shall I talk to Professor Nicholson about the body? And get Daze's consent?'

'Are we okay doing this?'

'You mean—ethical?'

'Yeah. Because—'

'I'll be discreet. We're supposed to try and see a wide range of—. Jenny, it's a lost opportunity if we don't.'

Lost opportunity?

Max probably means, *to investigate a statistically rare range of malformations.* 'Okay. We've certainly got the equipment. At Genetics. I should try to take Daze a few things.'

'Later would be better: she'll be drowsy from the anaesthetic. So, I could drop you back in Cambridge? I'm on my way home.'

I try to say no, there's a bus. But the temptation's too strong. We begin crossing the car park. Max has a sporty, but very second-hand, tomato-coloured car, a Ford Capri.

I say, 'Svelte wheels,' and he says, apologetically, 'My Uncle Euan's cast-off. Don't ask.'

I'm still stunned by it all: Max, Daze, the baby. A thought detaches itself. 'Max, you don't think … Have you ever seen anything like that baby before? D'you deliver babies from my father's fertility programmes here ever?'

He responds in that evasive, clinician way that can be very annoying: 'I'm only on a six-month rotation, I can't comment.'

'Six months' rotation?'

'After graduation, once you're qualified, to access the GP training scheme you have to do two years' Senior House Officer jobs. In fields that'd relate well to general practice. Obs and gynae, geriatrics, psychiatry, A and E, paediatrics … Newcastle had no space for me to do the kids' placement. I was fortunate to come back here.'

'And, you don't want to commit yourself over whether neonates you get in the special care baby unit are ever conceived at Dad's clinic?'

'Did I say that?'

'Exactly. So I know not to push the issue, don't I?'

As we drive, I see ahead a field of parked, hippy-style vehicles: the Traveller's site? 'Stop—that looks like Daze's place.'

'Here?' Max queries. 'You want any help?'

'I promised Lily I'd report back. She'll be upset. Maybe I'll pick up some clues, like drug habit, environment? And the stuff for Daze … She'll hate being in a hospital nightgown, she'll want something to read and a wash bag.'

Max slows, and draws into the entrance of the site. Avoiding a pothole or two he parks, leaving the engine running, and turns to me. 'If we're going to do cultures, we'll need to set that up soon. You should take photos. I remember your lovely Pentax: you still have it? How soon can you manage?'

'Yeah, the one Dad gave me.' S'pose he recalls our cliff walks with that camera! 'How soon can you?'

Looking at his watch, Max says, 'I need to sleep. Late this evening? Or in the morning? That's the furthest we should leave things.'

Seems we're planning to work together on a project, and still emotionally entangled after four years apart. The chugging engine indicates Max isn't wanting to get into talking about that just now. 'Tomorrow,' I say. 'About nine?'

A look passes between us. Should've been a kiss. No it shouldn't: he behaved so badly I shouldn't even talk to him.

Detached? Were me and Max ever detached?

I jump out, slamming the door a bit too hard, and in a second he's gone.

I accelerate, once I've turned the car around, giving the appearance of a person who doesn't look back on old stuff. Of course, I do. I'm fleeing back to wound-lick in my masculine lair.

Jenny Guthrie.

Why was I at that Forum Guthrie organised? Rational thought says, because today's general practitioner must be aware of all the developments. Because Wil happened to ask me along. *Interesting to experience the famous father,* he said. Of course, I took a risk. And of course, once back in Cambridge, I suppose I'd been waiting for a right time. Even for circumstances to decide for me. My approach to life: a pendulum that swings between risk and caution.

Switching off the ignition, I hurry from car to house, hope to close the front door on my own thoughts, go straight to bed. Pausing only to use the bathroom, fling off my clothes, close the curtains tight shut.

But, it's like she's still here with me. That silent look between us: pure pain. She's resurrected the past. Women have this talent for saying what you don't want to say. And that you wish they wouldn't because it's already a thought, a memory too raw to touch. Even verbally. Especially verbally. It's hidden in your heart, hidden to save your feelings.

Jenny's right. I was cruel. I was weak; I acted, in essence, like Dad. Who re-interpreted the first hints of his MS twenty years ago as God calling him out of the RAF and into full-time ministry. Damascus Road? In med school I soon learned that his temporary blindness must've been the not-unusual precursor of his neurological autoimmune disease. Which then hit the Pastor while I was working at Jenny's mother's GP surgery. 1984. It was like God telling me not to betray my family in their hour of need.

Or am I worse than Dad: pulled back with a twitch of the parental dog lead ... emotionally afraid? This disgusts me about myself. Duvet over my head.

I can do everything through Christ who strengthens me. My mother's favourite text, hanging in the downstairs cloakroom: my mother the obedient wife, the true saintly Christian woman, a pattern for feminine living. Mum would've accepted that letter, and submissively, silently, lived with the unfairness of being thrown aside.

Why the hell was Professor Nicholson's other SHO then late today? Lying in bed hung over after a stag night? Causing me to be thrown the task of an extra shift—which included Daze Potter's admission to have her dysmorphic baby. And why ever did life—or God—dish me this twisted train of events? I thought I wanted to forget Jenny!

Sleep, from exhaustion, is a gift. It envelops me for several blissful, emotionless, thought-free hours.

Takes me no time to spot my stepsister's home among the six painted hippy buses bathed in silence and heat. A converted coach painted with black daisies! The sun's face smiles on the front of the bus, and the moon's on the back.

I picture Daze, dark, slight and bony, driving this heavy, ancient vehicle, with its vast steering wheel, its old-fashioned gearbox, its black exhaust fumes. Rattling down country lanes, travelling to a festival. With or without the father of the pathetic thing we've left in cold storage in order to investigate its problems? Gives me pangs of complicated regret, desire, anger, to think of Daze and her man, just after meeting Max.

Back to practicalities. I try the door: it opens. Scents of incense, diesel, and humanity pour out. I step inside. The sun streams through dusty windows on dancing motes, spiralling in the fetid air like the flower fairies Daze make-believed live in the hedgerows. As kids we popped blackberries from those hedgerows into our mouths as we walked up from the village store. Tried to form cowslips into the balls mentioned in an old children's book Daze's mum gave her, before she disappeared. Unlike daisy chains, cowslip balls are very difficult. Even for dextrous children like us.

And Cornish hedgerows are beautiful enough without fairies, and real Cornish fairies are mischievous as hell: to be honest rather like Daze. Yep: an elf, Cornish-style. Living here, pregnant, making a home and life for herself. Then the Thing is born. Braver than me: I'd have crumpled up to find myself pregnant—imagine …

Did Daze really care for the baby's father? Or just have sex and move on? Did they share this home?

So much stuff! Herbs and garlic bulbs hang in strings from the roof. They brush and knock my face as I move around, mirrors (where I see my face—surprised, exhausted), a string of brass bells, several rosaries.

Organised, in its own way. Clothes in hampers, and clothes on hooks. Trousers, skirts, a black crushed-velvet dress. A basketful of underwear and tops. I shove a couple of pairs of knickers into my shoulder bag, don't see anything else she could decently wear in bed in a hospital ward, grab a couple of long skirts and a shirt. I'll buy her a nightgown or at least a big T-shirt in town. She *might* even thank me … We don't hate each other, we don't exactly resent each other.

Shelves of dried peas and beans, plants in pots. A bowl of over-ripe fruit. Nature books, art books, poetry.

Paints, brushes, oily rags, pencils, pastels, strange-looking tools and bottles of medium. An odd chickenwire creation, like a woman's body: dressmaker's dummy? Sketch books. I flip the pages: drawings of little mice? Latter-day Beatrix Potter? Mouse embryos? Careful, realistic drawings. And stuff you'd only see under an electron microscope. Current science. Like my father showed at the Forum. Daze copied state-of-the-art microscopy in Colombia? Dad said she was doing admin.

Doesn't make any sense.

Back outside, I look around. The site's pretty primitive: no proper facilities. On cracked dusty ground at the top of the field, surrounded by mire and a few buckets and bowls with washing soaking in them, there's a standpipe. With a rag tied around its neck, it looks like a person.

'You from the council?' The speaker's a woman, her T-shirt hitched up and a naked child, maybe eighteen months old, on her hip, latched onto and sucking her breast. 'It's people like you force us to break the law by putting a fence of laws around us,' she carries on without waiting for my explanation.

'Chill out: she's Daisy's sister.' Thank God, here's Lily. Kids clutching onto her like fruit on a branch.

'We're all her sisters—'

They look more like her than I do.

'If you mellow out a bit,' I say, standing there with Daze's clothes draped over my arm. 'It's not about the site. I've come to collect her stuff.'

'It's okay,' Lily smiles, scooping her smaller child into her arms. 'Corralled here like Native Americans in a reservation, we can be suspicious of what's coming next. Forced onto polluted land.'

'You know it's polluted?'

The women give a collective shrug. 'Six months and we'll be gone. Called having a choice.'

'Suppose this land can be proved to be polluted,' I begin. 'You know what it's been used for, before? Have there been premature births, any problems?'

Shrugs, and vague suggestions. 'You need to press the Council to tell you. You should contact Environmental Health and—' But as I try to fire them up to action, they're rightly more concerned for news about the birth.

'You've not said how they are. When'll they let them home?'

'The baby, to be honest, was far too early, too small to live. Daze will need a bit of time to recover.'

The whole group howls, murmurs, offers sympathy. I feel terrible: although I don't want to describe the Thing to them, the site may hold clues. I spend a few minutes accepting comfort for my own experience and on Daze's behalf. Quietly, later, I must speak about the site with Lily. If there'd been another like the Thing, though, surely they would've told me?

Walking back into Cambridge, something about those women makes me wish for a moment human beings could really live free as they do. I left that behind to grow up. But without medical care, how many of those mothers would be here, how many of the children?

And then, I bump into Laura outside a café where I was going to buy a coffee. Laura squeals, 'Jenny, have you seen your results?'

I wake disorientated, mouth dry, naked in bed, yesterday's clothes on the floor. Imagine a Mullins who drops his clothes on the floor! Brightly sunny outside, it's still today, and there's that dysmorphic infant in the fridge at Maternity, and my pledge to Jenny. Wasn't there another way we could've met again, and revived a civilised relationship? Apparently not.

Shaking my head, I pad off to take a shower, throw on decent casual clothes, and even hang my suit up. Over a mug of tea and a toasted sandwich, I page through notes on chromosomal abnormalities.

I was writing an essay for Professor Nicholson on Human Aneuploidies when Jen and I first met. I took Jenny to visit Serafina, a mosaic Patau's syndrome baby: Serafina's amazingly still alive, according to Nicholson's registrar. Can almost see an ironic smile on the face of the Almighty. Irony, or maybe encouragement?

Back at the hospital (would prefer not to be here on my time off) I take the lift up to see if I can talk with Nicholson. The Prof gives ponderous approval for research, and reminds me about requesting consent. Emphasises he's off for the weekend and won't be around to view the body until maybe later next week. 'I leave it to you to talk with the mother. Be gently persuasive. I wish you success.'

*

Daze's been put, out of respect, in a side-room, away from mothers with babies. I knock, hesitating before I walk in. If it's right to give her privacy, who am I to waltz in merely because I'm the doctor?

'Yeah?' comes her mumbled voice. I enter, check her obs, and then I sit down by the bed. 'Daisy?'

'Yeah?' Small, pale, woozy from the anaesthetic, the shock of the sudden birth, loss of blood, and the loss of her child, she makes an effort to focus properly on me.

'Daisy,' I say, 'you know who I am?'

'Max Mullins,' she says, almost smiling. 'You were there. Paediatrician on call. Ain't life weird, hey? Thought you'd left Cambridge for good.'

'And I hadn't.' I smile at her. 'How are you feeling now?'

'Like shit. An', she left somethin' on my bed—it's over there?'

Jenny's precious, expensive video camera—doubtless bought for her by Dr Guthrie—lies precariously on the side of the sink.

'Thanks, Daisy: she missed it.'

'That letter you wrote: Jenny chucked it down the toilet. That's my sister!'

I pretend her IV lines are more interesting to me than her stepsister—continuous antibiotics as well as whole blood, syntometrine and saline. Daze abruptly changes the subject. 'So, you're the paeds guy—what you here for?'

'Well as I happened to be on duty when your baby was—born—it's my job to ask you a few questions. Is that all right?'

'Ask away: jus' your job an' that—' she says, the words blurry like she's had one too many on a girls' night out.

'Okay. Daisy, it was all a bit much to take in earlier, and you probably don't remember too much about it.'

'Some I do.'

'You know why your baby isn't here with you?'

'She died.'

'In—in my arms Daisy—she just gasped and—'

'And you know why this baby couldn't have led a normal life, do you?' Her accusatory voice is fuzzy. 'And you've put her somewhere—Do we have to talk? Or can I see her?'

'Daisy, you're allowed to see your baby if you want to.' I try to plough on, feeling she's almost palpably vulnerable. Even so, must she mention my inept letter to Jen? And what's her real attitude to her lost child? I try to regain objectivity while being gentle with her.

'It's quite a bit obvious how your baby didn't grow normally, the reasons she couldn't have lived outside you. But I could bring her in,' I say. Although I know the genitals are somewhat ambiguous, if Daze wants it to be a girl, why not. 'She'd be all wrapped up, you don't need to see anything you'd find distressing. Other mums like you—well, this makes the whole thing more real—you don't just feel empty—'

'God,' Daisy mutters, angry now. 'Distressing? Max how would you know? You're just a *guy*.'

'We find—Look, it could help you to hold your baby to say goodbye—mightn't it? Jenny could be with you when you see your baby—if you like? And then, or maybe before then—once you're on the ward, Jenny could bring your things, you'd be happier to have your own nightie—'

Silence.

I wait. I glance at my watch: and remember, absurdly, my father and his regimental-style timekeeping. 'Daisy, I'd like to sit with you here but I have to see other patients.' (Not quite true just now!) 'Would you like me to bring your baby in later? Or would you rather have a nurse do that? Shall I ask Jenny to come over?'

'No,' she says. 'Don't bother. An' no need to mention to Jenny: prob'ly even you'd do better.'

'Right. Okay, Daze.' I almost put out my hand to reassure her that she—at least—will be whole and happy again. But I stop myself. 'Anything else I could do for you?'

'What exactly went wrong?'

'With your baby? We aren't sure, but, something which happened very early.'

'As early as conception?' she emphasises.

Does that give me clues?

'That would take some time to discover. If we ever could. We don't usually—Daze, let me ask you a question—did you have proper antenatal care?'

''Course,' she says. 'Weight and wee and dietary stuff—I'm always careful what I eat—'

'Blood tests for rubella and—?'

'Yeah, yeah—Look, Max, it's a mother's right to choose,' she says. 'Yes, I had a scan. Yes, they murmured about a problem. No, I didn't want a termination. Okay?'

'Right. So you carried on. They kept an eye, did they?' I glance at her notes: a significant gap where antenatal checks from about twenty weeks should be. And remember they warned me, *girl from a Travellers' site, may be a few problems.*

'Them? A Traveller woman who's a trained midwife kept an eye, as you call it,' Daze says.

'And she lives? Name?'

'Rosie. All over. She checked me when she came by. She checked the baby was alive.'

'Right.' I make a note. Traveller midwife, name of Rosie, no surname, always on the road. Not a lot of help. 'Daze, two more things.' She sighs at me. 'One, do tell the doctors about this next time—that is, if you're ever pregnant again?'

'Yeah, 'course.' Sullenly. Like taken as read.

'And, there's something we'd like to ask you to do for us.'

'What?'

'Just to help other mothers like you, to help us to understand what went wrong—'

'You want to take my baby for research?'

'If you are agreeable—only if you really feel—'

She hesitates. 'If you do that, what'll I get to know? Like, shall I be involved, shall I get to see what you do? Will she be—be—'

Here I'm on the spot: what can I say? 'We'll do hand and foot prints for you.'

Daze raises herself on an elbow. 'Max, you know what I meant: can I be involved, see what you're testing for?'

'I—don't think so—I'll—Shall I come back another time?'

'Nah. Jus' make sure I see her, right? Before? An'... what happens to her if I say no?'

I hesitate: Daisy says harshly, 'Okay, I'll say it: I'm guessing they don't do funerals, do they? For prem babies?'

'Not ... not usually ... this size.'

'Okay. So, better she's got a future.'

'A future?'

'What you asked. Research. Do it.'

I say quietly, 'Daisy, thank you. I just need you to—sign this—I'll read it carefully so you know what it says?' I read out the consent for research form. 'Informed consent,' I say, 'means that you are fully aware of what you are permitting. You can ask me any questions you need to. I shall try to answer them.'

As Daisy signs away her rights to her child, I'm amazed she's so down to earth. But then, I don't know Travellers, do I? I'm a conventional guy, I live in a house and work in a hospital, and can have no idea how her mind works. I recall she once drew a child crucified on a woman, as I watch her form the careful italic words: *Daisy Potter*. 'Max, you do something for me, okay?'

'If I can.'

'Treat your next woman right, okay? An' I hope she's worth it.'

I swallow, can't answer. 'I'll let you get some rest,' I say quietly, crossing the room. 'Someone will arrange about your baby.'

Feeling horribly chastened—she's put me through it over Jenny in a sisterly kind of way—I go downstairs, collect a coffee from the machine, and standing outside in the usual gathering place, light up. Should not. Recall Jen's comments a few hours ago.

Patty—an agency nurse we have working for us on Neopaeds—appears. We enjoy the early-evening sun, comment on its Mediterranean heat, talk about the upcoming hospital ball. Ticket prices are such that after buying one, we cannot afford a holiday, we joke. We do not discuss work.

Then suddenly she says casually, 'I was at the Drey until last week—you're seeing the med director's daughter aren't you? You two were in the canteen.'

I throw away the half-smoked cigarette and stamp on it. Saying, 'I know Jenny, yes.'

Patty says, 'They're pushing on the boundaries down there. Pay's good though.' And then she stamps out her ciggie and turns back inside.

All those questions: and the ambivalent attitude. Does Daze know more than she's telling me?

JENNY. SATURDAY 18 JUNE, CAMBRIDGE

I should be so lucky: Saturday morning, and Kylie Minogue, belting out of Laura's radio in the bathroom.

I got a First!

Daze produced the Thing, Max is back in town … and I ended up with a migraine. My unworn ball gown hangs on my door, reminding me that I should've been out at a May Ball last night.

After Laura, library books under her arm, finally dragged me off to see my results, there was my name listed in the small select band of First Class degrees! We bought champagne, popped the cork, danced around: me and Laura and several other finals people whom we don't actually know that well. Capering, laughing, hugging.

And at home, '*Maeve, I got a first!*'

More hugging, more celebrating, Maeve's got an upper second, spurred on with her studies by me, she said.

But then I told them: 'My stepsister had her baby ... it—'

'She went into premature labour? And is the baby—?'

Simpler not to describe the Thing. 'Tiny, unviable.'

'Oh Jenny ... oh how awful.'

'And, Max Mullins was the on-call paeds guy ... we had a coffee. And we're still, you-know, involved.'

'Max who dumped you? Why'd you even hang out with the guy one minute?'

'Because ... because, maybe, Daze gave Max her honest assessment, right there from the delivery bed. "*Max who dumped Jenny!*" I owe her one: I'll try to see we get a proper explanation of her baby's defor—reasons it died. And, maybe I want to show him I'm tougher than a person who'd crumple when they come up against their ex. Or maybe I even think he might have a decent explanation for what he did? Seeing he came over and talked to me?'

I was looking at Maeve, but one of her eyes suddenly wasn't there. Instead, a zigzag arc of coloured lights danced. They almost buzzed.

Now the headache and nausea's almost gone, I begin to think again. Why didn't Max scarper quick as he could?

The extraordinary experience of sharing Daisy giving birth.

How and why did she become pregnant?

Would she tell me? No.

Last night, late, I managed to call Mum: who was delighted by my news, devastated by Daze's. Insisted they'd leap in the car and drive over. 'I can manage what needs doing,' I told her.

'Sure you're okay, sweetie?'

'Yeah—yeah I'm all right.'

'Bless you. Jenny, you did so well. Listen, we'll be on the road first thing. Have you called your father?'

'Tomorrow. He'll be all over me to do some enormously complicated, expensive celebration. Or, he'll be too busy to do anything. Mum, guess who was the paediatrician they sent down? Max—remember him?'

'He's qualified? And in Cambridge? *Darling*—I remember. How dreadful.'

'Just make that *unbelievable*.'

Now, I throw back the duvet and carefully swing my legs out of bed. Mum and Des, devastated by Daze's news, elated by mine, will be arriving around lunchtime. My favourite jeans are spotted with Daze's blood. Leaving them in a heap, I pull on an old pair, a shirt, run a comb through my hair.

'Why *ever*, after Daze's baby, did you have to hang out with that jerk Max?' Laura asks.

'The locked door,' I mumble through my dry toast and mug of tea.

'What?'

'Locked door: theme in masses of stories. Peter Rabbit: a locked door, into the forbidden garden. Chased by Mr MacGregor, loses his coat, and gets sick from stuffing on lettuces.'

Laura laughs. 'What if whoever it was hadn't stepped through the wardrobe into Narnia? What if James hadn't entered the Giant Peach?'

'Yep. Lewis Carroll's Alice glimpses an amazing garden through a tiny door ... eats the cake, drinks the drink. The best stories happen when the protagonist takes the risk—you know they will have an adventure. I want an adventure. I want to prove to Max I'm not unable to work with him now and I want him to know just who he lost!'

*

Max swings by. Heart does not need to pump so fast, as I slide into the car. This is purely a work relationship.

'Camera,' he says, looking envious. 'Yes, same beautiful SLR.'

My fourteenth birthday present from Dad.

'Camcorder,' Max says, passing it over.

'Thanks. Bit heavy and bulky, prefer taking stills. But you know—' I stop. Let's not talk like we knew each other well before. 'So Daze managed to look after it! How is she?'

'Bit dopey, but decisive, when I saw her. Quite the photographer, aren't you? Second string to your bow, Jenny?' He smiles.

'Always was, I think.' *No guy's worth it*, I tell myself, clutching at resolve. After all, he's patronizing me, isn't he?

And as Max drives smoothly, confidently, towards Addenbrooke's, almost as if he's part of the car itself, I stop myself blurring the edges of natural caution by thinking of the Thing, our project, left in cold storage. That, and only that, is why I'm here with him today. He is a pompous male, no doubt about that.

'And the consent? She was okay with that?'

'She was astoundingly cool about it. Asked a couple of questions we might find useful.'

'Which were?'

'How early did whatever it was go wrong. And, could she know what we're testing for, could she be involved.'

'She never responds as you expect. Once we'd found a chrysalis and I wanted to cut it open—we were only about nine or ten—Daze hung about, telling me not to. But afterwards, she took the thing, showed it to Hat, and kept it in her room, part of her nature museum. Her interest isn't objective, scientific: it's kind of personal. She is weird, you know.'

'Och, well, you might appreciate this: Daisy told me off about that letter.'

I am amazed.

'Oh, and she wanted to see the baby.'

*

Out of the sunny morning into the cold path lab, where we don lab coats and gloves. Max unfolds the small green paper parcel. Can't not recoil. The object of our investigation was, when I saw it last, still warm, and smeared with drops of blood. Now it's stiff and cold. Weird human-oid, a baby and not a baby. In tune with the Goth posters and music Daze was into when we were at school.

'This is so unfair,' I manage, 'I'm going to have to talk to her about it.' And I touch its cheek, gently, almost to show myself—and Max—I count this person human.

'I gave her a strong hint. Can you ask about any environmental influences?'

'The Traveller women mentioned polluted ground. But they weren't precise.'

'Is that so? Now: let's make a start. And can we forget the past?' Max kind of half-smiles: embarrassment? Good, he should feel that.

'Did I bring it up?' I offer him the camera.

He shakes his head, no. 'You're the photographer.'

'Black and white—I'll develop it myself.' There's more irony: Daisy's father, Des, taught me all I know about photography and developing.

Max positions the body: I take shots and shots. Details of the omphalocele, the spinal stuff, the face. 'You okay with this?' Max asks, as he turns the Thing over.

'Yeah: could always stand back. Detach. From medical things, not emotional—'

'Should've been a doctor,' he says.

'No—prefer to keep out of the personal stuff.'

'Sure about that?'

'Yep.'

'This no exception?'

'Nope.'

I take two more shots—close-ups of the omphalocele—and I'm done. I stand back. 'Two rolls. Not too sure about the model.'

Max gives me a look. Was I too flip? 'No need for autopsy, the department will do that,' he says.

'So just pics and the blood analysis?'

'Biopsies are better for cell cultures,' Max reminds me. 'Skin, thymus or spleen—preferable to relying on a blood sample when the infant is moribund.'

'You sound like a textbook,' I say.

'Sorry: probably was a quote. Retaining detachment?'

'Yeah.'

'So let's do it, then,' Max says.

We work well together: Max leading with the clinical stuff, me when we prepare samples for cell cultures. 'We'll take these over to Genetics, we've got a new process,' I tell him. Max looks at his watch. 'You have to be somewhere?' I ask.

'No—'

Efficiently, with teamwork, we clear up, so when we're finished the room looks like we've never been there. The Thing's in a clean metal dish, on new green paper towels.

'So—what happens to—?' I hardly want to ask this. 'After Daze sees it?'

'Someone will come by on Monday and take it for autopsy, then to be disposed of,' Max says coolly.

So Max might toss Daze's child into the incinerator? Part of me can't believe what paediatric neonatology does with these babies. Did he tell Daze?

'Look, you don't believe in abortion and chucking away abnormal embryos and—stuff—well, you didn't ... and yet you're so cool about—disposal.'

'That's how it's done in hospitals, Jenny.' Shaking his head. 'She'll see it first: we can arrange that. And I'll get hand and footprints done.' Pulling off his gloves, and chucking them in the bin. Its metal mouth clangs shut and he attempts to usher me out of the room.

'But that baby isn't latex gloves.' Did I say that? These non-objective emotions are weird. New. First day I had that lovely camera, I was an arrogantly scientific fourteen year old who mercy-killed a rabbit.

A rabbit in a gin trap, up at Botallack, my fourteenth birthday. It was screaming the way animals do: its leg was all mashed and I took one look and told Hat—who was imploring, '*take it to the vet—quickly!*'—I told her 'No: it won't survive, Hattie, that leg won't heal, the muscles are torn, the bone's shattered.'

I sent Hat to pick flowers and dig a grave. I handed Daze my precious birthday present camera to look after, telling her, 'Cross the road and turn away.'

And I took that rabbit and walloped it against the wall of the ruined chimney of the tin mine. Its blood was suddenly on my jeans. I cried then, and shook with cold. Maybe I should've strangled it instead. I didn't know what to do, really. I wanted to be brave and tough and put it out of its pain. Daze said, 'That was gross, Jen. You're gross. I think I'm gonna be sick!'

She wasn't. Next day she produced a perfect drawing of how the muscles and tendons had been damaged. By memory, out of her head. Took it to school. Showed it around, told the story to a whole group of girls in our class next day. I got the label: Jen the Bunny-Killer.

Now, 'You can't keep it,' Max says, 'just let it go.'

'So the man of faith really would chuck the body,' I needle him.

'Jenny, you know this is impossible. It's not done. The chaplain wouldn't want to get involved, an undertaker wouldn't deal with it. So there's formaldehyde or the incinerator, which do you prefer? And let go about my faith, can you?'

'Yuck, Max—do you have to put the choices like that? It's a baby! You go along with one set of morals and then—you're inconsistent. You smoke and drink and take out an unbeliever, and then you obey your dad the minister,' I say, forgetting my resolve to be cool. 'You're a mess.'

'I know,' Max says, 'I know.'

So now I hear his pain. I've pushed too hard, and my resolve is set to crumble.

Max leans back on the counter, I stand in what'd be his path to the door. Seeing his complex emotions: sadness, fear?

From Maeve, I've learned fundamentalists don't make relationships outside their own group.

'Did you ... did you deliberately ask me out, a non-believer?' Max takes a couple of steps towards me, then changes his mind. Quietly says, 'Research or—a clean neat destruction—we don't yet have other options—'

'Fine,' I mumble. And I turn, and touch the baby's cheek. Human.

'Jenny—I believe that baby isn't just a body—the real person it is, that person is somewhere else now. You can tell Daisy that. She'd agree.'

'But I don't.'

'I know you don't.'

Is he disappointed? If I did would it not have ended?

'I will tell Daisy. Where you believe it is.' Maybe that's a better kind of lie—in Max's book—better than saying Hospital Policy.

'Jenny—C'mon, next step?'

As we work at Genetics, 'We might even write it up,' Max suggests, 'Somewhere. Sometime.'

'Brilliant,' I say. 'Mullins and Guthrie, nineteen—'

'That'll be Guthrie and Mullins—' Max says, placing me as the assistant on the paper's title. Which cues me to thump him—not too hard as he's got vital evidence in his hand. And he slips his arm around me and then—stupidly—I let it happen. We start kissing, mouth to mouth, Max like he wants to suck me inside himself.

Until, extricating myself, I push him away, both hands against his chest. 'Don't. I didn't mean that.' I don't even know if that's a lie or not.

He looks abashed.

Very formally, I say 'Now if we're through here,' and take the samples from him to place the rack in the incubator cupboard. Max leans on the bench, waiting. He has that unreadable look again: fear? Desire? Regret?

'Daze'll see it wrapped up.'

Shouldering my camera by its strap, and re-tying back my hair, I end his sentence for him. 'Yes, she won't need to know how bad ... although its face isn't exactly ... Listen, I have to go: the parents will be here.'

'Of course.'

'We'll maybe need to consult when I've got the photos and the karyotype. And anything else.' As I leave, I realise I never told Max, so I turn around, 'I—I got a First,' I say, as if it was a thing to be ashamed of.

'I'm not surprised,' he says. 'I knew you would.'

Well, Daze stuck up for me when she was *in extremis*, I'll do the same for her. I'll use Max's interests and contacts to help me find out what went wrong with the Thing.

FEE MULLINS. SATURDAY 18 JUNE,
A SMALL MARKET TOWN IN NORTHUMBERLAND

While Jenny Guthrie and Max Mullins are preparing cell cultures from biopsied samples of Daisy's baby, Fee Mullins parks her car in a small Northumberland town and takes the grocery-shopping list from her purse. She hands the list to her daughter Kirsten, seventeen.

'And this is for Max,' she says, producing a small parcel.

Kirsty scowls at the parcel, holding it as if it's hot. Dad's Sermon.

Fee hands her three twenty-pound notes. 'Remember, only take up any special offers on items I'd buy anyway—no treats—And remember at the Post Office, Dad prefers that goes recorded delivery.'

Kirsty opens her mouth to say something, and closes it again. 'I'll meet you at the tea shop and we'll have a bun and a coffee.' Fee adds.

'Go for it, Mum,' Kirsty says, and they hug.

Fee locks the car, and disappears inside Annie's Salon. Kirsty turns the parcel over. Is sending Max Dad's sermons Mum's way of easing her conscience about updating her image? Is the change from the groceries enough to cover a choc-ice, as well as this month's *Cosmo*? (Can she keep the *Cosmo* hidden in the tree house?) She goes to the supermarket via the chemist's, buys shampoo to enhance blond hair, and a tube of sun cream which claims to tan you without help from the sun. Northumberland is not the sunniest of counties and boys like girls with brown legs ... a twinge of guilt: beauty's supposed to be an inner quality.

Fee meanwhile smiles at Annie-Marie Price, once a member of the First Truly Reformed Sunday School. Notes the amount of make-up she uses. Annie-Marie sees Fee's pursed-up mouth, but smiles all the same. 'I've booked you the manicurist to do a make-over on your nails while your hair dries,' she says.

Annie-Marie hands Fee a pale blue wrap, ties it around her, and settles her into a chair before a long mirror. The salon smells of self-indulgence: of scented shampoos, conditioners, perfume. Women chatter to the girls who snip, snip their crowning glory into fashionable styles.

As Annie-Marie unpins, and then holds up, Fee's long, blonde tresses, Fee feels within her a gasp, a missed heart-beat. Alisdair. His strong fingers in her carefully brushed hair: but, it's heavy, it's fading, it's impractical. She isn't a girl any more, by a long way. A short style is simply something he will have to get used to.

Sanctification, Fee thinks, as Annie-Marie says, 'a nice Lady Di look, I think: your face can take it.'

A cleaner's whipping a mop around under the beds, a notice stands in the middle of the doorway: CAUTION WET FLOOR. Cleaner has a smile on her face.

Daze feels odd: empty. After the squirming of the baby, it's a sense of ... loss. More discomforting than she expected.

'Pardon?' she says, realising the cleaner's been talking at her.

'Your mum's on her way—you'll feel better then—would you like a wash, love?'

Daze reads the name-label: Nursing Assistant. Why then the mop? For a wash? Bizarre. 'Oh, sorry. Yes. My stepmother,' she says.

'Oh—well, be nice to see her—won't it?'

'Yeah. Yeah. She's a doctor, you believe that?'

'That's nice.'

Why? Daze thinks. Bizarre again, or stupid. 'Nice?' she asks.

'She'll be here soon.'

Next, Daze, unsure how much she wants to see Caroline (a step-mum never replaces your real mother) and explain herself (not at all) is examined by a midwife. Midwife smiles, adds something to her notes, leaves. Daze fitfully sleeps.

Someone else comes and insists on fastening a blood pressure cuff around her arm and pumping till it hurts, writes in her notes, and—thank God—then disappears. Where's Mum? Halfway between here and Cornwall, it's a good long drive!

'Daze—hi kid. Can I come in?'

'Lils!' In this chemically clean place, Lily is the best sight yet. Scented with patchouli and woodsmoke, purple silk pantaloons disgracefully alternative. 'Finally someone half-sane!'

Lily plumps herself down, the bed gives a bit, they hug. 'Came soon as I could. Jenny said the baby didn't make it. Whatever was wrong?'

Explaining that the baby was 'What they called unviable,' unwelcome, surprising, tears well up in Daze's eyes. Taken aback, and seeing Lily's crying too, Daze wipes them off on the sheet.

Lily fetches green paper towels from the dispenser above the sink.

'Thanks. Everything they do here, they do it in kiddies' medi-speak,' says Daze. 'Let me just pop this into your vein, can you cough for me, have you had a wee this morning?'

They laugh.

'And look—' Lily blows her nose, then points at the yellow cone left by the cleaner. '"Caution". There's a deal of other stuff they could caution us about these places—the energy here ...' They laugh again. A passing nurse eyeballs them: 'Beds aren't for visitors.'

'So,' Lily says, 'Your baby had a few problems. But you got to hold her, didn't you?'

'They were in a huddle, then I had a few problems—' Daze indicates the IV lines which are still replacing lost blood and fluids, delivering antibiotics—or whatever they do.

'But then—?'

'Get this—,' she lowers her voice, 'the paediatrician was my sister's ex-boyfriend, the one who screwed up her first year. An' I did a stupid thing: he wanted the baby for research—'

'God—heartless bastard! But—was it—' Lily looks concerned, and bothered, 'really, really bad?'

'Really really. Judging by the way he pussy-footed, mincing words, *grody to the max.*'

'Oh my God!' She clutches her mouth with horror: it was she who persuaded Daze—she thinks—not to have the offered termination. After the scan. 'But you haven't?'

'Not yet.'

'All life is sacred, even if it's a bit different ...' Lily says, swinging her feet (the bed is very high). 'We thought, Rosie thought, Down's or something, didn't we? Hare lip, cleft palette, repairable. I'm so sorry, Daze.'

'Thanks. Not your fault. We did the right thing: shouldn't kill a baby. Anyhow, yesterday, I went with what they wanted—Max is a nice guy, conventional but decent.'

'Daze, think about it: that baby's *yours.* Once you've seen her, held her, she must have a proper burial. And a name—it was a girl?'

A sense of possession, of holding onto what you've got, of not being deprived of your heritage, hits Daze between the eyes. *Mine.* My little girl ... maybe there is a future for the tiny scrap, other than being given over to the hospital to mess around with?

A name comes to mind, which'll fit with what Lily's suggesting. 'There was Persephone. In Greek mythology. Lived underground, married to the god of the Underworld?'

'Cool. We'll plant pomegranate seeds—those are in the myth, aren't they?'

Daze smiles.

'Better. Your sister was up at the site yesterday. I told her maybe pollution with chemicals: we don't know what the land's been used for. It's obvious, isn't it? We should try to sue the Council.'

Daze's smile fades. 'Jenny?' She grabs Lily's arm. 'Jenny was snooping about?'

'Just picking up some things for you—clothes—I'd have done that but—'

Did she leave her sketchbook open? She can't remember properly. Was that wire mould draped? 'Shit. Jen's been through my stuff?' The pains got so bad ... Lily insisted this was true labour and even if it wasn't ...

Lily remembers putting the sketchbook back on a shelf, shoving a little packet of grass into a drawer. 'I don't think so. Listen, what's with your attitude? You don't want to challenge the Council, you don't want Jenny to see your stuff? I'd have kept her out if you told me. I've got

43

lawyers in my family—I'd even get in touch with them, if they could help us nail the council.'

'I'm—I'm not sure—' Daze says, more quietly. Certain things might even shock Lily. 'Let's—have the funeral first. Most important is I see her.'

Lily is mollified. 'That's cool, then. And whatever they think, we want a funeral.' Then she shrugs. 'I'd take them for all they're worth though—it's Persephone's life we're talking.'

Daisy swallows down more discussion on the whys and the possibles. 'The food's shit here,' she says. 'Can you sneak me in some fruit and proper yoghurt?'

*

Lily returns by lunchtime. A carton of orange juice, bananas from the market. Plain yoghurt, cashew nuts, dried apricots, from the whole food café where she works part-time.

And then, there's a knock on the door, and Caro smiles into the room. Carrier bags in both hands, 'Darling Daisy—'

She's followed by Des who presents Daze with a bouquet of Cornish wildflowers—ragged robin, scabious, foxgloves, even thistles—picked from the drive at Chapel House.

'So—here's your mum and dad.' Approvingly, Lily spots the wildflowers. She hitches her mirror-work bag onto her shoulder. 'Demand—don't let them frighten you!' She turns, and nods to Caro and Des, 'I was just leaving.'

'Friend of yours?' Caro asks. 'Now how are they treating you?'

'Mum—' They kiss hello.

'Darling: did they let you hold your baby?' Caro asks, when she's done the hugging thing and handed over the bags: breast pads, bath seeds, and sundry other chemist's items.

'I'd like to now,' Daze replies.

Caro notices the IV lines, and even leafs through the notes in Daze's file at the end of her bed. Snaps it shut.

Des hugs Daze. 'Princess,' he says.

Once Caro's established that Daze still needs to retrieve the body from the hospital's possession, Daze wants her to chill out. 'Mum—there's a machine somewhere—could you get me some tea? Could you get us all some tea?'

'Good idea. Shot of caffeine.' Caro makes off down the corridor, eager to sort things. Daze munches one of the bananas Lily brought, crunches some brazil nuts. 'Dad, you have to help: I need to get my baby back like permanently.'

'They should never have taken her away—you want me to make a complaint? D'you want me to get Caro's medical solicitor people?'

'No, Dad—I said they could do research. But now, I want to give her a name, and return her to the earth she came from.'

'Sounds right to me.' He leans against the windowsill, back to the panoramic view. She sees him pass his hand across his face. 'Do they have a chapel here?'

'Up at the site, we're Pagans. I thought a woodland burial might be nice. Lily's organising—'

'Pagans? Lily? Your friend who was here?' Des shakes his head. 'I don't think that'd be allowed, Princess. Wouldn't a nice church ceremony be better—maybe a small headstone? I know a stonemason—'

'Unitarian Chaplain!' Caro beams, returning with four plastic cups of tea on a tray, and a plump brown-haired person in tow.

JENNY. THAT AFTERNOON

Laura or Maeve must've let them in, and then scarpered out of respect to my family. In the hall there's a clutter of their stuff: Mum's brought their duvet, the big picnic hamper, and a weird pillow I've seen in our district midwife's car. Champagne.

*

It's already mid-afternoon. Hunger gnaws my insides. Mum's stuffed the fridge with food from home. Fantastic. I grab a pasty.

No, it's still deep-frozen. I eat bread and cheese. Decide not to go shopping, instead fold one of my own nightshirts into the bag I collected of Daisy's things. Catch a bus to Addenbrooke's. Thinking of seeing Daze reminds me of the violent, shocking, scary, birth. And that when I lifted the Thing out of its cot and looked at it, it was like her art. Like covers on the albums she buys, like sci-fi fantasies she likes to read. How's Daze taken it all, really?

Des imagines she's like him: creative personality, needs space. Makes the excuse for her that her mum ran off when she was little. I don't buy it. I've tried to all the time we were growing up. It's not nurture, it's nature.

Since leaving school, and when she was at Greenham and college, I've not been around her much. Hat's always got on with Daze okay. Hat wasn't in the same form at school, didn't have to share classes: 'the scientist and the arty one.' We weren't bloody twins! Not even sisters!

Maybe asking Hattie I'd get some clues about Daze's motivations?

The bus approaches the hospital. I stand, holding onto the bar, bag of stuff in my other hand, ready to leap off. I told Max how detached I could be. Working on Daze's baby, was I detached? Is detached helpful here?

Does what Max thinks of me matter? He was detached, when he wrote that letter. He detached from me. Because he couldn't tell me about his father.

Men are different. Could Dad be detached enough to use Daze—show off his work to her, con her into relationship?

45

A sharp, sudden tap on my shoulder. The bus has stopped, and I'm blocking the way for a plump woman with a big bunch of flowers and a Get Well balloon. 'Are you getting off here dear?'

'Oh, yes, sorry.'

*

Daze's door's closed: as I knock, voices murmur within. 'It's Jen. Daze, can I come in?'

Mum's voice rises above the others. 'Darling!' as I enter.

'Okay: all kinds of personal bits,' I drop the bag of her stuff onto Daze's bed as Mum and Des embrace me.

'God,' Daze says. Rooting in the bag, pulling out and inspecting the contents. 'Lils told me you went poking about in my bus.'

'I went to find you some clothes you'd think half-decent. Stuff that's your own.' I sit sidesaddle on the bed. And notice another pair of brown eyes in a concerned-looking face, across the room, summing me up.

'Yeah—course.' Daze says. 'But a person likes to feel their stuff's like safe, you know?'

''Course it's all safe. I think Lily's a kind of watchdog on your property up there! All those women think of you as their sister. Hey, they sent real yoghurt?'

Daze takes the lid off, and sniffs the contents of the jar. I remember the images in her sketchbook.

'This is the Reverend White, Melanie White,' Des says. 'Unitarian minister: we were wondering about a proper funeral for the little one.'

'Funeral?'

Despite I was turned off by Max mentioning the incinerator, I hadn't thought of real alternatives. A proper funeral ... has Daze withdrawn consent? Fighting Daze's choice would cast us as body snatchers, instead of cool, objective scientists.

They're all looking at me.

'Sorry: I hadn't thought—it'd be unusual.'

'I said Max could have her, but I changed my mind,' Daze says to me. 'She should be buried, Dad's in favour. And Lily. So what's with the freaking? Did you know...?'

'I—' I begin, frantically.

'Max have her? For what?' Mum interrupts, frowning at me. 'Daze? Jenny? What is going on?'

We speak in unison. Daze says, 'Max wanted to do some tests,' while I say, 'Nothing. Told you, Mum, Max just happened to be on-call paediatrician.'

Mum's absorbing what all this might mean, while Des asks Daze what he probably thinks is a practical question that'll help solve things. 'What about the father, your boyfriend? Or is he shirking his responsibility?'

'Dad, I wasn't—we weren't—in a relationship. Like, it's cool, I didn't want him involved?'

Des and Mum are further put out. Des looks hurt, like he understands all those fathers whose partners have said *My body, my baby* before having an abortion. In fact he's looked really, really shocked since I first saw him.

'I can't understand your attitude, Princess. But if that's the way you want it, no father ...'

Mum says, as if Daze wasn't there, 'Jenny, can't you persuade Daze to let us into her life a bit more?'

'Leave it,' I say. 'When have I influenced Daisy?' Mum makes a tight mouth.

The brown-eyed person (rounded and comfortable in shape) leans forward, asking Daisy in a soft, kind voice, 'Daisy, do you want to contact your baby's father, to include him in our arrangements?'

'Look, the father's irrelevant.' Daze is calm, bordering on insolent. She's not breaking down about the guy leaving her, or blaming him for the malformations. She's not psychotic. Or ordinarily upset. She's just determined. 'I'm the baby's mother, I make the decisions, okay?'

'Well, now. If you're sure,' says Melanie the minister-woman, casting a smile at Des and Mum. Out comes her notepad and pencil. 'We should get on with the details. I have an arrangement with the team vicar of a little medieval church not far away from here.'

Des, worried by it all, says aside to me, 'Jenny, is that normal, to investigate?'

'Dysmorphic children are born for all kinds of reasons,' Mum interrupts. 'I hardly think—in fact, Jenny, perhaps we should talk further away from here? While Des and Daisy ...' I hesitate.

'Jenny—' Mum says. Rising from the chair she's been sitting on, and picking up her jacket. She's determined to leave Des and Daisy (and Melanie) together a while. 'What for?' I ask, feeling cold. Came here to be a good sister, and get hauled out like a child.

'See ya,' I say to Daze, hoping that'll be understood as sisterly empathy, and follow Mum into the corridor.

'If Daisy wants the baby to have a funeral, do you know whether it's in a fit state for her to view?' Mum hisses at me, *sotto voce*. 'As a past medical student myself, I can understand your interest. But your sister's child?'

'*Step*sister. I'd never do that to—a relative! We're interested in human development, but we didn't cut it up, you know,' I say defensively.

'We? You and Max? An unofficial autopsy, or just what are you two doing?' she persists.

'She always liked him,' I say. 'It wasn't really—it's not the size that qualifies for a funeral ... he said.' My emotions waver: am I remaining detached?

'I suppose it's official and above-board, seeing Daze told us she signed a consent form.' Mum says.

'Tissue cultures,' I say, 'photos. Of course it's all official.' As we pass the nurses' station, an agency nurse lounging over a file gives me a look.

'And Max is in charge and your relationship to Daisy isn't known?'

'I suppose.'

'Suppose?'

'That they don't know. I'm not a blood-relation, anyhow.'

Mum and I reach the lift. 'Aren't we going to wait for Des?' I ask.

Mum summons the lift, and leans on the wall beside the lift-shaft waiting while we hear the works grinding it upwards from below. Floor indicator lights go on and off, a bell dings. 'Sweetie,' she sighs, smiling a bit now, 'life is full of surprises. We're all in shock.'

*

'Daisy's always been such a puzzle,' she muses a few minutes later, as we step out into the sunny early evening. A cool wind blows across the hospital complex. I shiver, Mum pulls on her jacket. 'Greenham. Colombia. Now this,' she says. 'You really don't know anything about how she got pregnant? Why must Daze be so evasive?'

'It's her nature,' I say. 'Is Des okay? He looks really unwell.'

'Stress,' Mum says. 'He's rushed over here after spending all hours directing the college musical. So, who knows where the baby is? Daze needs to see it.'

'Max does. No probs.'

FEE. LATER THE SAME AFTERNOON

All's quiet at the Manse—unusual for a Saturday afternoon—as Fee dials the Cambridge number she knows by heart. It rings a long time. Just when she's about to abandon the call he answers, curt for a moment. 'Yes?'

'Oh there you are pet. I hope this isn't a bad time?'

'I was emptying rainwater out of the dustbin.'

'Oh—have you had a storm?'

'So, sorry I if sounded— Anyhow, Mum: everything okay at home?' Fee recounts the morning's daring activity, ending, 'Annie-Marie assured me, "a nice Lady Di look, I think: your face can take it. You've the same classic features" she said—as Lady Di, I mean—no going back, once she set to with the scissors.'

'And Dad—is he—' Max hesitates.

'Reluctant acceptance,' Fee says. 'You know your father, not a person for sudden change.'

'Not a person for anything over which he doesn't have control,' Max says quietly. 'I'm sure you shouldn't feel what you did was wrong.'

'Yes—well—I've posted you the latest sermon—I know you said being sent Dad's sermons week by week wasn't really helpful, that you have very little time ... but time for the Lord, Max?'

'Speaking of time, you'll be pleased to know I've some holiday. I thought I'd come home and have a chat with Uncle Euan. Interviews for the GP training year have begun.'

'Lovely!' Fee's heart leaps: Max at home, a person whose support for her branching out a little into projects of her own—like the Special Needs Sunday School—carries a bit of weight with Alisdair. 'We shall look forward to it.'

'Of course, it's meant as study leave—the Diploma in Child Health is coming up.'

'Right: I know my place.'

'I hope that's not a serious remark, Mum.'

'Of course it is: sitting up in that attic day in, day out isn't going to be a holiday.'

'Don't worry,' he laughs. 'You will see me. That's only a warning to keep the Twins out of my hair. Speaking of hair, I can't wait to see you as Diana.'

'God has a Diana for you somewhere.' Max is silent.

Fee knows not to push further. Instead, 'By the way, Rachel and Colin adopted a baby,' she adds. 'From Eastern Europe somewhere. He's a bit skinny but he'll grow.'

'I have to go now: see you in a couple of weeks?'

DAZE

Daisy puts a few things together in her head. Max isn't in professional research. But Jenny could be. Why ever hadn't she twigged! If Jenny and Max—no—maybe yes? How long's he been back in Cambridge?

Is this why Max seemed evasive yesterday? He did, didn't he? Busy with the medical stuff, not meeting her eyes. Could be he visited partly as Jenny's representative.

And Jenny's insinuated herself into whatever, whoever, is involved in this research team? Jenny could get her name all over any articles. *Jenny could further her career chances by using Persephone!*

Daze always had her own plans for Persephone, and Jen's cassette is safely in her locker. What reason is there for abandoning those plans?

She rings her bell: a nursing assistant arrives quickly. 'You rang?'

'Yeah—I'm okay, but, look, could I use the phone?'

'I'll bring it over.' Time passes. Nursing assistant wheels in phone trolley. Daze, momentarily, sees not a phone but a baby in plastic cot. Goodness: hallucinating! No ... just a twinge of guilt maybe? Or even maternal instinct?

'Could you pass my bag over? And, is there a listing, like, you-know, of people who work here? Numbers? I have a friend I'd like to know I'm here? Thanks.'

Nursing assistant demurs a bit, then agrees when Daze adds 'She's a chaplain, Melanie White?'

She returns some while later, with the number on a piece of paper. 'Thanks.' She hangs about.

'You can go, really—I'm okay—'

She leaves.

Daze feels around in her bag for coins. Dials with cold, sweaty hands. Breathless. Waits.

'Melanie White's home: Melanie speaking.'

'Oh, Melanie?' Daisy uses a very passable imitation of her stepmother's voice, omitting 'this is Caroline' and assuming Melanie will assume it is. 'I'm with Daisy—yes, we're discussing the funeral. She'd very much like to invite the young doctor who was so helpful after the birth—Max Mullins, that's right. The paediatrician. She'd like to thank him for being so gentle with the bad news, so concerned, and visiting her on the ward. Do you have his number? Oh, right—so where can we find it? Oh, you do have a listing of junior medical staff—would you mind? Lovely! Thank you so much. Yes, we're so grateful for all your help.'

And then, it's easy. Though an answer-phone clicks in: a heavily accented voice says something like, *You've reached the home of Dr Wilhem du Plessis.* Daze nearly jams the receiver back again—she gave me the wrong number!—but the tape continues, *and Dr Max Mullins: please leave a message.*

She leaves no message, but makes sure she keeps that number written in her address book.

MAX. LATER, AT HOME

After maybe half an hour, that phone rings again. It rings and rings. Under the car, looking at the rust on the underbody of Euan's old Capri, I should be safe from Mum's worries and Dad's reactions. The whole haircut thing's ridiculous and points up their absurd areas of concern as old-style Evangelicals.

But the phone won't leave me in peace! It stops only to start up again.

Squeezing carefully out, I dash indoors and grab the receiver in my filthy black hand, leaving the front door open. Thankfully, not Dad, but Daisy Potter!

Can I bypass all hospital regulations and produce her baby's body for her? Now?

'Let's take a few steps back,' I say. 'Do you remember much about the birth and the baby at the time?'

'You've put me through all that crap,' Daisy says. 'As did my stepmother. So please drop the medico stuff—you were there, for God's sake.'

'Yes, I was. You had a nasty experience, and it'll take you a while—'

'Cut the crap, please,' Daisy interrupts. 'I don't want just to see her. I want you to *get me her back*: I've changed my mind about the research.'

'I see.' If she's signed it over to us to become a research project, it's no longer hers. Would be harsh to tell her this, until I'm absolutely sure. And over the phone. 'I'm not sure I can do that.'

'You still don't get it. I am her mother—she needs to be protected from being used for research. She's having a funeral, it's all arranged.'

Yes, I see it all. I understand from what I've seen of mothers of prem babies—yet, returning this particular one, which is such an interesting case—I was planning how to do in-depth questioning about the pregnancy, their diet, lifestyle, any drugs.

Jen should investigate Daisy and the father's karyotypes, possibly visit the Council offices, maybe with Lily, see if they can view any maps or plans, documents on its past use.

'So you're saying you are taking back what you said and signed?'

'C'mon, Max, you aren't a retard: you're buying time and there isn't any. I am planning this funeral, for my baby: why fucking prevaricate?'

'Daisy, I'm sorry.'

'Good. So'm I—so will you do something?'

'Yes—look, is there a nurse around? Try to talk to someone. Have a cup of tea—'

'I don't need one: I'm not in shock. Dad and my step-mum found a Unitarian—whatever that is—to do a service in a church.'

'It's the weekend. But I'll see what I can do.'

I know where we left the body. I should've contacted the pathologist anyway, and got him to prepare it for Daze to see. How to explain to Nicholson that the mother's had a change of heart? 'Daze—did you discuss alternatives with anybody?'

'Max, I'm discussing with you. This may surprise you, but I trust you!'

'Daisy, hang in there. I'll try my best.'

I replace the receiver quietly. Wiping the phone free of black grease, returning to the street outside, I wriggle back into the stinking dark cramped space beneath the Capri. Bugger all that, I was trying to deal with some rust, a simple task compared to human emotions.

Though now I wonder: Daze caught me on the hop. Should I've told her no go, she's made her mind up and it can't be changed?

Point to learn here: how to listen with fairness, while not being manipulated by the patient.

*

It's a child, of sorts. It could've lived a few hours, maybe days. It could have been a Serafina. And so I apologetically call Melanie White. She suggests tomorrow mid-afternoon for the viewing. And seems to think it's Caroline who's organising this: anyhow, she'll be the necessary pastoral helper when Daze sees the infant. Paperwork I'll deal with later. When Nicholson's around.

Having arranged to meet up with Harrison the pathologist, I fetch the body from the fridge on Maternity, wrap it up, and hand it over personally. Harrison's sympathetic: he's Presbyterian himself, we understand about people who'd request a premature stillborn to have a proper burial. And, he's privy to the ways of the mortuary. He'll have tidied it up, leave it ready waiting in a refrigerated drawer.

I refer to the samples I gave him Friday afternoon. And ask about which undertakers we use if there are no relatives to make that decision. I even speak to the guy, name of Blunt. 'As a doctor, I would value having a practical insight into your work,' I said. 'We have a friendly vicar who's loaned his church for Wednesday morning.'

'You want a nice wicker basket for that,' Blunt says. 'I'll have everything ready. My daughter can weave some flowers into the wickerwork. Suit you?'

*

Wil returns home. Notices my mood. 'Guthrie's daughter refusing your invitations?'

'Actually there's been a bit of a debacle over the research project. I'm wondering why I didn't just stick with ploughing on with my clinical work. Why'm I helping push the boundaries of knowledge by investigating that malformed scrap of humanity?'

'Curiosity.'

Could be an even baser motive.

JENNY. THAT EVENING, AT HOME

In their rush to minister to Daisy, Mum and Des forgot to book a B and B. Maeve offers her room. 'Your mum and dad said they wouldn't mind the floor, but I'm away home in the morning and you've the worry of Daze yourself, Jenny.' They accept.

In a crisis, Des (so unlike Daisy) focuses on other people. His eyes are bloodshot, he has a worried frown, as, hand on my shoulder, he asks, 'You're okay, are you?'

'Yeah. Bit of a shock, all this after finals, but I'm fine. Can I do you a hot drink or anything?'

'I'll just turn in, thanks.' We hug. 'You girls are all being splendid. Maeve, Laura: you've made good friends.'

'Yeah. They're cool ... I never asked, how'd the play go? West Side Story?'

'Great. It was great,' Des supplies.

'*Everything good in Ame-ri-ca*—or whatever,' Mum sings. Yeah, they try to be upbeat, to lift the atmosphere.

'Until my lovely daughter interrupted the romantic scene where the director and worn-out GP go off together under the stars,' Mum smiles.

'There's that bit?' I say, playing along. 'I'm sorry.'

Mum yawns. 'Haven't had a proper night's sleep for three days ... You did phone your father, didn't you?'

'He wasn't there.'

'Predictable,' Mum laughs, without malice. '*Everything good in Colombia!*'

I suppose she means he's off over there, checking out the work. 'Anyway, if it's fine tomorrow sweetie, how about a celebratory picnic? That'll avoid being too upbeat when Daze is around. Are there friends you'd like to bring?'

*

In my bedroom, as I flick on the light, a hump on the floor under Maeve's flowery duvet wriggles to a sitting position.

'Oh God, Maeve: I'm sorry you have to doss down like this. I'm screwing up everyone's lives.'

'Sure you're not, you silly woman. I like sofa cushions. Reminds me of when all the cousins come to stay. We're a large family.'

I say nothing: everyone's being so kind. Could sleep in my clothes. But pull them off, toss them onto a chair. And slide into my unaccustomedly hard bed.

'Mine won't fit two, so I added your mattress alongside,' Maeve grins from her cocoon. 'You're on the divan base, Jenny.'

I lie listening to Maeve's steady breathing. Daze has withdrawn consent: can she do that? I've my tape of the birth though. And photos. If Laura had a video player, I'd get that cassette processed and play it back. Though would that tell me anything more about the baby?

Mum thinks I would be privy to Daze's private life? I know how Daze sees me: arrogant, know-it-all Jenny, always the little adult, bossy-boots Jen, the class intellectual. Who now wants to take this poor malformed infant to pieces and find out why it is how it is.

But Daze herself poked into how things worked, when we were kids. Was envious when Dad got Max and me tickets for the Hox gene lecture, four years ago. Homeobox genes which govern the shape and development of all animal embryos including humans, totally relevant to what we've ended up working on now. Does she remember any of what I told her about them?

I could ask Max about the consent. Though if I let myself think about him, I feel that rough, spontaneous embrace again. He'd no right to do that. And in the path lab, surrounded by the clinical instruments and with the Thing in its dish looking on. He took advantage.

He fired up my feelings. His excuses for the coldness of his letter are unconvincing. His father has MS: why not just tell me straight?

MAX. LATER, AT HOME

The girls who lived here before Wil: what did they put down the bathroom sink? Unblocking the wastepipe's become our task for the evening.

Coming up for air, grasping the handle of the plunger, I glimpse my face in the mirror. Push back, with my other hand, the flopping, overgrown black fringe, and there's my father, gazing back. Face a little too long and grave, eyes a little too heavily lidded (or is that the hours we keep in hospital?) Mouth a touch too sensual for a minister? The plunger's not right: I reach for a sponge. Balancing it on my palm, I demonstrate. His pointing finger, his voice filling First Truly Reformed from the pews to the balconies and the rafters.

'God created the world in six days, God ordained the names of the animals. The complementarity of male and female. In Genesis, the tale of Adam and Eve clearly explains how suffering entered the world through human disobedience. *The desire for knowledge has its sorrowful conclusion in that men must work and women must weep.* Adam will find the ground hard and unyielding, Eve will suffer the pains of childbirth.'

'Man, you taken leave of your senses?' Wil appears behind me, a bucket in his hand. 'Move aside: we'll unscrew the pipe underneath. What was the sermon for? What's with the sponge?'

'Bible. Sermon's on human disobedience: the pursuit of knowledge. Seeking after knowledge: not a good way for a person to earn a living!'

He laughs. 'How old are you, Max?'

'Twenty six next birthday.'

'So what's the problem?' He attacks the wastepipe: it doesn't yield.

'I would do that more gently ... feel your way, till it gives a bit ...' I squat beside Wil, 'put the bucket underneath ... let me.' I take over, cautiously least the thing goes all at once and showers us with black slime. 'Yes, well, doctors sometimes call themselves plumbers you know. As a clinician I know that the welfare of the patient—Daze—is more important than the satisfaction of the researchers. Is where I came in, thinking about that. I've agreed to help her see the bairn, and I think that may be as much as anything to demonstrate that I honour Daze's mothering instinct above my own curiosity. Demonstrate to Jenny, I mean.'

'You've lost me.'

'Jenny wondered, did I deliberately ask her out because she was a non-believer? No. But my faith isn't inconsistent. And if it is, Jenny's no better: she named it *the Thing*, then argued it's human and shouldn't be incinerated as waste. In fact from either side of the religious divide, we feel the same. We agree on the need for research and future prevention. Consistency can be the chilling mark of a closed and inflexible mind, such as my father's. Don't you think?'

Wil nods, 'The curse of fundamentalism. I'm an expert.' Neither of us want to get into discussing the politics of his homeland, so he ends, 'It was pretty borderline, as a person.'

'It was a child. In First Truly Reformed homes,' (we have the pipe unscrewed: I carefully remove it. Black slime slides into the bucket, and as Wil runs the tap, water follows, as I, steadying the bucket, continue), 'marriage is a blessed union, a pattern of the Church as bride of Christ. The man is the head of the woman, the woman cares for the children. *Find a good Christian woman when you are ready to provide for a family. Do not marry too early: your family will starve. Do not delay too long: your sexual needs will not be met.'* Wil laughs a kind of snort. 'Don't mock!' I say, 'it works for some people!'

'Your dad maybe: five of you aren't there? And six of us, back home.'

'Enough! Enough water. Turn that tap off! Pipe's running clear!'

He does. We complete our task, throw out the slime, replace the pipe, and clean ourselves up. Meanwhile, I'm finding myself expanding on my dilemma. 'Does my father's teaching fit me and Jenny? Our attraction's not based on an exchange of sexual and housekeeping needs and being a provider. It's the desire for knowledge that holds us together, isn't it? The task of modern genetics to iron out of society the misery to parents and children of birth defects and inheritable diseases.'

'And you're not even—'

'No: inconsistency dictates I'm firmly on the path towards general practice. I do actually enjoy the clinical side.'

'Man, your life's a mess.'

'I know. Damn Presbyterian teaching, damn the Mullins family and First Truly Reformed! Forget I said any of this?'

'But, you're—what? Twenty-six, qualified, and have the means to provide. If that's what grabs you.'

JENNY. SATURDAY NIGHT, SUNDAY MORNING

Jumping out of bed involves leaping carefully over Maeve. I tear across the landing, the phone shrieking urgently into the darkness, and rush downstairs. They left Harriet home alone: is she okay? Has Daze developed a problem?

Orange streetlights illuminate the hallway: I grab the phone receiver.

'Jenny?'

'Max?'

'Jen. Jenny. We should talk. I need to apologise: today in the lab?'

'You're forgiven. These things—' I'm trying to act cool, demonstrate how I've matured. This woman is neither bemused by you nor in love with you, arrogant guy, calling in the depths of the night.

'No, they don't and they shouldn't,' Max ploughs on. 'You have a right to be aggrieved: my evasive letter, my behaviour.'

At last admitting he was hurtful?

'My father's teaching messes up the head of anyone who tries to live by it.'

'But we all—'

'Have to live by some kind of rules?' Max offers, interrupting. Not what I was going to say. 'Jenny, we don't have to hurt each other. When I arrived home from Cornwall to find my father seriously ill, I didna' turn my back on you because I wanted to. I saw it as we're taught: care for my family, abandon what I wanted for myself.'

'So you've added detail to what you cryptically said in the canteen. Is that meant to explain taking advantage? Did you even think how receiving that letter would feel?'

'Och, Jenny, you're making this difficult.'

'How? How am I *making it difficult*?'

'You dinna' ken how my church thinks ... or how I—'

'I know how I think.' My hand's now sticky on the phone receiver. I don't want complications. Or the hurt of imagining what might have been. Max puts his family's beliefs before my feelings. 'Did you hear Daze has withdrawn consent? They're planning a funeral. End of our work,' I say coldly.

'I—I heard from Daisy: and there's no need for this to be the end of anything.'

'*Daisy* phoned you?'

A beat passes. Then Max says, firmly, 'We don't need the baby. We've our cultures in the incubator. Chill out, Jenny. I've even talked with the undertaker. I'm taking the baby in for Daisy to see: I wish I could take you as well, but that's Daze, not me: she wanted only the essential professionals.'

'Figures,' I say, disappointed that Max has adapted so well to Daze's request. I've not: I'm angry. Just as I am with him obeying his father.

'Jenny, there's something else.'

'What's that?'

'Och—well—I do want to see you—outside of the labs, I mean ... I wondered ... Would you agree to starting again, if I can keep my father's teaching out of it?'

'I don't know. I don't ... know.'

My irrational self wants to jump back into this swimming pool, where I nearly drowned before.

'If you don't trust me, I understand.' Trust? Could I? Should I?

'We're doing a family picnic tomorrow. Suppose you came to that, on probation?'

'Okay, I'm accepting.'

I tell him where to meet. 'So tell me, how long have you been here? Again?'

'Just for the paediatrics—they had no places in Newcastle.'

'And you didn't—'

'I'm a bit—cautious,' he says slowly. 'But, we've met now, haven't we?' I have no comment! Max adds, 'It's the Scottish guilt, Jen: I havena' wanted to—'

'Explain?' I finish for him.

SOME HOURS LATER

'Jenny—love.' It's morning. It's Mum, with a mug of coffee.

'Can't sit up if you're—' I say, as she plumps onto the bed. 'That's better,' as she jumps up.

'Letter for you!' Maeve's left me a card. Inside, a little rhyme, like autographs from primary school leaving day:

> Roses are red
> Violets are blue
> All God's children are precious
> And so are you ...
> Has been great working with you, may you discover the meaning of life
> and your heart's true desire,
> love,
> Maeve (McCarthy)

'Leaving card,' I say, dropping it onto my bedside table. Maeve, who secretly bought and wore frivolous underwear. Who delighted in viewing life through a microscope, exclaiming at the wonders of God's creation. Who sees a pattern in everything.

'Whatever's the time? Maeve's not left, has she?'

There's a lot of noise downstairs. From the landing, I peer between the banisters: the front door's open, a taxi chugging outside, and Des is heaving Maeve's last bits of luggage into it.

'Hey Maeve! Max rang! Hey, keep in touch, woman! Thanks for the card!'

'Well it's just the meaning of life you need now!' Maeve calls back, dry as ever.

'Could murder you, girl, if I didn't know you better! Have a good journey!'

The taxi door slams: I turn away. 'Mum, life's so unfair! I get a First, Daisy produces a dud child.'

'It is,' Mum says, and she squeezes me tight. 'Max rang, you say?'

'I suggested he come to the picnic. After all, Maeve can't.'

'Oh sweetie. Should I be glad for you?'

'Tell you later.'

We stand, still hugging, silently communicating. It is all too much for words to capture. The sun streams over us like honey. 'Glorious day ... whatever else.' Mum says, letting me go.

*

As we lay out the food, Max appears. He looks shyly at all of us, especially me. I'm not sure how to act. 'Des and I really want to thank you for being there when the girls needed a familiar face.' Mum says. 'For your caring about Daze's little one.'

'There was nothing I could have done—you know that?'

57

'You did what was possible. We're all grateful. Jenny—pour Max a glass of that—yes, the champagne! Later, you can fill me in on how paediatric clinical is going. Now, we all need to toast the new graduate! To Jenny!'

So here we are, celebrating my success, larks ascending over the cornfields, the sun through the leaves dappling the grass.

I brought the camcorder along: Mum insisted. But I hadn't time to put in a new cassette before we left: now, when I go to do it, it's empty.

Turning to Max, 'Look. Was this exactly how she gave it you?'

'It's yours: I didn't open it up.'

'Then Daisy took out the birth film.'

'Maybe she couldn't bear the thought of anyone ever playing it back?'

'Maybe—though not very Daze.' Curious. What's she done with it? Everyone else agrees with Max's theory.

We munch our way through exquisite Cornish pasties, and toss pleasantries around. Laura's talking about how she'll miss travelling in Europe this summer since her folks want to see her at home, and helping herself to more potato salad. Mum's telling Max about an interesting case and assuring him that life in primary care does actually have some cutting edge. Couldn't look more like one of those Arcadia-type paintings Des introduced us to on our art gallery mystery tours. In which I'm certain there is always some wobbly romance pushing up the heartbeats of two of the people arranged so casually, neither touching the other, on the picnic rugs. Just like us here.

Des grins across at me and, first swallowing down my bite of pasty, I say, 'Don't we look French Impressionist?'

And he says, 'I'm relieved we'll be giving the little mite a proper funeral.'

*

'Now, Jenny—don't let us split up the party, but we ought to visit Daisy,' Mum smiles, as we finish the food. 'Max, was lovely to meet again. I'm glad Cambridge kept its arms open for you. And best of luck! He's about to take the DCH exam, Diploma in Child Health,' she adds, aside, to Des, while packing the picnic basket. 'Max, you know where I am, don't you? If you need anything any time, like a reference?

Max is still sipping his second glass of champagne, and smoking a cigarette. I watch him trying to look cool, and remember he once told me that coming from his father's church meant he feels like a person in an E. M. Forster novel, observing the poised society to which he'll never belong.

'Of course you will—you do,' I'd said. After all, wasn't he four years my senior and wasn't I just a kid, back then?

Rug shaken out, chairs folded, Mum and Des evidently mean to leave the three of us to return in our own time. But Max, folding the rug, stops them, 'Daze called me late yesterday. I didn't want to discuss all this in detail. But I know from her about the funeral plans—I've promised to take the body for her to see. I've to meet the Unitarian pastor in,' he glances at his watch, 'less than a couple of hours. And stay with her.'

He lays the rug on the back seat of the Volvo. 'Thanks for lunch.'

DAZE. AFTERNOON, SUNDAY 19 JUNE, ADDENBROOKE'S

When Max and Melanie the minister appear, Melanie asks kindly, 'Daisy, you are ready for this? Sure about it?'

Daze thinks, why the hell didn't I ask for Lily?

Lily's earthmother instincts would take over emotionally. Lily would start yammering again about pollution. These two: they're used to doing things formally, for strangers.

'Daisy—Daze?'

'Yeah?'

'She's all dressed up, wrapped in the shawl—but—we can't warm her up. Or make her the right colour. Or—you saw her face when she was born? She hardly weighs anything.' Daze half looks at Max, and the white bundle in his arms. 'Daze—you ready?'

Yeah. So don't make me nervous, Daze thinks. Reaching out.

Max hands over the baby. Daze unwraps the shawl.

Purple, waxy skin. The head and face oddly shaped, the eyes hardly present. An upper lip, but split in two, mixed up with the nose. Ears set far too low.

If beauty is symmetry, then this is simply an asymmetrical face ... Daze holds one tiny, cold, fisted hand: it won't uncurl. Slips off the bootees and examines the feet: curved soles, six toes.

Finally strips the body. Dress, all-in-one towelling suit, even a nappy. Yikes. What's this? Extra bits ... A bubble of skin containing the—inner organs? She swallows. Bites her lip. This formed itself inside her? This kicked and squirmed with life? Did it know it was alive? What the hell have I made happen?

She feels a touch on her arm: Max. 'Daisy: you don't have to look.'

'I do.'

Max murmurs bits of information. About chromosomes which get mixed up and give confused messages at an early stage of development. Yeah, yeah: what Dr Guthrie explained years ago, in the Barbara Hepworth Sculpture Garden. They'd met by chance. She'd asked about the lecture Jenny had gone to in London: he explained Hox genes: a toolkit, he called them.

Guthrie's such a great teacher. And suave, creative, the power pulsing in his veins like an almost visible energy. Really, a scientist complementary to herself, the artist. Totally unlike her own dad, an ordinary art teacher.

Daze, repeatedly returning to the Garden, had contemplated Hepworth's work. A large oval piece, reminiscent of an egg, had a hole, laced with thin wires, at its centre. What should now fill the hole which Hepworth wrought as a window on nature?

What is nature? How does technology alter or complement nature?

Anyhow, that part of the project's not what's important now. Remembering that Leonardo da Vinci drew all kinds of people, all kinds of things, 'So can I,' Daze thinks, carefully running her eyes over and over the malformed body on her lap.

It's my baby. As Lily pointed out.

Like Leonardo did, *so can I*. My project was always meant to question nature in today's world, to demonstrate that our relationship with it is un-natural.

'So dear—anything you'd like me to do?' Melanie breaks into what's become a long silence.

'Sorry? What?' Daze carefully re-wraps the baby. Persephone?

'Anything I can do?'

Whyever's she here? Oh, because I rang ... Knowing she deceived Melanie in order to obtain Max's phone number, Daisy gives the Chaplain her best smile. 'Can't think of anything,' she says sweetly.

'Oh ... okay.'

'Tea,' Daze says, inspired. 'Mum found a tea machine: maybe we should all have some, while we plan the—service? And chocolate bikkies—from the shop on the ground floor?'

That's got rid of her.

'Right, Max: I'm gonna name my baby.'

'You—Melanie—we don't baptise babies who—'

'You don't think a baby like this is human?' Daze challenges.

'Daze, let me explain—' Max begins.

But Daze lifts the meadow flowers Des brought out of their vase, and lays them on the bed. She dips her finger in the water, and shakes drops onto the baby's face.

'In the name of Gaia, the great Mother, we name you, Persephone, dweller in the underworld. Lie in her arms, feed from her breasts, dance.'

Daze takes up some of the flowers, threading the stalks between the tightly clenched fingers, so that the baby appears to hold them.

She hesitates, then kisses its weird face. In a strange logic, that name had suggested itself. Yesterday. Popped into her head, a pun, a black joke. Persephone, created to live below ground.

'Persephone ... Right, Max: swear you'll not tell anyone I did that. We'll work out the burial when the lady returns. Hey?'

Max is caught looking nonplussed, as Melanie sweeps back into the room carrying plastic cups of tea on a tiny tray, and with a packet of chocolate digestives under her arm.

'Persephone,' Daze smiles at the tea and biscuits.

'That's a lovely name, pet.'

Daze shudders inwardly at Melanie's use of that intimate *pet*: supposed to cosyfy everything?

Persephone's inside her head, now. In her eyes. Can't be forgotten.

Daze rests.

But when Lily arrives again, she's busy covering the back of the hospital patient menu-sheet with drawings in the spirit of Leonardo's. Persephone's strangely distorted face looks out from the centre of a flower.

MAX. EARLY EVENING, AT HOME

We can't and don't baptise a dead infant. As I told Jenny, we don't do anything with them if they're born that early, tiny, unviable. But ascending in the lift towards the maternity wards, words had come to mind. *Suffer little children to come to me, and forbid them not.* And then, I was shocked, and strangely moved, by Daze's little ceremony.

These texts run deep, tugging me back to follow along the Lord's path. The life of service. How can a doctor draw lines? We learn triage ... but *First do no harm*: I think we're doing the right thing. Daze has a point: if we count these dysmorphic babies human, why don't we think out some rite of passage, some gentler way for parents to say goodbye?

Driving home, I recall my first meeting with Jenny's stepsister. 1984, when as part of the student clinical course, I'd found that perfect opportunity to spend time with Jenny. The argument for working in a rural practice with an unknown team (rather than at Uncle Euan's) was accepted by the parents, and of course by the University—which is what really counts. So, I'd a placement at Caroline Guthrie Potter's surgery in Sennen, far West Cornwall. Lodged in the rather grey little town of St Just. (*Just* visiting, *just* about restraining all my male instincts, *just* here for the clinical experience ...) Getting to know Jenny and her family.

My first evening, Caroline asked me over for dinner. As I arrived at the house, a golden sun dropped between strips of grey calico cloud and into the sea. That ever-changing Cornish sea which shimmers emerald, turquoise, navy, indigo, reminded me of life before First Truly Reformed. In Cyprus, a very long time ago.

A girl was sketching, out on the porch step. Glancing at her picture, expecting something vanilla to do with the landscape, I saw it was a classic Crucifixion: but the Christ-figure was a child. And the Cross subtly constructed as a woman's figure. A child, crucified on a woman? 'Shocked, are you?' she said. The West Country accent far more pronounced than Jenny's.

'No. Just surprised.'

Her reaction was a shrug. 'An artist has to push the boundaries.'

'You're certainly doing that.'

'You're Max aren't you? I'm Daisy—Daze.'

Later, her face and mine appeared side by side in a mirror. Me passing behind her down the passage, the bathroom door being open.... Daisy applied dark purple lipstick, grabbed a sheet of toilet paper, pressed her lips together on it. Then, 'What you starin' at? Cornwall's full of magic, you should respect that.'

'Sorry—nothing—not very hygienic, Daisy—was looking for Jenny?'

'S'my life, s'nothin' to concern yourself with. Jenny's cookin' dinner—I think.' Daisy closed and locked the bathroom door. I went on downstairs: Caroline was still at the surgery. From Des Potter's studio, *Carmina Burana* suddenly burst forth. And from the kitchen came the scent of something Mediterranean, rich with herbs, and more memories. Jenny, her back to me, was taking a casserole from the oven ... *moussaka*.

A crucified child? Nailed to a woman?

What kind of a family?

JENNY. THE SAME AFTERNOON

We drive silently back into Cambridge. Mum and Des are obviously hurt about Daze only wanting the professionals present when she sees her baby. Once home, Laura calls a cab to take her to the airport bus.

Helping unpack the car, I pick up the rug we sat on and a couple of small, rectangular objects fall out. Quickly, I slip them into my pockets as Laura's cab arrives. 'Remember, Jen, he picked you up on your interview day,' she says.

'I could've refused.'

'You didn't.'

'I can handle it!'

'Yeah, like wildfire.' We hug, she climbs in with her bags, tennis racket, backpack. 'See you in the Fall!' Slams the door shut. The thing chugs off down the road.

'So, any plans?'

'I've photos to develop. Shall I walk you and Des to College, and you can browse the gardens?' Posters are displayed on our route: one advertises a typical Cambridge musical offering, Purcell's *Dido and Aeneas*. The other an art exhibition: *New Perspectives from the Pacific Rim*.

'We'll look at the new art,' says Mum, linking her arm through Des'.

Beginning when we were nine years old, he taught us everything about processing our own photos: my introduction to chemistry. He'd transformed the dingy tiled cloakroom in our converted chapel into a darkroom. Out came the old lavatory, the big cracked sink, the lead cistern. Took him a couple of months, and we had a new, shallow sink, benches, cupboards, blinds and equipment. I told my friends: *we live in a chapel and have a Darkroom where my stepfather does magic.* Even that first time, as the pictures appeared in their chemical bath, I knew it wasn't magic. Though to kick off with, we felt like the magician's acolytes, the sorcerer's apprentices. We adored it that once the blinds were pulled tight, the film had to be loaded onto the reel in total darkness. Daisy insisted there were ghostly Methodists watching us!

'Ghosts are just stories—now, this is facts, and it's where science meets art,' Des said. 'Let's see some peace, concentration, precision.'

So, when Dad gave me the camera, Des had already taught me the skills.

Today, fetching the departmental darkroom key, I will that it won't be already occupied. That I'll be able to use it for some rather grim magic. It isn't. I slip inside, turn on the red light, and lay out, in order, the tools of the process. Pull the blinds and go through the ritual of transferring the film onto the spool.

Precision is calming. It's brilliant, after the events of the past days. Two rolls of film go into in the tank. Didn't tell them my pictures were of the Thing.

Which is actually a person. Whatever it looks like, all of us, Max, me and Daze, seem to agree on that. Thinking of seeing it again, on film, I wonder: should Daze have let Des see it? When I looked at pictures in Mum's textbooks, later when Max and I broke up, could I have imagined this scenario? Daze bringing us back together? I shouldn't indulge in remembering his passionate kisses. Be very careful. That father of his isn't going to go away ... Think about something else.

I set my timer and wait, leaning on the bench, listening to its soft click. Since I was a kid I've known you don't touch your negatives till time's up.

If that site's polluted, if Daze arrived there before the end of her first trimester, then my photos could prove very useful. Might be an una-voidable argument. Cambridge Council would have to take notice and investigate. Daze could get compensation. When exactly did she join the travellers? When did they arrive on that site? Where else did they go? Daze isn't co-operating. Better to ask Lily.

I imagine putting together a dossier on the Thing for Dr Woods. A lot of research papers to locate, cite or even include the abstracts, to back up my argument. Gather the evidence, a long and tedious task—then, Beep! My timer goes off. Turn on the cold tap and lift off the tank cover, carefully pull the film from the tank and hold it up, taking a first proper look before clipping it up to dry. Initial glances tell me yes, nice and clear. Looking at the Thing again catches me out: that could've been a baby, a real proper baby ...

I clear up, leaving my negatives to dry. Locking the room.

MAX. AT HOME

Shake my head, entering the house: dysmorphic babies are just part of life. Dad would say: of the fallen world, disobedient to God. We'd explain it in science differently. If they live, we try to fix them up a bit. Like Serafina, doing well in her own way. Though still in and out of Addenbrooke's. Walking with a frame. Communicating through squeezes of the hand, tears and laughter.

Hunting in the fridge for food, I think, I could write up the naming. A young mother's loving reaction to her malformed child ... for a journal: Psychology? Child Health?

Considering the angle I'd take, putting together the elements of a snack to make in the sandwich-maker, I find bread, cheese, and hunt for chutney: none. Marmalade wouldn't do—would it?

I'm sorry I can't describe the naming to Jenny, that Daze made me promise. Might help her towards—towards appreciation of the spiritual dimension?

The front door bangs and Wil bellows, 'Anyone in?'

'Kitchen. I saw you bought groceries.'

'Bloody Sunday. How was yours? Family lunch with the ex-girlfriend? How'd it go? How's the princess of micro-manipulators?'

'As good as could be expected,' I remark evasively. He grins. I open the lid of the sandwich-maker, grab a knife from the drawer and, avoiding melted cheese burns from its oozing filling, flip my supper onto a plate. 'Yeah, it was okay. You would've enjoyed the food. And Laura: Laura's interesting.'

More congenial than his present female: Patty the agency nurse from Maternity. 'She's looking at the concept of immortality with reference to the death of cells in normal development ... I suppose looking at why death is necessarily built into life. Dying in order to live.'

'Exploring in nature a paradox that lies at the basis of the Christian gospel? She's doing this in what discipline?'

'Philosophy? Theology? I don't know ...'

Wil loses interest. 'So what's bloody about Sunday?' I ask him.

'Man, the department's deathly quiet. Canteen's shut. I've spent the day toiling through some routine stuff. Passaging cell cultures. I'd have got someone like your Jenny to do it, if she'd been around,' he says, pouncing on a tin of lager, then putting it back in the fridge, and filling the kettle. He takes down mugs, and spoons in coffee. 'Putting together what we think will be the optimum growth factors.... Did Jennifer G's stepsister see the child yet?'

'Today.' Kettle boils. I make the coffee. Wil opens a tin of sardines.

'How did she react?'

'Surprisingly well ... I don't think Jenny would like to be called the princess of micromanipulators—'

'Aagh, man—she can take it. Skilful hand-eye co-ordination, despite the short sight. No trouble with sliding the nucleus from a cell. Perfect choice if we were to want to create chimeras ... So, thanks to events—that baby—Jen Guthrie's succumbed to your charms?'

'She's thinking about it,' I say dryly. 'If I was her, I'd think long and hard before joining up with a Manse family.'

He raises an eyebrow: 'So it's on again, and serious? Move overseas. Australia. They're doing excellent work in her interest areas.'

'Possibly. I'll take this with me.' Picking up my mug of coffee, I leave Wil to his sardines. Years ago, Daze drew a child, crucified on a woman. Bizarre.

Possibly how she sees herself?

JENNY. THE SAME TIME

It's late afternoon when I wander down to College wondering if any of my friends are still about. The person who's about is Mum, on the bridge, watching a punt full of tourists slowly circling in the middle of the river. They're puzzled how to proceed using the pole.

We grin.

'Des?' I ask her.

'Gone home for a doze. Grieving the baby, I think. Wishing he'd visited Daze before, while she was pregnant? I was thinking, if nature doesn't quite take its course and a flawed embryo survives, well, Daze isn't the kind of person who'd want a termination. So the best thing happened in many ways.'

'You mean, that the baby didn't live even a few hours?'

'Des wished it had. But, better this way: Daze can put this behind her and forget it ever happened.'

'She can?'

'Well, not totally: it'd be wise to have a few checks before she gets pregnant again. But she's forewarned. And most likely—oh most likely it's a once-off.'

'Yeah. I do wonder though, what caused its flaws.'

'Sweetie,' Mum says, covering my hand—resting on the parapet beside one of those senseless stone balls on the bridge—with hers. 'You do have a lot of your Dad in you.'

'You mean I've inherited his thirst for finding things out.'

'And his objective attitude. Don't … don't feel you must be too objective, will you?'

'I found a couple of Max's things folded in the picnic rug. I wondered if he meant to leave them there, for me?'

'Max is very human, Jenny. You two be careful of each other.'

*

We're eating supper. The phone rings. '*Dido and Aeneas*? Purcell?' I ask.

'That's what's on: you've always wanted to see it before you left Cambridge, haven't you?' Max says, with a touch of humour.

'Of course: I forgot for a moment. I can't miss this opportunity can I?'

It's brill to escape the tension of my parents and the Daze situation. I do know this is unwise, but I want to go, and I think I can handle it, not be overwhelmed by hormones. Though whatever my resolve, as the Queen of Carthage sings of her deep love for with the shipwrecked Trojan, our hands finally join as we share a programme. Softly, Max kisses my ear. I

65

let him get away with it, and on the way home, a little more. I have given in. Should be more careful!

Morning always arrives too fast for Fee: the alarm clock buzzing at 6.00 am. Again at 6.15 am. She silences the clock: it falls under the bed.

Monday … Alisdair's weekly day off … retrieving the alarm clock, Fee thinks, Max: why so tetchy and edgy on the telephone?

Fee has no day off. Showering in the en-suite, she can't stop herself polishing the taps, squeezing blue gloop from the toilet duck into the loo, washing out the bath, meanwhile with the other hand, rubbing her damp hair with a small, slightly frayed towel. Dressed, she creeps downstairs to the kitchen, keen as if to meet a lover or a dear friend. Sets the kettle to boil, and pulls down her Bible from the shelf of recipe books.

Bible, pencil, notebook, and her special mug. She smiles: Erin's first commercial commission. *Save the Soup Run*! Maybe Erin does love the Lord: at least she was his hands and feet, working for a homeless charity the year after graduation.

Now, Fee hears the phrase in her heart (complete with Biblical reference): '*Therefore, my beloved brethren, be ye steadfast, unmoveable, always abounding in the work of the Lord, forasmuch as ye know that your labour is not in vain in the Lord. 1 Corinthians 15: 58.*'

My labour is not in vain. But also, it's not what I'd choose.

She sips tea, runs her finger down the worn page-edges of her Bible: the gold leaf is almost gone. *For my dearest wife Fiona, on the safe arrival of our double blessing, all my love, Alisdair*—such wear and tear, in so short a time. And Alistair is so very male … Wouldn't it have been lovely to have been given an eternity ring? Sapphire—like Sophia—Wisdom. Across the title page—King James Version, 1611—a chocolate smudge. God works in mysterious ways: why did God add to their family by sending twin boys, when a pastor's wife's responsibilities are never-ending?

Bible or prayer? The Bible falls open at her favourite page: the Lord Jesus approving Mary's leaving the catering to sit at his feet and listen and learn. Crumbly flour-dust is in the crease of the book: Fee brushes this off the thin, crinkly paper. Pictures herself as Mary at the Lord's feet.

'Decent and in order': practically the Presbyterian watchword. She grasps her pencil: so much to praise and thank for, so write a list … But prayer pours from her heart, unbidden, almost unworded, *Lord, Why me?* Always on display, when I never enjoyed sticking out of a crowd? At least I can cast my cares, the weight of the public life, on you. For you care for me.

A kerfuffle breaks out overhead. A door bangs. Their feet resounding heavily in this big old house, the twins descend in the middle of a lively argument.

'Boys!' It comes out sharply, as she springs up, her precious morning routine interrupted, to fling open the kitchen door. And then—quietly, finger to her lips as they see her—Alex swinging around the newel post with a fading grin—'Boys—Sshh! Your father's sleeping!'

The boys leave for their paper round: Fee re-settles. '*I can do all things through Christ which strengtheneth me*, Philippians 4: 13.' Does any one of the family know why she cross-stitched that text and hung it in the downstairs cloakroom? To visit and remind herself, when she wants to slip off unnoticed. For James 4: 7 instructs her, '*Submit yourselves therefore to God. Resist the devil, and he will flee from you*'—slip into the bathroom and set my eyes on that text—*I Can Do All Things*—because *Christ will give the strength*. Counselling, baking, encouraging, raising the family, entertaining the congregation, speaking to the women's meetings. Cross-stitch—how apt.

Swallowing incipient tears, Fee pulls her mind back into shape ... *Ye know that your labour is not in vain in the Lord*—

Another person's up now: 'Kirsty!' Fee smiles. (Lord, you have sent me this interruption—it is my work as a mother not to mind.) Sunbeams, falling through the window, accentuate Kirsty's golden hair: Fee, with a yearning love, touches it.

'Mum, don't do that!'

Fee, stung, makes toast, and waits, quietly spreading marmalade.

Kirsty flips India-paper pages which rustle in the silent kitchen. 'Your swimmers are in the laundry room,' Fee says.

'Cool. Mum, Max was snapping at you on the phone last night: I heard him. I heard you. Does he have a girlfriend down there? Again?'

'Max has study leave soon: he was a bit ... preoccupied.... We should cast our cares on the Lord, Kirsty—and rejoice in him as Scripture says.'

Fee's bothered about her whole family. Beset by such complicated emotions. Towards Alisdair: love, fear, respect. Alisdair is a passionate man, not just in the faith. Oh Lord, the husband you gave me. Sometimes I have only wanted to sleep and not to meet his needs. Forgive me Father. I know that it is wrong for me to deny him. Towards being a pastor's wife: such a full life ... Everything's like a dance, a reel, to Alisdair's tune.

What about Max? Does he have a girl they don't know about? Why'd Kirsty think so?

Fee speaks to God in her heart. 'Lord, give me private time, time when I'm not mum or wife or public person.'

And the vision comes: sipping a cup of coffee, alone, in Fenwick's restaurant? When she has to be in Newcastle, anyway, shopping for the family?

Thank you, Lord, for showing me how—and where.

JENNY. CAMBRIDGE

Monday: seems '*no guy is worth it*' has become meaningless.

Back from my run, I peel off my T-shirt and tracksuit bottoms, and get under the shower. I'm curious to check the Thing cultures, soon as I can get away. And Mum wants a girly day with lunch and indulgent shopping.

We meet in the hall. 'Let's have lunch at the veggie café where Lily works. But I've stuff to do first.'

At the department, the secretary calls out from her office, 'Jennifer Guthrie! Jenny, I gather you did very well in Tripos Part Two?'

'Yes, it was kind of a surprise.'

Woods isn't yet free, so I put on a lab coat, and open the incubator cabinet. Reach in for one of the containers, and take it to the window. If I were put a few cells on a slide, what might I see? If it weren't for my date with Mum, I might even have time to properly prepare them, and use the electron microscope—or the new, state of the art, confocal.

Woods taps me on the shoulder. 'Looking good?'

Thankfully not a reprimand.

'Wondering if they're using up their food resources, and ready to be transferred to new media on a clean dish. I think they may need passaging. What d'you think? And can we maybe take a look, on a slide?'

Rich Woods is calm and sceptical. 'Those cells have to grow through a few more passages before you can—well, you know that don't you?'

'I was hoping we could maybe—use the confocal?'

'The confocal? Today?' Woods shakes his head. 'You look disappointed. I'm afraid we must learn patience is a virtue in this work. Now, I wanted to see you because there's a chance for research work at Roslin research station near Edinburgh. Studying the cell cycle. Which of course we need to more fully understand. I suggested you'd be a possible candidate for interview. You'll be receiving a proper invitation, but you'll need to be there at the beginning of next week.'

'But these cultures—I need to be here!'

'Gracie can see these are safe—' he says, referring to his doctoral student who's ahead of me by a year.

'She won't—?'

'No—she'll just look after them for you. Passage them—once I would think—they are your project, Jennifer. Post finals, a break is prescribed. You've only just completed your tripos—spend a bit of time at home.'

'Yes,' I smile. 'Thank you.'

'Let me see your notes and photographs, and we'll review—let me see, I'm away—so, in a week to ten day's time?' A big smile.

I feel patronised. Ten days? Can I trust Gracie? Will my cultures really last till then? Is Woods simply sidelining me?

'I'll read whatever you throw at me before you go off anywhere. And Jenny—remember patience is a virtue, don't run before you can walk.' He smiles, then glances at the clock. 'Past lunchtime: I suggest you go and relieve your mother before she thinks I've swallowed you whole!'

'Special today's the falafel,' says Lily, plumping a menu on our table. She might've chatted, but the woman on the counter calls to her, and she says 'Sorry: we're busy today!'

I pick up the card, 'Falafel and Greek village salad? Dessert—vegan flapjacks? Huge sticky ones—shall we share? Dr Woods says I might get an interview in Edinburgh.'

Once I've explained a little about Roslin, and we're into our meal, Mum says 'Remember Aunt Val? Dad's twin sister? I think she moved to Edinburgh.'

'Just about. They visited soon after we moved to Cornwall? They haven't since.'

'Val and Dad always fought. Val joined a commune in the Western Isles same time Dad came to Cambridge. He needs a woman to spar with, he took on a replacement—me!'

With a ding of the bell, like an old-fashioned shop, the café door opens. Admitting a slim, short guy in Levi's. He crosses to the counter and interrupts the two women there, busy putting out more bowls of salad.

'Seriously,' I ask, thinking of Max and me, 'was it too difficult: Dad in research, you in clinical?'

'Darling, every couple is different. You and Max, take it slowly, see how things pan out. This place is nice: Daisy could do worse than—'

As Mum speaks, the words 'Daisy' (and is that 'Colombia'?) in a male voice drift across the café. The thin guy's talking with Lily at the counter. Lily shushes him, I strain my ears: and Mum says, 'I thought you were interested in Val.'

'Yes, sorry, I am.'

But I notice Lily looks over at us as she hands the guy a coffee and a slice of pie on a plate. He nods goodbye, and takes his snack to a table, on the way collecting some of the leaflets from a rack of information on organic and alternative foods, Yoga, animal rights … 'Mum?'

She pulls out her address book: I copy Val's phone number. I'll call her myself when I have the interview letter. Then I seize the moment: 'I keep thinking about Daze working at Dad's clinic. Where I guess she met the father. But why'd she go there? Weird.'

'People are weird, Jenny. Or rather, human behaviour is. I've ceased to be amazed by it. We see more youngsters with PIDs than we used to. A shame. They don't know these can lead to tubal scarring and the lesions can present a problem with future fertility. Then, they request IVF.'

'Doesn't everyone use barrier methods since AIDS?'

'Parties, festivals, people don't always think.'

Yeah, girls like Daze, having sex with guys they know nothing about. Though why Mum's got on to that—I want to know what prompted Daze to take that job in Colombia.

69

Very cautiously, I probe about the Colombian outfit. 'What's Dad doing there that he can't do here? People gossip. I don't want to think it's questionable. This Forum of his I went to was inspiring. That's why Max was there: that's how we met again.'

'Your father,' Mum says emphatically, 'is far, far too ambitious to screw up by totally ignoring or transgressing the ethical boundaries.'

I decide not to tell Mum that I saw—when I was in his office once—a file on two women in a relationship, who'd requested IVF with donated sperm, in order to have a child together. I've an idea that'd cause furore in some moral circles. He stretches the boundaries, even if he doesn't transgress them.

'If you're implying anything about Daisy, I'd not imagine he'd give her IVF treatment whether she needed and thought she wanted it or not. He's clever and intuitive. He knows where the perimeter fence lies.'

From her expression, I discern not only that Mum understands my unworded thoughts, but that despite the quarrels and the divorce, her feelings for my father remain. Which Mum admits is true.

'That's weird as well,' I say, 'after he abandoned us all!'

'Darling, you and Max?' Mum says.

'Max—that's different!'

But it's not. She's indicated I'm going where she has gone, and it'll end in grief. Me and Max, Mum and Dad: it's like a gene insertion. The person's in your DNA, and do what you will, they'll stay there. For ever. Marriage, divorce, whatever.

'Listen, what I really want,' I say, desperate by now to end this subject, 'is a pair of stone-washed jeans … and,' (Mum's face is behind the menu) 'I'd like an Irish coffee—skip the flapjack, I don't need the sugar—'

'Irish coffee?' she says. 'Yes—they do it.'

I decide not to share with Mum my thoughts about that guy: I shall call Max, later. Maybe come back and talk to Lily.

*

As we shop, Mum asks if I think Max'd like me in some tight jeans I'm trying on. Adding casually, 'I hope you remember about—having something with you—now you're not only seeing him as a work colleague.'

I say, '*Mum—*'

And she gives me the look, '*I know better than you,*' which mothers will do, whatever—and picks out a pair of jeans, wrong size for me—which she'll buy for Harriet.

I say, 'Don't. Harriet's nineteen now—she'll un-shop, on principle, anything you buy her. And thanks for the teen clinic advice!'

Conspiratorially, 'I'll write a prescription, just ask. Because you—I know—are totally smitten. But Max's father's word is a very powerful influence. If you—I know you—you'd never want to …'

We let the unsaid 'destroy Max's baby' hang between us: I know, Mum knows, we understand each other. Max is my John Guthrie. And she and I are moving on, to a more adult mother-daughter relationship.

We then buy girly luxuries to welcome Daisy back and enfold her with female empathy, even though this may in her view be calculated, scientific, and unwanted. It's peaceful and cosy to indulge in retail therapy with Mum. Lastly, we drive to Addenbrooke's, meaning to bring Daisy home to my place.

*

'Daisy's had a rather disruptive visitor.' A nurse draws us aside as we approach Daze's room. 'He's gone now, but she's a bit shaken up. So we're keeping her in another twenty-four hours and screening her visitors.'

'Well, I'm her step-mother—Caroline Guthrie Potter—and this is my daughter Jenny.'

Nurse smiles. 'Yes: we met before. I'll just—' she goes to Daze's room, knocks, and puts her head in, 'Your mum and your sister, Daisy. Is that okay?'

'Yeah, great,' Daze growls, resigned.

'So—who was it? Not—?' Mum asks. As a cleaner dodges past with a dustpan, mop, and bucket.

'Not?' Daze repeats.

'The—father?'

Daze gives a shrug. She's never bonded with Mum, there's a huge barrier to sharing her intimate adult life. I look around, intrigued about what mess the cleaner'd been clearing. Then 'May I?'

'Yeah, dump your bum on my bed why don't you!'

'Well, sweetie, was it him? And did it worry you?'

'Nah,' Daze says.

We're all silent. Till Daze adds, 'Guy who worked at the Clinic. He was doing a trek round the world: he's back, came to see me. We had a few words, was all.'

'Came to see you?'

'Yeah: his folks live somewhere near Ipswich. He was passing. You know.' She gestures, flapping her hands.

Mum doesn't push further. I say nothing.

Using a word she often avoids, 'Mum,' Daze says, picking up something off her locker, 'it's okay—Look, they gave me foot prints—and I'm planning to paint her. She's got a name: Persephone.'

Mum's mouth kind of drops open a second: then she realises, swallows, and smiles. Holding out her hand for the little card. 'From the myth? Original, and nice.' I go over and look, too. There they are: six-toed prints, in pink paint.

'Daisy, this is a really sweet idea. You could put these in a frame.... How's your blood pressure? D'you need to talk about it more, sweetie? Would you rather talk to me or maybe Jenny?'

Daze's brown eyes single me out. 'Jen, really.'

'I'll be outside.'

'You don't have to,' I tell her as soon as Mum's closed the door.

'Have a grape,' Daze says, indicating her green plastic fruit bowl, full of assorted gifts. 'Lils brought them.'

She drops her voice. 'Jen, I told you, it's not complicated. A guy I knew at the clinic came by. I didn't want to see him, and that's it. End of story. Do not tell your father: swear you won't.'

'What'd I tell him? Why?'

'That the technician came by. Links with the clinic? Digging the dirt an' stuff?'

'Is there dirt?'

'Did I say dirt? ... Hey, the foot prints: what d'you think?'

She's not going to talk. I'll get nowhere today. 'I think they're a good idea. And okay: I won't tell Dad.'

'Naff, though. Listen, Jen, whatever else, Max was decent about Persephone. Can you drop your investigations? I don't think Max'd have trouble with that. So, don't barge around giving him grief, okay?'

I get up and walk to the window, where I can look out instead of looking at Daisy.

Turning round, the light behind me, 'Daze, when a baby like that gets born, they like to do tests. So you have some idea—'

'Yeah, yeah. Maybe if I ever want to get pregnant again, I'll know to ask for those.' I wait. Neither of us speaks. Then Daze tells me, 'Max isn't bad as a doctor: he's, like, human.'

'Yes: he is.'

Wish, oh wish, Daze and I were closer and this whole thing hadn't happened the way it did. Wish Dad was around and I could talk to him about what she might've done in Colombia. People grow drugs there. Maybe that's the obvious answer?

But she's being nice about Max. 'And, Daze, I know you didn't want to talk to Mum about anything. But don't suppress it. Do you talk, like really share stuff, Lily and all of you?'

'I'm okay,' Daze says, by way of answer. 'I'll be out tomorrow: could Dad collect me?'

'I'll ask him.'

'And Harriet's coming to the—service?'

'Yeah, 'course.'

So annoying that Daze can't be persuaded to talk! Mum had set up the celebration lunch for me: maybe there should be something similar for Daze, what's called a rite of passage? Might even get her to trust me more, if I suggest it. 'Daze, d'you want a—one of those—a meal after the service? For your friends?'

'Lily said something.'

'I could see about inviting them to my place?'

She takes a little persuading. I agree I'll talk with Lily. That'll give me a chance to ask some other questions.

Finally, 'Did you—you didn't chuck something at him, did you? That cleaner—'

'My visitor? Yeah—hospital supplied an overripe tomato, lunchtime. And a square of foul green gooey pud!'

We laugh.

'God, Daze, what'll they think?'

Passing the nurses' station, I see the nurse who pulled us over. 'Daze's visitor,' I ask, 'was he a kind of shortish guy, thin, long dark hair in a ponytail, Levi's and a check shirt?'

'Could've been,' she says, only slightly wary. 'I did notice the lack of height.'

'Mum, Daisy'd like a meal after the service,' I say, crossing the car park a few minutes later. 'I said I'd discuss plans with Lily. Okay?'

So she takes our purchases home, while I return to the café.

*

'Mum and Dad would like it at my house: is that okay with all of you?'

'Cool: whatever you people want,' Lily says.

'Right, we'll do a proper funeral tea, and you'll bring the kids along? Would Daze want that?'

'Cool,' Lily says. 'I can bring stuff from the shop.'

'Don't want to put you out.'

'Nah: s'cool. We'll celebrate Persephone, whatever sarky Shane thinks.'

'Shane?'

'He's not interested.'

'You mean the father?'

'The bastard.'

'You know him?'

'Nah—he was in earlier, overheard me telling one of our other suppliers about Daze's baby, and barged into our conversation.'

'So, he isn't one of your crowd ... But he's one of your suppliers?'

'His mum's farm supplies goats' milk and vegan burgers. I didn't know he knew Daisy, but he seemed very interested about the baby.'

'They've a farm, and it's local?'

'Over Ipswich way.'

Just where Daisy said the technician guy lived. 'How long's Daze had that bus? When did she join your group?'

'Spring.'

'When in spring?'

'Way before Ostara—that's the Equinox.'

'Is that your Easter? How far gone was she?'

'Maybe four months. Listen, is Daze coming, when we go to the Council? 'Cos, sometimes, like now, I kind of wish there was a good solid reason to kick the buggers up the bum!' she adds wickedly.

'Lils, don't get your hopes up. If Daze arrived at Easter, then she'd probably be past the time when pollution from the site could harm the baby. Though she could've encountered it elsewhere.'

This disappoints Lily, but I have questions for Dad. Did he have a technician called Shane? Is that guy likely to be here now, in Cambridge? When precisely did Daze leave Colombia, and is there any reason to imagine she could've encountered pollution there?

*

Hat and her boyfriend Tom arrive for supper, rucksacks on their backs, like oversized snails.

'Hi kids. Maeve's lent the parents her room—Daze'll be using Laura's—you're welcome to my floor—' Harriet looks a little peevish, I'm reminded of her at age four when she didn't get a chocolate ice-cream. 'Or you're welcome to find a B and B?'

'Floor,' Harriet says. 'And this one can have the sitting room,' she adds, digging Tom in the ribs.

Having Hat around is better than expected: she takes a lot of trouble with making the room welcoming for Daze: lays out on the bedcover a velvet jacket I bought at the market for her, and the soap, and jojoba shower gel. Arranges flowers in Laura's favourite vase, opens a packet of incense sticks and places one, ready to light in its little holder, on the desk. Beside it, ready, a matchbook from the burger chain place they ate lunch. Candles on saucers on the mantelpiece.

She turns back the duvet just a small triangle, and places her small sympathy card on the pillow. Harriet has developed style. I have a cool sister.

Max calls: rational and detached, I report on Daze's visitor. 'It's possible the father's here in Cambridge. Somebody who worked for Dad. At the Colombian place.' I describe him. 'Shane, apparently. Lily supplied the name. She certainly thinks he's the father.'

'Lily?'

'Daze's friend from the site. This Shane's parents' farm supplies a café where she works. Daze won't discuss it further, but could be the same person?'

'Lily knows him?'

'Not really. But, from what she said, Daze may've been past the first trimester when she joined that group. Which would mean it's no go about pollution at the Site.'

'Pity: was a possibility.'

'Daze was very complimentary about you.'

'Och, it's my job: but, she's not the usual kind of patient!'

'You won't make it to the funeral, will you?'

He has to assist at a heart op on a tiny Downs baby. Just as well: I keep forgetting Max is only with me on probation.

*

Tuesday dawns cool with high, white cloud. Rich Woods has gone wherever he was going, and all I can do about the future of the research is nail-bite or relax. At least the Thing has a name now. *Persephone*. Odd. And I've a possible name for its father. I shop for party food and wine with Mum, Harriet, and Tom. Harriet insists we buy balloons and streamers: pink, white and lilac. And while in W H Smith Mum, thinking of the Traveller kiddies, buys chunky crayons and colouring books.

Back home, the Roslin letter's arrived. I wonder if Dr Woods mentioned the work I'm doing right now, and whether I've still got the option to complete it. Daze appears coming downstairs, her black shirt hardly hanging on to its buttons over her milk-engorged breasts. Harriet squeals, 'Daisy!'

They hug. Daze yelps, 'My boobs!' and Harriet jumps a mile high, 'God, I'm sorry—'

They rock each other, standing on the bottom step. Daze never had much bust before: I wish she had had, would be easier then not to be so aware that this is a baby she's had, not a research project I've been handed.

They go in the kitchen to make cocoa. Comfort food. 'Jen? You coming? You want a drink?'

We hug our mugs. 'So what's the—plan?' Hat asks, avoiding the crucial words.

'Service in this ancient country church and the Vicar's letting us have her … buried there as well,' Daze says, faltering on *buried*. I would too—we're all lost for what to say. Tom quietly sips his drink. Harriet gazes into hers, stirring and watching the bubbles.

I quietly open my letter: Wednesday week, three p.m. Interview and tour of the Research Station. Next chance I have, I go to the phone and call Aunt Val. 'You're through to the home of Valerie, Harris and Lewis,' says her answer phone. My cousins are named for islands!

*

I'm glad it's too busy an afternoon to think. The sun breaks through with sudden intense heat, Daze is sent off to rest, we tidy and decorate the house. After supper, as we're all heading for bed, Daze asks Hat to do tomorrow's eulogy.

'Oh my God!' Hat goes pink. 'You know I can't do words—' she says, squirming.

'C'mon—I'll help,' I offer.

'I'm not about to write a treatise,' she says. 'I'm the practical type.'

'Yeah, but Daze asked you!'

I ban Tom, sending him to lay out his sleeping bag in the sitting room. He's probably asleep at once, but Hat lies on top of her bag beside my bed, in her bra and pants, and the heat of the oppressive, thundery night fills the room like an invisible tog-20 duvet's been laid over us.

'Not—you know—not quite a person—so what can I say?' she complains, chewing her pen. 'You saw it—I wasn't even there!'

Daze's fetus, my raw materials. Inwardly, I clutch at Dad's wonderfully scientific attitudes towards embryos and early fetuses: not a person, not a person. Outwardly, I have to participate in this also apparently reasonable grieving ceremony. Wish I could call Max, who'd know what to say. But his firm's on take: in other words, he's up at the hospital in case there's an emergency for the Consultant's team he's been assigned to. 'Oh give me that—' I snatch at Hat's paper. Amazed at my own impatience.

'I can do it!' Hat hisses.

I'd like not to be here. I'd like to be anywhere else. 'I'm sorry,' I say. Yes, I am. Telling Hat I need a drink of water, I slip out of my room. 'Coke?' Hat calls after me. 'In the fridge?'

Des is in the kitchen, just staring out of the window at the night.

Am I such a jerk I can want use his baby grandchild to gain academic prestige? All science is part of a majestic whole—the pursuit of knowledge for the common good, I counter myself. But since Persephone's arrival, since the conversation Max and I had at the path labs, some new, persistent, inner voice has welled up. Inside or outside me? Is it Max's influence? He hardly ever talks his religion.

Des suddenly represents everything that's good, comfortable, and consequently ignored: crossing the room and hugging him hard, to somehow quieten that inner voice, I almost frighten him.

Recovering his breath, Des gasps, 'Lovely—but what's it for, our bright star?'

'For being the best stepfather—sorry if I startled you ...'

'No, no, Jenny. I was just, thinking. Quiet, back of the house, isn't it? But those sodium lights: glad we live in the country.'

'More stars,' I say.

'An illusion of more stars.'

Maybe that's all he was thinking? Really sorry I shoved my own problem away by snapping at Harriet, I reach into the fridge, and take out a can of Coke Laura's left. 'Brain stimulant,' I tell Des.

He shakes his head.

*

Wednesday, Funeral Day: how odd this feels.

I tell myself I'm participating to help Daze. Around eleven, having helped lay out the party food, I put on a black strappy sheath party dress—bought at Cambridge market for College cocktails and wrong for both the weather and the time of day. And, seeing bare shoulders wouldn't look right, my blue denim jacket.

In the kitchen, Mum and Des are arguing in whispers: *Pie Jesu* or *In Paradisum*.

'Oh, and Granny Ianthe sent you this,' Mum says, handing over a padded bag. I rip it open, at the same time shoving my feet into kitten-heel court shoes. Hmm: congratulations card, and a letter saying she's really sorry she can't do a visit to Cambridge for celebration dinner as she's off to Bhutan, the foothills of the Himalayas. 'The last home of *real* Buddhism!' Granny writes.

Ianthe Lavenham, my mother's mother, has never grown out of being a scientific *enfant terrible*. An early champion for supplying contraception to unmarried women, she chose to have a baby with her lover: the baby grew up to be Mum. Which makes my family, even without Daze, hardly normal! And my present's a six-by-four inch second-hand book I've seen on her shelves: *Facts and Faith* by J. B. S. Haldane. Not sure I either need or want this: I've already dipped into it at Granny's, it's dry as a desert. A normal Gran would send money, or a book token, or even something pretty!

Mum interrupts my thoughts 'Now, Jenny, I can't stand Crem tunes. Daisy's chosen something from her favourite album, to open proceedings. So, to process out to the churchyard, we'll have something classical. *In Paradisum*, from Fauré's Requiem. On tape of course.'

'You're still choosing music?' A picture flits through my mind: the hospital incinerator. 'It isn't a Crem. That's the whole point.'

'Let's think of Daisy today,' Mum responds. 'The Fauré is divine. You've sung in it haven't you? That college choir thing I was sorry to miss.'

'But on a tape? In a boom-box?'

'We can hide the player behind the organ. The Vicar told me. He often does, for funerals and indeed for—'

A ring at the bell. The funeral cars arriving.

Daze appears: black skirt, black satin boob tube, Doc Martens, Susie Sioux make-up like she wore before she did Greenham, and several chains, one with a big Maltese cross. And the black velvet jacket. Opens the front door, and squeals, '*Max!*'

Not Max. A burly middle-aged bloke in a dark suit. Holding out a tiny white wicker basket, the lid closed and tied down with pink ribbon. Decorated with pink and white rosebuds, mock orange, carnations. Obvious what's inside: a brass label reads *Persephone, June* 1988.

'Max said he'd take care of the Undertakers for me. This is Mr Blunt. His daughter did the basket for Persephone,' Daze tells Mum.

''E said 'e thought you'd like to see it first,' Mr Blunt tells her.

And she smiles. 'Thank you so much for showing me. It's beautiful.'

Why can Max be so thoughtful, to Daze? Even as we lose our research subject?

I cast Granny's book away, recalling how I argued about Max's view of the Thing's destruction, right after the birth. From my shock of mixed-up pity and almost warmth towards it. 'Max seems to've colluded long-term with Daze,' I say to Mum. 'This all makes everything far too human.'

'Everything?'

'The ... baby,' I say. 'What was to be our research.'

'It is human,' Mum says.

Yes, like Serafina. It's just challenging my presuppositions that's difficult.

Des is wearing a suit, which he must've hired, seeing they didn't know Daze was planning this. Mum has on a smart navy outfit bought yesterday as 'suitable for work'.

'Everyone ready?'

We pile into the cars, the Undertaker reverently handling the basket.

MAX. SAME TIME, ADDENBROOKE'S

While Jenny watches Persephone committed to God and to the earth, we—Sarah, Professor Nicholson's junior registrar, and I—will be watching and assisting at a very intricate heart procedure on a very young baby. The heart op—correcting ventricular septal defect, atrial septal defect and patent ductus aortas—is not going to be that simple and its outcome will not necessarily be either. The infant has Down's Syndrome—and indeed the whole case is not straightforward.

Sarah is not the easiest person to work with. She's from a great medical dynasty, and I'm a nobody—though used to it, as I told Jenny in a letter, soon after we met. Went a bit like this: *Just to say, we have more in common than you think. Being a minister's child is always a good reason to attract teasing, I've lived all over, and finally we settled in this small-town place where we had the wrong accents—empathise there too. But Cambridge opened up another world for me. Don't worry, Cambridge will do that for you. B/wishes, ever yrs M.*

Wrote that in the train to Northumberland. 1983, a few days after I met Jenny. Hoping to talk with Dad about possibly moving from clinical medicine into research. How did our talk end?

'*I'll not hear more of this, James Maxwell—you're away down there having thoughts unworthy of you put in your head. God's image is marred by human sinfulness, not by disease or defects.*'

'*I—I'll leave you to think about it. It's maybe a lot to take in?*'

'*It is a lot to take in from you.*'

Jenny, I discovered, was the famous John Guthrie's daughter!

I wonder how she's coping with Persephone's funeral?

JENNY. LATE MORNING

Outdoors, brightly humid: inside, dim, cool, almost chilly. Smells of damp stone. Stout pillars, decaying hymnbooks and carpet, uneven flagged floor, pink flowers in a brass vase on the font. Hat, Tom, and I find seats together.

There's Lily with both her kids, several other women, and kiddies who squirm and drum their feet on the pews. And a couple of the nurses who looked after Daze. Nice of them to be here! Then the little procession enters, to Daze's favourite Goth song from the concealed boom box. Des carrying the basket, Mum one side of him and Daze the other, leaning on his arm. Melanie the Minister behind.

Melanie's service is a bit more sparky than the one in TV dramas and films, beginning *I am the Resurrection and the Life*, said in a sepulchral voice. We kick off with the Our Father and while other people's eyes are closed, I swivel my head carefully round to look behind us. Has Max got time off? No.

We sing a nice children's hymn: *All Things Bright and Beautiful, All Creatures great and Small*. Reminds me of the elegant London pre-prep school, where I went before Dad moved out ... green blazer, green kilt, regulation T-bar brown shoes ... even bottle-green knickers! In Cornwall, we all went to the village school. Uniform was green, again, though. Next new girl was Daze!

Don't think about it!

Mum and Dad argued about sending Hat and me off to private boarding schools: Mum insisted we all three went on to the local comprehensive, no distinguishing. And certainly no Dad paying for Daze, which would insult Des!

We're halfway through the hymn: Mum's got her hankie out. Even though she doesn't believe the Lord God made them all. Then Harriet succumbs to its seductions. Daze clutches her mouth and can't sing: Daze and Harriet hold onto each other, swaying.

Lily's written a poem. It doesn't quite fit, unless Lily knows a side of Daze we don't.

When mothers unwrap babies,
they count their little toes,
but we're all individuals,
and baby's one of those,
She wasn't sent to live here,
she knew I wasn't ready,
she just came on a visit,
and to collect her teddy
but in her land she's pretty,
and in her land she'll sing,
We've learned some lessons from her,
we've learned what babies bring—
So, Gaia sent an angel,
and not a changeling elf,
all wrapped in human being,
and totally herself—
we'll give her back to Gaia,
our sweet Persephone,
and when her turn on earth comes round,
she's going to visit me—

Hat blows her nose, stands at the brass eagle: 'I haven't known Persephone' (I glance at the white basket again: our focus) 'but I've known Daisy since I was about six years old. When we went to live with Des and Daisy, I didn't want to go. But then, I got a new big sister who spent time with me. Des had a wonderful studio—which he still has of course—and we'd look at his oil paints and Daze taught me the exotic names of colours. "*Do you know your colours, Harriet? They aren't just boring red, blue, green and that.*"'

'Daisy made you really look at things—just like Des did—she described the sea and the sky in words I'd never heard—*eau de nil, indigo, Payne's grey, ultramarine.* She called the colours *hues.* Daze told me a sunset over the sea was *crimson lake, shot with gold.* Daze told me that white light is split into the rainbow by prisms, and even that *the colours are waves* ... Daisy loves the wild things in Cornwall as well: birds, rabbits—'

Hmm: when I killed that bunny at Botallack, Daze was happy to draw it, dead!

Everyone's involved, everyone's part of the grief-focus. Except maybe me. Too much objectivity? I take a look at Daze. Inscrutable, or what?

'And so I know little Persephone is going to—going to love those visits with Daisy, and when she has—a brother or a sister—well Daisy is going to be—such a good mum—'

But it's a dead body in that basket, Hat, I think. Have you got religion or something?

Melanie says she won't preach a sermon but she has a few words for us all. *If the seed doesn't fall into the ground, and die,* she says, *then the plant will never grow, will it?*

And then, it's like from inside the basket, the Thing—Persephone—shouts something at me. *If you're so scientific and objective, how come you were cut to pieces inside by Max's cool factual letter, and not reconciled with his explanation, his valid and logical reasons for what he did about his family's need?*

How come my sterile arrogance and cool objectivity is cracking apart? *Apoptosis,* Persephone suggests.

Apoptosis? The necessary death of cells which takes place in order to properly form a developing creature. If it weren't for apoptosis—the planned and orchestrated death of certain cells at the correct stage of development—we'd have webbed fingers and toes. In fact, some people do—the Thing has—it's a birth defect. Apoptosis can also be sparked, after initial development, by a stem cell which is damaged: this prevents possible malignancy in whatever organ that damaged cell is part of. If there isn't apoptosis, cell-suicide for the greater good, the opposite happens: things can go really wrong.

It's central to Laura's thesis on Immortality. Physical immortality is simply not good. Though Laura's philosophised about why we desire it.

Prayer begins again: I sink onto my knees and hide, my head on the pew in front. It's all about God, isn't it? Apoptosis, the death of something to bring ... healing? The idea's so destructive: someone dies to save somebody else ... but we do it all the time. On the lifeboats. You can't grow up in Cornwall and not be aware of the lifeboats! And in medicine, fire-fighting, mountain-rescue: why do we do it? People throw themselves into danger to save other people. Max felt he had to go home and help ...

That is not the same ... Jenny, you would not have done that!

Who's in a mess: Max or me?

Hat nudges me: we're meant to be processing outside. It's time for *In Paradisum*, which does at last prickle my eyes and constrict my throat. We're playing this, which is so beautiful, harmonious, moving, for Persephone Thing? Who's supposed to have an afterlife with God. That's the myth, isn't it? Of Paradise?

I don't understand my feelings, as we stand around a very small, deep hole in the ground, throwing in earth, and flowers, on the little white basket. Like J. B. S. Haldane says (in that very dry little book which Granny Ianthe enclosed in her parcel), *When I set up an experiment I assume no god, angel or devil is going to interfere with its course: and this assumption has been justified.* It's obviously rational and normal to discount some eternal, unseeable Being who orchestrates everything and demands our notice and allegiance. Isn't it?

Fauré just put together harmonies which would create certain emotions in us, due to associations from other parts of our lives. Didn't he?

MAX. LUNCHTIME, THE HOSPITAL

Lunchtime, Sarah and I are in the locker room, having spent the past five hours toiling with delicate instruments inside the tiny, bloody space of an eight-month-old chest cavity. I kick off my white clogs. Open my locker, remove my scrubs, chuck them into the linen basket.

'Patient's yours now,' Sarah says, doing the same. 'Should be straightforward.' I stretch, and rub my eyes. The return to the world, and a full afternoon. How was the funeral? I'm buttoning my shirt and thinking about Jenny, Daze and Persephone, when Sarah asks: 'Wasn't it you, Max, that Nicholson put on the track of what screwed up that Potter kid?'

'Sorry?'

'That grossly dysmorphic stillborn? Pretty good luck to get a chance from Nicholson to make a study when you're only on GP training rotation.'

'Well yes—as paediatrics is a special interest of mine, of course I'm grateful.'

'Well, the general practitioner is I suppose a specialist at being a generalist,' Sarah (who has recently failed an exam) says somewhat sourly.

Okay: now I understand that Sarah's passing me a tricky piece of medicine—following up that sick baby—in return for being, apparently, one of Nicholson's chosen. 'Oh did you hear that?' I respond, throwing her a deliberately ambivalent answer.

'Am I wrong?'

'Sorry—I've got a clinic in half an hour.' Pulling on my jacket. Thinking whether the canteen's still serving lunch.

'Arrogant sod,' Sarah mutters as the door closes on me.

Arrogant? Hardly. Sarah's problem is with herself, not me.

I'm only involved with that baby to help Jenny, to try to get back in her good books after letting her down so unkindly, under my father's influence. Or am I?

*

Later, towards evening, I'm on my way to SCBU—the Special Care Baby Unit—to check on that tiny heart op patient, when Nicholson falls in beside me.

'Walk with me,' he says, and talks of the patient I'm about to visit. Then, lowering his silver head from its great height above my slightly-above-average one, speaks in guarded tones: 'It is wise to know who one's friends are.'

I agree.

He mentions Serafina—the child who Jenny came to see. 'Serafina is doing well. You will recall she had similar severe heart problems, but it looks possible now that we can anaesthetise her long enough, with sufficient degree of safety, to do something about her eyes. You recall her eyes?'

'Very small, malformed, one lacking ocular globe?'

'Precisely. This is causing a distortion of the face, which could be improved with surgery, perhaps with the insertion of a prosthetic eye. You should—if you are a hoping to pursue your interest in the futures of dysmorphic children, attend in theatre. The operation is scheduled for—for—my secretary will give you the date ... about a fortnight. Make sure you are returned from study leave, Dr Mullins.'

'Thank you. I shall.'

As we arrive at my destination I'm thinking what a privilege to be invited to see Serafina's operation. And Nicholson comes with me through the double doors. Returning to wisdom about one's friends. 'I understand you are seeing—I think they call it—Miss Guthrie, daughter of the Medical Director at the Drey? And that it is she who is sharing your present research project. A little unwise, seeing that dysmorphic fetus was, I now have reason to believe, some kind of a relative of hers by marriage?'

Inwardly, I die. How could Nicholson know about Jenny and my relationship? Saw us in the canteen? Hardly. Was informed by the obs team about Jenny's presence in the delivery room? And assumed?

'Her stepsister's, sir.' I survey the ground ahead of me. Depressing grey-green highly polished vinyl.

'I am presuming you did not know. And I suspect the cultures are in the Woods lab at Genetics? More care next time, I think, Dr Mullins?'

I understand exactly what he means.

'You are on call for our small patient of this morning? I have an interest in him myself.' Nicholson pauses, consults his watch. 'You have an interest in Miss Guthrie. How about a visit this evening?'

My mouth almost drops open. What does Nicholson imply?

He smiles at me. 'Go: go on, I am suggesting an evening out with your girlfriend would not come amiss. Your work impresses me. Just: be careful about your friends. And perhaps she might benefit from your example?'

JENNY. AFTERNOON, AT HOME

I feel so moody going back for the party. In the car, squashed up with Hat and Tom, I pull out of my bag the things Max left folded in the picnic rug: a packet of Marlboros, a New Testament and Psalms.

So: a guy pulled in two by the prevailing culture and the Manse upbringing. Will that help me, in my present mood? The book's edges are all furry with thumbing. And when I open it, there's writing inside the cover, spidery sloping fading black ink: *James Maxwell Mullins from Grandad, Thy Word is a Lamp unto my Feet.*

Dated Max's birthday, 1974. Max would've been thirteen.

That's his grandfather's writing. Isn't it odd how when someone means so much to you, everything they possess is interesting? Isn't it a contrast, his Bible-reading Grandpa, and my Granny Ianthe? But it's not a surprise: grandparents so want you to carry on family tradition, they push who they are at you, hoping you'll swallow their teaching!

Flipping through, as we drive, a phrase Max used in an argument we once had about Dawkins's Selfish Gene stands out: *Surely I was sinful at birth, sinful from the time my mother conceived me.*

'Here it is,' Max told me, finding the page. '*Just what it took scientists so long to discover: did we really need Freud and analysis, Dawkins, and let's see—Skinner? We've always known it. Sin: well that's just wrongdoing, isn't it? The human spirit left alone is just as the ancient theologians said, desperately corrupt—bent towards carrying out whatever destructive desire—self-destructive, destructive to others, greedy—whatever comes into our heads. We can't help it. We think of something, we know it's wrong, we let that guilty feeling creep up and whisper naughty but why not? Is altruism built into our genes?*' he added ironically. '*How surprising to find it isn't!*'

'Dawkins re-defines altruism as survival instinct.'

'And so he kills it dead: altruism redefined as self-serving. Doesn't that make you despair?'

What's wrong with wanting to survive?

Max shares Maeve's talent for tying everything up so that God is a necessary part of the equation. And anyway, his stupid cigarettes illustrate his bent towards self-destruction—*apoptosis?*—no, not that.

83

Finding myself drawn by the Fauré and the apoptosis stuff towards too much self-analysis, I throw myself into partying. Though the afternoon's such a mix of gaiety and sadness, it's hardly helpful. Heaps of food and drink, kiddies roaring around the house. A lot of flushing in the downstairs loo announces their fascination with watching the paper being sucked away: something you can't play in a chemical toilet in a caravan.

Lily finds my guitar. She has a gravelly, folksy singing voice. The women persuade Des and Mum, who only know some of the words, to perform a duet from West Side Story. Me and Harriet circulate endlessly with the wine and the finger foods. The kiddies stuff down food, and spray crumbs around, then Oh my God, Laura's furniture! They finger-paint the coffee table.

Hat's Tom gives them piggybacks. Daisy takes photos of her friends.

I take a break in the only place you can hide from a crowd. From the bathroom, I listen to the continuing noise downstairs. Champagne: my head's full of cotton wool and confusion. *Wake*: enough to wake the dead … is that why …? Maeve would know … Maeve and I had fun sparring over the status of the embryo. I seduced her with the promise I'd go to church if she'd join the Choir: we sang anthems in the Chapel, she with guilt and me with disbelief.

We sang that Fauré.

I wish my friend with the Irish brogue and the unshakable faith in God was here. To explain apoptosis and me.

Eventually the kids, overtired, overactive, or curled in corners asleep, are gathered up by the women and the whole crowd of Daze's friends trails off down the road together, a straggling circus. Mum kicks off her shoes, collapses on the sofa. Tells Daze, 'You should come home and recuperate.'

'I'll think about it … maybe catch a train in a couple of days.'

Hat and I make coffee. Tom eats some of the sausage rolls Lily removed when she found her toddler sucking on one and was afraid he'd get a taste for meat.

A couple of hours later, the family's ready to depart. 'Mum, Des,' (I hug them) 'it's my place: I'd rather do the clearing on my own. Get on the road before it's too late, hey? And Hattie, your speech was amazing. I never, like, noticed all that stuff about Daisy you found to say.'

'Cheerleader stuff. I wanted to make her happy.'

The Volvo's packed: and my surprise at my little sister is complete when it's Harriet who catches the keys which Des tosses across the hall to her, and gets behind the wheel. There you go: all grown up, I think. Hat's driving. Daze had a baby. I've got my degree.

The early evening's purple and thundery. I wave until the car indicates at the end of the road and turns the corner.

House stinks of alcohol and strong coffee, of Mum's perfume and Lily's patchouli, of incense, and sausage rolls. I'm picking up glasses, chucking away paper plates, scrubbing at a wine stain (or is it the finger-paint the kiddies were playing with?) on the carpet and eventually I plump myself down on the sofa, stretch out full length and close my eyes. Yuck! Something soft, cold and damp! Eyes fly open: half a well-sucked sausage. On my way to the kitchen bin, a flash of lightning, and someone knocks on the door.

Max?

'Hi, kiddo—just picked up your message,' Dad says, as I fling the front door wide, and catch my smile just before it totally slips off my face. 'A First! Of course, there were no doubts, were there?'

'Doubts?' I laugh. 'You may've expected it, I didn't!'

Huge bearhug. Dad's wonderful aftershave scent all over me. 'What'll we do—' he begins, and then, looking around, 'What's been happening here?' he asks. 'Celebrations? Did I miss the party?' (A rumble of thunder.)

'Stuff,' I mumble, then, 'Everyone's gone—you can come and drink coffee while I clear up a bit.'

'Better, I'll take you out to dinner and we can talk—my diary's clear.' He dumps himself on the sofa where the half sausage roll just was. 'Well. Jenny. Can I guess what this was about?' (I'm standing in the doorway, waiting to ask him *coffee, tea or leftover champagne?*)

'Party was—did you hear? Daze's baby arrived. It was not exactly normal, and it didn't live that long.' I'll try to sound like I couldn't possibly imagine he's involved. How will he react? 'Party was a wake.'

'I heard something,' he says, crossing his legs and wriggling one foot, in a casual expensive loafer.

'How much? And coffee or something else?'

'Aw—coffee's fine—heard she'd had the baby and it was seriously mal-formed.' He pauses. 'One of my nurses does some shifts at Addenbrooke's: they were …' (Is this an innocent act, or not?) '… talking about it.' A plate with a few slices of cold pizza still sits on the coffee table: I stare at it, con-sidering whether, where, and how to ask him the questions in my mind.

'I thought of asking you along to the church—seeing that Daisy's worked for you,' I say, watching his face, 'I thought she might appreciate that—but you weren't answering the phone.'

'Been away,' he says, popping a bit of leftover pizza into his mouth. No more. Thunder rumbles again.

'Come in the kitchen: I've stuff to do,' I say.

'Better I give you a hand.' He removes his silk tie and carefully rolls up the sleeves of the Ralph Lauren shirt. Off comes the Cartier watch, as well.

In fairness to Dad, he does a good job washing glasses, swabbing down the kitchen counters. While I deal with the living room and then the downstairs loo: paper, as streamers, litters the floor like an Andrex advert.

'This all in the trash?' he says coming by with a rubbish bag, 'jeez, that puppy's gone ape in here hasn't he?'

We laugh, stuffing twisted lengths of clean, soft pink loo paper into the bag. 'Now: dinner out, Jenny-Wren?'

'You haven't called me that in while.'

'I've hardly seen you in a while. I heard you're back with that guy who's dad's a minister—' Dad ties up the neck of the rubbish bag, and reaches into what he'd call his pants pocket, 'and I thought you'd find this interesting.' A folded newspaper colour-supplement article.

'So who told you about me and Max?' I ask, unfolding it. The article manages to be both cosy and sensational: a run-down Presbyterian church brought alive by *'straight-from-the-shoulder Gospel preaching, with funky evening-service music from a band.'*

'Cambridge has a grapevine,' Dad replies dryly.

'It's not only Christian parents who're looking for something better for their children, says RAF fighter pilot turned minister Alisdair Mullins.' Flicking through, I learn that an attached primary school, teaching Creationism and 'family values', has now upgraded to offer secondary education to GCSEs at sixteen. And there's a proposed Health Centre for which they're confidently raising funds.

'Creepy.'

The photos show someone clad in a good-quality dark suit who could be Max in thirty years' time. And a blonde woman beside him, wearing a flower sprigged shirt and denim skirt. Her smile too adoring to be real.

I fold the thing up. He wants a reaction, but I equal his uncommunicativeness about his sources with assumed coolness. 'So—well, thanks for bringing that over.'

'You're a geneticist. You know what my work is: developing PGD, plus the male infertility treatment, possibly improved pregnancy tests for home use—money-spinner as well as convenient. And you still want to—?'

'Max and I have a project. He doesn't have to agree with his father over all that.'

Dad raises an eyebrow.

'We're adults, we can manage working together. Max was brilliant with Daze. Talked her through the blues I think. He fixed for the undertaker to use a kind of lidded basket that gave you the idea—just the idea—of a Moses basket. He also encouraged her to give it a name. Persephone.'

'Don't let them seduce you—you were raised on enlightenment thought. That kid, whatever lovely things were said, was just a—a mistake by nature. Best it didn't live.'

'Max rejects his background. Not his humanity.'

86

'Well, neither do I. That sort—we have plenty of them in the US—will throw everything they can at biotechnology, because they're prejudiced and ignorant. They've been made aware of the progress being made, and they're looking to roll out a raft of pro-life legislation. The body's a machine, a wonderful, intricate, highly evolved machine. We need to be able to clone human embryos so that we can develop perfectly matched human stem cells—the right cell for the right job. And no space has been found within an embryo for a soul. Period.'

He sighs loudly. I've just been delivered a short lecture on scientific doctrine, lest I should be giving in to propaganda. 'Let's go eat—what d'you fancy?'

Actually, I'm tired: unwilling to dispute his dogmatic materialism. He's simply made me feel protective of whatever it was which nudged me during the service towards opening up my own mind (or soul) to possibilities beyond. And more than ever resentful of being torn in two by loyalties.

Although, I do have questions for him. 'Why don't you fix me something? At your place? Could you?'

'Sure. If that's what you want.'

*

The custard-coloured Merc crouches under the purple sky: I'm transported through slamming heavy rain to the Drey Clinic, where Dad has a little apartment. Rain stops, sky's clearing, and there's a certain amount of coming and going at the main entrance of the Drey. A van arriving as we swing towards the staff parking and Dad's Medical Director's slot. What's that delivering?

Twisting in my seat, I recognise the packaging in which human organs and tissue samples are transported. While Dad's pulling his briefcase out and locking the car, I watch the organ box being carried into the clinic, and another one carried out.

A couple arrive in an expensive car, and are greeted by a nurse with a clipboard. Dad doesn't even pretend to notice the new patients: not yet time for him to see them. We go around the side and in at his private entrance.

'What d'you make of the research papers we're beginning to see on stem cell work?' I ask him—knowing the answer, and mentioning Wil's mice, produced genetically identical like batches of fairy cakes. My curiosity's been alerted by the short lecture on research without moral constraints.

'Fantastic breakthroughs. Future of medicine. Do away with transplant surgery: organ transplants'll be called the age of the dinosaurs by—well, we're in 1988, say 2003? Fifteen years? Remember I taught you nuclear transfer?' Dad says, mounting the stairs.

'One of your associates did.'

'Jenny, the long history of medical research has always depended on willing donors and patients who agree to try new things. The doctor-patient relationship, nowadays, is a contract. Between equals. No more paternalism. If my students or my staff or my patients want to earn a bit by contributing their oocytes, well and good. Or their embryos. You know that theoretically, the wasted oocytes of an aborted female fetus could be grown up and used to grow stem cells for medical research, or even treatment? It isn't far away.'

'Of course. We all know about the possibilities of growing and using cells immunologically matched to the patient, using embryonic stem cells. There's an enormous amount of work to be done, though. Isn't there? On cloning. Are you into that, here or in Colombia?' Seeing Persephone's pathetic little body in my mind, I add: 'You and I've both seen what aborted cloned calf fetuses can be like—haven't we?'

'Science moves on all the time,' Dad says, not missing a beat. 'A whole raft of possibilities stretches out once we truly understand the cell cycle.'

A raft stretches out—I want to smile at the phrase, but don't. 'I may even be working on that—at Roslin—you know it?'

'Well, then, you're gonna unlock its secrets!' he says, flinging wide his front door. His trendily decorated, batchelor-pad living area with large sofas, massive TV and music centre, and leathery bar, is revealed.

I kind of laugh. 'A tiny corner maybe, Dad!'

'But key!' he says. 'What can I fetch you?'

I sink onto a sofa to browse his Clinic brochures, sipping the glass of white wine he has pressed into my hand. While he heads for the kitchen nook and makes pasta with mascarpone and mortadella, and a rocket salad.

'You look a lot like your mum,' he says, total change of direction. 'Caroline's hair with that shimmer of gold.' Creeping into my good books? But I'm here to discuss Daze's baby. The scrappy humanoid we buried earlier. 'I'd have been happy for you all to come over to Caltech with me.'

'No, you and Mum parted over more than the brain-drain.' And I glance at his bookshelves and immediately notice the photo: an athletic-looking girl in skiing togs. 'Anyway, let's see … that's Karen, isn't it? Is it—long-term?'

'You'll be the first to know, babe.'

'Shouldn't Karen be?'

He lets a beat go. Then laughs, 'Good point,' he says, shaking his head.

I let the banter pass me by. Karen—one of his senior scientists I met on our tour, the summer holidays after Max dumped me—is now Dad's girlfriend. He's not ever going to remain celibate. Why should he?

But Mum keeps a special place for him, in her DNA. Despite she's been with Des for thirteen years!

'Madame est servi!' he exclaims, and I, recalling my schoolgirl French, move to the smoked glass and steel table.

'A great window of opportunity,' Dad says, continuing on the Roslin theme. 'Co-operation goes ahead in many different centres.' He adds, passing the rocket salad, 'You'll be in the van.'

'Hope it's a comfortable one!' I grin. 'So. Although you've got all the resources in the US, Carter and every president since have considered the interests of the moral majority. They've banned work which harmed or destroyed human embryos. You can't work there any more. So, the venture capitalists who think private labs will beat the academics to the answers moved in, and you can dodge government regulations?'

'Right on the money, kid. The US is the engine for biomed research worldwide, with substantial public resources devoted to basic and applied research. But, we need as permissive an environment as possible. A secular state with a strong government. Easier to get that over here! We don't need schools like your Reverend Mullins', dragging God back into the equation.'

'Just like in Russia,' I say dryly. Less complicated for research scientists to view all life as a kind of machine. Until it's given a religious burial. 'Like you said earlier, creation really means putting the right bits together and shooting an electric shock through. No more no less.' Back on track, wondering about Shane, I continue, 'Describe Colombia?'

'Set not far from a little Amazonian forest township, that clinic is doing remarkable things.'

Remarkable things: raised on Haldane's wonderful futuristic visions, which you might mistake for the plots for science fiction novels, I'm alert to the phrase. Gene therapy, gene insertion, crossing species characteristics to improve on humanity ... I intended to ask about the location, and possible pollutants, but as we're discussing the justification of experiments using human life, let's go with that first. 'Do they contribute their oocytes? Your staff in Colombia? Painful, isn't it, for a woman to produce lots of ripe eggs instead of the usual single one per month?'

Dad ignores my question. 'Nicholson mentioned your project to me.'

'Professor Nicholson? God, you didn't let him connect Daze and me?' Dad's introduced this subject deliberately: knocked my breath away.

'Our paths do cross, Jenny. He knows who you are.'

'Yes—but ...'

'Jenny—Jenny—' Dad holds up his hand to stop me. 'Babe, Nicholson knows nothing! He simply admires what he knows of *you*.' Laughing at my fears of Nicholson's wrath. 'We exchanged enough words for him to convey to me, in that dry tight-lipped style, his congratulations on passing on my genes,' he grins.

His eyes crease up when he turns his special look on you: a look kept for the women in his life: me, Hattie, Mum ... now Karen.

'Phew: imagine if he knew.'

'Listen,' Dad adds, 'you two may've made some crazy connections, that kid arriving so soon after the technique you heard described at the

Forum, but, *read my lips*, the new technique—the male infertility treatment—is safe, nothing wrong with it.'

We're both silent. It wasn't his technique I was meaning, it was Nicholson's stamping down on the ethics of my involvement. But he's picked up on my mistrust.

And now, responding to the oocyte question, he lays down his fork, and covers my hand with his: warm, dry, and ever so slightly rough. 'Jenny. Jenny. I appreciate your concern. I do. But no, I did not recruit from within the family—even my ex's stepfamily. Yes, Daze was in Colombia; no, she was not part of an experimental programme. As for the new answer to male infertility: needs further fine-tuning, but, heck, the first babies were normal and you never saw anything as thrilling as the look on the parents' faces. Men who thought they could never be fathers.'

'That lovely warm feeling,' I say.

I hope what he's said is true. Success—in terms of the gratitude of people who he's given what they want most—is what he craves and lives on. Like an addict. 'You tested the technique on couples who otherwise wouldn't be amongst your clients, people who'd never afford the treatment ... They were totally normal phenotypes? All of them?'

'The first babies were born perfect.' He stands and removes our plates. 'Fruit, baby? I have strawberries in the fridge.'

'Love strawbs. In South America?'

'I was there in the delivery room. We flew the couples to the capital, big modern hospital, everything you need. Paediatrician checked 'em over, nothing wrong. All kinds of tests. Perfect. You want ice cream? Home made by our chef?'

'Please. And, I was there in the delivery room, when it was Daze's baby. So, your ideas?'

'Kid, I don't know.' He scratches his head. 'One of nature's mistakes: obviously not picked up by scanning. PGD'll change all that, babe. Hey,' (smiling like he's offering me a lollipop) 'I show them their embryos before we re-introduce them—introduce them to their possible kid— fertilised embryos that we care about as much as the clients do. The look in their eyes: like kids—'

'In Disneyland?'

'You come down to the lab, after this, I'll show you.' Moving to the fridge to make dessert.

'No, tell me about that technician you mentioned before—the one Daze ran around with?'

'Ooh—Shane McShane?' Dad places ice cream topped with strawberries in front of me.

So I was right about Shane, who was at Lily's café! And now, I have a surname for him.

'C'mon, tell me?'

Dad spoons in a few mouthfuls, then says 'Shane's a good degree in biochemistry, and a few crazy ideas that led to his giving himself a gap year travelling.'

'Crazy ideas?'

'Some friends into saving the rainforests. Daze went along on a couple of trips. He'd yak a bit about what's in essence marginal philosophy, which tries to impact on our work. Hey, remind me: I'll give you a shirt! We fertility experts actually don't need to re-define the usefulness of humans and animals. We're only helping couples have what they want. Pro-life in fact!' He laughs at his joke. 'They were more thrown together than they were an item. And there's your answer: casual sex, I suspect. What did Daze say about him?'

'What do you say: did this guy use? Like, drugs? After all, it is Colombia.'

'Not allowed on site. Does Daze?'

'A bit.'

'Jenny, I don't need to make excuses. I have nothing to hide!' Dad spreads his arms wide, as if whatever I think he might be hiding is going to be in the inside pockets of his jacket, or even his armpits. 'Zero! Zilch! Jenny, always think the simplest solution first. When that's eliminated, begin to think the bizarre ones! One of nature's mistakes slipped through. What tests are you planning—on your samples?'

I describe what we've done and what I plan to do. Karyotype. Photos and literature search. Looking at chemical exposure or drugs. 'Going the right way,' Dad says.

'Cool. No factories with noxious fumes or effluent nearby your place?'

'You kidding? First thing I'd want to avoid, baby!'

'Of course. You'd locate in a nice non-industrial area ... Daze was mega-impressed with everything. And the archaeology. When was it she left? Did she fly straight home?'

'Company jet to Miami I think. From there scheduled flight to Heathrow. March. My PA booked it. Gold Museum's impressive: you must come over some time with me.'

'Daze said same as you. When she left, she seemed okay?'

'Babe: let it go. You know—my next project? Assisted hatching—'

'*Persephone*: you're an expert on pregnancy and you noticed nothing? Daze was well, was she? She wasn't like, throwing up, feeling queasy?'

'I'm an expert on *fertility*!' he chuckles, as if that and pregnancy are unconnected.

*

I let him show me the embryos: Dad (or one of his colleagues here) made those for somebody who's going to be so thrilled to have the baby they've been longing for. And he hands me a T-shirt with a logo about saving the rain forests, in Brazilian Portuguese. Then he drives me home.

91

As I'm climbing out of the Merc, 'Go for it, kid. It's your project! I do appreciate you wanted to come over,' Dad says. Then adds, 'The myths your Reverend Mullins peddles have always been the enemies of progress. Thank God we now have people like Dawkins and Singer who've articulated a rational approach based on Darwin.'

Then, is it the emotional rollercoaster I've been on with Max back in my life, my degree results, thinking I've located Daze's lover, Persephone's father—or is it just funny anyhow?

'Why you laughing?' Dad asks, bemused.

'Because of what you said—*thank God for Dawkins*—thank God you don't believe is there for the guy who denies his existence? I know what you mean—but—funny—so I laughed.'

Dad shakes his head dismissively. Waves as he drives away.

*

Dad: fraternising with Nicholson. That's disturbing. Nothing to hide? All I've learned, and not learned, about Daze's time at the clinic is interesting input. Plus he's confirmed Shane's involvement with Daze.

I open the door: the dark silent house, empty of my family, waits. It almost hums, or is that my own ears? Laura and Maeve gone.

Family gone.

Just me. Take a few steps into the hall, switch on the light: there's a note on the mat.

'*Unexpected free evening, & thought you could do with some support after the rigours of today, but seems I missed you! See you very soon. Love, M.*'

Oh. Lean on the door to close it, re-reading the note. He came looking for me, and I was at Dad's! Do I want to look for him, now? *Love*, he wrote…. And I have information.

Max the paradoxical: the incinerator, the church service. Fauré, apoptosis, that white florally decked basket.

Dad and Karen … Mum's attraction to him … Daze and Shane?

Love? Hormones? What's love if we're machines?

Look at my watch: it's not late. Instinct prevails over common sense.

As I cycle towards Max's house, the streets are still shiny from the pouring rain, but the moon and stars are out.

*

I love that shy grin. It spreads from his eyes to his mouth to every part of him, and he sweeps me up into his house like I'm just what he's been waiting for. 'Hey, I need to lock my bike!'

'Better put it in the hallway,' Max says, leaving me and hauling it inside. 'So: how was it? Today?'

'Confusing.'

'Life can be confusing. You've never been here, have you?'

'I was at Dad's: he mentioned Professor Nicholson.'

'Did he?'

Max closes the door. I look around the hall: my bike has joined another bicycle, a couple of hockey sticks, and a tangle of shoes, trainers, and briefcases. A leather jacket hangs on the newel post. A British Medical Journal lies on the bottom stair.

'Nicholson gave me an evening off, and I'd been hoping we'd have a meal out. Take your mind off the confusions of today, and maybe talk about the project. Can I offer you a coffee? Music?'

'Music?'

'Therapeutic. For the confusion. Which you've highlighted.'

'It wasn't *that* confusing.'

As we move towards the back of the house, several raised voices start up behind a door. Max says, 'Wil and his cronies with a curry: you won't want to meet them, we'll go upstairs. First left on the landing, I'll bring the coffees.'

Tidy room! Bed, desk, chair, clothes cupboard. Open window behind the desk. Again, everything belonging to a person who's important glows with significance, like the Bible and the ciggies he left me. Like a dossier on their personality: what they own, how it's kept, what they've touched, what they do with it. On the desk, piles of books, some open, anglepoise lamp. He's studying for the Diploma in Child Health: *Nelson's Paediatrics* lies open at a page on some nasty skin diseases. Across the back of the desk, supported on two piles of cassette tapes, is a black-painted plank forming a shelf. On this sits the skull from Max's bone box. Every med student has a bone box, but Max has used the skull as a feature: it wears a panama hat with a red spotted scarf tied around it, and shades. Sellotaped on.

This is such a guy's room, I think, turning away, and noticing the squash racquet, and the violin case, behind the door. The bike repair and Ford Capri manuals, both well thumbed, the pile of *New Scientist* magazines stacked by date. At least it smells clean, with a touch of TCP.

The skull surveys me as, head sideways, I try to read the titles of the tapes: what kind of music will my therapy be?

'Och, you found those!' Max is back with coffee steaming in mugs. 'Dad's sermons. You don't want to listen—do you?' he jokes, placing our drinks on the desk beside the books.

'Really? And there's Fauré's *Requiem*. They chose *In Paradisum* today. I let it get to me. Since when Dad's been underlining his mechanistic universe attitude combined with a few swipes at religion, typical Dad.'

'You poor wee lassie! But I thought you weren't religious? Am I wrong?'

'Whose recording?'

'That? Those are a few wee pieces of my past I didn't want to leave behind at home.'

'You've gone pink: you sang in it? A solo? When?'

'You don't want to know. Now here's something ...'

Very carefully Max is removing a tape, without the shelf sloping or the skull sliding. He puts it into the player. When he presses the button, there's a few bars of sorrowful, lilting fiddle music, and then a girl's voice, one of those sweet sad northern folk songs full of longing, with a rhythmic beat that demands a slow dance.

Our eyes connect. We connect: each out reaching out, into an embrace, and begin dancing. Circling on the spot, swaying gently. The way Max strokes my hair back from my neck sends signals to parts of me that evolved for a purpose I didn't come here for, and my brain instructs those parts not to listen to basic instinct.

'You're on probation,' I say, suppressing a wobble in my voice, and gazing into Max's eyes (hooded by too much work). Max slides his hands lower and lower down my back until he's pressing me against himself. Feeling his hardness against me. I want it, I want him. I move to put my hand over his erection. He kisses my earlobe. 'Pearl studs, is that new since I was in Cornwall?'

I pull my sensible self together. All very well, my brain says, about him being aroused, but he's untrustworthy. And even if he isn't, he can be made to wait. That straying hand moves away, as I say, 'Everything is new since you were in Cornwall: you wrote a rather unpleasant letter, and it changed things.'

'I apologised.'

'Yeah, so you're on probation.'

'Yeah, I am. Own stupid fault.'

'Yep.' And he loosens his hold on me. I don't let go of him, though. 'Dad confirmed my suspicions, anyway.'

'About me?'

'No, about Shane. He worked for Dad, he's hung out with Greenpeace types, he was a friend of Daze's in Colombia.'

Max raises an eyebrow.

'I came here to tell you. Shane fits the father slot. I think we might consider, that is I'll check out, male drug use and chromosomal abnormalities. What recreational drugs might do to male fertility, or to the spermatozoa? If Dad's technicians in Colombia contribute samples for the research, which are stored, then maybe there's a sample of Shane's DNA just waiting there?'

'Och, Jenny, you do change the subject suddenly!'

'Yeah, well, it seemed appropriate somehow. Maybe something reminded me?'

'You are a witch. You know that don't you?'

'Seriously, I do. Oh don't look at me like that: okay, it's funny!'

'In an ironic way ...'

'Dad also told me he hangs out with Nicholson sometimes.'

'Yes ...' The erotic danger passed for now, we sit side by side on Max's bed, sipping cooling coffee while he tells me how Nicholson has warned him off working with me on Persephone's genetic profile.

'Hell,' I say. 'She's not a blood relative.'

'Conflict of interest all the same. But it wasn't for nothing, was it? Or was it?'

'God. Apoptosis. Word stuck in my head at the service. Thought of you: the death of cells for some useful purpose, I knew that's how you'd see it! I'll try to at least get a look at the cultures before he hounds me out of the way: it's you he's warned, you work for him. I don't.'

'Time I took you back, I think?'

'I've—got my bike ...'

But I push it, and Max walks with me, and as we kiss on the doorstep, I wish this probation idea wasn't in both our heads. Just imagine, we walked all the way discussing the fertility solutions Dad offers his clients, even the ones who can't have a child together because they both have the same sexual organs. Dad doesn't see why not, in some cases he makes it possible, and he's very discreet.

'*An artist has to push the boundaries*—I quote Daisy,' Max says drily.

DAZE. THURSDAY AND FRIDAY, THE TRAVELLERS' SITE

All that flummery over. The stuff they wanted, the ceremony they chose. Back at Lily's bus, Daze struggles with herself. Without the family, find her own solutions.

The Traveller women have been served notice to quit within a month: Lily presses Daze on the subject of polluted ground. 'If we can prove this place's a total shithole,' says Lily. 'We might be able to swing a better deal next time. You'd definitely get compensation. Isn't there a human right to a clean unpolluted environment to raise kids? If not there should be!'

'Clean water,' mumbles Daze.

'C'mon: isn't your sister into all that? A medic boyfriend?' someone suggests.

'Yeah, yeah: but, you know, making waves; I don't want to.'

'Aw, Daze ...'

'God, can't you lot all *shut up*!'

The group are stunned: almost physically they move back from Daze, who seems incandescent with fury at their understandable suggestions. Daze sways as she sits on the mattress Lily's covered with bright throws and cushions, and curtained off so she can have privacy. Back and forth, softly banging her head against the side of the bus. Think, think. Persephone: named and given to the earth. That creeping sense of loss trying to assert itself. Loss of—? A sense of—guilt?

This was never meant to be.

What to do, how to manage everything?

Make it happen! You thought that in the hospital, girl. Have faith in yourself, nobody else will ... Then, light at the end of the tunnel: she puts on a tape of whale songs. Universal mammalian sound, deep wordless communication. Eyes closed, sink into those sounds ... Yes ... reconnected with her determination when she reclaimed Persephone for her own ... Work alone, at her own pace. The project's gonna be a lot of work, the casting'll be quite a performance. Resin. Fibreglass?

Stupid to let Dad drive the bus back: and God! With the Project inside! And her money, in fact all her really important stuff. Bloody idiot!

But, how about working there, Sennen? Share the studio? Dad's a wus, but a cool one: won't ask questions, believes in trust. Even, share the project with Dad? Get his advice on casting?

No way! Thank God she had her wits about her, less than a day after the birth, nicked the cassette out of that snazzy camcorder before Max took it back to Jenny. Didn't pay enough heed to the techie stuff at college, though. Now, she must perfect videotape editing. Who'd know how? One of Dad's colleagues? Nah. Bryn Williams, used to go out with Jenny Four-Eyes! Who's still in St Just, the family electrical business. And his hobbies include video recording and editing.

Shut the door on Dad and Caro, who're too busy at work to interfere, either with sympathy or advice, and on the Traveller women, and any grand schemes to challenge Cambridge council. Emerge from the chrysalis a butterfly with purpose.

Meanwhile, the women decide Daze's retreat from them is pure grief. It must be. They're all mothers, and how would they feel themselves? Gutted. Maybe they shouldn't have approached the subject so soon after the Wake: insensitive. So they creep around, apologising, offering little crumbly bits of comfort, a choice morsel of food, a scented candle, a share of a spliff, an offer of a massage or a quiet walk together. They try to keep the kiddies occupied away from Daisy. Watch and wait, the women decide.

JENNY

Next morning, I arrive at Genetics, full of the information I've put together on Shane and that warm feeling that Max, though on probation, is back in my life. Rich Woods appears. Shouldn't he be on holiday? 'I was hoping you hadn't left, Jenny.'

'Yes? I've found some leads about the baby's father, ideas to follow up—'

'Can I stop you there? I was called back from leave. We've had a bit of a ... disaster.'

'Oh?' My mind's a mineshaft down which his words fall, clanging hollowly as they hit bottom. 'What happened?'

'I'm afraid someone—it wasn't Gracie!—foolishly flicked the wrong switch. The incubator cupboard was turned off for long enough to—'

'Kill our cultures?'

When I set up an experiment I assume no god, angel or devil is going to interfere with its course: and this assumption has been justified, Haldane wrote. But a human being can and has.

'Jenny, come into my office.' Dr Woods corrals me along. Once we're inside, he closes the door. 'I am truly sorry,' he says, indicating me to sit in the spare chair he keeps for interviewing us on our progress. And furrowing his brow. 'It's a nasty shock to lose your work.'

'It was such an opportunity. Who could be so stupid? We have notices to remind us. I should've been there, I should've—'

'Jenny, regret is natural, but we can't lean back on it and beat ourselves, or others, up. Sometimes the experiment will fail, you will lose cultures. The lesson to learn is this: don't give up when things work out in unexpected ways.'

I bite my lip. Dr Woods continues with advice: the Thing project wasn't a solid piece of my career. The Roslin interview is far more likely to lead somewhere. Cut my losses, put it behind me, go to Edinburgh ready to confound them with my brilliance. Or rather, to perform well and look poised and enthusiastic.

'But—' I begin.

'You have photos? Yes. But, Jenny,' (he looks meaningfully at me) 'loss can sometimes teach us patience, creativity, endurance. I gather Professor Nicholson gave permission for that project before he knew there was a conflict of interest. You might be wise to just forget you began the work?'

Yeah, I might.

Though I'm furious as hell this has happened. Momentarily I even think Nicholson planned it—but no, people don't behave like that. Do they?

'I'd advise you collect your negatives, do something about destroying them, be nice to your grieving stepsister, and prepare for Roslin. The letter arrived?'

I mustn't let Dr Woods see the sweat trying to break out, the incipient angry tears. It's an effort to smile and say steadily, 'Yes. Interview Wednesday week.'

'Good. I wish you luck.' Woods dismisses me. I creep from the lab, collect my photos, and go to recover alone in the loos.

My father's pride in describing his work gave me so much information and clues about areas of Daze's possible involvement. And now, the door slammed on my careful detective work by the careless flick of a switch! *Apoptosis*: so something else can live?

What? My chance to work near Edinburgh? My relationship with Max, whose boss—Professor Nicholson—yatters with my father?

*

As if it still matters, I spend the day reading up on the effects various recreational drugs can have on male fertility. And puzzling about whether Daisy could possibly have *wanted* a baby. Seems unlikely. Research may've shown teenage girls who get pregnant want someone to love and call their own—but not Daze!

So what zany idea might working at Dad's clinic have suggested to her peculiar brain?

Early evening, it's me who's unlocking my bike outside college when Max comes by. Doing a really wicked thing: he's heard from Wil du Plessis about the disaster at the Woods lab and he's come straight from work to find me!

'So how bad is it?'

'Just everything that was in our incubator cupboard destroyed—all the Woods lab work, so that means our project!'

'Oh no: that's terrible.' I let him put his arm around me. At last, somebody really important cares.

'Woods told me to destroy my negatives! He was so complacent! You should've heard him. "Live, learn and accept" ... and then he mentioned Nicholson, and avoiding conflicts of interest. Nicholson should be pleased, every scrap of evidence is gone ... it makes me so cross. I hate failure!'

'You haven't failed. Somebody destroyed our work, that's not your fault.'

We begin walking, me pushing my bike, and letting go my bitterness. 'Doesn't make anything better, does it?'

'Why should it?'

'S'pose you've got a point. Why should it? We were victims.'

'Don't go down that road, Jenny!'

I look at him, picture of maturity, coolness, calm. Feeling defeated by his rationality, I choose my words carefully. 'After all the cutting edge stuff he told me about yesterday, for a moment I thought they could've all colluded. Woods, Nicholson, and Dad ... to hide what Dad was into. But that'd be nonsense, wouldn't it?'

'Colluded? I wouldn't think so. Though with the conflict of interest, possibly solves any problems. I'm as sorry as you are about losing our project, but we can't bring the cultures back and we're clear of any wrongdoing an ethics committee might've accused us of.'

'The voice of common sense,' I say, a touch ironically.

'It's often best to take our minds off things. Let's do what we can do: let me put that bike in the car, and drive you home.' As our eyes meet, after heaving the bicycle into the Capri, where it only just fits, Max adds, grinning with evil, 'You can cook me dinner!'

'Hey, Max, where've you been? I might be your girlfriend, but never your slave! And what about probation?'

'Just trying it on! We'll cook dinner. Unless you'd rather go out?'

'In would be nice. I've a prescription to collect and then ... listen, I've been reading up on the possible effects of the hippy lifestyle on the germ line DNA.'

'Lighten up, Jen! I've had a hard day as well. Will we grill a pair of lamb chops or go by the chippy on the way over?'

What did Mum say? 'You two be careful with each other'? Max was so thoughtful, knowing I'd be desolate and coming to find me after work. Now the chemistry between us is buzzing again. We're trying to ignore it and cook a meal, when the phone, which lives on a shelf just inside the kitchen, rings. Max leaps to pick up the receiver, then moves with it into the hall, closing the door further and further until I can't hear the murmured conversation. I meanwhile discover real garlic and a jar of dried rosemary in their store cupboard, and use these to enhance the dinner.

He returns smiling that it was his older sister Erin, with a lot to say.

'Jen, did Woods talk about Roslin?' he asks then.

'Roslin? Yeah, I got an interview. Woods was all positive, it's my future so forget the cultures, blah, blah.'

'Good.'

'Good?'

'That the food's ready and I discern we use the same recipe. Now,' (laying knives and forks, and dividing the food, and managing to look very desirable performing this ordinary task) 'do you recall what your father said about aneuploidy screening?'

'He's working on developing pre-implantation diagnosis—as we are here—of course, typically, he mentioned it as a source of income! Screening all embryos. It'll have to be pretty safe if they do that.'

'*Aneuploidy screening brings a new class of patient,*' Max quotes. 'He's keen to haul them in, yes. That being the case, with reference to Daze's bairn, we can discount that your sister took part in any experimental programme. Since it's hardly likely he'd use any even slightly doubtful-looking embryo. Any connection between Persephone, as Daze called her, and the Colombian clinic, would either be coincidence—the damage done early in the pregnancy or present in the germ line—or the fault of some other practitioner.'

He's thought more clearly than me. Max, though a medic not a research scientist, has made the sums add up.

'You realised all along, didn't you? Even though he's my father, I suspected he could use a family member in a research programme, and then lie about it when things went awry. But you perceived the influence of Dad's ambition. That restrains him.'

'I know *my* father's ambition, and one day I'll tell you more about it. Yes, people can be dishonest, and they can be cruel. But the wily ones don't jeopardise their own career.'

Silently eating, we consider this.

Still silent, I look at Max, at his hand resting beside his plate, a male, long-fingered hand, holding a fork with a piece of lamb chop impaled on it. The slim but powerful-looking wrist, the large watch with a beaten-up old leather strap. My feelings nudge at me, remembering the touch of that hand on my neck, sweeping aside my hair, and his mouth kissing my ear.

'All kinds of things happen,' he says, 'and we have to get over them. When I was thirteen, my father destroyed something precious to me. An antique microscope.'

Whether or not it's wise, I'm about to tell Jenny a story that's central to my family.

'My Uncle Euan, who's a GP, received it from an elderly patient. A lovely antique instrument, and great fun to use. On my thirteenth birthday, a big rectangular brown paper parcel was on the doorstep!'

'He gave it you?'

'Euan loved the romantic idea of being the successor of generations of scientists—which he isn't. But then, he noted the lust in my eyes, taking a look at that microscope whenever I could. Before I met you, you see.'

'I'll take that as a compliment, shall I?'

'Och, well ... in my class at school, there was an overweight, early-maturing boy, rather unpopular, who'd been in hospital—Slipped Capital Femoral Epiphysis. Some of us had visited: he wasn't best pleased, as the treatment back then involved plaster incarceration in a humiliating pose while the hip healed. When we were minded to try out that micro-scope, repeating van Leeuwenhoek's experiment—you know it?'

'Oh no you didn't!'

'No—listen: when we decided to, this guy's voice had broken, and we reckoned he'd maybe produce a better sample than those of us who could still manage the treble solo in Monteverdi's *Beatus Vir*—which I'd to sing at the end of term concert.'

'You sang in that as well as the Fauré?'

'Sshh—The experiment was well on its way: we had our sample,' (she giggles) 'Och, the rude bit's not the point.'

'No?'

To amuse her, I adopt a broad Scots accent, 'Would you pay attention, lassie?'

'Long as you're understandable.'

'We're peering down Uncle Euan's microscope, when Dad throws wide my bedroom door, entering like an Old Testament Prophet.'

'How did he know?'

'My father has special powers ... He flings out my friends. Hoists the microscope through the open attic window.'

Jenny gasps, 'Max, he didn't! How could he?'

'Easily. What we'd done he saw as wicked. He ranted Scripture at me: Genesis chapter 38, which tells us not to spill our ... seed.'

'You didn't deserve that. It was completely irrational. He's a man after all—and—and that was utterly outrageous and violent! And ignorant! A precision instrument.'

'Jen, the point is, these things happen and—Och, it isna' at all the same but it's about sudden loss of something I found important. And it was supposed to help you cheer up and stop greeting over your lost cultures. No good crying over spilt—'

We both laugh. I think she's over the worst. 'Of course, the loss of the cultures is devastating. But we can learn from what happens that life goes on. That incident eventually led to me being here, doing medicine. Which is good. So, apoptosis, you thought of that in the funeral service, and you wondered why?'

'Yes?'

'Maybe what happened to our research was meant?'

'Meant? Who by?'

'Well, d'you not feel there was no further need ... the project's served to bring us back together.'

'No I don't. Are you hauling in God here?'

'Jenny—'

'I was feeling good, then you say God orchestrates our lives! Of course he doesn't! We've got free will. Some idiot was thinking more about their date or their exam results or what they'd have for dinner, and threw a switch!'

'I only meant that the research isn't vital to us being together! You silly woman! Och, I was a clumsy idiot.'

'You were.'

'Jenny, Jenny! My Dad's idea of God is up to him of course, but I do not think that he would—'

'Religion is attractive maybe, but it's illogical.'

'Let's be clear and logical then. We've established you are my girl-friend, Daze is your sister. I certainly have to cease having anything to do with Persephone.'

'Shouldn't I be treated autonomously? For who I am, not whom I'm related to?'

'It doesna' work like that. Anywhere. The world's all connected up, related or not, we have responsibilities to each other. And as a professional—'

'Obeying authority's so important to you, isn't it?'

'Did I mention obedience? Non-cooperation with my superiors would be irresponsible. As far as you and I are concerned, I canna' believe God would play cat and mouse with our affections, I canna' believe he'd bring two people into a relationship and then chop them both in half because of some cultural differences ... Oh hell, Jenny, I canna' deal wi' it all.'

Find myself miserable, and angry: raking my hands through my hair, accent exaggerated by emotion. Jenny didn't mean it, but she's put her foot fair and square into the shit in my life, and spoiled our chances of a romantic evening. 'You've seen the sermon tapes,' I rant, 'weekly arrivals.'

'Do you listen to them?'

'Would you?'

'Probably not. You know that my father preaches scientific material-ism as hard as yours preaches belief in God.'

'There's our problem: how to escape their certainties and maintain our own integrity.'

'I guess. But, in the sluice room you and I agreed—'

I make a decision here. It's been hanging about the edges of my brain, wanting to be offered to her. 'Jenny: you've an interview at Roslin. I've some study leave. And I need to see my Uncle Euan as well. I'll be driving to Northumberland. You'll be travelling to Edinburgh. So, meant or not, would you agree we might journey north together, and you'll come to meet my family?'

'Is it maybe *meant* when it's what you want, and *not meant* when it isn't?'

'Touché. Let's just say the jury's out. You're invited. I'll have to do some study, of course.'

'I might just fit that visit into my schedule. And while I visit my aunt Val you can have a few undistracted days.'

JENNY

I'm curious to meet the rest of the Mullins clan. And I shall put the Pastor straight on a few things while I'm there, maybe.

'Don't you think Daze might want to move on? Max asks over the washing-up. 'She asked for a burial: that suggests she's putting this gradually into the past. Though it'll take some time.'

'Whatever Daze thinks she wants, she's still in shock. I'd want to know everything, and be glad I'd a sister who could help. I want to do this for her. Try to heal our differences?'

Still brandishing the mop, Max gathers me close against his side. 'Jen, it's kind that you want to find this out for Daze. But if she doesn't want to know, that's her prerogative. And the results of any findings from the blood samples I took just after the birth will be recorded in her notes and I will ask that this information goes to her GP and ... Shall I make some coffee?'

'Not yet. Nicholson?'

A silence. Then, 'Yes, it goes to Nicholson of course.'

I say, half joking, 'He's theme of the day, isn't he?'

A pause. I find it in me to laugh at myself. Flinging my arms around Max. 'Hey, I'm sorry ... I was a cow earlier.'

He drops the mop back in the water, and holds me so close we're like one person.

'Mooo.' I feel his laugh, low down in my body as he leans into me.

We both laugh, my face buried in his shoulder. And then, our mouths search, and meet, a long while. Finally, I say, 'One day I'll do proper research and look back and know Persephone wasn't important—'

'Good. That's a relief.'

'You're off probation, if you want ... let me,' I wriggle so I can reach into my pocket, 'I thought, maybe, some time we could test drive one of these?'

Max stares at what I've taken from the pocket of my jeans: for a moment, I think what I've done was very mistaken. Hoped he might laugh, but he looks into my eyes, seriously. Not hostile, but it's complicated to read. Then he kisses me on the nose. 'You're a witch,' he says, and pats my bum.

Surprise myself by squealing, 'Don't do that!' But I'm damp and full of longing, brain totally defeated, far too easily aroused. 'Granddaughter of Ianthe Lavenham, who campaigned for contraception for unmarried women? What else can I be? Mum gave me a prescription, but ... those things take time to work, don't they?'

'You're wicked. Don't let my father know or he'll call you my practice affair, and that is not what's intended.'

What's Max meaning? Our biochemistry is about to take off like a rocket. There in the kitchen, and up in Max's room, under the stern eyes of that Skull with the Shades, figuring out the mysteries of the condom, so essential since HIV ... thank God we forgot God, I could say. Along with Dad.

It's such a thing I wouldn't have done if Laura and Maeve were in Cambridge! Maeve would've totally freaked. 'Max Mullins is one of the untouchables,' she used to say, 'the medics who swear they've foresworn women till they're good and trained on account of having so much work! Then they marry pretty little airhead nurses ...' So what if she knew, what I know, later: the untouchables are human, and can groan *Oh baby, baby*! when you locate the right places to touch them?

I shan't tell her.

MAX

The seduction wasn't quite as I'd expected—though if I'm honest, it was near to a tempting daydream I've often had ... and not always even tried to suppress.

Now, thankfully, there's not enough time in the working day to think about the future—our future, certainly *ours* not *mine*. *And they shall become one flesh*—a text for everything, whispering into my ears.

But no time to dwell on what most people around me would regard as nothing to worry about. No time alone is good—even buying a sandwich for lunch—'Hey, Max—over here!' and I join a table of colleagues—or even having a quiet pee—'Ah, Max, I was looking for you, about the Down's syndrome twins ...'

It's going home, and her scent is everywhere, and she's left a note with X's all over it ... By Dad's standards, I'm lost. My imagination filled now with the scene, his wagging finger as he stands in the pulpit, railing about moral uprightness, Christian exclusiveness, seen especially in that we have No Sex Before Marriage! Our defining principles summed up by our intimate behaviour!

Seeing I intend to marry Jenny—seeing I always intended to, and was caught up by an inappropriate and childish response to Dad's need some time back, I now have a sense of peace and resolution about everything. If it weren't for, what? Guilt, at my own decision making? Fear, for Jenny being branded a tart by the family, because she's not a believer? As much as because of what we've done and will do again? Which they will *assume* we've done even though they do not *know*.

I move towards the phone. To call my mother and inform her I'm bringing a guest with me. A guest I am not ashamed of. Mum, though obedient to Dad, will nevertheless attempt to make Jenny welcome.

I picture them all, their lives bent to Dad's will. The Christian Family: I wish. So much is hidden beneath the smiles, but it is not hidden from God himself. If God forgives our human weaknesses, why then doesn't Dad, his self-appointed representative?

I'll leave calling Mum till Sunday evening—he's guaranteed to be out then, preaching to the Youth Group Sunday Evening Fellowship, ensuring they remain exclusive from the temptations of the world. Of course I perceive how our sexual morality relates with our broader morality—but couldn't we think a bit more about the wider issues, about the destructiveness of greed, and violence, and lying, instead of being known for our obsession with relationships?

FEE. SUNDAY EVENING, THE MANSE

The house is quiet: the kids at church. Despite the deeply ingrained command not to work on a Sunday, Fee finds herself pulling out the chair to sit at her small desk in one corner of the bedroom.

A typescript's lying there: a talk she must give to the assembled Pastors' Wives at the upcoming Clergy Conference. The title, *The Complementarity of the Helpmeet*, given her by Alisdair.

She's neatly typed a Scripture passage at the top, and her opening words: *In the passage we heard read, the Lord makes clear we women are to be helpers. The Lord says 'It is not good for the man to be alone. I will make a Help, meet for him.'*

Why that sentence makes her uncomfortable she can't think. As she considers, the phone rings. 'Mum?' Just hearing that voice, her whole demeanour changes. 'Max! You beat me to it.' she smiles.

He laughs.

'I'm glad you rang, pet, because I was thinking, when you're here, would you be able to pop in on Rachel? See how she's doing?'

He doesn't reply immediately. Then, 'Rachel's having a hard time?'

'Colin's so busy at work, and the baby ... She's maybe a bit lonely, tied to the house?'

A pause. 'Och, I can fit her in, I should think. Now—' Fee's immensely proud of Max. Handsome as Alisdair, a hard worker, in a good profession. And thoughtful for others. 'Now, it's just possible—Mam, line crackled: you are still there?'

'Sorry, pet—you were saying?' Inwardly, she berates herself for dwelling on her love for him instead of listening.

'I rang about the visit: you've nobody using the spare bedroom that weekend?'

'The weekend you're home? Nobody.'

'Well, it's just possible—I might want to bring someone for you to meet.'

'Really? Well of course we're pleased—but it's rather a surprise.'

Max gives a nervous laugh. 'Not to me: I've known her a while. Her name's Jenny.'

'Jenny?'

Jenny? Who Max knew in Cambridge, who was studying genetics? 'Do I not recall you knew a Jenny, once?' Alisdair had been concerned that this Jenny could be having undue influence over Max's views on the new biotechnology. Right before the MS struck him down.

'Yes. The same one.'

Now deeply disturbed, Fee doesn't respond.

Max breaks the silence. 'Well, anyway, as I say, it may not happen.'

'Well, if it does, there's a bed here, pet. And you'll pop in on Nat—the baby—and Rachel?'

A couple of goodbye sentences later, Fee replaces the receiver so quietly it hardly clicks. *Jenny.*

The reason behind his seeming pleased to return to Cambridge for the six months' paediatric placement?

A knock at the door. 'Who is it?'

'Me, Mum. You got a minute?'

'Did you not stay for the youth programme, Kirsty? I thought you liked the choruses with the band?'

'There's never time to talk. To you. I came home early.'

'Come and sit with me, pet,' Fee smiles, patting the dressing-table stool. Although she's disturbed now by the accusation of neglecting Kirsty's needs.

Kirsty approaches, but doesn't sit. 'What're you doing?'

'Reading my talk. What can I do for you?'

When Kirsty doesn't answer immediately, Fee's aware that she's reading the typescript, upside down. 'Mum, that's just stuff Dad would say. God can speak through women—you just have to listen!'

'Your father, Kirsten—' Fee begins, folding away the paper under a book.

'That's right—change the subject and use my whole name. Dad's hotline may actually sometimes crackle a bit.'

'Really?' Fee's eyebrows rise.

'Suppose God has a different plan for my life? One Dad doesn't know about?'

Fee frowns. 'What kind of a plan, treasure?'

'Like he doesn't care whether I swim for the county or not?'

'Oh.' Fee relaxes, though taking a proper look at Kirsty. Pale and tired. 'I thought that was going well? Dad'll be thrilled if you're chosen.'

'This isn't about Dad—it's—it's—never mind, I can fit it all in. I can do it. Only ...'

'Yes?'

'Nothing.'

'Listen, pet.' Fee's decided a conspiratorial mother and daughter plan might help. 'Max is bringing a girlfriend with him—'

'Oh wow! I was right. Are they—?'

'I don't know, pet. But can you make friends with Jenny, try to find out a bit about her—and, shall we both ask the Lord to guide how the visit goes? I've yet to let your father know of this development.'

Kirsty's look is penetrating. 'Dad was so wrong about Rachel, wasn't he? That's what I mean: Dad doesn't always know.'

Fee lays her hand on Kirsty's. 'None of us do, pet. We have to trust. It seems Rachel wasn't for Max, and Rachel—'

'Yeah, God spoke to Rachel—not Max—see what I mean? About women?'

Fee shakes her head. 'Shall we commit this to the Lord? I'm not certain she's a Christian girl, Kirsty.' Fee is certain she isn't.

A prayer later, and Kirsty gone to find her books for school in the morning, Fee reaches again for her talk.

God has called us to ministry no less than he has called our husbands. When the Lord created Eve, it says he brought her to the man to be a Help, meet for him. You may want to ask, What in today's world does that Scripture mean? The point, rather, is what the scripture means—period.

... What the scripture means, period.

Kirsty gone, Fee considers the Americanism: why not 'full stop'?

Full stop has a finality she doesn't want to introduce. Her talk will emphasise the on-going, eternal, everlasting words of Scripture: a God who is unchanging, and forever. *We have a God whose words at the beginning of time are valid for all time—the woman was created a help, meet— suitable—for the man. To be called to be the helps suitable for our minister husbands is a high calling. It can be a wonderful service—*

'Och, look at you—slaving over a typescript—' an ironic voice says. Fee startles. 'Alisdair! I wasna' working on it.'

'I wouldna' imagine you were. But reading it over? Yes? Let me see ...' he says, his voice gentle, almost wheedling.

Fee moves a little in the chair. Alisdair leans over her shoulder, reading the text. '*To be a help meet for him—we have a God whose words at the beginning of time are valid for all time—*' That's good—that's excellent ...'

Actually her message doesn't sound so good in Alisdair's voice. It— lacks something. It—doesn't quite ring true with her own—self? That it shouldn't fit is disconcerting.

Her experience as a helpmeet is the journey from shy young faithful Presbyterian girl, to air force wife, chaplain's wife, now wife and helpmeet of a very successful, ambitious pastor who's turned around an ailing church and draws a huge Congregation to hear his preaching. In tandem, from virgin to mother of five, from self-effacing withdrawn young woman, to visitor and comforter of all manner of suffering souls, who's discovered an empathy with special-needs children and their families.

Does that have relevance to the eternal, changeless commands of Almighty God? How should she encourage others setting out on this dusty, dutiful road?

'Going well,' Alisdair commends her, then consults his watch. 'I'll be away to my study a wee while. Would you know what Max is planning for next weekend: we'll no be here after Monday lunchtime.'

Fee wishes Max would choose a weekend when she can spend more time with him. It's almost as if he doesn't want to see his family.

JENNY. CAMBRIDGE

I call Val again: this time, she's home. Sounding pleased I'm begging a room for a night. 'You'll stay a couple of days with us? You remember your cousins?'

'Harris and Lewis, yes.'

'I'll make sure they show you around; Edinburgh's a wonderful place, d'you go for architecture? And history? Bring your warm jerseys, we've a cold east wind. Our place is a typical tenement, top flat, lots of stairs, amazing views.' Translating, in my head: *tenement*, old-style word for a high-rise block. And imagine a tiny flat hardly big enough for Val herself.

'And you'll tell me how Daisy's getting along now?'

'You remember Daisy?'

'I remember all of you. I'll expect you in a week, then.'

Max laughs at my fears about the place being too small to fit in a visitor. 'Wait till you see how Edinburgh does tenements on the grand scale.'

Max studies most evenings, preparing for the Diploma in Child Health exam: actually, we both work.

Max hints at our future being in the North. *Ours*? I'm a Southern girl despite the Guthrie name. Is my future at Roslin? Won't two days at Aunt Val's doing the Edinburgh sites in a keen East wind be terribly boring? What will the Mullinses really be like?

Sneakily, I'm still reading up anything and everything on dysmorphic infants. Causes. Syndromes. Unknown reasons, once-off phenotypes and strange cases. As well as what's going on at Roslin Institute. I'm not a pro-lifer. I'm totally happy to work with early embryos, and destroy them when I'm done. But as I read, as I watch articles I need to keep for reference roll off the library photocopier, I increasingly see these babies as human. It's because ... because Persephone was Daze's baby, not a number or a case history. A person we buried, to the music of Fauré, and celebrated with a wake.

Most nights, when we pack up the books, Max stays over at my place. We work really hard till bedtime, *to earn our pleasure* (his phrase).

*

Friday morning Max implies I should pack my stuff.

'Relax: we don't leave till Sunday.'

'Och, maybe, but it's as well to be ... Jenny, what d'you need for this trip? Not all those photocopies on the desk there?'

I say nothing.

'You'll need a pair of walking shoes,' he says, 'I'll be showing you the wall Hadrian built to keep us Scots out of Caesar's beloved angular island!'

He leaves for the hospital. I pack a few things, including those disputed photocopies. And head for the shower; am hardly out of it when there's a ring on the bell.

Hair wrapped in a towel, throwing on Max's rugby shirt over nothing more than a pair of knickers, I dash to open the door. Just a crack. 'Daze?'

She's her house on her back: an even bigger one than Hattie's. 'They shut the site, fucking towed the buses away!'

'Daze—they didn't!' I gasp, hauling her inside. 'Your home.'

'Council sent a couple of hit-men with an excavator and a notice to quit, started dragging the buses away before I could rescue my shit.' Her phrase for her precious possessions!

'Oh Daze—I'm so sorry. You must feel gutted.'

'Yeah—like a fish, filleted,' Daze says.

'Anyhow, take off the backpack, you shouldn't be hauling that around.'

'May as well go back to Sennen. But all my cash's in the bus: can I borrow some off you, Jen? I'll pay you. Don't have a card—no fixed abode.'

'Where's Lily?'

'You seen her again?' Daze asks edgily.

'No—why? How come the council gave you no warning? How come they didn't allow you to take your things, or know where your bus is?'

Daze shrugs.

'Look, is this a story you're telling, and if so why? You need cash. How much, what for really?'

'My ticket home.'

'Okay. Let me get properly dressed. We'll go into town, I'll buy your ticket, and see you onto the train.'

She follows me upstairs. 'Fooled you didn' I? Dad drove it back and was stupid enough not to ask me to take out what I needed!'

I nearly use the f-word. But, 'No: I was pretending when I was sorry for you,' I say heavy with sarcasm. 'You really are going home? Thought you'd prefer staying with Lily,' I say, pulling in my stomach to fasten my jeans. Hunting a top that's really mine.

'Yeah.' She walks about the room, examining my things. 'Lils and I're not that close. Hairdryer: not necessary, not natural. It's summer.'

'Okay ... thought she was your friend.' Wishing she'd keep her eyes to herself.

'Trainers bit massive for you, Jen? (I kick Max's trainers under my bed.) 'C'mon, Jen—' Daze waves a packet of Marlboros at me. Left by Max: I'm trying to persuade him to give up. Daze grins, 'Hey, you don't now, so, tell tale signs, and in the bedroom! Can I have one?'

I say nothing, feel bad about having a boyfriend when she's lost hers, as well as her baby. About to remove the other alien object on my desk but she's too quick. 'Bible-thing's his? Figures.' Flipping the India-paper pages, 'New Testament and Psalms. Here's one. The Lord is my shepherd—how about that? Remember learning that one at Sennen Primary? An' I was the class little black sheep—I don't think so!' She re-zips the leather cover and puts the New Testament and Psalms back where it was.

I put on my watch. 'Thought you were in a hurry?'

Daze tamps a cigarette on the edge of the table. 'Those aren't natural either,' I say. Daze lights up, inhales. Says, 'Who else among medical types would've let me change my mind over Persephone? And deliver her back tucked up in a basket?'

'That was like he tuned into what you'd want, wasn't it?'

For a moment, we connect.

'The man's got soul: you mightn't deserve him, but hang onto him. You don't need to work together to do that.'

'What d'you mean?'

'He's one of those genuine types. He *really likes* you, Four-Eyes!' Daze emphasises. Seemingly without irony or malice.

'Thanks a bunch, Daze.'

We smile. She appreciates my dry response. I almost introduce the topic of Shane. Her words stop me, as I grab my bag and keys. 'So you don't need to *make* a reason to meet.'

Okay, I perceive her meaning. I won't pursue it now, but I can't drop my curiosity like that.

*

On the way to the station, I drag Daze into a café to have breakfast. 'Can't travel on an empty stomach.'

I buy a coffee and Danish, Daze has a black Earl Grey and a flapjack, 'Better've been made with vegan margarine!'

I'm noticing the sharp contrast of her dark wavy hair, and her pale skin. Can hardly look at Daze without recalling her, groaning and swearing and then Persephone swooshing out. What's it like? Giving birth? God, what's it really like? The ultimate purpose of having a sexual relationship, the reason our hormones—. Don't think about it now!

Hope she's physically up to the travel.

'Daze, after the birth, you are okay?'

'Yeah—yeah. Midwife signed me off.'

'Really? Do they let you off that quick?'

'Bugger midwives: Mum'll know all the stuff, she'll cluck about checking me, won't she?'

'What'll you do, at home?'

'Work.'

'Paint, you mean?'

'Yeah, yeah, paint, as you put it. Maybe some photography.'

Photography: what about my video cassette? Something stops me asking ... Could the destruction be a legitimate act? Does she find the thought of anyone watching it too painful?

Is spending time with Max is affecting my way of seeing people? Things he said about my being more interested in my own cultures than in how Daze is suffering with grief and stuff?

Picking up my coffee, I try empathy. 'Max said soon as you saw her you named her ... that was kind of nice.'

She snaps back in her usual style. 'Look, I don't want to talk about this, okay? How'm I meant to feel? I dunked her and named her: I was kind of still anaesthetised I expect. I'm putting it all behind me now, getting on with stuff.'

'Max said—'

'Stop it, Jen! You're so like Mum! I told you, right?'

'Sorry—sorry—no need to go into meltdown.'

Daze catches herself, maybe because she's dependent on me for her train ticket. 'No: I'm being a cow: I'm sorry.'

''Sokay. Like I said, time's getting on, I've got work to do. You want to catch that lunchtime train at Paddington, don't you?'

I pay the bill. We move off towards the station, me insisting on wearing the backpack. I buy her ticket: King's Cross, Paddington, Penzance. And hand over her luggage. 'Take care, Daze. They do know you're coming?'

She shrugs.

'I'll call Hat, shall I?'

'If you want.' We hug. 'You can go now,' (how typically Daze to dismiss me!) 'I'll mail you the money once I've found work.'

And that's Daze, really: private, but a toughie. Is she safe to do that journey? Max would know.

*

I find a phone box. 'Hat?'

'Jen?'

'Impressed Des gave you the Volvo keys!'

'Yeah: cool, wasn't it?'

'Listen: I've just put Daze on the train.'

'What?' Hat sounds incredulous.

'Get this: she spun me a tale that they towed the buses away!'

'Her stinking bus is here, I'm looking at it!' Hat says. 'Should've seen Des driving it: clouds of black smoke stream behind like an *arty fart* ... Des brought it back, Daze said she was moving in with Lils.'

'Whatever, I bought her ticket right through: and that's, like, not cheap! Wanted to make sure that's what she did with my cash. Des had better pay me back, she's his—responsibility.'

'That's mean, Jen.'

'I don't think so—I have to live on my grant an' that, don't I? And I've got nothing now until I land a job same as Daze. And she treats me like— Okay Hat, Daze and I don't hit it off. Anyhow, can you meet the train, make sure she's okay?'

'Sure,' Hat says.

I give her the time Daze should arrive. She says, 'Maybe she's freaked because of the baby. Suppressing her feelings, makes her act weird?'

'You're the A level psychologist! Hattie, could you hang out a bit with her, see if she says anything?'

'Shouldn't we leave her alone? It's not that un-Daze to be weird. Remember she used to climb out of the window and go to perform at the pubs in Penzance with her poetry group?'

'Penzance Pixies?' We laugh. 'I climbed out once, and went with her.'

'Okay, Daze exaggerates and tells stories. But she takes her Goth side seriously. Like the beating heart art project?'

Daze's counter-response to my prize essay on the first live-born, healthy IVF baby caused such a row. Des had to defend himself against the Head's accusations that he was encouraging nihilism and violence in the art group. He'd had nothing to do with it.

'What did Mum think when she announced her Colombia trip?' I ask.

'She was like, *great idea, Daze could use her schoolgirl Spanish.* Doing something that doesn't involve—you-know, Mum's bit about Daze drooping around in second-hand clothes and her room smelling like the Oxfam shop on a bad day?'

'She came back in about March didn't she?'

'Just before Easter, and went pretty much straight to Cambridge.'

'Okay ... and alone, no guy in tow?'

'I'd have told you.'

Same as Dad's and Lily's accounts, and no time spent hanging about elsewhere, encountering a chemically polluted environment in her first three months of pregnancy.

'She said, the College thought she'd make the Turner prize some time,' Hat says. 'That huge conceptual art thing, sort of concrete philosophy— Saatchi and Saatchi, big bucks? You need to do a splendiferous exhibition, then they discover you and put your name forward. The art critics.'

'Well, you're more on her wavelength than I am: thanks for looking out for her.' Daze may tell stories, but what Hat's said makes sense. Specially since I've just been with the real, out of hospital and dramatic baby's funeral setting, Daze. Maybe I was on the wrong track imagining her involved in some kind of a sci-fi type experiment which went wrong. She's an artist first and then some. Unless, of course, she was getting paid!

'Glad to be of help,' Hat says, with some irony. 'The surf's great. You coming home at all?'

'I've got an interview up north. And, I'm invited to the Manse—like, Max's Dad's vicarage!'

'Wow, you and Max: properly back together! It's truly madly in lerve this time, isn't it?' my little sister teases, pronouncing 'love' Elvis Presley style.

'We're going to his see his family, yes,' I say, curling my toes.

'I hear wedding bells!'

'Tinnitus!'

Travelling

Tomorrow we leave. Outside the engine of the Capri coughs sporadically. If Max has his head under the bonnet, I may as well drift back to sleep.

'Coffee! Toast! Up, lassie, we've places to go, things to do!' I wake properly. 'You'd be up for a day out, before we're surrounded by relatives everywhere we look, wouldn't you?'

'Where?'

'Surprise?'

'Right. Smart? Casual? What should I wear? Car okay now?'

My packed bags and interview outfit have disappeared. There's my clue. Imagine myself writing to Maeve: *Max booked us a secret location for the night before we stayed with our relatives …*

*

Some hours later, as we bump down a farm track, 'Erin's husband's a Yorkshire lad,' Max says, 'He's a little place they're doing up around here … and I think—yes, here we are.'

It's a tiny brick cottage: peeling green paint, straggly honeysuckle and roses climbing the walls. Bathed in late-afternoon sunshine.

'That conversation with your sister Erin, after the cultures were destroyed? Plotting?'

'Looks that way!'

Up the path we go with our overnight bags, between absurdly flowering cabbage plants and a tangle of snapdragons and willowherb. Inside, it smells of fresh paint and sawdust, of new carpets and floor varnish.

There's no teapot, one mug, six wine glasses, and the instruction booklet's still tied to the oven door.

'Well-equipped kitchen!' Max laughs ironically, holding up the corkscrew and indicating the pasta-machine and big wooden block of kitchen knives. A note on the pine table: *milk in the fridge, brandy in the living room cupboard. Have fun!*

We look at each other. Fall into an embrace, laughing.

'How about we see what's upstairs?'

A yellow-painted nursery, a bedroom with a huge, low bed, black sheets, and duvet. Black and white striped pillows. 'This is really your sister's place?'

'Or someone's who's mailed me the key.'

We're relaxing in neutral space, neither mine nor hers, wonderful. An opportunity to explore each other's lives. Then Jenny asks about my interview with Uncle Euan: who he is, why he's important.

'Euan is mum's brother-in-law. He's easier to get along with than my father: you'll like him.'

'He gave you the car: why?'

'Och, because he didn't think it suited his lifestyle any longer. You know what he said, back when he so generously gave it me? He told me the car's performance and mileage to the gallon, in terms of journeys between Cambridge and Northumberland!'

I laugh cynically. Jenny doesn't get it.

'My father's wanting to further develop the Christian presence in the area: adding a health centre attached to the church. *Waters of Life* surgery! Euan dislikes the idea: but he's no mind to have it out with Dad. And while he doesn't, I've no inclination to work with him. I've applied for something in Cambridge. Which maybe makes Wednesday's interview a farce.'

'Don't do it then. Just tell him.'

'It'll do me no harm: it can be a dry run for any other interviews. More important, to update you, when we're at my parents' place, Mum's asked me to drop in on one of my father's congregation.'

Her eyebrows draw together. I'm already nervous: but I ought to tell her about seeing Rachel. 'Where's this going? Do I want to know?'

'I need to explain. She's married, now, with a child, but, it's someone who—who my parents thought should be—important in my life. Mum requested I visit because she's worried about Rache.'

'So? You don't have to go.'

'Yes, I do. There's some things you need to know.'

'About your religion?'

'Listen, Dad and Uncle Euan grew up in the same church. Theirs weren't well-off families. Dad was already in the RAF, the air force was paying for him to study for his degree. Euan was at med school. There was a devoutly Christian family with two lovely girls, Fiona and Margaret?'

'Your mum and—?'

'Yes. Dad could afford to get married. Euan waited till he qualified and was earning to marry Margaret. You understand? In places like First Truly Reformed—my dad's church—the idea's taught that we look around for guidance and God will lead us to the right girl. And, guidance isn't left to your own feelings. There's nudging, a bit of a push, a suggestion.'

Jenny looks at me, horrified as if I was describing something obscene.

'No, Jenny, it's okay, it's all okay. You already know it didn't work out, but…. While I was back with caring for them all, when Dad was ill, Rachel met all the criteria and was kind of picked out, for the son of the Manse—' Jenny bites her lip, silent. 'It sounds bizarre?'

'More like disgustin': bein' handed a wife!' Her West-country accent's as exaggerated as Daze's.

Coaxing, I slip my arm around her, 'You're not wrong. I was twenty-two, but I was First Truly bred … flattered by Rachel's attentions, she is nice looking, in a fragile way.'

'Your father *offered* you this woman? He's crazy. They're crazy.'

'No: he's an evangelical. What he believes God wants comes first. I need you to know how they think and act. But Rachel … I should never have got involved … I'm so convicted.'

'*Convicted?*'

'Accused. I *thought* God was calling me back to do my duty, I'd been given a kick up the backside. Shouldn't be hanging out far away, with a non-believer, which is called by them being *unequally yoked*.'

'What'd your God think about betrayal and rejection? Two-timing me … talking crap about my being too young to get serious? Writing that something had come up?'

'I never took Rachel out before Dad's MS struck him. I hardly knew she existed. You and I were hardly going out.'

'We were almost having sex that afternoon on the cliff top. Something *came up* that time!'

Yes, I could go with her tasteless joke, but we're discussing something serious. I ignore it.

'We didn't because I didna' want to exploit you. Besides, your mother was, in effect, my employer.'

She says nothing.

'Okay: I deserve your contempt. All done to please them.' I take a long breath. 'It wasna' anything like us. And Rachel soon called it off.'

'Crisis of faith in God's planning?'

'She wanted me to run her life—where we went, what clothes I liked her in. What we planned for the future. I never want to play that role, that absurd headship of the male. And it is a role.'

'She dumped you because you didn't tell her what to wear?'

I laugh, grimly. 'Inwardly, I compared her to you, all the time. Our talks about embryology and genetics research, about clinical medicine, our different ways of looking at the world. Your excited letters about coming to Cambridge, the Hox genes lecture. Rachel was never a threat. She's a dream my father had.'

Slowly, quietly, Jenny puts her arm around me. 'Everything's about him, isn't it? When we met, you'd smoke, drink, party … I was eighteen, we'd got to know each other, we weren't strangers. Sex is fine between people who care about each other and take precautions. You give in too much to powerful guys. Like Nicholson. And your Dad.'

I see where she's coming from. But, 'Sex is fine, is it?' I say quietly. 'Don't let him hear you. He'd conclude that proves his mistaken, convenient belief that sex is why we're together. As someone outside our church, I can have a relationship with you and use you ... Even now Dad might expect I'll get rid of you when I want to settle down. Select some nice girl from his flock who's under twenty-five and likely to submit to—obey—me, and bear me children. In his eyes, you're practice, if we mess around.'

'You're serious?'

'Serious about you. That's why we're going to meet my folks. It's what I shall try to implant in their minds. Our relationship isn't a game.'

*

The evening settles down again: hours later, in the pink, birdsong-filled dawn, I wake a moment. Do I see Jenny naked, kneeling up on the bed, squinting through her camera lens? I pretend I'm asleep.

I wake again: time to eat breakfast and part. One of the hardest things. We'll not see each other again until we're together under Dad's roof.

MAX. MONDAY, JESMOND, NEWCASTLE

It's mid-morning as I reach Rachel's house, in the nice part of Newcastle where the University lecturers and such live. Mum doesn't fuss about the congregation without cause. *Lonely and tied to the house* will mean more, as I see when Rachel opens the door.

Her bushy, carrot-coloured hair's tangled and her complexion—always translucently fair—emphasises the grey under her eyes. She's in a blue fluffy dressing gown, the end of a pink nightie showing. The whimpering baby's strapped to her front in a sling.

'Max!'

She steps back into the hall, still clutching the front door.

'Perhaps not a good time?'

Rachel's struggling with herself, then 'Come in,' she says, low-voiced. 'I'll go and put something better on—it's disgraceful you find us like this. You'll have to excuse the house.'

Trying to reassure her, 'I'm used to young mums,' I say. 'He's not a good sleeper, then?'

When Rachel returns, her *something better* is a long, flounced, flowery skirt and modest T-shirt. And her over-domesticity's just like Mum's: with our coffee she serves homemade biscuits.

The washing machine grinds. Rachel says brightly that Colin prefers her in feminine clothes. That he's well, the school's doing well. My father's church is full to overflowing, God works mightily through his preaching.

'And I'm praying for you, Max,' Rache adds. Earnestly regarding me over her mug. 'Your mum mentioned a girlfriend? Who's maybe not one of us?'

Mum requesting support meeting Jenny? I can imagine it, at the Women's Fellowship!

'She's a lovely Cornish lassie,' is all I say. 'So Rache, how are you, in yourself?'

Rachel hunts for answers among the knots in the pine tabletop. Nat fusses in the sling. She lets him suck on her fingertip.

'You said young mums. Okay, Nat's restless, but it's his age, and settling in—he was left on the step of the orphanage when he was hours old. *Hours.* Maybe it'd be different if I could—you know, breastfeed. I read books that claim all kinds of miracles but I don't produce milk. And he needs a lot of love.'

'He's not allowing you to eat or drink: shall I take him a while?'

From the relief on her face, I get the feeling she'd not mind if I took him for good. I begin, surreptitiously, to take a closer, more clinical look. Mum told me they'd adopted a five-month child—who'd be all of six months by now. He looks more like three to four months. He's a peaky little face, slightly strange features, a thin cry, low-set ears. What does that tell me?

Cautiously probing, I discover Rachel's also concerned. So, it helps that I've still some friends at the hospital, and that I'm working with Nicholson at present. Rachel's initially reluctant about acting so fast, but I manage to set up an appointment for her to take him to the paediatric assessment clinic.

JENNY. TRAVELLING TO EDINBURGH

The Intercity train speeds northwards: Max will be at Rachel's now. The bothersome thing's not that he's gone to see her, it's knowing how she was chosen by his parents. The culture of First Truly Reformed sounds like what some Asian girls at Cambridge told us: being offered in marriage to a guy they didn't know.

And the microscope incident: an indication of his father's controlling violence? I wonder a lot about Max's family: if I was him, I'd try to walk away from them. Not hang around dutifully.

And another thing to ponder: Daze's motivations. How her mind works.

*

In Edinburgh, mid-afternoon, I lug my suitcase up some rather worn stone stairs. Val's door's already flung open. In the hall, there's a hatstand draped with coats, tweedy wraps, floppy hats, topped by a knitted tam-o'-shanter.

'Jenny! *Must be*—won't say how you've grown!'

Flat, and aunt, aren't how I imagined. Val, Dad's twin sister, arms out to hug, wears flowing unbleached linen trousers and a shawl. Though she's the same brown hair, broad forehead, and sharp, intelligent eyes as my father.

Looking down the hall, over my shoulder 'Harris? Lewis!' she calls. 'Thought we'd be meeting your young man: where's he?'

'My young man?'

One cousin appears, blond, gawky, maybe sixteen? 'Right—Harris never here when you want him—Lewis, here's your cousin Jenny.'

Then, 'Kitchen—bathroom—living room—' Val leads the way, waving her arm at rooms as we pass. For a top-floor flat, this place has high ceilings and loads of space. The sun shines through big windows. *How we do tenements in Edinburgh.*

It's cluttered, as if they've lived here a long while, the place and the people grown comfortable with each other. The Oriental rug in the hall's thinning: the paint's chipped around the doors, the sofa in the living room sags a bit, and is piled with cushions. Lots of plants in pots and baskets, masses of books. Everything worn, but not shabby. Smells clean, and homey, of baking.

Val flings wide the door of room at the very end of the hall. 'Most important, where you'll sleep! Your mum mentioned a Scottish minister's son—Max? Jenny, you ken that's going to cause trouble? Lewis? Take Jenny's bags in, can you?'

Lewis dumps my bags on the huge double bed, genuine Victorian or Edwardian—mahogany head and foot, massively plumped-up duvet with a heather-coloured woven rug flung across.

Val had assumed we'd both be here, and not thought separate rooms? Wicked.

'Now, expect you'd like a coffee—or maybe a herbal tea? And some Dundee cake? Come to the kitchen when you're ready. I don't know where Harris has gone.'

'There's blackcurrant and ginseng tea, or peppermint?' she beams a few minutes later. 'See, I promised Dundee cake and Dundee cake you shall have—albeit sunk a bit in the middle!' She cuts hunky slices of her steaming, fresh-from-the-oven cake, the centre weighed down by the traditional topping of blanched almonds.

'I live mainly on nuts and seeds—and salads—but I don't expect young people to go without.'

My other cousin lopes in, 'God, Mum, when did you last make a cake? Hey, Jenny, I'm Harris.' His dark hair's a mop, jeans and trainers very worn. But the walk, and the deep pools of dark eyes: Dad. Even the grin. 'I made you jump!'

'You're only the spitting image of my dad!'

'Oh no—not that!'

'S'pose I can get used to it.'

Val produces the teapot, containing a vile alternative Daze-style herbal brew: 'Infusion of garden weeds, my apologies,' Harris says, darkly, dumping a mug in front of me.

'Eye of newt and toe of frog,' Lewis grins, 'isn't it, Ma?'

'None of your nonsense!' Val bats at them both. And I notice on each finger she wears a different silver ring.

'D'you two remember us?'

'I've this vague image,' Harris says, scratching his head in a gesture like Dad's. 'You, Harriet, who's called Hat, isn't she? And a kinda scrawny kid, Daze, who ran around with her.'

'D'you go for Goths?'

Harris laughs. 'Figures. An' your dad, we never met: Mum's spun us yarns about Dr Frankenstein.'

'Not wrong. Get this: Daze thinks he's kind and generous. He thinks he's here to help people.'

'Who's that you're describing?' Val asks archly.

'My father,' I smile.

'Daze uses such terms to describe my brother?'

'How come you left for the Isles when you were a teenager? What's the rift with Dad, if that's not rude, raking up the past?'

'Identity crisis! As a twin, either you live the daily three-legged race or you get out! I was tired of being the extra leg—'

'Seriously?'

'Seriously, your dad and I were still wrestling in the family womb. I needed to find myself.'

'Dad's always on about how IVF twins is not a good idea—'

'Be that as it may. I heard of some people teaching traditional crafts in the Western Isles—years before traditional crafts were trendy—I'd hated school so rather than wasting time on college I went to be trained.'

'By old people who hadn't lost the arts?'

'Stepped back into another world. You want to see weaving for tourists, go to one of those places around here they've set up. But I'll show you real traditional weaving.'

Harris and Lewis roll their eyes, pick up their mugs of tea and seconds of cake, and leave. Val leads the way to the spacious living room. One end's occupied by the loom, a huge frame with different coloured wools all threaded up ready, and a half-woven piece of cloth in pale beiges and misty blues. By the hearth there's a spinning wheel. Though a gas fire grins complacently from the bricked up fireplace.

There's a basket of raw wool: Val demonstrates the process of carding, running the yarn through her fingers. 'The lanolin softens your skin. But, sniff: smells like wet dog? Never store wool wet or too hot. That will make the yolk—the lanolin—rancid. You'd not believe the stink of that!'

She explains spinning. As she didactically demonstrates her crafts I see how Val and Dad are alike.

And I see something she'd appreciate: 'The spindle: this is really clever. In order to separate out the DNA from the two parents, and then combine a strand of each and reject the inevitable extra bits, in the actual process of fertilisation, the fertilized cell kind of—in layman's terms—devises this bit we call the spindle ...'

Val supplies a used envelope, and a pencil: I sketch a diagram for her on the back. '*Before I was woven together in the womb ...*' she murmurs.

'Sorry?'

'Apposite quote. Popped into my head!'

'So you and my father—his work makes the weaving in the womb literally possible. Babies happen for infertile couples. Though it's in a dish not a womb!'

Maybe it's fanciful, but, it's like, are there patterns, meanings? The word I want is *elegant*. That's what mathematicians call it.

Val smiles: even if she and Dad can't get along she's pleased they have a twin-thing. 'It's hand-eye co-ordination, isn't it?' Though her rather chunky Guthrie fingers are very similar to Dad's, and mine aren't exactly willowy. We smile, seeing familial traits.

'Yeah, I'm good at that. You take off the rings while you spin?'

'Oh yes: have to. Let me see your hands: yes ...'

Val with some effort removes the ring, patterned with stars, from her right little finger. 'Right hand, Jenny!' She slips it onto my ring finger. 'Links,' she smiles.

MAX. THAT AFTERNOON, HEXHAM, NORTHUMBERLAND

I'm at Euan's well before afternoon surgery, with that good feeling I've already done something positive today. Euan introduces me to the practice nurse. And his part-time GP partner, a rosy woman about thirty-five, mother of two lively boys. And leaves me to look around with her while he goes out on a couple of visits. Then I sit in on his consultations as his registrar, and afterwards we discuss the most interesting cases.

Tuesday, more surgeries, visits, the antenatal clinic. It's all lovely Dr Finlay stuff, my Cambridge friends would say, cosy and nostalgically backward looking.

Euan retains his natural avuncular attitude, though he insists I drop the Uncle from his name. The attitude in which he handed me the keys to the tomato-red Capri, his cast-off car, a couple of Christmases back, 'I'm getting older, and our wee Chrissie's growing up, and a young lad like you has more use for a sporty car than I do.'

With Margaret and Chrissie away (at *Women Christians in Golf ... Includes children's Bible Camp!*) we spend the evening in a pub restaurant which serves excellent steak and chips. And play a game of darts with the locals. 'Medicine's set to change,' he says, as we walk slowly back to the house. 'I don't like everything I see coming: I worry about technology forcing out the essential humanity. Tomorrow we shall visit the new Hospice—one of the good developments—and the old Community Hospital. Community hospital is set to close, they're wanting to centralize everything in Newcastle. Darwinian evolution seems to mean the survival of the fittest—or more aggressive—in every sense.'

'Must that happen?'

Euan shakes his head. 'Darwin might've kept quiet about evolution: it's not the truth of it which worries me. It's the use of it. Will we share a dram before we turn in, Max?'

Back at the house, in his study, Euan pours the whisky. He asks shall I see Rachel. I tell him I already have. He sighs thoughtfully. 'Is it no' strange they had no idea of his problems when they signed the papers?'

'Her being a nurse, I can't think why she wasn't alert to the signs.'

'People can be desperate for a child: willing to do anything. You'll see that in practice.'

Cautiously I approach the subject of the modern fertility treatments. Euan looks troubled. 'I have enormous compassion for the problem, Max. You ken the time it took Margaret to fall for Chrissie? Eleven years of unexplained infertility. And we already had David.... I've no ethical problem with the basic IVF but you'll be aware of those that do, probably among your father's congregation. The method of obtaining the sperm bothers them. Never mind the rest of the process.'

'I'm aware it's an ethical minefield ... out there the research is way ahead of what ethicists can cope with.'

'I know your father's views on pre-natal testing: I see things from a doctor's viewpoint, as you do.'

'IVF and pre-implantation testing could solve problems for couples who wouldn't want to risk termination of affected fetuses.'

He takes a long breath. 'Of course, you and I believe the Creator has a purpose in how he forms families and individuals: the culture is moving towards an attitude I don't welcome: babies off the shelf.'

'If a Christian hasn't the integrity to deal with it, who has?'

Euan gives me a sharp look. Then, 'I doubt we'll be the ones who'll be asked to decide anything,' he says gloomily.

JENNY. THAT EVENING, EDINBURGH

It's a huge, comfy bed. But I'm so missing him: what exactly is our relationship? We've plunged into something deep, but there's no boundary, no certainty. The now is lovely, but what's the plan for next year? Five years' time? Is there one? Or is this what they call a fling? He says not. And awful stories about how wives are chosen in his religion. Or cult. Whatever it is. Max's assertions that his God isn't his father's God are confusing. What's Rachel like? A preppy little nobody? I'll outshine her, whatever.

If we stay together, might he want me to convert? Is the m-word assumed in the equation? Will Max be sucked back into the family, join his uncle's practice? Does he expect it to be cosy, with me over the border working at Roslin? What did he mean, other interviews? Where?

Where does *my* future fit? Research means far more self-discipline. There are restraints. That'll be hard. Would my curiosity carry me through the meticulous, routine focus on one tiny aspect of the puzzle of the cell cycle? Is a doctorate simply expected? What am I good at? Lots of things: photography, music ... (all this time, down the passage somewhere, someone's persistently playing the flute. Who?) Even baking: all hobbies. Never thought of doing any of them seriously. Look at what Val does!

I wish Dad was right out of the picture: then I could be sure I'm not applying for research to impress him.

Those thoughts had all been waiting, hadn't they, for a solitary space when they could bother me!

I wish Max had phoned. He'd appreciate how Val's like, and unlike, Dad.

*

In the morning, led by a delicious, unexpected, scent, I find Harris in the kitchen. 'You want breakfast? I'm making bacon and sausages.'

Harris does not look like a person who lives on fried food. A treat? After Val's Peter Rabbit rations? 'I'd love some.'

'D'you work out?' I ask as we eat. Expecting some kind of a snide Dad-like response.

'I run a bit. You people surf all summer?'

'Harriet surfs all *year*. Well, if you've the right gear for it— Where's your Mum?'

'Picking berries. Done the flute practice.' So Val's the musician.

'Picking? Where?'

'Not really. She probably buys them frozen.'

Val appears, a box of fresh raspberries in her hand, making dire and humorous threats about people who eat all that greasy stuff.

'Anybody'd think you grew up in Scotland!' she jokes. Chucking the fruit into a bowl, adding fresh yogurt, and spooning it in, standing at the counter. 'Been up for hours, I went early to market. Not all of us up here eat so badly.'

Later, my cousins drag me off to see the Castle: grey, gloomy, mounted on its rock, presiding over the cold, windy city.

As time goes by I worry more. The Persephone research could foul up my interview. Nicholson just gave Max a warning. It's more serious for me: if a whiff of that work got out, I've realised too late, the academic community will assume the Guthries share not only a name but a dubious ethical outlook. How stupid to embark on a risky project.

But, Wednesday, the interview seems to go well. They slide quickly through a few references to Dad—'Guthrie as in John of the Drey Clinic? Did your father's interests inspire you?'

'He was in the States when I was in secondary school: when he discovered my interests, of course he encouraged me. Then after I'd applied to Cambridge, he invaded my territory. I was astonished to hear that the Drey was opening on my doorstep!'

The interviewers nod, wisely.

And eventually hand me over to a young research scientist who shows me around and takes me to lunch.

But will they decide I'm just another Guthrie, more curious than circumspect?

MAX

Interview day: it's awkward: I must for now appear open to the Lord's leading, as the family would expect.

Euan ends with probing about marriage. He would prefer a junior partner to be wed already. Have I a lassie in mind? 'There's someone I'm bringing to meet the folks at the weekend—she's up for interview near Edinburgh.'

His eyebrows rise. 'I hadna' any idea, though I was hoping ... What does your father say?'

'They've not met Jenny as yet. We'll be at the Manse this weekend.'

'I see.' Those two words convey as much as a paragraph. 'May I inquire about this Jenny of yours?'

He asks about her qualifications, my intentions, and even, obliquely, whether or not (once he knows she isn't our kind of Christian) we've slept together. When I try to fudge that, Euan just looks, knowingly, and slightly disappointed. 'And how's Jenny feel about moving to the Border country, Max?'

'It's maybe how I feel, Euan. I'll admit, if she gets this place at Roslin, I'll need to think carefully about what that means for the future.'

'I'd have thought you'd see it as the Lord's guidance, or is that not so?'

'I—quite honestly, I'm thinking there may not be space for me and my father in the same county.'

Euan casts me a gloomy look. 'Laddie, I'm no' surprised you feel that. Though it's a disappointment to me.'

'And he'll act if I've rejected more than working for you. Well, nothing's—fixed. Just ideas.'

Euan rubs his forehead, and frowns at me, drawing together his bushy eyebrows. 'Max, you may think now this Jenny's a companion and a helpmeet to you, but if she's after a career of her own, have you considered what kind of a doctor's wife she'll make? When the bairns arrive, you'll have heavy commitments to your patients. It's hardly going to be possible for you to take a big share in the raising of them. So, d'you want your children given their tea and tucked into their beds by a series of young girls here to learn English?'

'Och, Jenny'd no' be out in the evenings!'

'It's not intentional, but a career brings business trips, meetings, conferences. What if the Lord calls you to work for him overseas? Is Jenny going to up sticks and follow on to somewhere she hasna' any chance to find work in her own field?'

By this time, I'm as gloomy as he is. Though I recall Wil's advice that we should move overseas to escape the family and further Jenny's career—and am grimly amused to put the two ideas together.

*

Later, in the evening, he returns to my personal life. 'Well, Max, you ken the Borderers' Club? We've a ceilidh planned for Friday. Maybe you would care to invite your lassie?'

I understand this means Euan's decided he and Margaret should vet Jenny. They'll be sweet as can be. But they'll stand back from any obvious support. As they did over Erin's marriage.

He grins mischievously. 'Of course, Annie-Marie, whom I recall was in that Folk Group you had, when you were both teenagers, will be playing in the band.'

'I've no objection to Annie-Marie's band playing!' I say. 'Maybe we'd give them a wee bit of help? Or a challenge?'

He smiles slowly. He and I were a fine pair on the fiddles at a ceilidh, during the three years I spent at Newcastle med school. 'I think Jenny might rather enjoy that.'

'That's a grand idea, then: you bring her over, Margaret would be happy for her to stay. A grand way to let her down slowly into the family!'

He concludes this conversation speaking of me and Dad in terms of a Biblical story, Jacob wrestling with the angel. 'Keep on wrestling, Max. Remember Jacob persisted until dawn. He gained what he asked for, but not without a lifelong injury to remember the strength of that angel.'

I understand this to mean he sees Erin's marriage and voluntary exile from the family as an injury. A self-accepted wound. Odd. But in keeping with my strange church.

JENNY

For supper, Val serves vegan risotto. Then produces a large photograph album, which she opens on the cleared kitchen table.

'Our community in the Western Isles.' Long-haired men and long-skirted women, half-naked children, dogs. Sheep. 'Where Harris and Lewis were born, hence the names—'

'And the next bairns would've been Egg, Muck, Mull, and maybe Rum—' Lewis says, 'so it's as well our Dad—'

Val stops him, so I don't hear what happened to their father. 'Ah, here we are: the core group.'

We all pore over the album. 'Me,' Val says, 'with Lewis—inside at the time—and Harris, that's him in the backpack—' In the picture, Val's enormously pregnant, clad in a tent-like caftan. 'Robert—my ex.' Tall and bearded, his blond hair streaming in the gale, wearing a kind of framed rucksack-like contraption on his back. Harris, a big toddler, leans dangerously out of it to wave.

'And here's—goodness—how colour prints fade!' (She stares, smoothing the picture, as if that might help.) 'Yep, the Joneses from Pembrokeshire—and there were one or two others—let me find them— this lot all met on the hippy trail,' she smiles, 'guy turned up with two girls on his arm—if you ken my meaning—he and this one paired off— she was Loose—funny name. Shortened for Lucy, some kind of a joke.'

Loose is dark, petite, with a determined chin. The guy has his back to the camera, and the other girl's in shade. Not a good photo!

Val turns the page. 'Fishing boat we used to bring in supplies from the mainland—that's Old Tam—or Old Jock was it?' she says, stabbing at a bent elderly islander with her forefinger. 'Can't remember—one of them'd make a terrible stramash if we wanted him to come out when it was his day off—especially he'd never come out if it was a Sunday.'

'He was a Wee Free,' Harris adds. 'You know they lock the public toilets on Sundays in the Western Isles?'

'Aye, folks should be away in their own homes on the Lord's Day, you see. Not striding around other people's countryside. Whether or no, the Sabbath was made for man—and woman of course—who the Lord made physical beings ...'

We laugh. Harris then points out a picture of a small child, and pokes Lewis, 'Sunshine—remember him?' but Lewis shakes his head.

Val's on a roll: 'We bred sheep. We tried to breed sheep. Actually, we got quite good at it. Jock—or Tam—they were very knowledgeable. Everyone had nicknames: Dozy Des and Lovely Loose ... the Murky McShanes ... Jewels was known as Jellybean.'

Bells ring in my head. 'May I?'

I turn back the pages. Another look at the core group. That's surely *our* Des, under the long hair, and floppy face-obscuring felt hat. 'So, this girl with the baby ... they're not—'.

'Des'd already joined us, then when Jack and the girls arrived he paired off with Jewels, Loose's sister.'

'So both Daze's parents, and one of her aunts, were all on your Commune?'

'I didna' expect anything serious would come of it, but I just mentioned to your mam that one of our commune members was moving to Penzance with his little girl. Des, your mam, I'm the link.'

'Oh—my—God ...' An avalanche of thoughts.

'Caroline's not told you?' Val stares.

'No. Jewels bunked from Glastonbury, Daze remembers that. No one's ever mentioned the Commune. How long were you there?'

'Och—maybe ten years? Nineteen sixty-five to seventy-five, about?'

'Longer,' Lewis interrupts. 'I was born there, and twelve when we moved.'

'I was fed up with the sheep breeding, and a pretty good traditional spinner and weaver.' I have to wait while Val explains her otherwise interesting career path. So frustrating! 'Plenty of housewives wanting to learn the old crafts—well, that's cynical maybe—I wanted to take my skills out to somewhere I'd get paid for them! Needed to put the boys in secondary school. So, we quit.'

'Who were the McShanes? When did Des and Jewels leave?'

'Des and Jewels? They found teaching posts. Art. I teach spinning, weaving, some dyeing—natural dyes—I'm not sure about the others: we haven't been back.'

Val recounts the visit she and the boys made to Cornwall, which I just about remember. 'Well, by then Des had bought and converted Chapel House. I was astounded you were all moving in with him. Never dreamed Des and your mam would shack up!'

'They even got married. Daze and I both remember that!'

What secrets have been kept!

And then, the phone rings. Max wants to compare notes on our interviews. Then he says, 'We have an invitation. Have you ever been to a ceilidh?'

'No, never.'

'Your education was sorely deprived, Miss Guthrie. Suppose I pick you up from Edinburgh tomorrow? Aunt Margaret's invited you to stay overnight.'

'I've nothing to wear.'

'Excuse to go shopping!'

'Max! Now listen properly and don't tease. Val introduced Mum and Des!'

'You and Daze never knew this?'

'We've been left ignorant! Val's talking about their Commune: Des's family lived there. When Daisy was born. There was even a family of McShanes there ... same surname as Daze's possible boyfriend?'

Max is all warnings, 'Jenny, be careful: families often keep secrets to stop people getting hurt. We'll talk at Euan's, I have to go now. Miss you.' Those last words almost mumbled into the phone.

*

Max's call interrupted my chat with Val: when I hunt for her to complete our talk, and thinking really way-out theories, Harris appears. 'Mum? She went out. To tootle on the flutle.' He does an exaggerated demonstration. 'Wednesday evening, her chamber group meet.'

My next opportunity is Thursday morning, shopping for Scottish dancing shoes. Val also spies gathered tartan skirts: but I find a plain rose pink cotton in an Indian emporium.

'Aunt Val: can I ask you more about your Island days?'

'Over a cup of tea. First, as you've grown up with no knowledge of your heritage, we've more essential sightseeing. John Knox. 1572. The crucial facts and date.'

'What about the crucial facts of how Mum met Des?'

'I didna' ken you'd not been told,' she says, 'but there's more to visiting Edinburgh than twenty-year-old gossip!'

'Aunt Val, you're as didactic, and evasive, as Dad. And you didn't grow up in Scotland any more than I did.'

'Indeed? The Guthries are not members of the Scottish diaspora? And the homely weaver is merely a front?'

To pay for drawing her out about the Commune, I've to see Knox's statue, *erected by Scots who are mindful of the benefits conferred by John Knox on their native land*. He looks disapproving about that, and indeed looks down upon the whole of Edinburgh disapprovingly.

She tramps me round St Giles's Cathedral, pointing out a few bits to smile at. *Seat: Part of the furniture of the Antechapel of the Most Ancient and Most Noble Order of the Thistle, St Giles, the High Kirk of Edinburgh* reads a note on the base of a chair. 'See,' Val says, 'a quiet humour beneath the stern outside. You didna' ken your great grandfather, did you? No, you wouldn't have. Like John Knox there: a minister of the Kirk.'

'Grandpa left Scotland. You came back.'

'The call of the Islands! Jenner's!' Val exclaims, leading the way. 'You'll need to take a wee gift to the Mullins family. We'll find something there.'

Jenner's is good for quality tweed women's suits, and wedding hats: Val tries on some hats. We view cut glass and light, warm, very itchy, tartan throws. Val finds Guthrie tartan. I buy a Maxwell tie for Max.

'Not Guthrie?' Val exclaims.

'Would you buy a man a tie in your tartan?' I ask. 'Wouldn't that be the next best thing to a noose?'

I expect a laugh, but 'Och,' Val sighs. 'Now, don't forget you've to buy shortbread to take back ... Time for tea.'

Earl Grey, and a fruit tart, in the café.

'The Murky McShanes: nicknames have a basis, don't they?' I ask.

'Och well: mine was Ian.'

'Ian?'

'Val, Valerian, Ian?' She laughs. 'My ex was Bunny. Mr McGregor, Peter Rabbit, Bunny?'

'Aunt Val, you're winding me up.' I coax her. 'Your nickname stories are great, but, what about the whole of Commune life in the sixties? Woodstock. The Isle of Wight festival. How festivals started.' Cradling my cup, I gaze into her eyes. 'What was the free love thing like? Before AIDS? It's mythological, and we were born too late!'

'Right: the Commune.' A sip of tea. An earnest look: 'Jenny, it wasn't romantic, it was hard grind. Learning the old skills and being self-sufficient when we'd mostly been brought up soft middle-class townies?

Going to bed cold by candlelight and getting up to your clothes still damp from yesterday's rain?

'Of course we had some good times and of course we did learn enough to run a functioning smallholding. But it wasn't like a movie or a fairy-tale, singing to our guitars, wearing flowers in our hair, smoking dope. Oh no. The dope-smokers got a kick up the backside from the lifestyle and they left. Or gave up the weed!'

'Des and Jewels left.'

'Yes—tell me about Daisy. Scrap of a bairn, but determined and busy in the studio, painting the floor with flowers, I recall. Defying your mother.'

'Daze's mythological side definitely survived Mum's scientific upbring-ing. Proof of genetics? Though that's unscientific of me to say.'

We laugh. Then, 'Aye,' she says, thoughtfully. Like Dad in the States, Val's adopted the style and accent of her chosen, or rediscovered in her case, culture. 'More tea? Another cake? Or a scone? What your mother may've decided not to talk about, Jenny, she may think is not my place to tell you.'

'So you're not going to? Suppose it was something I, or Daze, needed to know?'

'Is it not for her father to tell Daisy?'

'I suppose.'

'As for the nicknames: it was all a bit of fun. Murky McShanes was unfair: you said yourself it was the free love era.'

'And?'

Val shrugs, and offers the last scone on the plate. 'There was ... Des decided he'd had enough of the Western Isles, and took his family back to Essex! Jewels's parents actually did have a real farm. Suffolk? That was all around sixty-seven, soon after that photo was taken. Next thing I heard was five years on: Jewels abandoned Daisy at Glastonbury Festival. It was in the newspapers.'

'What did the newspapers say exactly? Wasn't Des with her?'

'A wonderful story: *Mummy said she was buying me an ice cream.*'

Val won't say more. Just asks whether I *dig* Bob Dylan.

FRIDAY

When I rush down the steps outside Aunt Val's, and cannon into Max, and hug him tight, for a moment he doesn't respond.

'You are all right?'

'Sure I'm fine. And you?'

'Do I get a ... kiss then? I've a present for you—which you should wear with that.'

The tartan is Maxwell, and I have never been anywhere with a man in a kilt! It's a funny feeling I have looking at his legs. And the family's obvi-ously proud enough of their roots that they preserve the Scottish lilt: his heavier accent's something I've noticed in our phone calls.

But not this reserve.

'Val wanted me to buy Guthrie—I told her no.'

'Och,' Max says, and laughs. We get in the car. At last we touch and kiss properly. Max lays the Jenner's bag with the tie in it on my lap.

'Is it too personal, or dreary? Like an aunt would buy for Christmas?'

'Oh no—I do like it. You're a dear, sweet lassie.' Max changes his tie, not looking at me.

'Is being given things—. But your car, the microscope?'

'Recycled around the family!' I make him look at me. I see something very deep, almost painful, in his eyes.

'Val gave me a ring. Recycled.' I hold my hand out.

'Pretty.' Max holds my fingers a long second.

'Look, all this isn't really over a tie, is it? It's something else.'

'Let's—get on or we'll not arrive in time.' I get another kiss, just on my forehead. And he starts the car. The atmosphere's totally wrong to discuss the McShanes, and how Val carefully forgot them.

'So, where is this we're going? I thought you said your aunt was away?'

'Hexham Scottish Borderers Club: my grandparents—Mum's parents, refugees from Edinburgh—founded it. Margaret had to be back—even from the *Women's Christians in Golf annual event, with evening talks led by the Reverend Anthony Field-Plowright*—or she'd be letting the side down.'

I glance sideways. Max is grinning wickedly.

'Christians in Golf?' I ask. 'They have a special club for that?'

'Very important: you can have Christians in anything—medicine, law, science, sport—golf's merely a subdivision of that ...'

'You serious?'

'Of course. A great opportunity for the gospel and fellowship,' Max adds dryly.

I take another look at his legs—long fawn socks like we wore at primary school—well, not quite like ... his usual shoes, but in the shop I saw the kind men wear for the dancing. Pumps with crossover black ribbons ... and yes, driving with a man in a kilt is weird, when you're not used to it. Doing anything with one.

'Chrissie—my wee cousin—she's likely been in a Bible Club or something they run for the bairns. Or, being a gifted child, she's been helping with the babies or learning a bit of golf herself. It'll be good to meet my relatives this way. It's a deal more relaxed in their house than at the Manse.'

Max has a key to Euan's front door. I wait in the hall while he goes to find his aunt and uncle. Golf clubs (Margaret's?) stand sentinel, their duck-like heads poking out of their tartan holdall, surveying me.

When the relatives appear, Euan's exactly as I expected: big, broad, clad in a kilt, and those dancing shoes. He grasps my hand and shakes it hard and long. Margaret's in a conventional green dress, her honey-coloured hair clasped back with combs. Chrissie's a plump child of eight or nine, pink furry deelyboppers dancing on her head above the bottle-green tartan silk party frock.

'Max, are you going to marry Genetics Jenny?' she giggles. 'You can choose what kinds of babies to have, can't you? They look at the ... *embryos*,' she emphasises the word. 'And then they pop the one you want inside. I've read a book.'

My God, what a child.

Leaving the Capri in the drive, we pile into Euan's Land Rover. Not forgetting two fiddles in their cases.

At the hall, the windows are flung open wide, the music's folksy and wild, not at all buttoned-up and Calvinist, and the kilts and the gathered skirts swing, the feet in those black pumps pound the floor. For the first half of the evening, Max and Euan join the band. Margaret, Chrissie and I join the skipping, hopping, junketing mass of humanity. I am twirled and whirled by partners whose names I don't always catch as we pair up for yet another fast, complicated figure, and then, eventually by Max, and Euan.

Problems and worries fly out of those windows along with the sweat and the humid breath and the noisy music.

As we arrive back, three or four hours later, the phone's ringing. Euan strides indoors, then comes back out to me. 'Your father, Jenny.'

'Oh my God—' Then, I clutch my mouth: I'm in the house of a member of Christians in Golf! 'Thank you—I can't think how he found this number.'

'He's waiting—' Euan says.

'Hi—Jen—honey? It's Dad—' Yep, deep news commentator voice an' all.

'This is Max's Uncle Euan's house. Who gave you the number?'

Reception's useless, his voice breaks up. Meanwhile, they all tramp by with the fiddles, a bottle of whisky won in a refreshment-break raffle, and a bunch of roses someone presented to Margaret in thanks.

Suddenly Dad's back, he's on his cell phone, must've moved around. 'Hey, don't blank me out, sweetheart. Easy to find, Alisdair Mullins, smart pastor, big church, Christian school—'

'Who passed the number on?'

'Cool it kid. Fee Mullins? Max's mom?'

'Really? Dad, everything all right?'

'Jenny, listen kiddo. Interview go well?'

'Jury's out. Seemed okay.'

'We need to celebrate your degree: you up for safari? I can book three weeks in Kenya next month?'

'Dad ...' My head buzzes with the tunes and the rhythms of the evening, burned into my ears and feet. That and my relationship, and Daze's mysterious life events, all take precedence over any expensive holiday he's cooked up because he thinks I moaned enviously about Daze's Colombian trip.

'Or if that doesn't appeal, snorkelling in Elat?'

'Can I think? I'm—'

'Sure you can think! But not too long ... And before I let you go back to your Scottish dancers, a follow-up to the Forum: I believe there'll be a piece in one of the tabloids this weekend.'

'Really?'

'Don't be worried if they've jazzed it up a bit. Highflying researchers are always near the edge, private companies are the envy of underfunded academics. And the media enjoy digging the dirt.'

'Is there any?'

'No way! But they may've sensationalised. Today me, tomorrow someone else is flavour of the month. End of story.'

'My tutor says the ethics committee's still out on using your new techniques, other researchers have developed similar treatments but they're waiting till it's legal.'

'Exactly! All anyone needs to know is, the trials proved the technique's safe. Okay, baby? It's an enterprise culture, you wait, my pushing ahead will be everybody's style in a couple of decades, less.'

'Okay, Dad.'

'Anyhow, what's with the cocooning in a Presbyterian minister's home, kid? Scuba-diving's far more fun.'

Need I explain myself, simply because biology made him my father? 'I've been learning Scottish dancing. Max and Euan played in the band a bit. It was amazing. You should try it some time.'

'I've danced a reel or two. You pouring with sweat now, then? I'll get off the phone and let you shower.' He chuckles.

'Dad—listen, they're nice people and I've had a great evening. But about the media—'

Suddenly the line goes dead, Dad disappears.

'Everything all right?' Euan asks, passing with a mug in his hand. Horlicks?

'I have to apologise for my father: he thinks he can barge in whenever he wants. Wherever I am.'

Euan raises an eyebrow. 'He most likely likes to know where his daughter is and with whom,' he says. 'I'm no' sorry for the compliment.'

Nice people, had a great evening with them.

'Max, my father: we don't need a sensational article on my Dad just when I'm about to meet yours!'

They've made sure he's sleeping on the sofa: Max has a duvet and two pillows clasped in his arms. 'Is this the Sunday papers we're speaking of? My father won't see those and neither will the Congregation. No buying or selling on a Sunday.'

'What about newsstands? They can't not read a screaming headline outside a sweet shop on their way to church.'

Max smooths a flat sheet over the three plump cushions which form the seat of the sofa. 'I'll deal with that. Dad and Mum are away to Carlisle midday Monday. I'd imagine Dad'll be holed up writing on the Christian family in the modern world until then. There's a fair bit he'll have to say on that … The paper might not use the story anyway.'

Euan's at the door, quite obviously sent to check on us. 'I didna' think—would you like a Horlicks before you turn in? You'll be needing a few wee moments to catch up, seeing we stole Jenny away from you to dance. A Strathspey reel is no place for conversation between young people who are courting,' he adds dryly.

Max, politely, accepts for us both. And 'Look—my father's not me—yours isn't you. We have a choice. We can be, think for, ourselves.'

Once he's brought the hot drinks, Euan remains. A three-way conversation covers my father's activities, and my mother's practice, in a general way.

He then regards me thoughtfully, 'You'll find Fee's a warm person, very much involved in caring for her family.' She'll be nice to me, but she'll not want to give up Max to any young woman? 'Alisdair can be a touch aloof, challenging—but he's a pastor, you must remember, he has a deal of souls in his care, and responsibilities.'

Then looking at Max, 'Will you be wanting to show Jenny around the surgery tomorrow morning? We run an emergency clinic, but I imagine she'll be happy to fit herself around that?'

'All right with you?'

'Fine. Good.' So they think Max will work here? And assume we're moving straight towards the m-word, not passing *Go* on the Monopoly board? Where do I come in?

'Well—if you've finished that,' Euan says, 'I'll take the mugs …'

Margaret appears, to lead me to my bedroom. Next to theirs, the hall light left on for Chrissie. Pink floral duvet, matching curtains and lampshade. *Scottish Field* and *Good Housekeeping* by the bed.

ALISDAIR AND FEE. THAT EVENING, THE MANSE

Fee scrapes the last of the chocolate fudge icing from the bowl, and smoothes it over the top of the large, rich sponge cake. The kitchen door opens. Alisdair enters. 'Ah—*a good wife who can find*?'

His favourite quote from Proverbs, she thinks, scattering walnuts on a sheet of greaseproof paper. She folds the paper over, and begins crushing them, using the rolling pin. Leaning on the wooden pin, she can feel the nuts give as they fall into pieces. 'And did you complete your message for the Kings School end of year service?'

'Is a minister's message ever complete?'

Alistair spies the fudge-icing bowl, the sides still thinly coated with chocolate mixture. He begins to wipe the inside with his finger, licking off the collected chocolate. Fee puts down the rolling pin, releasing the crushed nut mixture, and scatters nutmeats carefully, silently, over the top of the cake.

Alisdair lays the bowl aside, and the next quote's from his favourite Burns poem: '*O my Luve's like a red, red rose That's newly sprung in June: O my Luve's like the melodie? That's sweetly play'd in tune!*'

Fee's well accustomed to this. She begins washing up her cooking utensils. Alisdair advances on her from behind, his arms meet around her waist, and he feels her relax against him. He touches a bit of chocolate frosting on his fingertip to her lips and whispers into her ear,

'*As fair art thou, my bonnie lass, So deep in luve am I: And I will luve thee still, my dear, Till a' the seas gang dry.*'

'Go on now, you daft man,' she says, as she turns, kissing his chocolate fingertip and then his lips. 'You know I have work to do. Will the things wash themselves?'

'They'd maybe try—'

Fee, who is tired, and anxious about Max bringing this Jenny home, wishes they would. Also—more so—that Alisdair'd let her go down to London to see their first grandchild instead of having to act out the dutiful wife beside him on the conference platform next week. Married love? Marie Stopes was wrong: the hardest part is not the question of contraception. It is the question of duty.

Alisdair sets her free, and she scrubs at the mixing bowl as if chocolate icing were an enemy. 'And when do our visitors arrive?' he asks. 'You keep the social diary: what have you arranged?'

'Max and Jenny will be here in time for tea.'

'Good. And this—' he indicates the cake '—is in their honour is it?'

'You know it's his favourite.'

'Hum. This is someone who works in a genetics laboratory. I'm wondering how Max found her again? What is his purpose, in bringing her to visit?'

'We've always encouraged them to bring their friends home. D'you think—d'you think he's considering ...' Fiona stops herself there. The idea Max could have a serious relationship with a girlfriend which he hadn't previously mentioned remains difficult. Margaret's passed on her impressions: 'A nice wee lassie, polite and a good mixer. Even told me her great-grandfather had been a minister! She fitted in, and enjoyed the ceilidh. Max is obviously very smitten.'

Fee remains worried. The girl isn't a believer ... 'I don't know—maybe at one of those church weekends—we girls used to enjoy those—even if we spent more time cooking—'

'You think Max goes on church weekends? We don't even know which church he attends, down there!' Alisdair idly flips the pages of Fee's recipe file. Angel Food Cake—he's rather partial to that. 'And what do you imagine her angel food cake is like? Do we know she can cook, this lassie? Or merely dabble with cells?

'We'll have to see, won't we, Al?' Fee says, gently humorous, untying her apron. She hangs it on a hook, and picks up the milk bottles to place on the doorstep. 'Maybe as we get to know her—' Alisdair takes out his keys to lock up. Fee would like another woman in the family: a good woman, of course.

Friday night is traditionally an early bed and a cuddle, on Alisdair's initiative. Alisdair quotes the final verse of the Burns poem as they mount the stairs, Fee giving him a steadying hand. He adds, 'Were it not for the MS, you understand.' He seems to enjoy his own grim humour, though at present, in remission, the disease doesn't strike at his performance in bed.

FEE. SATURDAY, MID-AFTERNOON, THE MANSE

Fee's on her knees at the rose bed, weeding with a small fork, when she hears the car coming up the road. Leg of lamb with garlic and rosemary's already in the roasting tin, fruit cake on the table ready to ice, angel cake cooling upside-down over a Coke bottle, as advised in her American cookbook.

Stock still behind the roses, Fee squints between the leaves and almost-overblown yellow and pink peace blossoms, as Euan's car slows to a halt on the gravel. Of course, it's no longer Euan's car: he handed it to Max. But for so long, it was Euan's trade-mark, his sporty wheels, his pride and joy.

First the driver's door opens. Max has long legs like his father, today in grey trousers and black shoes. He bends slightly, stepping from the car, clipping sunglasses to his shirtfront (stripy shirt she hasn't seen before), sweeping back that black hair she always tells him shouldn't fall into his eyes.

He goes round to the passenger door, but it's open already: the girl comes out laughing, stops. To do what? Pull on her shoes! Strawberry blond hair over her face as she leans forwards. Overbalances, hops, laughs. Max's hand under her elbow: more laughter. Jeans are too tight: what's that written on her T-shirt? Handbag's a basket, like you buy on holiday. Tosses back her hair. *Spectacles!*

They're hauling out their luggage: heads together. Max has the girl's overnight case: an argument, she takes it from him. She reaches back into the car to pull out a khaki army-surplus shoulder bag, like Erin's school bag. Erin scrawled ban the bomb signs, and flowers with faces, on that bag ... Jenny's is stuffed with what looks like files and papers.

And then Max—that horrible sports-bag-like holdall thing he likes to carry his baggage around in swinging from one hand—is moving her along, one arm loosely around her waist. Eyes locked into each other's, then glancing up at the house, the girl saying something—*microscope?* Not *microscope*, surely!

Max speaks: Fee can't hear. The girl shakes her head, and smiles. Max moves his hand to her shoulder.

Now is the moment: Fee rises from behind the rosebush, pulling off her gardening gloves. 'Max! Pet—and this is—?'

'Mum, this is Jenny—my mother.'

'Jenny. Of course.' She smiles: 'Fiona Mullins. Alisdair—Max's father—is counselling in the study,' Max knows that signals *quiet, please*. 'We'll all meet up at tea.'

Jenny dips into that basket: hands over shortbread from Edinburgh, and a cube-shaped tartan box. Hard to know what to say at this stage, Fee thinks, except thank you, you shouldn't have. Box label says inside is small crystal vase. She'll make sure it's on the tea table, filled with sweet peas.

'Mum, the hair's great.' Max holds her at arm's length, admiring it: a shiver goes through Fee, her oldest son so like Alisdair at the same age. 'You'll not be getting the headaches from the weight of it any longer.'

No, but over this: he evidently *belongs* to this girl, this Jenny. Jealousy is a sinful emotion.

Though righteous judgments over relationships ...

Fee leads the way inside. A door opens behind them: Alisdair showing some worried person out. Fee nearly stumbles on something, stubs her toe: a skateboard!

Her toe's so painful, forgetting herself, she calls loudly, 'Alex! Ian! Skateboard tidy, boys!'

Nobody answers. Is that a giggle from Jenny, as Max drops his bag and replaces the board on the special rack Alisdair constructed for the boards, helmets and kneepads his brothers dote on?

'Max! Hi—and Jenny? Hey—I'm Kirsty ...' Why do the young hug? Fee wonders.

'Where're your brothers, pet?' Her blonde daughter's barefoot in track bottoms and a grey T-shirt—*Kings School Summer Camp* across her breasts in pink. 'Mum—'

'Kirsten?' Fee smiles (at the same time noticing Kirsty's maroon toe-nails), 'Would you show Jenny where she'll be sleeping.'

'Mum—'

'Kirsty.' Fee stops her there. First entertain the guest!

'Yeah, sure. Jenny, where's your things?'

Girls despatched, Fee hopes for a word with Max before Alisdair reaches him. 'Let's go in the kitchen: I'll make a pot of—. Max, where *are* your brothers?'

JENNY

Fiona—Max's mum—a bit wooden ... pretty as that smiling photo in the newspaper Dad gave me. But I want to like it here, to like them. Except the minister. Kirsty's human. Look at the painted toes!

The hallway's organised like it's a school or something. Wellington boot rack, umbrella stand with umbrellas, bicycle pumps, and a walking stick, coats neatly hanging on hooks, and that skateboard tidy!

We divide my luggage, and climb up towards my room. Cool green with twin beds: so unlike Val's. Let it be different in a good way ... Kirsty's

135

found me green bath and hand towels, 'Sorry they're a bit frayed. Jenny, isn't my brother a sneaky—'

'Yes, he's kind of private about stuff.'

'So, can I see the ring?'

Ring? She's thinking First Truly isn't she? Have to play along here.

'Um—haven't yet got to the shops.'

'That means he's going to give you Granny's!'

Oh. My. God. Their tradition, the one planned for Rachel!

As I think this, Kirsty's inspecting me from under her hair. Her serious grey eyes (like his) are hunting for clues. *You're wondering about me*, I think. *Yes, the Max who's your big brother is different to the Max I know.*

'Where did you meet? What do you—do?'

'My dad heads up a research lab—Max and I were at a kind of academic meeting there?' (But did she know we were together before this?)

'So you're a doctor? A med student?'

'Oh no—I work with cells. And …' I stop myself over embryos—maybe Kirsty's too influenced by her dad for me to mention them. 'I'd like to help find out a bit more about—when babies have problems—like Down's babies? But it's all very slow—each person does tiny bits, I'll just being looking at one aspect of what one part of a cell …' My explanation's drowned as a kerfuffle breaks out downstairs, and Kirsty clutches her mouth: 'Brothers! Do you have brothers?'

'Two sisters, younger.' A door slams shut. Another's wrenched open: the scent of roast meat drifts upwards.

'I need you here, now, Kirs-*ten*.'

'Mum—' She tenses like a scared gazelle, then skips away. 'I'll see you—'

Is she really nearly eighteen? Fiona has seriously more clout than our mother: Harriet wouldn't skitter down the stairs like that.

MAX

Both parents make appeals. Mum's ballistic in a tight-lipped way. 'The boys, I left an angel cake cooling: Alex and Ian … Max, do you go and sort them out—'

Meanwhile, Dad's heard the shock waves, and appears at the kitchen door. She grabs his arm, 'Al, stay here, it's not possible for you—'

'What have they done?'

'Max can deal with it.'

My brothers are in the tree house with the empty plate. Hauling them out, I warn them, 'Dad's in a bate. You'll be away to your rooms now but not until you've apologised to our mother for causing her grief—and,' I pause, making an effort, 'to Dad for breaking whichever commandment—look up the Scripture passage, and I'll warn you in advance, he'll have you learning a psalm for this.'

'Och, man, he doesna' make us learn things,' they complain.

'He maybe doesn't, but I do … away with you—both!'

So, a quiet cup of tea with Mum in her domestic setting? Jenny and Kirsty to join us? No. Dad's finished on the Congregation for today—and now's his opportunity to haul me in for some counselling of my own! His scheme to *have a wee chat* was expected: but as soon as I walk through the front door?

*

His study's a place of shadowy green darkness, and memories. On his desk, the family portrait photograph: Mum, Dad, Erin, me, standing. Kirsty, Ian and Alex sit in front. Everyone smiles except Alex who's evidently just been poked by Ian.

Beside that photo, he has the Robertsons—Euan, Margaret, David. On Margaret's lap, Christine, smiling. *If you're happy and you know it, then you really ought to show it—* Under that ever-so-straight fringe, she shows it with a big smile. My gifted little cousin: destined for great things?

Every good gift, every perfect gift, coming down from the Father of lights.

'Did Euan tell you where David is?'

'I heard he's away to Australia.'

'Surfing!' Dad scowls, dismissing Chrissie's elder brother.

I don't comment: we don't have to be like our fathers: we can be, and think for, ourselves. Telling Jenny that was the first time I said what's been in my heart for years. All through med school. *I do not need to be like him.*

'So—you didna' think to share your plans at any stage?' my father says. 'Would you sit down, James Maxwell, and not pace the room like some wild creature reluctant to be here?'

Extremely inauspicious. I stop pacing, and I shrug. 'Shall we both sit, then?'

Dad takes his place in the leathery swivel chair, beside his huge desk: seated sideways like someone consulting in a surgery. Like me, in my adult life away from him!

I'm forced to perch on that velvet-covered two-seater he keeps for couple counselling: well below him in height. 'Colin and Rachel,' I say, looking upwards at him, 'I'm surprised they adopted so soon. They've been married less than two years.'

'As I recall, Rachel knew Colin was left with the legacy of mumps in adolescence: however, that doesna' concern you.'

'I'm concerned she looks so worn out. Also that they failed to have that bairn checked over before they signed everything.'

'I'm certain they behave responsibly. Which is not what I can say of you.'

'Oh?'

'Max, families are mutually caring, families discuss developments. It pains me that you did not think to consider your family. You merely sprung this information on us and brought home a girl we have never met. Do I take this to mean that this person—whom we have never met—is to become one of us?'

'It goes both ways, Dad: Jenny needed to meet my family. You've taught me enough about an open home and hospitality: I brought Jenny here so that you could all meet.'

'Presumably you speak of an engagement?'

'Please: it is an engagement.' Right: I have said it. To him in advance of a formal talk with Jenny, too! 'Maybe I sprang it on you, but it is not talk.'

'Humph,' my father says. He rises and it's now him who paces around.

'Max—you are with open eyes about to be—maybe you are even now— yoked to an unbeliever?'

His way of snidely probing into our physical relationship. 'I can't listen to this—' I say, standing up to meet him eye to eye. 'I won't have Jenny insulted.'

'Oh—you won't?'

I move towards the door. Dad grabs me by the arm. I ignore that his limp's worse than I've seen it since the MS has been in remission. I shake him off. We stand, eyeballing each other. 'She's no' a Christian girl: when you have a church full of good women, any one of them would make excellent wives and good mothers. Who would rear your children in the nurture and admonition of the Lord.'

'Any one of them—really, Dad, I am not after mix and match—I am not selecting from a list—Och, Dad, Jenny is a help meet—does not Scripture say that? Suitable? To me? A challenge and a companion? My equal, intellectually and every other way.'

'And tell me,' he says, slow and thoughtful-styled, needling, 'how do you know that this is the woman you should marry?'

'How do you know that this is not the woman God has given to me?'

His eyebrows rise. 'A son of this family—and an unbeliever—tell me we are not to expect—'

I continue up the faith track, ignoring his second tasteless insinuation. 'The Anglican Church mayn't be to your taste but it isna' heretical.'

'The Anglican Church? She was baptised in the Anglican Church, was she? And what does that mean? An abode of woolly thinkers, who have no personal relationship with the Lord.'

'Right. Well, I'm not the specialist—'

'And Euan, although a competent practitioner of medicine—is neither a pastor nor your father.'

'Euan?'

'Who spoke highly of this girl whom you chose to take to his house before you brought her to meet us.' A pause. 'I am extremely disappointed with you,' my father says, 'You clearly sneaked this up with no warning because you were ashamed—'

'Would you just drop it, Dad? I am not ashamed. I brought a very beautiful accomplished woman into this house, with its reputation for hospitality, and I am outraged to find we are treated as children. I have the lives of children in my care—I am no longer a child.'

It's gone deadly quiet downstairs. What happened to tea? Bit of a contrast to Euan's comfortable family. Where's Max? I unpack a few things. Hang out of the window to see the garden. Nobody there. Flower borders and fruit bushes. A Frisbee abandoned on the lawn. Can smell supper though. I'll find the kitchen.

It's a huge family kitchen. Fee's at the pine table, hand over her eyes, in front of her a huge fruitcake, the trappings of a complicated icing session, and a Coke bottle. The Aga's set with pans of vegetables in waiting, there's obviously a joint roasting in the oven. 'Mrs Mullins—Fiona? Are you all right?'

'Jenny?'

I've surprised her with her public face off: she hurriedly replaces it: smiling, 'Yes. The boys—Just a bit of a headache. The weather, high pressure.'

I know the signs. Her speech is slow and slurred. The arrival of the unknown serious girlfriend has set off a migraine. What Granny Ianthe would call *one of her heads*. Used to puzzle me when I was small! I'm beginning to feel unwanted. Max shouldn't have brought me.

Fiona indicates the fruitcake, 'It's for a baptism party.'

'Yes—it looks lovely.'

There's also a recipe card: *Angel Cake.*

'I—love angel cake—' I falter, then kick myself for saying something inane. Start again, seeing I can't drop through the floor and disappear. 'Would you like some help? With anything?'

'Oh no—I'm fine—We should be looking after you, Jenny. The boys are tinkers: they should know better—'

Kirsty appears on cue to explain that rumpus we heard. 'Alex and Ian ate the pudding!'

'Oh! Oh, that's awful!'

'Max told them off!'

I see my opportunity to shine: I don't just *like* angel cakes, I'm rather good at making them. 'Look, why don't I, shall I, replace it? Would that help?'

Fee accepts. They have plenty of eggs, flour and sugar. She makes Kirsty run about finding the utensils, keeps apologising for her migraine.

'Once it's in the oven I'll fetch it out again, Jenny: you go and … Kirsty! Homework!'

'Mum, have a lie down!'

In the nicest possible way they kick me out of the kitchen. No sign of Max. A door I try is the downstairs bathroom. The open window admits a chilly fresh breeze, there's an odour-removing pink plastic thing standing sentinel beside the spare loo roll, and a little floral soap dish with a removable saucer and holes for the soap to drain. Shining taps. A framed text over the basin: *I can do all things through Christ who strengthens me—*

139

Don't Max's pre-adolescent brothers laugh at that?

Murmurous voices sound from the Minister's study, left of the front door. To the right, the sitting room, smelling of fresh paint. Cream walls, white wood, blue carpet, floral-patterned suite. Tiny TV and video hiding in a corner, bookshelves. Children's classics, travel guides, poetry. Dickens, Scott (Victorian editions?), the Brontës, P. D. James. National Geographic and The Raj Quartet. Knitting basket with needles sticking out, and a three-tiered sewing box.

I feel like I'm too large and gross for Max's family, all so neat and organized like dolls in a doll's house. And I so wanted to fit in and be accepted—and tell them—tell them what? That I'm not a monster because of my work? Why does this house make me feel guilty? I'm ordinary. They're the freaks, with their strange ideas on marriage and obedience.

'*Cast all your cares upon him for he careth for you*—1 Peter 5:7' is worked in brown wool cross-stitch beneath a picture of a rose-covered cottage—

Suddenly a heavy hand is laid on my shoulder. 'Family motto: You know the verse before that?'

'Max!' Try slipping my arm round him: he goes tense and pulls away. 'Where'd you *get* to?'

'Dad made us all learn this—*Humble yourselves therefore under the mighty hand of God, that he may exalt you in due time: Casting all your care upon him; for he careth for you. Be sober, be vigilant; because your adversary the devil, as a roaring lion, walketh about, seeking whom he may devour: Whom resist steadfast in the faith* … What's not up there is as important as what is. The unspoken as the spoken?'

'Really?'

'Time to eat tea—'

I'm then surprised how proprietarily Max draws me against his side. 'Jen, don't be scared of them. Believe me, it's better in the open right away.'

'What is?'

'Us? I've—spoken to my father.'

He takes my hand and leads me along. Spoken to his father?

*

No tea in sight, but the whole family's gathered, and Alisdair … Alisdair is physically so like Max thirty years on, more like than the photo Dad gave me, because he moves the same way. I'm breathless, as Max introduces us, 'Dad, everyone—Jenny—Jenny, my father, Kirsty, my mother you met—Alex and Ian.'

'Hello.' I'm inanely grinning and hardly hearing the minister's response.

'This is a great surprise.' I know how he means great: not as in wonderful. As he turns and gets busy with a steel and a carving knife, which he then hands over to Max, 'Do you take your turn tonight.'

Oh my God: same physique, tall, slim, graceful, narrow hipped, and the dark hair, greying and receding. The long nose, the grey, penetrating eyes. Those eyes swept over me, summed me up, and rejected me as strongly as Max, summing me up, can be woken by desire.

Heart pounding: how do I relate to this sterner, older copy of my lovely guy?

Nudge, nudge, 'Jenny?' Someone's pulled out a chair and they're making me sit down: God, it's Alisdair. I fall into my place, and hear Fee, in command, 'Kirsty—roast potatoes,' says Fiona. She's always telling Kirsty to do things.

I'm put between Max—still away from his place, carving the roast joint—and Fiona, supervising the vegetable supplies. There's a flurry of plate passing. I so want to like them—or for them to like me. It's so formal though. And his father, a horrible feeling being disliked on sight by a man so like ... Suddenly, Max is back in place and everyone's grasping hands—Alex or Ian starts up, 'Lord Jesus we thank ...' and the Minister—Alisdair—stops whoever it was, 'As Max is home, I think maybe he should lead us in prayer tonight. No more and no less than three minutes, of course.'

Is that ironic, or literal? Kirsty grins at me: I take that to mean it's their kind of joke. Max clears his throat and out come these just weird, religious phrases like we're in the sixteenth century, like we're people in the Bible, like we're at school ... I *die* inside! Can his father make him do this? How awful!

'Some hae meat and cannae eat. Some nae meat but want it. We hae meat and we can eat and sae the Lord be thankit. Father we thank Thee for Thy blessings on our journey and for your provision for our needs. *Bless this food to our use, and us to your service, make us grateful for all your mercies, and mindful of the needs of others ...'*

Squirming, inwardly, I wish I didn't have to hear this. Who was it helped me deal with the Persephone business? Where's the person at Erin's cottage, in the black-sheeted bedroom?

'... in the name of Jesus our Saviour, Amen.'

'Well now: as Max has no more to thank the Lord for, let us each in our own spirit of thankfulness begin our meal. Kirsty, would you pass the potatoes to our guest and I should like to hear how your swimming trials went today?'

'Alisdair—please—' Fee says. Smiling. Still looking tired. 'I think we've all been passed the vegetables. Jenny, do begin.'

I can't look at Max.

Alex passes a slice of his meat to Ian, and Ian passes Alex one of his roast potatoes. Or vice versa, which is which? It's a lovely dinner, though difficult to swallow in this company.

Max leans towards me, 'And afters will be your angel cake and Mum's home-made raspberry ice-cream ...'

Afters: I don't want to, but I hear my Granny Ianthe's comments on U and non-U, Us and Them. We're eating *tea*, pudding is *afters*. So, the sofa's probably a *couch* and the sitting room'll be a *lounge*. And they probably think I'm a snob. But it's just words: I don't believe in that stuff.

Now Alisdair's extracting a detailed account of something Kirsty's done: been chosen for the Under-20 County Swimming Team. Fiona (who obviously already knew this) makes another an effort to be nice, smiles at me, and asks 'Tell me—about your family? The Guthries of Arbroath?'

'I'm sorry—I don't know. My mother's a doctor—my parents met at Cambridge.'

'And your father? A minister's son?'

'Grandson. He's moved from clinical medicine into research.'

(A sharp look from this Minister.) 'Ah—medical family.' She smiles even more. 'Brothers and sisters?'

'Two sisters.'

'Jenny's the oldest,' Kirsty supplies. Alisdair glares. She's supposed to be talking with him, not listening to me and her Mum! 'Sorry, Dad—for interrupting.'

'All going the same way?' Fee asks.

'One's an art student. That's Daisy. She's—'

'Very talented, isn't she?' Max says. Lest I say, 'Just had a baby' or 'My stepsister and not a relation', while Kirsty says, 'Jenny works with cells. Isn't that exciting?'

'Wow: how do you see them? In enough detail?' asks a twin.

'A lot of it's done with an electron microscope—a great big thing, nothing like an old-fashioned optical microscope, like the one that Max—'

There's a silence. Everyone's looking at me.

Max comes right in with my name! 'Jenny,' he says, 'is a wonderful person ...'

MAX

I see her blush, but didn't I have to stop at source any discussion of antique microscopes, one we had here once in particular? And I plough on, 'a wonderful person. I hope you'll take the time to get to know her, because she's likely to become a big part of my life.'

They gasp, stunned by this crazy U-turn in the conversation. First the M-word, now the—well, second M-word, in essence. I know that was mischievous: but how else to prevent the family skeleton prancing from its cupboard?

Dad is silent. Meat on fork suspended between plate and slowly closing mouth. Mum lowers the serving-spoon she's held frozen over a dish of baby carrots, and breaks the silence, coolly. 'Alisdair?' she says, with a sharp look at him. He nods—just enough. 'Well, this is a—great surprise. Jenny, we shall have to get to know each other—Max has been very secretive. I hope your parents—?'

'I think it's brill,' Kirsty interrupts.

Ian asks, 'Do you play cricket?' and Jenny, who looks close to tears (and might be anyway, if the other subject had persisted), says, 'What? No, I don't.'

Dad meanwhile looks inscrutable. Already been told, but a great actor. Bent on demonstrating contempt of my important life plans, he turns to Mum, 'Perhaps you'd do the honours, Fiona—coffee, pudding—I have people to see this evening. Max, you must realise this is a surprise, a very great surprise. We would have expected—You have had ample time, no doubt, while courting to at least talk with your family about your friendship?'

'Dad, I have talked with the one who matters.'

'Meaning?'

'I expect you to know who I mean.'

Mum speaks up, 'Jenny, we'd really have liked to get to know you before this. I'm sure it must be quite hard for you—Max, really, you don't always think of other people.'

'I'm sorry you see it that way: I have thought deeply of other people. Life is fraught in Cambridge and this is the first opportunity—'

'I hope—I hope—' Mum says.

Dad rises from the table, meal only partially eaten. 'Would you be able to re-route that fruit cake you made for Erin's wee one so we can offer it for Nathaniel's baptism on Sunday?'

Mum's startled. 'That cake's for the family celebration. I made it to save Erin. I made angel cake … Jenny made angel cake … for you.'

'The Lord's ways are not our ways,' Dad counters. 'Colin and Rachel have asked for an early baptism for Nat. Of course, I hope Erin and that husband of hers will honour us by reappearing at First Reformed when the time comes for Cameron.'

'Of course, I can make another—'

'It is Colin and Rachel I'm to counsel tonight. Would there be some of that excellent chocolate cake to share with them?'

'I made that for—oh, there's enough of it there—'

I sigh: I am ashamed of my family: so tense, remote, concerned about—microscopes, and cake!

JENNY

What is going on?

I'll kill Max once we can get out of this room! For a moment I can't even hear what they're all saying. Babble, babble they go … Not only does Max's dreadful father plan marriages, but lest that stupid microscope gets mentioned, Max does as well. The relative importance of the two subjects escaped him. Couldn't he have let them rave, wherever microscopy might lead—would it have been so bad?

Thanks, Max, for saving your family, and leaving *me* isolated.

What're they saying now? Talk's moved on: an inane argument's begun over cakes. Their crazy Christian culture's totally far out, not like Euan's family who're almost normal.

Suddenly the whole party's breaking up, Fiona instructing the kids about doing homework. Max is gathering up plates. So I grab pudding bowls, and as we move towards the sink, I hiss at him, 'What the hell do you think you're doing? Saving a scene by telling them we're getting married?'

'Dad hauled me in to give me a *wee talk*,' Max says, heavily ironic. 'And believe me, you don't want to've been the person who dug up the past.'

'Really? Hasn't everyone moved on? So that's where you were. Discussing what?'

'I told him we are engaged.'

I dump the pudding bowls rather too hard on the kitchen counter, and face Max, 'You mean, you and he'd already— What are you up to?'

'It's the language he understands.'

'Right. I suppose if the M-subject hadn't come up, you would've asked me first? Before you spilt the beans over everybody?'

'I'll—' Max begins, but something brown and furry suddenly tears across my feet and scuds to a halt by the closed kitchen door. Alex and Ian pound in through the garden door, kitchen door flings wide, Fee appears, 'Boys—boys!'

'Dusky escaped and went for your lettuces Mum!' Furry creature, a huge rabbit, does a U-turn by the vegetable rack. Immense excitement. Over goes a chair.

'She's decimated your veg garden!'

'Dodge—head her off—'

'Tackle her!' Ian falls flat across the kitchen doorway. Rabbit skids over my foot again, then off around the table. Reacting like it's a match, I dive for the animal, the goalie rushing to deflect the ball. 'Awesome—did you see that? Max's girlfriend can tackle—'

Once it's in my arms, a lovely, huge, trembling creature, twitching its pink nose, I hand it over. Momentarily recalling Botallack.

'What else can you do?' Alex or Ian asks.

'Game of cricket outside?' Max's hand on my shoulder.

I shake it off. 'You can't get away with fudging and diversions: I deserve more explanation than your father's sensibilities and comprehension of language! Or I'm going home!'

But now there's a brisk ring on the doorbell. Fee bustles to open the door. Rachel and family! Willowy red-head in a long skirt, baby in her arms wrapped in a blanket, older guy.

'Good to see you home, Max!' Rachel's husband, big, bespectacled, and schoolboyish, near forty I guess, shoves forwards extending a beefy paw. 'We should have a game of squash while you're here—or is golf more your game now?'

'I've not a great deal of time this visit—' Max extricates himself quickly, knocking on the study door and calling through, 'Col and Rache are here.' Turning to them, 'Go in: Dad's expecting you.'

Then, shaking his head at me, like he's dismissing something unpleasant, asks his brothers, 'Where're the stumps, Alex, Ian? Ball? You using a real one? Or Dad still insisting on the tennis ball?'

So now there's cricket—with the siblings and even Alisdair once Rachel and Colin have left. And then, indoors, there's Scrabble. And no chance to be alone and sort our situation.

About quarter to ten, Fee sets the kettle to boil, and announces *supper*. She expects us all, except Alisdair who's working on his sermon, to sit obediently around the kitchen table with tea and chocolate cake. A third cake! A large part of it already consumed. Presumably by Rachel, Colin, and Alisdair, discussing baptism!

I need to discuss marriage.

MAX. NIGHT, HIS BEDROOM

Not an auspicious start: the wee talk, Dad over-exerting himself to play cricket, Mum baking herself into the ground and slaving over a hot stove, Rache and Col turning up, which rubs salt into Dad's wounds, and Jenny putting her foot into it—nearly—by mentioning the microscope. I told her, '*Remember church tomorrow: we all get up around eight for family breakfast. No need to worry about meeting Dad: he'll be giving the Message a final polish.*' Irony of course. But lost on Jenny.

Crept up here, to sink onto my bed: forgot how narrow and rickety it is! Reach for my Bible, leaf through the pages, their edges furry with use, looking at the well-known texts—how to balance *honour your father and mother* and *a man leaves his father and mother and cleaves to his wife* ... in a flat near Cambridge that goes with a trainee post at a rather pleasant practice? If Roslin does not snap her up?

Dear Dr Mullins (I pull the letter from my Bible, unfold and re-read it), *I am delighted to receive your application since as you know our prospective GP trainee (from the Indian sub-continent) has had to pull out due to visa problems. Could you let me know if you would be interested in the flat, which he was to rent over the surgery? It is suitable for a married couple ...*

A Spitfire, my last remaining Airfix model, hangs by the open window twirling slowly in the draught. Reminder of days when I wanted to be either a fighter pilot—like Dad was once—or, as they said at school, have a career in music.

Did neither.

How Dad could dare humiliate me before Jenny this evening I can well understand: it's his underhand war against us. Even Alex and Ian can't completely escape: last time I was here, he condemned their giving thanks for a meal.

'And this is the best you can manage, Alexander?' Silence. 'A two-minute jumble of childish thoughts delivered towards the top of this table in a mumbling voice hardly shows enough respect for our Lord—or do you disagree?'

My guts twisted with empathy. I remembered how once I'd realised you could master key phrases and string them together to make prayers, family graces could roll off my tongue easily and without thought. I gave them a lesson in extempore prayer!

What to do with this more serious situation? My autonomous life?

JENNY

Prettily decorated, but horribly chilly bathroom. Helps with the unwanted feeling that's filtering through: even Max has sneaked off to bed, with no reassurances.

What's Fee thinking? She acted like none of that wedding talk happened.

Close the window, turn the shower up hot. Sneak a look in the cabinet: cheap suntan-without-sun cream, maroon nail varnish, blonde rinse. Eye makeup stashed behind sanitary stuff. Kids' bathroom? Parents have an en-suite?

I saw how Alisdair glared at my rainforest T-shirt. Even without knowing Brazilian Portuguese, the message on it's obvious. And at Val's starry silver ring. Better not leave it on the basin! Val may be New Age: but the rainforest's God's creation in their eyes—surely? Shouldn't we save it? He'd have gone even more ape if the ring was a diamond solitaire.

They all cheered because I'd made another angel cake—'Jenny's made another! Well what d'you know!' Smiles all around the table, momentarily even Alisdair. They like it as long as I've a domestic side which could be developed. That *they* could develop. What'll I do? Call a taxi, catch a train, go back to Cambridge? I can't. Not run away.

It's so cold! Inside, their attitudes, and outside, minimalist tidiness. And jolly games. My statuesque mint green bedroom's a big contrast to the comfy pink sprigged one at Euan and Margaret's. Euan's description of the Pastor should've included *grim* and *controlling*. Alisdair's dominance is cruel and Dickensian. I mentioned the microscope incident, Max shut me up with something more awful. Fee quavered.

I guess it's this: Max has to be a different person here. The person who wrote that frightful rejecting letter: remember the look he gave me in the car, outside Val's? Sorry for me, being brought here! *You don't want to meet my family*, he said—back when—meaning, *I don't want you to*.

I'm so upset by all this, and having no time to share about the Commune, or Daisy's ambitions. Put my jeans and jumper back on, will have to find Max and try to talk. Opening my door, there's total silence, utter darkness. (More contrast to Euan's place.) Feeling my way, creeping up the attic stairs, one squeaks.

FEE. IN BED

Jeans too tight, T-shirt *Save the Rainforests*. Strawberry blonde hair, Max with that look in his eyes: I know that look, Fee thinks, feeling in her body the effect on her when it's in Alisdair's eyes. *My luve is like a red, red rose* ... But we're married.

The clock, downstairs, strikes midnight: her grandparents' grandfather clock ...

Train up a child in the way he should go: and when he is old, he will not depart from it. Proverbs 22: 6. 'Lord, please don't let Max depart from your way.'

In the dark, a hand fumbles around. Fee lies still. What was it Kirsty told her about that girl's work? A father who's a research scientist, work on why Downs and other babies come to be born disabled? On preventing that happening? Work on *babies*? Involving ... what?

That hand again: the headache gone, she is still exhausted. Love, and obedience...? What it is to be born a woman. She shifts, so her back is to Alisdair, and then she feels that isn't right, so she turns over and reaches out, clasps his hand.

His arms enfold her: she hears something. A door? Steps? On the stairs? She tenses, while also sensing he is not asking for her body, but for her self. 'Al? Shh ...' Silence again. 'You are ... all right?'

'I spoke to him. He is torn by it.'

'By?'

'What he must do. The grandfather may've been a believer. But, God has no grandchildren.'

'Oh—Alisdair—Oh—' Fee feels his pain. Clinging to him, she now wishes it was her body he was wanting—an easy thing to give. Only what is happening up overhead, in the attic?

JENNY

Light under the door. Sniff the air: not smoking: that's good. I open the door. Hand on the doorhandle, I look in. Stark desk, small narrow bed. 'Max?'

He leaps across the room. 'Not now.'

'No? You told them we're *engaged*—you never asked me!' Seeing a book, and a notebook on the bed, 'If you're studying—'

'No—I'm not.'

'Then what's wrong with me being—'

'Jenny—not a good idea. Isn't it enough that I'm busy and I said no?'

'God, Max, what's eating you? Don't be like them! Please!'

'Jenny, please? I have to conform. We'll talk tomorrow.'

'You said—'

'I said, *that's what he understands*. We really will talk tomorrow.'

'Max, what's Uncle Euan? To you? The microscope, the car? Why's he so important?'

'Well he's not my father, is he? Now, go?'

FEE

Feet hurrying down: door closes.

Fee lets out her breath. Relief!

Alisdair stirs, 'What?'

'Door banging: I—think maybe we left something open—wind's got up—hasn't it? Shall I go and—?'

'No—no—I'll go—'

'Let me.' She pads onto the landing. Looks. Listens.

Well, the moment's gone with Al, and what's more, there's nothing happening upstairs Max can't handle: he's sent her back.

Fee regrets the whole episode: after all, the MS might've made complete lovemaking impossible, but a cuddle would've been relaxing. Alisdair and Max are pulling her in half. And that is wrong: what God wants must come first.

Returning to bed, 'I'll help—I'll help—him. You shouldn't bear the burden,' she says. 'You did too much today. Cricket with the boys. You daft man ... He'll come home, and work with Euan—I'll speak with him.'

He kisses her cheeks. Which are wet.

Silently, they lie together. Enfolded, they communicate heart to heart. Now Fee finds herself longing for him, and recalling that look—in Max's eyes, at the girl.

MAX

Lost the plot? Open the window, stare into nothing and the stars ... Taking a long drag, I breathe out smoke over the garden, across the eaves of the manse where Pastor Mullins and his godly family lie sleeping. Far more needs explaining to Jenny. The unmentionable nature of the Microscope Incident. Our shock and dismay at Dad's violent act: God's minister, overtaken by his feelings. As he should not be.

I have to challenge Dad. I suppose Jenny needs to know what we're up against?

The incident was the first time: nobody won, but everybody got hurt. Though in my mind, the microscope incident and the living at Euan's and the path I'm on now are all connected up. Soon after the microscope catastrophe, I felt so ill at school Mum was sent for and took me straight to the doctor's. My appendix had been playing up for a while.

I remember hobbling down the oak panelled stairway, worried I'd miss my solo in the forthcoming school concert—Monteverdi's beautiful, grand *Beatus Vir*. Worried about how I'd hide the evidence of Dad's wrath from Uncle Euan. I kind of sensed that physical punishment wasn't normal for every family.

It turned out to be a locum doctor. 'What seems to be the problem? Right—I need you lying on your back.'

'Can't you just—it's my stomach, the pain's in my stomach, right here.'

He pulls up my grey shirt. 'I need to be able to feel it properly, James—something wrong with lying on your back?'

I watched Mum, Mam as we called her then: her mouth was buttoned shut. Once my shirt was off, he saw.

Not touching the places, 'Do you want to tell me about this?'

'My dad did it. But it's not his fault.' I said. Not his fault? Why protect him?

Because I was a child. Even at thirteen, knowing enough to want to repeat that experiment, to view our own sperm through my microscope, I was—Dad behaves as if I still am—a child.

'Whose fault is it then?' the locum doctor asked.

'Genesis 38, verse 9. *He spilled his semen on the ground—what he did was wicked in the Lord's sight.* Not me: but I was responsible, I asked a friend ... some of us—I've got a microscope, we were repeating Anton van Leeuwenhoek's experiment.' The pain came, I curled over. Mam said nothing. The doctor waited. 'My father would probably say God sent this pain.'

'I see.' The doctor pushed his hand into my stomach then suddenly let go: I retched. 'Hmm. What would you say it is?'

I might be the Pastor's son, but I'm no' ignorant, I thought, responding 'That it's appendicitis?'

'When's your birthday, how old are you? James?'

'Max—James is my first name but they call me Max—I'm thirteen.'

'A classic age ... I think we'll have to send you to hospital to get that appendix taken out.'

'They won't ask—about the marks?'

'Do you want me to explain it to them, so they don't?'

'He used his belt. He's a preacher.'

I was drawn to that doctor. He said, 'I'm sending you with a letter of introduction. Like Saint Paul in the Bible. You give it to the doctors. And I'll give you something for the marks, help your skin heal.'

'Thank you.'

'Okay, Max.' He smiled. After he'd finished the examination, 'Now, I need to speak with your mother. Can you wait outside?'

As I was leaving he asked, 'Did you manage to repeat the experiment—or did your father turn up too soon?'

'We observed them. They don't have little humans inside them, do they? Van Leeuwenhoek made that up.'

'Van Leeuwenhoek saw what he was looking for, because nobody had yet figured out reproduction sufficiently at that time.'

'He lacked scientific objectivity,' I said, and we both grinned.

In the anaesthetics room, I asked the consultant to give me the appendix in a jar of preservative after the operation. Home again, 'The Lord is well capable of stirring up the appendix,' Dad observed, holding up the jar. 'I am not convinced that school is teaching you what you should learn.'

'For my becoming a doctor?'

Here was my answer to Dad. Pleasing God, studying all the science I wanted to, having an interesting career of which he could not disapprove!

Leaning on my windowsill, tamping out the cigarette, I laugh quietly. I'd placed the jar with its contents centrally on the desk Dad had provided for doing homework.

And Dad, having frightened himself and all of us, never belted me again.

We are created for his pleasure, and saved from damnation for the life of service—

To God? Who is, I hope—*humane?*

JENNY

They creep about pretending to get along. They're secretive. Max has had to be secretive: then, he lets it all out, the way he sees our relationship! After only a few weeks!

How'm I supposed to sleep? Books in here are all missionary biographies and how-to-be-good manuals! So, I have to pull out my photocopies, and try reading about how broken chromosomes lead to broken lives.

What a family! The car, the microscope? A replacement? At least, he's not *my* father!

*

Morning, first thing, a knock at my door: Kirsty, with a cup of tea. She sits on my bed, wanting to chat. Blowing her fringe from her eyes, 'You know about the microscope?'

So she's here with an ulterior motive? 'Some.'

'He nearly killed me! I was five and Dad could've just slain me right there: didn't know his own strength!'

'You mean, when he threw it out of the window?'

'Yeah, well it was going to land somewhere! I was in the garden. It crash-landed on the lawn. Mum went ballistic. She was preggers with the twins, but she grabbed me, and ran upstairs, an' I was bawling my eyes out. 'Cos this great *thing* had whizzed past, and then, my mum was screaming at my dad—which just never happens.'

'Never?'

'I used to wake up at night and think, will Dad throw my toys out of the window if I'm naughty? Will he chuck my doll's house through the glass?'

Kirsty giggles at her five-year-old self. But the flip side of the grim, physically attractive, Alisdair's violent emotions is becoming clear. 'Is there more? I know what Max and his friends were doing—'

'Gosh, do you? Dad walloped Max! I *heard* it.'

'Walloped him? Does he—wallop your brothers? Does he—has he—walloped you? Isn't it illegal?'

'He doesn't do it *much*—and he doesn't wallop *me*. But it's in the Bible, isn't it? *Fathers, discipline your children* ...' I'm shocked. She changes the subject. 'D'you like your tea? It's Earl Grey, I bought it. Erin says it's what everyone drinks now.'

She walks around, like Daze, slyly inspecting my things. 'So—' (sitting on my bed again) 'I brought you this.' A tiny Bible like the one Max left wrapped in our picnic rug. 'Thought you mightn't have yours with you?'

'Thanks.' She thought, *she doesn't have one*?

'The Bible's full of amazing stuff you know.' (Obviously!) 'It's not true that science and faith don't mix. The Bible tells us how God forms us inside our mothers. So about the cell science—you study one little bit of a cell and how it works?'

Cautiously I begin explaining. Kirsty's fascinated. Is she wanting to ditch the creationist beliefs she's been taught? 'Pass my bag over—I'll do you a diagram.' I need to demonstrate meiosis—the combining of the DNA of two parents.

'I like your bag. Where's it from?'

'Crete. I was there on holiday.'

'You know Max was born in Cyprus? They lived there till Dad had his eye thing like St Paul.'

'What thing was that?' I pull out the letter inviting me to interview at Roslin, preparing to draw on the back.

'One of his eyes went blind—well, fuzzy—and he had to land the plane without being able to see properly. Like see the instruments? After that, he had the Call—to the Ministry—they came home. I wasn't in Cyprus. Max and Erin used to go on and on about it ... So, fertilisation ... Hey—' she leans over me, 'Jenny?'

'What?'

'That's you? On that letter? Jenny *Guthrie*?'

'Why?'

'Is he your dad—the fertility guy in Cambridge—the one who works with IVF and was on the telly that time?'

'Maybe. I don't know if Dad's been on TV.' (I do know, actually.)

'Wow. Interesting. And what you do's what he does?'

'No—not exactly—'

'Kirsten!'

'Gotta go—Mum! Have you finished? Shall I take your cup?'

Well, thank God for that. Saved from further discussion with Miss Nosey.

So, I'm beginning to understand. It's the violence isn't it? He rules by threat. He walloped—as she put it—Max. With his belt? Utterly barbaric, *cruel*, humiliating. Max was *thirteen* … What's that do to your feelings for your Dad? Screws them.

Surprised he's so normal.

Kirsty pauses, half-out of my door. Swings around it, adding helpfully 'You know Rachel and Colin who came by? Max went out with her, before. Dad and Mum were rooting for wedding bells there. Only it didn't happen.'

'Obviously not.'

'Kir-*sten*!'

Appalled by my discoveries, I must go with them to church! My mind snaps back to the canteen, right after Persephone's birth. Max's apologies, for that cold letter …

Downstairs, Max gives me a thumbs-up sign as we pass in the hallway. I can't speak to him now: when will I be able to? Fee smiles, approving my rose coloured skirt and plain T-shirt, passing me the toast-rack after saying Grace. 'No eggs: we ate them in the angel cake!' she laughs.

How can she collude with her husband? After all that she knows about him?

*

We walk in a bunch: me, Max, Fee, Kirsty, Alex and Ian. Strictly no hand-holding. As we arrive, a couple of girls seize Kirsty and drag her into a huge huddle of First Truly friends.

First Truly Reformed is solid, mock-Gothic, with huge oak doors hooked back to reveal a triangular flower-arrangement in pinks and white—gladioli, scented stocks, baby's breath. Obviously from some green-fingered church member's garden. Inside, little knots of people mill around, chatting. The tinted windows filter and dim the incoming sunlight.

Max silently sweeps me along up the aisle. Suppose, being here, I'm colluding? Women pause, whisper among themselves, sneak a peek at us passing. The church has a thousand eyes. Here's a great-looking guy, who belongs to the minister. (And what did their minister do? They don't know, do they?) Evidently to them, Max belongs to Alisdair, and that gives them a right to comment on his life, the bit they know about. I'd like to enlighten them!

Our stolid dark wooden pew, right at the front under the pulpit, has a long blue meagrely-padded cushion on its seat. The pew back's at ninety degrees to the seat, and feels like it's pushing me forwards.

'Do we need to be right under your father's gaze?'

'It's our pew!'

'All that whispering gives me goosebumps. Plus, I hope that journalist found something more sensational to write about than Dad's clinic and the male infertility treatment. If not, it'll be Dr Guthrie on the front of some grubby newspaper!'

Max pretends he hasn't heard, opening the hymnal and flipping its pages, searching for the hymn. Uncle Euan and Aunt Margaret arrive:

they sit behind us, but Margaret leans forward smiling hello. Chrissie's thick brown hair's tied in bunches with pink ribbons. She takes off her dancing fluffy pink deelyboppers, and lays them on the pew seat.

Where's Rachel?

Max sits quietly, thoughtful, ignoring me and everyone. By now, every square foot is crowded, and the church buzzing with excitement, or expectation, like a hive: Sunday worship's an Event. I'm feeling like a freak show. Fee slips into place late, beyond Kirsty, just as the organist strikes up.

O Lord my God! When I in awesome wonder
Consider all the works Thy hands have made.
I see the stars, I hear the mighty thunder,
Thy power throughout the universe displayed.

As this hymn, apparently about the natural world, unfurls, some of the words are unsingable. About having my *sin* taken away? By the Son of God I've been taught maybe never lived at all? By some vile sacrificial act?

I tune out as much as I can, but the sermon's hard to ignore: Alisdair up there in the pulpit, powerful, passionate, jabbing at the Bible with his forefinger, railing at us down below. Theme is God demanding all our everything. Yeah, even physical punishments? I consider this, surveying his handsome face. More prayers, then the final hymn: *Great is thy Faithfulness* ... More provision, more thankfulness, more being glad he's removed our sin. Very singable tunes. Emotionally beguiling. Putting a smoke haze over how they all really live.

Then Max puts his arm around me and draws me up close to his side. Ownership? Uneasy, I pull away.

Not over yet: there's a coffee hour, an urn on a trestle table, green cups and saucers, Malted Milk biscuits. The women serving wear flowered cotton dresses. Max's church friends are yuppie guys with earnest faces and their women have small babies and clinging toddlers who demand biscuits from the refreshment stall. I'm keeping an eye out for Rachel.

'Hey Max: introduce us!' Two young mums, Emma and Zoë, nursing friends of Rachel's. Emma has a baby tucked up in a sling. Zoë has a couple of kiddies dragging on her hands to show her their Sunday School drawings. Emma's back on a few shifts from tomorrow: her husband's a med student and they need the income. She looks terribly ashamed to've found a child-minder.

'I wouldn't worry about the baby: Dad was doing his PhD and I wasn't planned. So Mum went to work when I was tiny. The childminder had a little baby and she was feeding, so she fed both of us, like twins! She's my godmother.'

What've I said? I was trying to reassure her, but each sentence seems to've piled up on the last until Emma's staring horrified! And Max is frantically trying to tell me we have to go now. 'Why're you being weird?' I ask, but Fee appears and whisks him away.

Someone says *Hi*, behind me. I turn. Rachel. We stare: then she asks where Fee's gone. I look around, notice Kirsty, talking with Colin on the other side of the room. Rachel then asks about Dad: 'I read somewhere— it was on TV wasn't it?—he hopes to come up with an IVF solution to male infertility. Will that be soon?'

And then, there's Colin. Down comes his hand, firmly on her shoulder: 'Rache, time we were off.'

'Col, I was just talking—did you meet Jenny, Max's—'

She'd have said *fiancée*, but he stops her, crass and rude, 'We're aware of what your father's doing in Cambridge: as Christians we can't have to do with anything so demeaning to God's image.'

'Demeaning?'

'Involving behaviour the Bible clearly condemns. Rachel?' He grabs her elbow and hauls her away. Over her shoulder, she throws a word: was it '*Sorry*'?

Max reappears.

'What did your Mum want? Why's everyone so weird? Emma stared like I was a witch from hell!'

'I told Mum we'd lay the table for lunch.'

'That's not an answer! Why did you try to haul me away from Emma?'

'Emma's ashamed to be going back to work. First Truly wives don't. You revealed your non-believer status. 'Nuff said?'

'I only told her about my childminder, Kim. Who's what they'd call a believer.'

'Yes?' taking my hand, and folding my fingers inside his as he tucks both our hands, linked, into the pocket of his jacket.

Now he'll say *Maybe it's all meant*! So, I withdraw my hand. 'Don't, I can't be close while you're like this!'

Once around the corner, Max produces the ciggies I hoped he'd abandoned, and leans against a wall, lighting up. 'Don't,' I say.

'No?' Max says.

'No. You don't need to.'

'You're right—' he says. 'He'll come around the corner and spot us. He's perfectly capable—if he catches me—of throwing me a look of pure contempt. Sermon was targeted at me.'

'Do you think you deserve it? His contempt?'

Max laughs ironically. 'No. Or rather yes. He would, and I do not.'

'You absolutely do not. Kirsty told me more about the microscope, which explained why—'

'Jen, can this wait?'

'No. Explains why it is unmentionable in your family, and why you said what you did about engagement!'

I've got through to him! He's ashamed. Confused.

'So, what've you got to say now?'

'Jenny, please, we're home: after lunch we'll really go into it all.'

And while we lay up and wait for the others, he talks professionally about some suspicions regarding Rachel's baby's health, and that he's arranged an appointment with a paediatrician.

'Is that your job?'

'Yes, and no. She's a First Truly mum … Soon, we'll be able to get away a wee bit. Be alone. You'll prefer that.'

'*I* would? What about *you*?'

MAX. AFTER LUNCH

How miserable we all are! Eating cold-joint leftovers and salad, Mum apologising for the small servings of lettuce since Alex and Ian's rabbit ate most of it yesterday. Dad ignoring Jenny as much as he can, really quite rude. Then soon as I can, I corral Jenny in the hallway, beside the skateboard tidy. 'Let's take the car and I'll show you a bit of Northumberland.'

Her response is heavily sarcastic. 'Northumberland. This I have to see: you'll *really* explain the m-words?'

'This atmosphere. It's no' you—or anybody. It's all me.'

'You, is it? I've not noticed your father's very friendly!'

'No. He isna' given to being friendly. You needed to know about my family: and here we are. Will we spend the afternoon together being a little more friendly, ourselves?'

'Whatever.'

She grabs her denim jacket from one of the pegs. I pull on my leather one (the one the family don't like, and she calls *rather sexy*) and reach for the cigarettes. And poke my head around the kitchen door where Kirsty is clattering plates. 'Will you field Alex and Ian? We're going out.'

'Where's Mum and Dad then?'

'Sunday afternoon?' I say, demonstrating after-lunch nap. 'Then after-noon tea for the Deacons and their wives, and evening service?' Kirsty rolls her eyes.

We drive in silence towards Haydon Bridge, possibly we'll go as far as Hadrian's Wall. It's a cool clear northern summer day, a pale sun, a wide sky.

'So: everyone wears masks. Rachel's out of Stepford Wives. It's another planet.'

I laugh: sardonically. 'You're not wrong. I live between two cultures: to understand me, you have to understand the one you didn't know.'

'And let it speak for itself? Like your ciggies and your Bible, that you left me in the picnic rug. "*Families keep secrets to stop people getting hurt*", hey? I need to know how he hurt you. Kirsty told me about the microscope, her version, including how your father walloped you. That is illegal.'

'What d'you expect Dad said to Euan?' I say, embarrassed by my sister telling Jenny all the details.

'I've no idea. Euan should've handed him to the police!'

I shrug: 'They'd not do that, to a fellow believer. And what passed between them, would they tell me?'

'God—'

'What they did about it: I boarded with Euan and Margaret, after the Incident. All through secondary school, in term time. They were living in Scotland back then. I was educated in Scotland. Hence the accent.'

'Hence a lot of stuff: you're close to Euan, aren't you?'

'We all lived at Euan's when Dad left the RAF. But after the Incident, yes, I went back there, because Mum had twins to care for, and Kirsty, and Dad was building up First Truly—'

'And so they boarded you out? Max, is the secrecy over the microscope stuff about sex, which I can hardly believe, or is it about violence?'

A question I avoid. 'Euan's been good to me. He's moderated Dad's influence. Hadrian's Wall?' Slowing, as we drive into a petrol station, 'some nice quiet spot?'

Newspapers are displayed by the forecourt shop. A touch of guilt, an imagined tap on my shoulder, as I buy the one with the photo of a smartly-dressed middle-aged guy striding across a concrete campus. Dr John Guthrie: *Dr Miracle*, the headline proclaims.

'So they printed it: Dad's on the front!'

'His likeness, aye.' Does God have an ironic mind?

Jen grabs at the paper. 'Let me see: what'd they write? Dr Miracle: that's daft. *Towards a baby for every infertile couple.* At least they got the title of the forum right. If your Dad's church is hung up about sex, then I'm dirt literally, aren't I? Like Dad works day in day out with reproduction! But it isn't. You've not got a problem there. It's control, isn't it? Power games.'

'Jenny, please.'

It is too different a culture to explain in a word, while driving. Jenny's silent, awaiting explanations.

At Housesteads, we park and walk along the wall a bit, admiring the wide blueness of the sky, the freshness of the air, the quiet, the Roman building techniques. I'm seeking a private, grassy hollow I know. The tension, our separateness, is painful. God, or Dad, is watching.

Soon as we sit down, Jenny skims the newspaper. 'Pre-implantation diagnosis. The new male infertility technique explained, almost correctly. Dad's also let it out to them about assisted hatching. You're certain the congregation don't buy Sunday papers?'

'I'll be finding a litter bin for this well before we walk through his front door.'

'But might *they*?'

'He's their messenger from God, Jenny. They do as they're instructed.'

She looks thoughtful. 'Your father does more harm than mine ever could. He'd do anything to get his way! I could misquote you, *it's not me, it's all them!*'

'My father's not someone you need in your life ...' Sliding my arm cautiously around Jenny, fully expecting rejection.

'He needs to orchestrate everyone's life. He runs his church to have an empire. I know: my father's powerful, but he isn't driven by emotions. Or is it something else? He even re-routed the Christening cake your mum made for your sister Erin's baby, and gave it to a couple who aren't related. Why?'

Heart sinking, I reply, 'Because of an explanation you won't like, and I find bothersome myself.'

There in our grassy hollow, I give Jenny a short lecture on the whole complicated, legalistic style of belief which lies at the base of Reformed Protestantism: the concept of God's oh-so-gracious Covenant relationship with his flawed and disobedient creation, Man. Ending, 'so you see, Nathaniel qualifies for baptism, for inclusion as a member of the Covenant Community, because his parents have professed faith. Whereas Cameron, Erin's wee one, he's right out of it because his mother's turned her back on reformed religion. Nat is more one of us than Cameron, in Dad's eyes. And as for a baptism, well, the Christening isna' going to make any difference to Cameron's status, in the eyes of God,' I say, recalling but not describing Daisy's sprinkling water over her moribund infant.

'So God junks an innocent baby because its parents don't go to church? That's gross.'

'Not *don't go to church*: haven't professed faith, spoken out, admitted they were lost in disobedience, and helpless to change, and that Jesus saved them from their sins.'

'So: it's all about obedience, rules and laws. He's not a minister: he's a dictator!' In my own heart and mind, I totally agree. 'Did you take me to hear those magical carols so's I'd give in to the laws, eventually?'

'I did not! Jen, whatever, whoever, my dad is, I spoke of engagement because I wanted him, and them, to understand exactly my intentions. Towards you. I care about you.... Remember I told you, about playing around with unbelievers? To demonstrate that I'm not—'

'Couldn't you have asked me first?'

'I had told you I'd not walk out on you again. Doesn't that imply everything?'

'Told me? Implied? Should you tell a person they're gonna marry you? Don't people ask?' *They do*, I think. They do. Outside of First Truly, where the women wait for the guys, as representatives of God, to direct their lives. 'So it's in their rulebook, is it? A woman's place is to obey. Everyone obeys God, and women obey men ... Does he obey God? Did he when he thoughtlessly destroyed a precision instrument? In a temper? Would you do that? How d'you think I felt then about joining your family?'

'That violence shook all of us. His version of obedience to Scripture. It wasn't right.'

'Scripture?'

'Some verse that's supposed to tell us not to spill our seed! Which is what people such as him have against IVF.'

'So it is sex? If you people believe God created everything, to work as it does ...'

I laugh. 'Remember I explained that sex is only for marriage. It's in God's Law, for First Truly believers. Mum was pregnant, Kirsty was in the garden. After Dad threw the microscope, he was terrified at himself: he might've killed Kirsty. He took his complicated emotions out on me. I haven't forgiven him, and he hasn't forgiven me. We all know about it, but it's never mentioned. And we can't forget it either. He's meant to be our pastor, who cares for all of us at First Truly. But we, the family, all know what he's capable of.'

Jenny's arm slides around my back. At last, I feel she understands my aloneness being his son. We hug, silently.

'Max, it's a horrible system. I'm sorry you're caught in it,' she says, drawing me close.

This renews a strong mixed response: as we lie on the grass, silent in the silence, my head on Jenny's lap, she's almost motherly. But then desire takes over, after all these celibate days. We kiss, my tongue parts her lips, slips into her mouth. One hand in her silky hair, the other over her neat bum, cupping her buttock, then clasping the fabric of her skirt, pushing it up, reaching beneath. Pressing myself against her, stroking her to wake up her desire.

'Max, please, I want to, but—not here!'

'Here: it's remote enough.'

Jenny has turned away.

'Jenny?' She turns back to face me.

I laugh a little, pausing, brushing stray strands of hair from her face. 'A while? Enough time?'

'What'll it mean, huh?'

'That I want you?'

'No!' she almost shrieks, and pulls away. 'No ... Not if you're gonna behave like him, with me ... Secrecy, obedience, ownership ...'

We sit, unable to discuss it. Until I pull out my smokes. Which brings Jen to life, and we tussle as she tries to take them away: end up laughing, rolling on the grass ... lying still. 'Look, we got back together. We have something so ... important.... If we're gonna get it right, you have to break away from them.'

'You're right. Of course you're right. In the normal world.'

'Have we to do anything else, back there, today?'

'Church, I'm afraid.' Jen makes a face. I laugh. 'Kirsty has a solo ...'

'"Funky evening service, with a band?"'

'That.'

Back at home, Kirsty wants to run through her solo. We go in the family room, where last night we played Scrabble around the table. Kirsty sings, I accompany on the piano. The Deacon tea party, in the lounge at the front of the house, can't hear. I wish in a way they could, as when Kirsty leaves, I break into a honkytonk version of the tune, to amuse Jenny. Showoff.

'Hey, you could earn your living in a night club!' she says, arms around my neck.

'Watch it, Dad has antennae!'

'Are we still sixteen?' Jenny shoots back. And then, seriously, 'I begin to understand about that letter.'

MAX. MONDAY

I'm woken very early by a cold sensation creeping across my face. Hand closes over a large green amphibian! Gross! Doubtless Alex and Ian's idea, to get a reaction. I throw myself out of bed, down those stairs, and they get their reaction, a rugby tackle of sorts, just as they're exiting the front door.

'*Gerroff Max*—can't take a joke?'

To everyone's surprise, as I yell abuse at my captive brothers Mum emerges from Dad's study clutching a large hardback book.

'Max! Leave them alone!' she admonishes.

'Weird parcel in the letterbox, Ma!' Alex exclaims, dodging from my grasp.

'Weird amphibian on my pillow!'

Laughing, they escape to their paper round. 'And Max,' (I dodge as she ruffles my hair), 'at least put on a T-shirt if you have to walk around in pyjamas with Jenny here.'

She lays the book—not one of those brightly covered domestically religious paperbacks she likes but a dreary-looking theological monograph—on the hall table.

'Okay, taking froggie back outside. You've been consulting Dad's commentaries, have you?'

'Max, it isna' your concern, but I've a speech to make to the Clergy Wives, on *The Complementarity of the Helpmeet*. It wasna' right: I'd thought to sort it out.'

'Shall we investigate what's weird in the letter box?'

Shaking her head, still quoting a text relating to her speech, '*The Lord God caused a deep sleep to fall upon Adam … and he took one of his ribs …*', Mum reaches into the wire letters-cage on the inside of the front door. There's an oversized envelope, with *The Minister's Family*—DO NOT BE UNEQUALLY YOKED WITH UNBELIEVERS! in huge black felt-tip pen.

'Oh no!'

She deftly pulls out the contents, and stares a moment at the front page of that tabloid that's never been seen in our house. As the words sink in:
Dr Miracle: Does this man hold the answers to desperate wannabe Dads?

Leaning over her shoulder, I read it a second time: *Dr John Guthrie, maverick Cambridge fertility expert who could have your future in his hands. He certainly has a way with embryos.*

'Has to be one of the Congregation did this.'

Do not be yoked together with unbelievers, For what do righteousness and wickedness have in common? Or what fellowship can light have with darkness (2 Corinthians 6: 14), has been carefully copied, and attached.

Parts of the article are underlined: *Towards a baby for every infertile couple ... Gently introducing the sperm into the ovum ... assisted hatching ... pre-implantation diagnosis ... could make antenatal testing a thing of the past.* And whoever typed this has also added a bloodthirsty reference to human sacrifice in ancient times, supposedly alluding to the use of embryos in scientific research.

'Mum—Mum, let's be rational. Jenny and I know about this. Her father's not conducting clinical trials here—'

As I say this, the worst happens: Jenny appears, in track bottoms and T-shirt.

'I was going for a run.' Her eyes dart towards the article and note, as Mum tries to pocket them. '*What's that?*'

I move between her and Mum, offering Jen my partially open hand, the other protectively ensuring the amphibian can't escape. 'Look what the kids put in my room! Froggie, my brothers' idea of fun!'

Dismissively, 'That's a toad! Don't play dim, you must know the difference! And don't pull the wool, someone here obviously buys and reads Sunday newspapers. Even if it's true your dad tells them not to.'

'Whoever's our guest, this person's no business using the Scriptures with such venom,' Mum says.

'Whoever wrote that's the one who's in darkness—ignorant bigot! Religious people just don't get it do they?'

Mum recoils. But then, 'We don't condone this behaviour either. However, whatever someone's done, please don't insult the Congregation.' She's white with anger. With whoever who sent the note. With my girlfriend who's caused their upset. With me.

'All my father does is try to give people what they want! I s'pose that's why Alisdair has such a negative attitude, and Colin dragged Rachel away from me? I know all about the microscope, I should've realised. No point in spending time with religious people: the only way to live's by Dad's scientific atheism. Because this—this blacklistin'—is what religion does!' The West Country accent's back again.

'This person was really upset: you need to show them some compassion.' Mum says, her voice trembling.

'Jen, that's why I tried to save you—'

She stops me, 'For God's sake! Unequally *yoked*: what's that mean? Apparently me an' you crazy people! Whoever wrote that stuff and pushed it into the letterbox, creationist nutter!'

We're freeze-framed, silent.

'I'll not have the Lord's name taken in vain even if you are upset,' Mum says steadily.

'I have to go,' Jen says, galloping upstairs, 'Max, don't come after me!'

That tears me in half. Emotions too stretched to intervene straight away: better wait. Better not to appear like Dad: irrational, irascible.

Mum picks up her dull book and folds away the offending literature inside, saying, through tight lips, 'I must away and do breakfast—' as she carefully smoothes down the cover as if to keep the text contained within. 'Max, would you take that creature out of here? And put on proper clothes!' she adds, bustling kitchenwards.

Disguising anger and despair, 'No worries, I'm away to let him loose in the garden.'

Knives, plates, bowls clatter in the kitchen, drawers are thrown open and banged shut.

*

I do have to break away. Do either of them understand the pain of it?

JENNY

I'm too angry to be with anyone. Should've gone straight out, pounded around the streets working out my feelings. Now I'm stuck here, and have been so rude to Fee I'll have to leave.

Thank you journalists, for handing this perfectly timed opportunity, this feature on Dad's work, to a First Truly person to have a go at Max for choosing his own partner. Instead of the one his father picked out. And thanks, Dad, for giving the interview, peacocking your achievements. Ten years on from Louise Brown, IVF still attracts readers. Described sloppily enough, *test tube babies* sounds creepy.

God, what to do? Pacing around, arms clasped around my body. Shivering. I've been crushed between two worlds. Look at this room, the photos of missionaries, the cross-stitched texts, the neat half-dozen bland books between carved bookends. Pretty flowered wallpaper, but somehow stark and forbidding. Why'm I here?

Far too angry with these ghastly people to know! The crazy Rachel marriage plan, their prayers before meals … and then the insults! Here we are on the set of *The Waltons*, it's so false, they're all actors in a grim ironic play. Each has a role. Mine's decided for me: the evil witch!

Near to angry tears, throw open my overnight case, start packing. In go the photocopies about malformed babies. In my present situation Daze would wrap herself in that great black cloak of silent drama she sulks under. But I'm not her: I brave things out. They've thrown a cape over me: their projection! If I behave like normal, fight the insults, I'm acting like the suspect non-believer they expect. If I smile, fit in, act nice, I'm like one of them. How do I win? Impossible!

Nothing's impossible, Dad says ... I simply have to discover the answers. Who besides Alisdair knows I'm Dr Guthrie's daughter?

That Bible Kirsty supplied, lying on the bedside table, tells me. Max's snoopy sister. Proud of Dad, maybe defending my own work, I told her how embryology was studied by the Victorians. Even how in 1891 someone grew four sea urchins by dividing a fertilised egg. Thought she'd find that interesting.

Who's she told, outside the family?

Colin. She was talking to Rachel's Colin after church! Colin's totally hung up on the natural, evolved, necessary workings of our bodies to reproduce, and give pleasure! Whether together or alone. What's the harm? Especially if it'd get them a baby? But, in his church, they're taught not to spill their seed! So they can't have IVF. He can't even give them a sample, to test it. That makes him mad as hell: he's in a bind, so he takes it out on Dad, through me!

I'd be sorry for him, if he wasn't so venomous. But that's his defensive control of the situation.

And, it's about how he deals with Alisdair's control of them all. Colin responds to the rules with impotent rage: he knows he mustn't blame Alisdair, or God. But he must blame someone!

Now, I'll refuse to play the role. I might say very politely that as I'm clearly not welcome, I'm leaving, saving them further embarrassment. That'd sound okay. I'll emphasise I'm sorry for my outburst.

But, what about Max?

He can't leave. I can't. Maybe we could confront them, together, on what the teaching causes?

Doubtful they'd listen. And someone's marching upstairs now: Alisdair, like the Gestapo—or like in Kafka: the not guilty, accused?

He wasn't awake. It's Max: I'll explain about Colin.

'Jenny? It's me, Fiona: can I come in, pet?'

Fee. Hmm. The colluding wifie. Better show respect, for now, and let her in. 'Wait: I'll open the door ... look, I'm sorry I was rude.'

She's brought me tea, which she sets carefully on the bedside table. And looks genuinely puzzled at my packing. 'Jenny, pet, what's all this?'

'I made a mistake: Max invited me, but I shouldn't have said yes. If he has to stay on to study, I'll take the bus to Newcastle and find a train.' A surprising burst of misery as I think of leaving Max here. I swallow. 'My Dad's not a bad person. He tries to help people. That article was an unfortunate use of news about his work—' Trying to sound objective and clear-headed.

Fee gives me a silent look. Like Max did, outside Val's. And makes a little move towards me, puts out her hand, and stops, like she might've touched me and decides no.

I introduce the Colin topic. Though it could be done better! 'I think, do you think, that person who wrote the note could be kind of jealous, of people who'll be helped by the new treatments? If in your church, in vitro fertilisation is, like, not thought a good idea because of something you believe—' I catch sight of her face, and stumble. 'I just, wondered?'

'Yes?' It's definitely not agreement, it's a question.

'Well you see, we, geneticists and fertility doctors, need to look at people's, well if we can see if their DNA isn't quite right, quite healthy, we can answer the question why they don't have a baby, or why they've had a baby with a problem? I thought, I just— The way Max and I met again, was over a baby that had problems.'

Gently, not angrily, she deflects the subject, lest we tread on dangerous ground about tests and terminations. 'Max says you've a concern for dysmorphic children. Did he tell you about my Sunday School class for special needs?'

And she asks about my work, and Dad's work. Takes no time for her to somehow draw me into discussing what Dad does, and what I hope to do, and the differences. We sit down on the bed. I draw the diagram I drew for Kirsty. Explaining how Cambridge buzzes with developments in cell science and biotech. Even how we use modified DNA bases which make up a probe for commonly known trisomies and Down's Syndrome.

'DNA probes won't work for babies whose malformations aren't a known syndrome. It's possible one of this baby's parents carries a balanced translocation: all the necessary genetic material's there, but rearranged. Then at meiosis—the time when the sperm and egg sort the DNA strands to make up a new person—the chromosomes may not have segregated as they're meant to. If the balanced translocated chromosomes break apart, they signal what we could call a different pattern. Like a knitting pattern scrambled up wouldn't make the garment you expected?'

Fee nods 'I see, a sleeve where the pocket should be, ribbing in the main garment instead of the edges?'

'Something like.' I laugh. It's so sadly apposite.

'We had some of this—less detailed—in my course in special education.'

'So you understood meiosis already?'

Whatever Alisdair is, Fee's a person with feelings and interests and skills, not merely an alien driven by Bible texts and fuelled with fundamentalism. If she could see me less as someone spawned by the scary, inhuman Dr Guthrie, what'd be the result?

I don't learn, because she guides us back towards what she calls Scripture: 'Jenny, isn't it amazing, how intricately we're made—in one of the psalms we read *you knit me together in my mother's womb ... I am fearfully and wonderfully made ... When I was woven together in the depths of the earth, your eyes saw my unformed body.*'

'My Aunt Val—Dad's twin sister—quoted that. So it's from the Bible? That's amazing, that describes what happens inside the nucleus of the haploid zygote! How could anyone back then know?'

'Back when?'

'Back when—when they wrote it down—the person who wrote that?'

'Och Jenny, one day you will understand, I think. Meanwhile, woven together—knitted—and didn't you mention a spindle?'

'Aunt Val's a spinner and weaver. We decided maybe it's just poetry, but she and dad, they both do creative work—Spinning and weaving? A poetic pun?'

A link's been forged whether I want one, whether Fee wants one, I think, glancing at Val's ring, which Alisdair's stared at with distrust as a New Age object. Am I becoming a believer in poetry and symbolism?

Fee waits. I say. 'So wouldn't you agree that infertile couples have a right to some hope?'

'I truly believe God always has a purpose and you have to find that and use it, and let him guide your life.'

'Well if you believe in God. A lot of people don't.'

'Why not?'

I shrug. 'Science? History?'

'It's often a kind of grief and anger that makes people deny God. He's not there to wave a wand over our lives. He's with us in whatever happens to us though. He cares about you, Jenny ...'

'Whoever sent that letter, their belief in God wasn't improving their life and attitudes. And they belong to your church!'

Fee hardly misses a beat. 'That's a person who doesn't understand that God wants to love them and come alongside in their grief.'

'Yeah, like he tells me I'm darkness. But I'd never wallop my child!'

FEE

Oh God says the girl, sobbing hard, tears streaming between her fingers. 'I'm sorry, I'm sorry: I shouldn't have said it!'

'Oh Jenny, whisht, oh you poor wee lassie.' Fee quietly hands over tissues. Even though she winced at that outburst, and the exclamation, she feels enormous compassion. Praying quietly, she requests that God hears Jenny's words as a cry for his help. From the front of the house comes the spluttering of a sick engine.

Eventually, closing one hand loosely over one of Jenny's, now clutching the last, damp tissue, 'Let's not be hasty: I glanced at the story and I'm not concerned. I do not want Alisdair to see it. Someone in the Congregation should be ashamed, and they'll not have the chance to crow, because nothing will be said from the Manse.'

Damply, Jenny smiles. Moves to replace her specs, and for the tea. 'That'll be stone cold: I'll make you breakfast.'

'I'm sorry to've put you all in this position.'

Outside, the car engine judders a bit, stops, then roars into life. The two women look at each other.

'I'm sorry if we got wrong ideas. The article's certainly not about you.' Fee stops, thinks carefully. Back to that first night and Alisdair's words, '*I have spoken with him ...*'

164

'I'm just annoyed with myself for not standing up for you more before this.'

'Really?'

'I've seen for a long while our Max could never marry a girl like Rachel, however sweet a lassie she can be sometimes. However hard Alisdair's tried to turn James Maxwell into another of himself, it'll not happen. He thinks too independently. And marriage isna' all about being submissive and willing and dependent. It's about being helpers of each other. If Max is to lead the life of service, it'd be better for his wife to have her own calling than to wait at home with only babies for company.'

She pauses. Jenny's blushing. 'Max has an independent spirit and a good mind, same as Erin. He needs someone who can match that, and stand on their own feet. That's true complementarity—that's what I'm going to have to talk about to the clergy wives.'

Fee wants to stop and leave this thought with Jenny. She stands, intending to slip away to her own sanctuary—the downstairs bathroom where nobody can demand anything—and renew her mind with *I can do everything through Christ who strengthens me*. Even give an address, which this morning's occurrences have prompted her to re-revise until it chimes even less with her husband's teaching.

'That's your title, but you'll change your talk? What'll Alisdair say?'

'He can't say a thing. I shall talk about the reasons we believe God created Eve to accompany Adam through life and that man and woman are meant to share in marriage. Not for one to be a doormat for the other. You don't think I can? But—well, things change ... In your generation, things can be different. I was so touched about the angel cake. You didna' need to make another, when the boys ate mine.'

Standing, turning away to fold a garment into her suitcase, Jenny is asking 'Where's Max, where'd he go?'

'He wanted to come up to you, but I said I had to say a few things first. That car, I suspect it's Max out there, working on it?'

'Oh.'

Downstairs, Fee takes that dreary monograph containing the folded note and hides it among her recipe books. Pegs out the washing.

The car starts up again. Sounds healthier. Drives up the road, then returns.

MAX. MID-MORNING, IN THE KITCHEN

Thank you Jesus. Wonderful visit, including an insane, vituperative note—Even the car's collapsing!

I'm at the sink cleaning off my oily hands and trying to prepare myself to speak with Jenny, when Mum appears. 'Max, would you use the laundry room for that and not splatter filth from your labours all over the clean pots?'

And Jenny: 'Men!' They nod wisely. They've apparently developed some mysterious understanding while closeted away upstairs, and now, they are teasing me, and exchange what look like genuine, verging on the conspiratorial, smiles as Mum makes Jen a late breakfast, well into the pastor's wife role but happily so.

'Jenny explained me some very interesting things from her father's work. We discussed the relationship between that and what her Aunt Val does.'

'Really?'

'The spindle, at meiosis. Your mum knows the same quote as Val: about being woven together? It's poetry.'

'Right.'

Jen sips coffee silently, spreads honey on some toast. Then, 'Where's she gone?

Looking around, I shrug. Mum's disappeared so discretely we didn't notice.

Jenny indicates the coffee jug. 'Want some?'

I fetch a mug. 'I must apologise for my father's congregation. They're dire. Ignorance reigns.'

'Your mum's quite a special person, though.'

'She is.' I pour myself coffee. 'Jen, the car's a bit dodgy still, but let's get on the road a.s.a.p., shall we? You don't want to hang around till Aunt Margaret arrives with Superchild, do you?'

'You don't either?' she grins.

'No way.'

'Listen—I know it must be Colin, who sent that note. Your sister's not to blame for mentioning my father—Colin didn't have to do that with the information!'

'Colin? You're certain?'

'He's got the motive for it.'

Jenny explains. 'I think I'll have to write to Dad about this, carefully. Meanwhile: packing? I'm ready to leave.'

AFTER LUNCH

Girls have so much luggage! Jenny stuffs bags, baskets, loose shoes into the Capri. I throw in my one bag, one briefcase, and a massive tome on paediatrics, hoping the car's going to be up to the journey.

And notice Dad limping as he trudges from the house carrying an overhead projector. I mention the limp.

'It's nothing,' he snaps.

Mum's transformed: her cool, in-charge Pastor's wife look, a pale blue linen suit, white sandals, nice new small leather briefcase, smile.

'Jenny—' Will she give Jen a hug?

No. A smile.

'Will you keep us in touch with developments, Max? And I trust we shall hear if you fix a date?' Dad says coolly. 'Jenny.' He turns to her. 'I regret we have spent so little time together.'

He opens the passenger door for Mum, then settles in the driver's seat.

'That Audi was a present from the Congregation, Dad's tenth anniversary at the Church. You've seen Mum's clapped-out hatchback, haven't you?'

Jenny gapes. 'They'd do that for him? However much did it cost?'

We stand and wave the parents off: they hardly ever go away without their kids and when they do, family tradition dictates this ceremonial. Jenny laughs at the idea, then remembers her own family.

'Max, I should call Mum about Val's revelations once we're back. All that's been put on hold by stuff here. Des hasn't been totally honest.'

'Some families are less open than others.'

Once the Audi's turned out of the drive, we can leave. I turn the key in the ignition. Phutt, phutt, the engine says, and dies.

'Bugger it.'

*

I call the garage. 'How long?' Jen asks.

'They'll pick it up today but—'

'God.'

'Possibly,' I say. This irritates Jenny enough for her to cuff me, and for me to hold her close until she snaps out of the mood. A silent apology on both sides for this morning's falling out. Then as the garage pickup's hauling my independent wheels away round the corner, a dormobile appears, parks, and Margaret jumps jovially out.

'Och, Max, what's up with it? Once Euan's pride and joy, Jenny—but I suppose it's growing older like all of us!'

Jenny looks like she's making a real effort not to say something damning. As Chrissie bounces up, 'Oh wow—what's up with your car, Max? I know! Flat battery? Carburettor?' she chants, '*Big End*?' she giggles.

'Take her away!'

Bags back in the hall, Margaret's finding things to occupy us. 'As you're still here, Max, would you do us a great favour? Fiona left this note about a baptism cake. If you and Jenny are to be stuck here another day, could you possibly … you'll take your mum's car—won't you?'

'You're suggesting we take the cake to Rachel's?'

'Rachel's!'

'You don't have to come.'

'Max, I do—if you go!'

'Well …' Searching for a solution, almost convinced we should make a stand.

'Just to punch him on the nose?'

'You'd do no such thing—would you?'

'He'd better be at work!'

'Ouch—fiery lady!

'Could be ironic: we turn up, looking happy and together. S'pose they wouldn't get it though.'

*

'Alisdair's being very practical,' Margaret remarks tersely, 'Nat's baptism is next week, and really, although they want Erin to bring her little one to First Truly for his, I don't think they can expect ... There—I'll give you this bag for it'—she nestles the cake tin into a large Fenwick's carrier bag—'and if you take Chrissie along, she can see the baby.'

When we arrive I give Jen another chance not to meet Rache today. 'You want to wait outside?'

'No way! I'm here to chaperone you!'

We knock and ring: no reply.

Chrissie climbs the rockery, and looks through the letterbox. Announces, 'Baby's crying! They're in.'

Rachel, inside, calls 'Who is it?'

Then we have a conversation through the door, she asks why we're here, and says she doesn't think Mum should've sent the cake. 'Couldn't you take it back and say thank you for the thought?'

Adding two and two, I know something must be wrong. Mum and Dad maintained the friendship after we broke up: there's no good reason she'd reject Mum's offer, Dad's insistence.

Jenny's right: Colin wrote that note.

'Max, you shouldn't have waited.' Rachel has the door open at last. And she's holding one arm protectively close to her body.

Chrissie struggles to lift the heavy tin out of its bag. 'We've got a baptism cake for Nat!'

'Careful, pet!' Rachel squats beside her, trying to help. 'Sorry, I hurt my wrist—silly, wasn't it?'

Suddenly all the women shriek as the tin topples to the ground, the lid flies off, and the cake rolls out. It bounces down the rockery, shedding hunks of thick royal icing and blue roses. Jenny leaps after it, gathering the bits as it breaks into dark, fruity crumbs. Chrissie giggles. Rachel slumps, ashen, on the step.

I kneel beside her: her right wrist is horribly misshapen and swollen. 'Let me look, Rache. That's quite obviously painful.'

She turns away, recoiling. 'Max—no—it's nothing,'

'Doesn't look like nothing. Can you move your fingers?' She can't. 'Rache, let's go inside, and I'll take a proper look.'

'No—please—I'm busy. The baby needs his feed.'

'Rache, please ...' Quietly, I try to coax her. Fearing why she might be scared.

Jenny joins in, 'Rachel, whatever happened, let Max help you.' Cupped in her hands is a pathetically broken blue icing word: *Nathaniel*. 'I tried to save it, but—'

Looking Jen in the eye, Rachel says 'It's my own silly fault, carrying the laundry downstairs I trod on a trailing sheet. Wasn't that stupid?' With a wan version of a grin, 'Good thing I wasn't carrying Nat, hey?' She takes a long breath. 'A sprain can hurt more than a break ... Max, I'm so sorry about the cake.'

'Cut it out, Rachel. Apologising, thinking of others. You've at least had a nasty fall, and I'm a doctor—will you let me examine you?'

She shakes her head, and then without thinking, flips at her hair with her good hand.

Jenny gasps.

I see why. 'And are those bruises? Rache, what about your eye?'

'Oh, the airing cupboard door? I'll take some paracetamol, I'll be fine.'

A pause.

'C'mon, your eye's swollen. What's been going on?'

'Nothing. No good at playing Mum!' she says, suddenly bright. 'I shouldn't have asked for a baby, should I?'

'Nothing? Nobody did this to you?'

'Max: I'm tired all the time. You don't know what babies are like.' Irritable, now, and obviously in pain.

'Jen? Can you help Rachel inside?'

And, despite Rachel's protests, and with Jenny's arm around Rachel, we all enter the house.

Strewn about the powder-blue hall carpet lies a tangle of baby toys, dirty washing spilling from an upset laundry basket, clothes and shoes. Rache tries to reach for a tie lying serpentine on the floor.

*

'So, Rache, I'll take a proper look. In here? The living room?' Half out of its box, a smashed-up shop-bought gateau lies on the coffee table between two tea cups, one knocked over and trailing a dark stain down and onto the carpet. The TV is talking to itself.

'Look ... someone's cut out a window!' Chrissie's gone ahead of us, and now, she's dancing about laughing through the front of that sensationalist Sunday tabloid which reported on Jen's father. 'I'm on the front page! Daddy won't let this in our house! Even round plants from the garden shop! And I'm on the front!'

Rachel tries to grab the paper. 'Chrissie—Chrissie pet, could you put that back where you found it? Colin bought it for the sport,' she tries explaining, turning to me, 'I'll get rid of it. Max, don't tell your father!'

'This was the *front*,' Chrissie observes. 'Sport's always at the *back*. Daddy buys it for the sport on our way home from church sometimes when Mummy isn't there, then he throws it away. The sport's *still there*, look, on the back.'

Another angle on my Uncle Euan! And of course, certainty about Colin's responsibility for the note, if we didn't have that before. As

Rachel gulps a few breaths, and Chrissie reluctantly hands the paper over. 'Yes. Thanks, pet.'

When did it all happen?

The house has told the whole story.

Rachel hunches silent, self-protective on the couch.

I need to get her to relax and talk about her life, 'Do you see your friends? Zoë? Emma?'

Somewhere, the baby is crying.

'Jen? Find the baby for us? Chrissie—look, can you tidy up the toys for Nathaniel?'

JENNY

I rush to the kitchen, with an awful feeling it wasn't only me, or my Dad, who caused this. Colin had to blame someone who wasn't Alisdair, or God!

I've not grown up in a rural community for nothing: guys in West Cornwall who're angry look around, and hit out. Usually about the lack of employment but ... infertility'd qualify. Their women were the mums of people at school with me, and Mum's patients ... What if it was more than Rachel who caught his anger?

Thankfully, the poor wailing baby seems okay, just snuffly and sad. I'm still amazed and appalled, lifting Nat out of his bouncy seat, at what these strange sectarians have made out of a positive, if sensational, description of scientific progress. The baby touches me with his tiny, cold, damp fingers; he wriggles and whimpers. As we pass, Chrissie is kneeling in the hall, concentrating rather hard on stacking plastic cups in size order and posting shapes into a red plastic letterbox. 'Max said to tidy this up.'

'You all right?'

She looks at me, her eyes round and scared. She's a kid, however educationally advanced. 'What did I do? That made Rachel ...?'

'Nothing. It wasn't you and the newspaper, Chrissie.' I shift my hold on the baby, whose sodden bottom's damp against my hip. His pale little face studies mine, his solemn dark eyes blink. I've a mixture of distaste and compassion for him. 'It was all done before we came here. *Yuck*, baby! You're soaking me!'

'He needs changing!' the kid says, flipping back reassuringly into know-it-all mode. And barging off to the living room, 'Rachel! Where's Nat's clean nappies? He's wet.'

'Before we do anything, let's make sure ...' I lay Nat on the sofa. Glad to give him to Max who knows what to do, whose voice is authoritative, clinical, as he undresses and examines the scrawny whimpering infant.

I'm more confident about my role with Rachel. 'Whoever hurt you, please don't feel you must protect him!'

'Colin may've bought the paper to read the story,' she responds inconsequentially.

'And then?'

'Jen—don't. Nat seems fine except for a nappy rash. Over to you now.'

Handing Nat to me, it's like he's forgotten I'm not a nurse who he's working with. My mind flips back for an instant to the tiny, bloodstained, totally unmoving, still-warm Persephone. A bit safer somehow. As I cast about for something to wrap him in lest he pee on me, or worse.

'Jen, please, deal with the baby, while I see to the mum … He's miserable. You're a capable girl: take him and sort him out?'

'I've never changed a baby in my life!'

'Always a first time. Nappy stuff over there? In the corner? Clothes, Rache?'

'Airing cupboard, upstairs …' comes a strangled little voice.

Cautiously holding the still-naked baby in the crook of my arm, with my free hand I extract a disposable nappy from the box. Chrissie rather more expertly (from helping in that crèche at Women Christians in Golf, perhaps?) lays out cotton wool and baby wipes on a change-mat.

'I'll fetch his clothes: I know where,' she says.

I figure out how to wrap these strangely shaped paper and plastic things around a baby's bottom, have the dangerous parts of Nathaniel safely covered, when Rachel murmurs from the sofa, 'Don't you see now why we couldn't talk more: Colin thinks your father's work is—evil.'

'*Evil*? When he helps people have the babies they want?' I struggle to secure the nappy, using its sticky tabs, and with their twisted way of seeing the science which is meant to help people. 'Rachel, his work is some of the most positive use I can think of …'

'I have to support my husband, Jenny, though I don't share his views. He's a very keen pro-lifer. I'm so sorry, I can't say more.' She sounds like a disapproving teacher! And leans back on the couch, closing her eyes.

Misplaced loyalty, and an admission of what they did. Is this what godly—as they call them—women sign up to on marriage?

What about my talk with Fee: what about what Fee acknowledged? That even she was changing her mind?

'*Baby-gro, baby-gro, I know how the babies grow!*' Chrissie returns with clothes for Nat, chanting a little song. 'Baby-gro, Jenny! And a vest!'

Try to be quiet, helpful, clinical: follow Max's lead … Leaning over, I try pulling the tiny vest over Nat's head. Same moment, the nappy unsticks and opens up.

'Yikes! That was nearly my eye—thank you, baby!' He looks as surprised as I feel.

'They all do that!' Chrissie giggles.

Rachel, ignoring everything, says wearily, 'The methods …'

'... are condemned in Scripture.' Rachel continues like a run-down robot, ignoring that Nat's almost peed in Jenny's eye. 'We should conceive children only as God ordained. And—we should accept what we're given in life. I was wrong: I demanded a child and look what's happened. I tried to have nothing to do with the newspaper thing. I asked Colin not to.'

'I'm sorry,' Jenny says quietly. 'He made you ... he did this to you ... because to him, I represent my father's work: I don't understand but ...' she falters, as Rachel shakes her head.

'No ...'

'Of course, if Colin—'

Rachel interrupts, 'I thought God was leading us when we heard the orphanage was keen to place Nat. Then I thought it was right to have him checked over, when he failed to thrive. I shouldn't have taken that decision alone. They told me fetal alcohol syndrome ...'

Jenny's holding Nat against her shoulder. He's wailing.

'I took the decision into my own hands ... to have him checked.'

'You did the right thing.'

'Rachel needs to be seen: can you let her be, Jen? Please?' By now I'm incandescent with anger: probably with Dad. I need to find compassion. Can hardly manage it for everyone at once! Hold onto my clinical hat, think of Rache, the patient. 'Rachel, hang in there, we'll go up to A and E in a minute,' I say, sitting on the couch beside her. She draws away. Pale, grey under her eyes, as I check her vital signs. 'And they'll care for you. Shall we not bother with an ambulance? I'll drive you.'

'Rache, I'm so sorry. I seem to've spoilt everything.'

'No—no ...' Rache murmurs.

I leap up. 'Okay, let's go!' to stop their endless examination of motives and fault. 'We'll leave a note for Colin.'

'I'll write the note! I'll find a pencil—where d'you keep them, where's your phone? In the hall? Mummy always has a pencil and paper by the phone!' Chrissie's bounded into life again, after staring at our adult analysings. She touches my arm. 'We need a bag for Nat's things—Mummy says, there's so much to take around when you look after a baby.'

'Jen—' (as I fish out Mum's car keys) 'you take Chrissie back in Mum's car—Rache—give me yours—we'll have to take that so Nat's in his baby seat. Insurance? Don't argue—anyone—it's the only way.'

*

Heartsink time: Zoë from First Truly is on triage. 'Rachel! Whatever happened to you, pet?'

'Oh just a silly fall.'

Rachel shivers as we sit waiting. I wrap my jacket round her. With her left hand she grasps my coat tighter, displaying the big engagement ring and the slim gold band that symbolise her so-willing submission.

A perfume I so associate with her wafts over me. Remember that Christmas I bought her a big bottle of it: and sneaked off to phone Jenny, only to find their household were having a party, and her sister telling me to bugger off, and not try calling again.

If I could leave Rachel here, or get on with the clinical examination, including for further injuries and bruising, and send her off to X-ray, I would. God, I ask prayerfully, why did this happen now? How many times before, comes the answer. This time, you were here to see.

Rache jiggles Nat's buggy (a pest to put up in the car park without her help) to keep him from wailing. Emma hurries by, does a double-take, and throws us a smile. I can't deal with it all. Don't even think of slipping outside for quiet drag! Think about Nat: what's going to happen to him? 'Rachel, shall I call Colin for you?'

'Oh no—he'll see the note. He's working late at school, don't worry him. It's all my fault, tripping up. Max, when do you think I might talk to your father?'

Emma returns, a wee bit furtive, probably lest I sneak to my father about her early return to work, 'Rache: your wrist, is it? Ouch. Wait shouldn't be too long ...'

A wan smile.

'Let's be practical: who's going to have Nat tonight?'

'I can manage. Or maybe—would your mum mind very much if ...'

I explain they're both away. Rachel looks at the floor, then smiles again. 'Your mother's just the right person to talk on the Helpmeet.'

And then, 'Rachel Eccles?' She's directed into a cubicle with an unknown nurse.

'Max, please, I don't need you to help me.'

JENNY. EARLY EVENING, BACK AT THE MANSE

Chrissie, supplied with juice and cake, is bored. Outside, there's a basketball post. Exercise would do this plump kiddie no harm. 'Let's teach you to shoot hoops.'

She giggles about how many times she misses.

I don't want to think right now about all that's happened, about Alisdair's church, and the beast that is Colin. I do think about Max, how comfortable he is in clinical mode. How whatever Rachel was once meant to be to him, he managed to be so caring, yet so objective.

'Hi guys: why're you still here?' Kirsty dumps her sports bag and school stuff on the ground, and catches the ball one-handed. 'And Chrissie?'

'We got delayed.'

Kirsty bounces the ball as she talks, 'Oh. Right. So where's Max?'

'Max went to the hospital with Rachel,' Chrissie says.

'What?' Kirsty looks to me, grasping the ball to her chest, open-mouthed. 'Rachel? What happened?'

'It's complicated,' I begin.

'Rachel got hurt,' Chrissie butts in.

'You mean—an accident?' Kirsty says, under her breath, to me. 'What about Nathaniel?'

'Uh—no. We had to take the cake over—'

'Stupid cake, Mum made that for Erin.' Kirsty lets the ball drop. 'Mr Eccles—Rachel's husband—he wasn't at school today. Is that connected?' I hesitate to reply. 'They didn't know where he—we had team practice instead of current events—how bad is she?'

'Broken arm, black eye—don't know anything more.'

We go inside. Aunt Margaret and the twins are arriving home. Chrissie lets out a garbled version of our trip to Rachel's.

Margaret's face clouds over, but in a moment she resumes a calm exterior. And I give her a bland, expurgated version of the facts, while Kirsty makes everyone milkshakes in the blender.

Margaret cooks a huge macaroni cheese, and Kirsty makes a salad. 'I knew something was wrong,' Chrissie says, 'when Rachel wouldn't answer the door and ask us in—she always—'

'Okay—we know, brat,' Ian says.

'An' I knew what to do with the baby, an' I found all his stuff or Jenny wouldn't have—and the baby has very funny sticky-out ears, put on kind of wrong—'

'Yes—well now—we can't do anything about the baby's ears, so let's find something we can do something about. Gather round, everyone! Max has let that hospital swallow him up, so, I'll say a few words instead.'

We bow our heads for Grace. I get the impression Margaret's assessed the Rachel situation but won't comment.

MAX. LATER, THE A & E DEPARTMENT

She's a long time being examined. People go in and out of that cubicle. I hunt through my spare change, thinking of calling Jenny on the payphone. Then as someone leaves the cubicle, I hear Rachel sobbing.

The sound tears me apart.

I don't call Jen.

But, the registrar knows me from when I worked here: when he looks at the X-rays, he calls me over, and includes Zoë and Emma.

'As you see, she has a spiral fracture of the ulna, which taken together with her black eye and some bruises on her neck …' We are all reminded that this type of fracture is typical of a domestic incident. The three of us consult. I describe our reception at the house. The registrar tells us his other findings: extensive bruising to the trunk and evidence of recent and possibly resisted intercourse.

Almost as soon as it's said, I can indeed see Colin ... know that I knew all along. And the girls gasp. Certainly we three all know how this could rock Dad's congregation.

Then outwardly, they recover. Emma jumps up, excusing herself. 'My shift's well over: someone should make sure the baby's checked ...' Head down, almost at a run, she disappears.

Registrar almost imperceptibly nods. 'And you could push off now, Max, if you want.'

But Zoë eyes me expectantly. In place of Dad I must care for the congregation. 'I feel some responsibility for the baby—I could take him over to consult with paediatrics, see if they ...'

Registrar shrugs. 'If you're a family friend—there's no need ...'

I turn the buggy around, off to find somebody with authority to say whether Nat needs to be kept in, placed with his mother, or given to social services. 'Poor little scrap,' Zoë murmurs.

LATER, AT THE MANSE

Is the Manse, where I at last return, my home? Where I fit in and want to be?

All quiet; cold macaroni cheese under a dinner-plate, and what's left of a salad. I begin to allow myself, consciously, to think through events. My array of complex feelings. How does a guy deal with this—the girl I was supposed to marry! Beaten and raped?

A man must love his wife as his own body ... The headship of the husband and quiet obedient submission by the wife supposedly ensures a happy home life! If I'd not brought Jenny here, and no journalist had written a sensationalist effort about Guthrie's work, then no provocation of Colin, no attack on Rachel?

Nothing's so simple. That wasn't an isolated incident. Rache's marriage problems were obvious as soon as Mum mentioned she was lonely at home. But marital rape? Here's submission's subtext, its dark underbelly. Colin masquerades as a fine upstanding member of the church community. He'd call it discipline.

I might put together some arguments and texts to counter theirs: where is love your neighbour? Where is the God who brings light to a dark world? Where is compassion, empathy, respect?

More relevant, consider Dad's behaviour over the microscope: his desire for enforcing control, the abuse of power, backed up by a conviction of being right. The need to be right. Forget being loving, compassionate, empathetic. Be right!

We're vile! First Truly is vile!

'Max! You were ages! Hey, don't stand there, holding the plate, the macaroni'll slide onto the floor ...' Jen bursts into my consciousness. Here I stand, plate in hand, and I forgot I'd even picked up that plate of food.

'Give that to me, you're about to drop it!' Jen takes the plate and puts it on the table. She flings both arms round me. Full of uncomplicated concern.

She's a lifeline. I hold her, loosely, bury my face in her lovely hair, scented with outdoors, and with Jenny herself.

'So, how's Rachel?'

I try to find words. 'Jen, it was difficult. It's been a long day … for us both.'

'I know. Rachel was your girlfriend. Colin …'

'More complicated. I maybe need to face this first alone?'

'Max, no: that's not right.'

'Right? Who knows what's right—ever, objectively? This problem's not you, it's not Rachel … It's maybe not even me …'

'You always talk like that: but you were–'

'Yes. I've been raised in an exclusive place you can't begin to understand.'

'There's more, isn't there? That emerged at the hospital?'

*

'Max, maybe you'd tell me—' We spring apart, Kirsty hurries on with her question, 'Chrissie said Rache fell downstairs, but Jenny's version is she'd been beaten up.'

'Jen?' I mean she's to leave us to talk alone, but she doesn't.

'Max has had an awful day: don't bother him!'

'Max is my brother, and I asked him a question!'

'You all depend on Max too much. If you need to know more, I'll tell you when Max and I have talked. Or we'll all talk. Later.'

This is the worst it could be. Kirsty's lips trembles, and she's trying not to cry, but she's angry. 'I'm not a baby any more than you are, either of you! Please tell me! Dad and Mum never will, so you have to! What is this wall I live behind?'

'We all live behind it, Kirsty. Jenny: can we, later?'

'I guess,' Jenny says, her reluctance obvious. 'It's the way you do things here.'

Bugger off, Kirsty, is what I'd like to say, as Jenny runs upstairs. Inside my head, I hear Rachel's voice, from the past: '*I want to be a good wife for you, Max: you keep giving me decisions to take myself, and I want you to be my head, as scripture says …*'

Taking my sister, and the plate of congealed macaroni, into the garden, I try assuming the persona Dad requires of me. The protective male, sidestepping over the more horrific aspects of human nature.

Kirsty discerns my disquiet. Maybe even that it's a disquiet at my obedience to Dad, and my divided loyalties. And wrings the truth out of me, bit by bit.

I watch them, from my room, head to head in the twilight garden. Kirsty needs to know the facts: today has taught me why I can't help her. Their code of honour, their exclusive attitude to outsiders, their regarding young adults as innocent children.

Eventually, Kirsty stands, takes the plate, and comes indoors. Max reaches for his Marlboros. He crosses to the tree house, where his brothers ate the stolen angel cake, and climbs the ladder.

I scuttle downstairs, and outside. It's completely dark, the tip of the ciggie glows from the tree house. I run across the dark lawn, and balance on the bottom rung of the rope ladder. 'Jenny—'

'I know about domestic incidents: we get them, rural practice, isolation, unemployment? I passed along what I know from Mum.'

'That wasn't your place.'

'My *place*? Max, your sister's nearly eighteen, she asked for the truth, I told her.'

'You don't know how in this family …'

I scramble onto the platform beside him. 'Actually, I'm learning.'

'It's the context. Dad's church, the First Truly ways, and …' he flips ash. 'It's complicated.'

'Domestics are gross. We all knew at school. Don't shut me out. I'm not ignorant, and I only want to help.'

'I know,' his arm slides round my back. 'Och, Jenny, what'll the Congregation say? What do we tell them?'

'The truth. They need to know.'

'Rachel's friends were on duty. Once they began to understand, I could see them draw back.'

'Why?'

'They'll be wondering what Rache did to deserve it. Or why God didn't prevent it. One or the other.'

'But once they have it explained …'

'By whom? It's worse than what you saw.'

'So, tell me. It's bad isn't it?'

'It is.' Trying to make him talk, I cuddle up, lay my head on his shoulder. He strokes my hair. Silently.

'Colin raped her didn't he?'

I know I'm right, as Max stiffens, his whole body responding to that word.

'This is totally not what you speak about with anyone. Rachel wouldn't admit what went on until they began to examine her and ask. But Colin did more than twist her arm, literally, to force her to use that article and inform my parents. If this was Scotland, she could press charges. It wasn't consensual, though she says she submitted. You understand?'

'If she didn't want it, that's rape. Your father's church parcels up women as pretty dollies, to hand them over at the wedding for the man to do what he likes?'

Max doesn't answer.

'You can't admit it, can you?'

'I don't know what to say. Jen, it's late. Tomorrow, we'll talk? Promise?'

'Please, please, don't hide the truth from them all. Tell your father. Everything. You have to. Let him see what—'

Max stops me. 'I'll deal with Dad. Rache is safe for tonight.'

'And you're tense as a wire. You need to unwind. Without the ciggie.' He stubs it out. Beginning a shoulder massage, 'I do this for Mum sometimes,' I say. Max doesn't resist. 'They depend on you. You were fantastic with Rachel, you were just amazing.'

'Och, I don't think so!'

'You were, you were. You handled it all.'

'You were excellent with the baby. He didn't appreciate you!'

We laugh. And silently, we sit entwined, with our own thoughts. Gradually I dare to nuzzle closer, and we kiss, I slide my hand inside Max's leather jacket. 'Afraid this smells of Rache's perfume,' he says.

'Do I mind? Hey, here were are alone together, and they're all asleep.'

'As we should be.'

'How about I extend the massage? Don't do anything: it's all me, this time!' We laugh at my use of the phrase. I make love to him because it's the only way I can think of saying: Leave them, turn your back, you are too compassionate for their rules. And because I need to re-establish the us-ness we lose by being here.

It's two in the morning when we leave the tree house, relaxed but scratched and bruised by its rough unyielding planks. I'm carrying my shoes as we cross the dark expanse of the garden, when Max suddenly seizes me and lifts me in the air. 'What?' I hiss, remembering to be quiet.

'You were about to step on a couple of amorous snails!'

*

Back in my room, there's my case still gaping open, those articles on malformed babies I threw in when I thought I'd have to leave here. Seems days ago, not hours. Not any more.

But I'd imagined we might have time here to discuss the Commune, and how Val's kept frustratingly quiet about anything she knows that could've contributed to Persephone's problems. Jewels and Loose are sisters: suppose the McShanes are Loose and Jack? Then the cousin Daisy met is their son. If both sisters carry a problem gene, then consanguinity could be the explanation. Especially if Jewels ... But I've no evidence. And all today's developments make it unlikely Max'll be interested in all that for a while.

Lying in bed, I imagine Max with me again. Our limbs entwined, his scent, his touch. And my mind insists on presenting the flip side: Rachel, body violated, wrist throbbing, in her hard white hospital bed. And where's the baby? Cot beside her? Nursery on another floor?

Nothing I can do for Rachel. Max mustn't feel it's his fault for not marrying her, I mustn't feel I was the reason why not. Somehow, I do. Shall I visit her, take her some stuff on empowering women? She wouldn't want to know.

TUESDAY 12 JULY

It's a cold grey morning, in keeping with the gloom here. Well, my jeans and jersey cover the scratches and bruises from the uncomfortable tree house.

Max is hurrying down the stairs. 'Hey, Max! Wait for me!'

'Jenny: I must call Dad straight away.'

'Of course you must. But,' I catch up in the hallway and take both his hands, look into his eyes, 'stay with me, Max?'

He frowns. 'I'm not going anywhere. What d'you mean?'

'Don't get drawn in, hey?'

His answer: we kiss, as he dials the number. Then gives me a pat on the bum towards the kitchen and breakfast: I shake my head. Not your little woman! And find myself grateful Margaret didn't catch us. Nobody's about, though. I make my own breakfast, first time in this house. And catch phrases drifting from the hallway as Max talks with Alisdair.

'... it's not only happened the one time. Marital relations have been—forced, shall we say—on more than one occasion. She's been unwilling and he's not taken no as an answer.'

Silence.

'It has not been consensual.'

Long silence: wish I could hear Alisdair's response. Then 'Well Dad, I'm telling you.'

'Paediatric ward, for assessment.' So he's asked about Nathaniel. So now I know. Poor kid: orphanage, home with Rachel, back to an institution, and he's only five months old. Suppose when she's recovered a bit she'll take him home? *Home*?

All this because Colin's against fertility treatment! How could he believe God wants ... Well, I don't know about God, everyone's views are different. Max, Maeve, Fee, even Val ... And Fee, she's seeing the light, she's going to tell the wives at that conference they're equal to their men. Or something like that.

'Right, Jen: that's done. Coffee?'

'I made tea. Kettle's hot though. Aunt Margaret's doing the school run. How's your dad taken the news?' I pop bread into the toaster, Max makes real coffee in a jug.

'He'll be over once he's given the breakfast address, he'll try to see Rachel. He doesn't want to be bothered with family as he walks through the front door. And, he *doesa' enjoy talking to me as an equal.*' Max assumes a broad accent so I know it's a quote, *'Could Euan not have told me this? It's hardly a conversation suitable between father and son!*'

'And Colin? He'll not be allowed to teach now, will he? Not only what he did to Rachel: normal people don't shove slanderous notes through letterboxes, whatever their views on medical research issues. Colin shouldn't be allowed to teach, should he?'

'You've got a point. But let's keep that to ourselves.'

'A *point*? That guy needs locking up. Assessing maybe, but shut away.'

'Cool down, Jen—listen. Last night, Rachel: I couldn't stop thinking: *One of us did this. A man. To a woman whom he ought to love and cherish as his own body.*'

'That's—what they say at weddings, isn't it?'

'Yep. And Col, he needs help, doesn't he? As well?'

'Yeah. Course he does. But, he's pretty far out isn't he?'

We hear Margaret's car in the drive, Margaret's key in the lock. 'You spoke to him?' she asks, in the kitchen, tying on an apron as if she's readying for a fight with the housework. 'Your father's way too solitary and independent in times of difficulty and stress. As if he has no need of anyone.'

'I—Rachel—is there anything we could do?'

'Jenny, that's kind. I thought we'd go over and just try to clear up that house a bit?'

'We could. Is there anything more: like, d'you have a rape crisis centre here, any counselling place?' Ignoring Max's wild signalling, I push on with what I believe should happen now, 'Should we not make sure she tells the police?'

'I would not object,' Margaret pronounces, splashing the plates in her washing-up water, 'to Rachel's husband being charged with something more than indecent assault. But in their—our—church—we do things another way ... Will your father not buy a dishwasher, Max? They're really quite standard now—with such a large family it'd save your mother.'

'They all muck in—'

'When they could make better use of their time! Well, I'm away after we've finished at Rachel's. Your parents will be here, and it's no place for Chrissie to remain if there's to be talk about the situation ... Thank you Jenny, for offering, we'll be leaving for Rachel's in about half an hour, then?'

First, on Margaret's instructions, I cut sweet peas from Fee's garden, to send over to Rachel. Max crosses the garden, slips his arm around me, whispers in my ear: 'Sail less close to the wind, if you can, Jenny?'

'I'll suppress my natural self, shall I?' Snip, snip, another sweet pea for Rache. Wish it'd undo the horrible thing that happened to her! Wake her up to exploitation! 'It's damn hard!'

'Yep, I do it all the time here, as you see.'

'Don't sell out to their attitudes. Stay with me?'

'Always. Margaret's taking the kids to some suitable movie in Newcastle, straight from school. An almost unknown treat. And we'll leave, once Dad's home.'

So Max has finally decided he's no responsibility for them all?

'Don't forget your golf clubs,' he reminds Aunt Margaret, a few minutes later, trundling her tartan bag of duck-headed irons across the gravel. Does Colin play golf? I hope not!

FEE. THAT AFTERNOON, CARLISLE

It was lovely, waking in the lovely quiet country B and B, with Alisdair for once in slow, romantic harmony with her. (Not that it had quite worked, and she'd had part of her mind on Max, and Jenny, and what's really happening there.)

It was a rush, re-packing the car to hasten on to the Conference Centre in time for Alisdair's Breakfast Address, planned to set the tone for the whole Conference.

And then, such terrible irony, this news from Max ... After the note, and God's blessing in the way the girl opened up to her. Whatever other evil might lurk beneath the apparently untroubled calm of First Truly?

She watched, praying ... She'd acted as a true Helpmeet. Mid-morning, Alisdair had gulped down a cup of coffee and outlined to the conference organiser his duty to return to deal with a sad crisis in his Congregation. Fee had packed Alisdair's bag and brought the Audi round to the entrance. She'd touched his arm in silent, loving, supportive communication. And let him go. He turned the key, took off the handbrake and drove away.

And now, she's on the platform, waiting to address the clergy wives. Scenes flow through her head as they sing a hymn. His MS is threatening to return, I saw the evidence ... Lord, keep him safe: he isn't really in a fit state to drive. And I, I have a message that he wouldn't want to hear.

I can do all things—Christ, please strengthen me to speak out.

'*And so we welcome Pastor Mullins' wife, his Helpmeet, Fiona ...*' (a titter through the audience as the Chair says this) '*to address us on,*' (she hesitates and adjusts her spectacles) '*on the Complementarity ...*'

Fee stands, moves forwards, holds the lectern lightly with both hands. Her notes stare up at her. How confusing it all is, Lord. Even her rewritten speech doesn't quite encapsulate the whole message she feels she must now give to these overworked, seriously faithful, vulnerable, stoical women.

She remains unsure about the wisdom of her own latest submission: allowing Alisdair to drive himself home along those winding roads. She's tempted by the thought that Rachel's situation wouldn't have come about if ...

181

'*Don't think that,*' Fee tells herself. '*Max wouldn't have been happy with Rachel. Max has chosen a life partner, and God's ways are inscrutable. Jenny has shown compassion for the suffering, and an openness to the Lord.*'

'Dear friends,' she begins, 'I asked the Lord prayerfully for a text and he surprised me at breakfast this morning: we were served what caterers call scrambled eggs ...' (A quiet ripple of laughter.) 'And I was reminded, *You can't make an omelette without breaking eggs!*'

The room stirs as one being. While Fee recalls in her own mind her night spent amongst Alisdair's commentaries, the strength she drew from the words on the pages. Before that note arrived.

'*Here is bone of my bone and flesh of my flesh* ... Not a Spare Rib, something hot and juicy to be enjoyed with barbecue sauce.' The wives titter with suppressed laughter; Fee takes a breath. Yes, she's sure of God's message. To her. To the pastor's wife ...

'What is a helpmeet? Two separate words which have become fused! Let's look at what the Hebrew says. Does it speak of an inferior being? Does it say a servant, a doormat? A person who can't hold a separate opinion? Translating literally, *The Lord God thought, It is not good for man to be alone. Let me make him a help matching him ...*'

MAX. THE MANSE

Can't concentrate to study. This manse, supposedly, outwardly, a witness to the calm smooth running of a godly family living out the gospel of *do not be anxious*, is a hive of contradictions. How will Dad deal with the Colin and Rachel situation? How—and by whom—will he be told about the article on Guthrie's work and its apparent connection to Colin's actions?

The landing window's needing a new catch: I work on that. It's been painted over with so many layers it's stuck, almost impossible to remove. As we at First Truly are bonded by layers of Dad's preaching, which points up our failings and puts the pressure on to be perfect.

He's not only hard on us: he's at least as hard on himself. He'll doubtless take the brunt of Colin's actions. And then deliver a sermon berating the Congregation for being a poor witness to God's goodness.

The catch suddenly falls free: I reach for the new one, glancing over and seeing the Audi drawing up outside. The engine runs on a bit. Then, he switches it off. The driver's door opens, Dad sits sideways, feet on the gravel, rubbing at his right leg. Inwardly I groan. He reaches into the car and pulls out his stick. How's he going to interpret a relapse in the light of God's purposes?

I'm on the stairs as he unlocks the front door. 'Dad—'.

Holding up his free hand, 'Max. I have seen Rachel. And now, I must be alone: I need you to respect that.'

Dad won't change. He can't.

Halfway up the attic stairs, maybe I should have insisted on remaining and helping him? He's struggled back knowing he's in a bad way.

But, I'm unwilling to be shouted at! I suppose I pray as I decide to leave him alone. Mount the reminder of the stairs, and, leaving the door open a crack so I can hear him, lie on my bed, waiting. Thinking.

A text (we have so many stored away from childhood onwards) comes to mind: *O Lord, thou hast searched me, and known me ... thou knowest my going out and my coming in.*

Rachel quoted those words at the hospital. I questioned her interpretation, '*It's not that God knows you, Rache, and that you are a bad person. Isn't it that God knows you, understands you, loves you? Suffers with you?*'

What it means to me is the support machines and monitors flickering, beeping, around those tiny babies in the incubators, deep at night in the neonatal ward. I'm going to miss the tiny babies, that closeness to the beginnings of extra-uterine life.

And the toddlers like Serafina. I'll never be at the cutting edge of improving the chances of couples who carry a chromosomal abnormality ... ambitions that floated through my head back when Jen and I first met.

*

After all my efforts at separation, the trap's trying to close. And with the self-same scenario as four years ago: bizarre. I fear his demands. And I fear that he shouldn't be left.

And go down to the study. Knock. No response. Worrying: silently opening the door a crack, glance around (wearing my medical hat, so to speak). I see him, prostrated in prayer.

And the silence rips apart.

'Getting that!' I dash into the hall, grab the receiver. 'Max? When might we expect your father back?' inquires a syrupy clerical voice: the conference organiser.

And the front door bell rings: stretching the phone cord to its limit, I open the door to Jenny. 'Hi,' a hug and a kiss, 'all done and a country pub lunch!'

JENNY

Max hauls me in, speaking meanwhile to whoever's on the phone. 'Oh: I'm not absolutely sure, we haven't spoken. Could you say I'll call back in around, say, fifteen minutes?' Replaces the receiver.

'What's happened now? We had a great time, cleaning and clearing, leaving you to revise! Then Margaret must've decided to vet me some more, 'cos we did a bit of a countryside crawl and ate a ploughman's and chatted about Cambridge. She obviously wanted to stay out till it was time to fetch the kids. So, what's gone wrong here?'

'MAX!' Alisdair's voice rings through the house.

'He's home? Is he angry?'

'He needs me: he's ill again.'

I'm left like a lemon as Max pounds off into the house: God, what'll happen next? We're stuck. What a lifestyle they have, though in fairness I suppose he can't help being ill. Max is gone a good while. I wander into the kitchen, and look at Fee's recipe books: Delia Smith, Elizabeth David, Mrs Beeton (updated), *Joy of Cooking, Our First Truly Collection of Favourite Family Meals* and … *Knowing God*? Curious to understand what makes these people tick, I open it.

Out flutters that note and the article! She hid them from him here, among books he'd never consult!

Folded into one of his though. Has he missed it? Where do those quotes come from? Here's her Bible: let's see … Corinthians …

'Jen? Jenny: I've settled him down.' I slam the Bible shut, not ready for Max to know I'm even curious about *Scripture*, as they call it. 'But, I'm afraid I must leave you again, I've to drive over and collect Mum, seeing he's unable to.'

'What? Me, and him?' What a frightful thought! 'Isn't there a—train, or bus, or if it's an isolated conference centre, can't someone from there give your mother a ride home? Can't I, even?'

'She wouldna' want to be beholden.'

'Max, really: in a crisis?'

Looking at the floor, he admits another of their weird ways, 'Truth is, Jenny, they'd not want to share this personal crisis with the wider clergy group. Or risk news reaching the Congregation until they've sorted how they'll—play it. Damage limitation? Keep it in the family?'

'Why make it a secret? And was the MS brought on by the stress?'

'No. Unrelated. But if the MS's struck again, at a most inopportune moment, it's no business of anyone else's how he'll handle the whole situation.'

'I suppose not. But I can't care for him!'

'He's in bed for now. He'll rest. He'll have blurred vision, possible dizziness on standing, weakness in limbs, maybe bladder weakness. If he calls you, you need to go up right away: so stay in the house.'

'Hang about: bladder weakness?'

'There's a plastic sheet: it'll probably not be a problem.'

'Max, I can't!'

'You can: you'll rise to a crisis won't you? And while I'm gone, how about you call the garage, see if the Capri's ready? And make yourself tea, and relax, he probably won't want anything. I suspect he'll want to be left alone.'

*

I can do everything through Christ who strengthens me! Above the washbasin where other people would have a mirror, Fee's cross-stitched text.

How do they access that strength? I pray, really I do! Please God may Alisdair not need the loo. Please, please, may he sleep quietly upstairs and not need anything! I'd rather listen to one of his sermons than be in charge of him, in an empty house.

Empty house: curiosity helps me cope. Here's an opportunity to learn more. I try the door, and enter the room where those sermons are written. Bible commentaries, large, small, popular and academic. Archaeology books. Manuals on what they call counselling and I'd call brainwashing. Referring to that note again, I consult the commentaries. Not all of them agree! And here's a counselling manual, giving the weird basis of the teaching on the headship of husbands and the submission of wives.

Do I agree with their reading of the Bible texts? About light and darkness, ancient Israelite laws, submission and love?

What is love?

'Jenny!' Suddenly he's shouting for me!

'I'm here!' At your service: reluctant untrained nurse!

'Door's not locked: would you come in where I can see you!'

He can't see me, really. I'm blurred, or maybe there are two of me—I'm not sure. Feels like two, one watching the other, as I move towards the bed where Max's parents sleep. Noticing double-fronted fitted wardrobes, a dressing table. And, horror of horrors: one of those nasty bottle-things a bed-bound bloke can pee into.

Alisdair, in green pyjamas, sits on the side of the bed, rubbing his leg. The pale green's accented against the deep rose-coloured duvet cover and pillows. The duvet untidily pushed back, a pile of books and a glass of juice on the bedside table. 'Come here, lassie,' he says. Quiet, softly accented, vulnerable. I hesitate, look past him: a breeze blows the net curtains inwards like angels or ghosts.

I've seen him tall and strong and let's admit it, attractive in an all-male, besuited, almost sexy way. Powerful, passionate, committed. Leaning over that pulpit, Bible in hand, that finger pointing as he thundered at us. All that powerful stuff from the pulpit is how I want Alisdair to be. Washing ova out of cow's oviducts, dissecting frogs, transferring nuclei from one cell to another, all that's okay. But there are things a person doesn't want to do. Like seeing their boyfriend's dad in a state of total human weakness.

'Och, Jenny, I dinna' bite. Could you help me walk across the room now?'

I look for where we're going: there's another open door. En-suite. Between me—us—a chair with his clothes thrown onto it: jacket on the back, a pile of other clothes topped with a crumpled blue shirt and white underpants. Why couldn't Max have packed away his father's worn garments before he left for Carlisle?

'Jenny: I think we maybe need to start off, now.'

'Okay …'

Some awkward heaving and breathing happens: Alisdair is heavy and expects me to take his weight and to guide him across the room. We're in the bathroom, suddenly he undoes his pyjamas and they fall around his ankles. I thought I'd leave him in here to manage, but it's like I'm doing everything, everything that isn't a bodily function. Holding my breath at the sour smell of him and inwardly berating Max. Did I ever, ever, want to be a doctor like Mum, let alone a nurse?

Back at the bedside, we both collapse onto the mattress, which makes a whispery sound that's the plastic sheet. I feel so awfully sorry for Alisdair, the humiliation of his helplessness. And for me, the unwilling carer.

'Would you mind bringing me my tea now, lassie?' he says. Passing a hand over his eyes, which won't clear them. 'A lightly scrambled egg maybe? And there's a radio over there—would you put that to Radio Four for the News?'

I switch on the radio and make an attempt at plumping the pillows.

I wish so much I wasn't stuck with that vision of his white skin, the hair at the top of his thighs, the parts of him I don't want to know. That picture of him relieving himself.

The irony is that I intimately know his son.

MAX. MID-AFTERNOON, BETWEEN THE MANSE AND CARLISLE

Yesterday, when they left, Dad must've already suspected an attack was coming on. Now there's the Rachel business. Driving to Carlisle (a route so well known from attending clergy family events, the five of us acting out being the perfect pastor's kids), I can't forget the anger, the hurt, and the edge of despair I saw in him. As we painfully mounted the stairs.

'Max will you no treat me like an idiot, man, will you no treat me as a patient,' when I suggested spreading a plastic sheet over the mattress. 'Son—are you diagnosing me now? Are you saying this will lead to that?'

'It's just good nursing procedure.'

'And you're seeing yourself as my nurse now, are you?'

'Dad, please. Let's just—let's just get you settled and taking some rest.'

'Would you pull the curtains then?' And as I left the room, 'Would you pass me the Bible—no, I canna read like this—would you read me—Och, we don't need the text do we?' And together, we recited Psalm 139—which is coming to be a theme of this crisis!

'Max, he knows us. Inside outside. More than we know ourselves. I have done a terrible thing. I have ignored what is before my eyes. I have failed as a pastor.'

I thought Dad would never admit he'd done wrong: but he seems broken in spirit, battling with demons. God loves and understands my father from the inside out? Strange new thought.

*

Soon as we meet up, Mum asks, 'How is he? How did you leave him?'

'In bed. He's better there for now. He can rest.' Stowing her luggage, I try not to tell her everything.

'Your father doesn't rest, he mulls things over. I suppose Margaret's in charge?'

Fudging, because she'll worry, instead of replying I ask about her speech. 'Bit stressful, maybe, without Dad here?'

'Oh no. No. Of course I missed your father. But everything was fine. Just a bit tired.'

'That person who rang said you were a sensation. A good one, of course. Dad was chuffed by that. The only—You don't need to worry,' I end lamely, as we start for home.

'Only?' she says sharply.

'As you can imagine, he's not happy to be ill but it cheered him that your address to the Wives went well. That someone from the Conference Committee was pleased with it.'

Mum seizes my hand a moment, squeezes it. 'Max, thank you. It's so good to see you.' One moment of intimacy. Then, 'Max, when you're driving, look at the road!'

'Mum, he did share the full story about Rachel with you?' I try, using this rather anonymous situation of travel to approach the delicate subject.

'*I will give you a new heart and put a new spirit in you; I will remove from you your heart of stone and give you a heart of flesh …*' Mum quotes. Then slowly, quiet and determined, she says, 'Colin Eccles … Of course, when we were in the Services … but the men weren't … believers. Maybe I'm speaking out of turn, Max, so you must consider this in your own heart, prayerfully. I think your father, who's seen some things in the air force, and counselled many rougher, supposedly less self-controlled and more physical men than Colin, must cope now with having deceived himself. He ignored that Colin's need for power exploited Rachel's misplaced desire to follow those misinterpreted Scriptures concerning the submission of women.'

Amazed at this admission, I glance sideways. Quickly turning back to the road ahead, 'Yes. It's going to be hard, dealing with everyone involved, with the Congregation, with his own feelings. But it is the world, Mum, the world we live in.'

'Exactly what I said to the clergy wives.'

'You did?'

'In essence. Not about what we're going through at First Truly, of course.'

I glance at her, a second time. Less innocent than I thought.

'Och, why do women collude in violent marriages? Rachel should've spoken out right away. Why have we interpreted what God has said in such a way—is there no middle way, between Erin's feminism and Rachel's submission?'

'I'm not so sure,' I say quietly, 'that Erin's a very extreme feminist. And from what you're saying you should approve of her!'

'You think I'm inconsistent, now. Your father would. Max, you avoided telling me who is caring for him. Cleverly, but I noticed.'

'Margaret's taken Kirsty and the boys—and Chrissie—to the cinema. Dad asked to be alone.'

'This is typical! He's surely not totally alone?'

'I—had to leave Jenny in charge. She's very capable, her mother's—'

'Jenny?' Mum says, startling me with her vehemence. 'You left that poor girl in charge of a man she hardly knows and is somewhat in awe of, when he's disabled with an attack which could—Max, you really don't think of other people!'

JENNY. EARLY EVENING, THE MANSE

At least we managed, I think in the kitchen as I crack eggs into a basin. Though putting bread into the toaster, I'm shaking. Why? Relief. At least that wasn't the disaster it could've been.

And anger? What is going on here, what is Max up to, and where do the rest of them think I fit in the family? Offering to do a cake is one thing, being left to nurse a sick, disabled adult male is another. I thought I was a visitor, not a useful spare pair of hands!

I take up the tray, and guide him through eating egg, cake, sliced apple. His face is alarmingly like Max's, the long nose, the grey twinkly eyes. He's probably as embarrassed as I am. And he starts telling me a story. Half way through, he says, 'Look in the Bible,' and gives me a reference to find. 'Read out the last verse.'

'About which of the three people was a neighbour to the injured man?'

'Who does it say?'

'The one who had compassion?'

He nods, briefly, just about acknowledging my reply. 'You're a good lassie, and I'm no ungrateful to you.'

And then, we both hear the car, the voices, the door banging shut downstairs. Spontaneously, we smile—at one another! As Fee comes bounding up the stairs, 'Och Jenny, pet, I'll take over. He can be cranky: you deserve a medal.'

*

Damage limitation? The family close ranks. Max, how can you be so distant? After saying you'd stay with me: you'd be on my side, our side, not be sucked into First Truly ways?

He spends the evening on the phone with Uncle Euan, with the assistant pastor, with his sister Erin of the black sheets. Consulting with his mother. Kirsty plays the good daughter, quiet, willing, eyes turned towards the floor. Everyone's hushed, anxious, tense. Even Alex and Ian creep around. Even the house seems affected.

What'll happen to Colin, if they do things so differently in their church that they won't call in the police? What'll happen to the School, to Nathaniel, most of all to Rachel?

It's weird, awful. A small, family prayer meeting is called. 'Jenny, you're not excluded,' Fee insists. Fee, not Max. Possibly she's only being polite. Without Max's encouragement to be there, I offer to do the washing-up instead. I can hear their murmurings to God, while my head spins with turmoil: scientific objectivity, clashing with personal emotions. Why'm I here? The genes don't mix, any more than Daze and Shane could have a healthy baby. Did Max bring me here to shock the family? Or to show me, sadly and regretfully, that us could never work?

MAX. THURSDAY, ON THE WAY TO CAMBRIDGE

It's a struggle, juggling Mum, Dad and Jenny's needs: I don't think I do it very well.

Eventually I call Erin with the grim news. She's cautious, seeing she and Gary are outcasts in the unbeliever category, along with their gorgeous baby with whom Mum's only spent forty eight hours so far, Dad putting the needs of the congregation before the wishes of his wife and daughter. I haven't met him at all.

'Max, come and see us when you're in London for your exam. Bring Jenny?'

Maybe.

*

The garage swore the car's up to the journey South. I hope so. After this break at home, I just need to escape. Thursday early morning, things arranged here, out on the drive, I suspiciously move aside the tea towel that's covering a familiar basket: 'One of Mum's travel-picnics! I wish she wouldn't!'

'Your mother's sweet.' Jen says.

'Too sweet, too other-directed,' I say, throwing my jacket in the back and settling into the driving seat.

'Family trait?' Jenny's tight lipped. 'Mine would give me the cash for a sandwich.'

'Maybe that'd be better,' I say, 'imperfection's honest.'

Kirsty's away to that swimming training she's trying to get out of, and the twins on their paper round. Dad's asleep: I'm not sorry. Mum appears: this time, she and Jenny hug. I watch, thoughts swirling ... Mum, with her emerging insights, is the one I'm concerned for. The others simply need to learn not to count on my being around. Euan will keep an eye on them all. But how's Jenny come through all this?

'Right: that's over. You needed to know why I told you that you don't want to meet my family!' I try a grin. She touches my hand. Reassuring me that we are together, no matter what?

Bach's Concerto for Two Violins plays on the car radio, as the traffic builds up towards the morning rush hour. Two Violins. Is this a quiet togetherness? If so, reassuring after all the mayhem back home.

In the pocket of my jacket is my letter to Euan, written last night. Explaining, *I can no longer belong to this tiny, inward-looking ethnic community*. Even though we agree on so much, and shared our convictions that Dad must be prevented from assigning any blame to Rachel in this latest crisis, I'm still going to disappoint him.

Along with the letter, I've another important item stashed away. One I've not looked at, simply dropping it into that pocket a couple of days back, to produce in due time.

'You're quiet,' Jenny says after a while.

'Aye. And you.'

'You're okay?'

'Better the nearer we are to Cambridge. You?'

'Mmm.'

'I'm desperately sorry about the Rachel business,' I say a few miles further on.

'Not exactly your fault ... Max, I thought I might go home.'

What? I think, silently.

'If Roslin want me, I mayn't have a lot of time to see them, at home I mean.'

We're well into Yorkshire, and the signs for a motorway service station appear: twenty miles, twelve miles. 'Jenny, how about we stop, have a coffee, maybe eat some of Mum's picnic?'

*

Ten minutes later, assuming Jen has total recall (as women seem to do). 'Another crisis we've weathered together,' I say, carrying our Formica tray of over-priced coffee towards a spindly table.

'What?'

'Déjà vu? Addenbrooke's staff canteen, Daze's baby, a rather tricky conversation?'

'Oh. Yes.'

'Jenny? I've not been able to talk, but I've thought a lot. The pull of First Truly is a false one ...'

'Not if it's real for you. It is for them. Low blood sugar,' she explains, sitting, and reaching for the little bowl of envelopes containing sugar. She takes one, pulls it open. Where's that brilliant hand-eye co-ordination gone? Grains of Demerara bounce across the tabletop. 'Don't criticise, don't even look.' She empties the remainder into her coffee. 'There you all were praying, yesterday. On another planet.'

'We'll both feel better when we're back we belong,' I say, reaching for her hand.

'Where's that?'

'Och, Cambridge, isn't it? Where we had a coffee after that shock of Daze's baby arriving? And got back together?'

'Cambridge.' Stirring her drink.

'Jenny?' She looks up. Huge, grey-blue eyes behind the big spectacles gaze into mine: turn my heart over. She is not happy. My fault again?

'No ... No, Jenny listen. Another planet, maybe. But I no longer live there. What use is seriously following the Creator of the world in a tight identically thinking bunch in one corner? All through med school and beyond, I've curled at the edges realising how the other students, the other doctors, all my work colleagues rightly view us Truly Reformed types. People of faith are meant to be out in the community, doing acts of love and compassion. Not huddling fearfully in a corner, trembling, afraid to move without advice from their Pastor!'

'Your Dad read me a Bible story about being a good neighbour. Maybe a kind of apology?'

I'm on a roll, not listening to her. 'And Euan, Euan's a lovely old-style family doctor, but he's no' the future of medicine is he?'

'It's not Euan ...'

'Jenny, that visit settled my mind. I've an interview, a practice near Cambridge. There's a flat which goes with the job: I thought ...'

JENNY

As he reaches into his pocket, I think it's for the hateful ciggies. But no, it's a tiny battered cardboard box, and inside is my future, as Max wants it, wrapped in yellowed tissue paper.

'Jenny, despite the family ...'

His hand comes towards me, across the table, holding the ring. I recoil, lump in my throat, can't speak. This is terrible.

'I—I ... you change when you're there with them. Who'm I with, who's asking me this? Can't we, can't we just ... This began with you telling them we're engaged, without asking me!'

'Jenny, you've no idea what it is to be expected to have a duty of responsibility towards your family.'

'Yeah? Your mum works like a slave. I've seen what Colin did to Rachel because your father teaches submission.'

He lets go my hand. And gives me a look so dark, his eyes full of some unreadable emotion. 'I'm not Colin, not anything like Colin: we talked about submission and you know what I—'

I try to pull back some of what I've said. 'I still wanted to try to respect your father, but I can't do those messy, nursing things. And I had to see his—his nakedness ... Don't you understand anything?'

Max looks from me to the floor. Mumbling, 'I do realize. I can't condone myself. But that all happened at my parents' place: you can't think I *wanted* to be the one who sorted it out?'

'I don't know, do I? How can I know?' I do really want to. 'You took me further and further along a road I can't travel: heaps of intimate stuff, caring for people.'

'I'd no intention of taking you up there for that; you must've realised.'

And then, he pulls a letter from some inner pocket of his jacket, 'I wrote to Euan ...'

'Where does that fit in? Is that about us?' Jumping to my feet, leaning across the table, 'I don't care about Euan, I care about us! What is it about him? You've a key to his house!'

Max jumps up, rocking the table, 'I told you! Jenny, people are looking. People are observing an ugly rumpus between a crabbit lassie and—'

'You!'

'Yes, me.'

'I tried so hard to empathise, I really did. Over Rachel. But then you piled it on, the caring.'

'I'm not two people! There was a lot of it to do, how else would we have managed Dad?'

Ashamed of making a scene in amongst all those people, the plump beige-coated elderly, the families with wide-eyed kiddies, most of all the couples, we sink back onto our chairs. Spilt coffee now lies on the table, the little box an island in a lake.

'God, we've made a mess,' I say.

Max retrieves his box. 'They'll wipe it up.'

'I don't mean the coffee. I mean, I'm twenty-two, I just graduated, I can't be a wife, I've not begun my life yet!'

'Oh look, Jen, I'm off to the gents' and when I get back maybe ...' Max shoves back his spindly chair, coffee splashes, this time, onto my lovely Indian vegetable-dyed skirt, bought for the ceilidh.

'Max!'

He spins round from gazing about for the toilets sign, 'Sorry!'

'Thanks a bunch for the stain: it won't come out. I'm off to the ladies' anyhow.'

*

A few minutes later, we're walking to the car, Max apologising again for spilling the coffee. An AA man is busy preparing a broken-down vehicle to be towed away. A downbeat-looking couple stand watching, their luggage beside them.

'Won't be a minute then we'll be off: long way, Exeter!' says the AA man.

''Tis a little place a few miles the other side o' that,' the woman of the couple says.

Exeter? And that accent, although it isn't exactly mine, has the pull of home, the West Country, the softer, more humid air. More than anything, I want to be there.

'Look,' I say, 'it's like that guy—see—the AA man, hooking that car to his van?'

Max looks. 'Could've been us! Good thing I got the Capri fixed.'

'Not the point. I got hooked up to you, and dragged to the Manse. With all your expectations ...'

'Did you no' listen to a word I said? About my father's church no longer having a hold on me? I was not asking, *will you be chained to the Manse family*. I was asking *would you* ... Och, it doesna' matter any longer.'

'Well, good. Then you realise I'm not made to be Mrs Pastor's-Son. You said it was you, once. Now, it's me. I'm—give me your keys, I want something from the car. I'm sorry. *Something's come up.*'

Thankfully, he doesn't argue. He hands me his keys. I haul out what I think is most vital, my canvas army-surplus shoulder bag, the photocopied articles on dysmorphic infants poking out of it. And dart across the car park before he can stop me, or I can change my mind. The AA man and the couple are climbing in, 'Exeter? Would you have room for one more?'

From the cab, I see Max and my heart twists as he runs towards us, but I've slammed my door, the driver's turned the ignition ... I reach into my bag, pull out my camera.

And focusing fast as I can, take two shots. The second one, Max has his hand in front of his eyes.

Resolutions

'Let's have a coffee? Catch up?' The project's going well. Daze has found Bryn's pretty cool, for a nerd. He's giving her a few video editing lessons. Wicked.

Today's dawned with a sea mist filling the garden: ghostly laundry hangs from the line. Daisy, leaning on her windowsill, watches as Caro emerges below, medical bag in hand, drops her keys, retrieves them, opens and climbs into her Volvo.

Daze considers Caro. Her bonnet's full of psycho-medical bees, in constant buzz. A lot of them to do with kids and growing up. First time they met, Caro looked down Daze's throat. Then, *'Anything else, Daisy? Daddy says mummy's not in Cornwall with you both. How's that make you feel?'*

Yeah, well ... mummy's a photograph. Jewels' been, on and off, face down in the bottom of a drawer. From when Caro and the girls moved in till now. Right now, she's out. The worst for wear since being decorated, in Daze's childhood, with smarties and jellybeans (for her nickname) stuck all around the edge to make a frame. Later, Daze sketched in Dracula giving Jewels a love-bite ... Persephone's foot prints have been shoved into the frame alongside, partially obscuring Jewel's face.

Get this for Caro-type thinking: each girl had a present of a full-length mirror when they turned thirteen. Daze's is cool: Edwardian, freestanding mahogany. Jenny's is flat, screwed to the wall ... Daze can tip hers to catch the sun, could make signals if she had a mind to. (Used to try it!)

Today, smiles into it: a crooked smile like Shane's, but hers the result of that tiny op in babyhood. Shane's, he said, was what? Like his Dad's? Her hair's like his: mad dark waves! And Shane: is she like Shane inside? In her head? Is what he said true—or a taunting lie? Whatever, he was the one to look stupid, her aim with that hospital kitchen tomato was spot-on.

She checks for stretch marks. Which she seems not to have. Stomach not too bulgy ... normal almost. Recalls her sore, inflated boobs oozing milk, that day he visited ... awful. Turns away, picks up some clothes from a chair.

Her tilted mirror reflects movement on the drive. There goes Dad now, off to the College ... Empty house till Hat gets home, 'cept for the dog, possibly the cat. Maybe I'd have enjoyed a little baby.

Yeah, gets harder, as the weeks pass. Having those pink foot prints doesn't help. Seizing the picture, she rips them out of the frame and tears them in pieces. Instantly devastated, *Daze you're bloody weird, you're a headbanger, you know that?* A sob rises: doubling over, Daze gasps, squeezes her eyes shut, takes control of herself. This project ain't grief work. Artists aren't weird: we're sane. We see the world clearly: violent, dark, unforgiving. Babies don't realise. People don't realise, or they'd not ask John Guthrie to make them a kid in a dish. She's conceived the cleverest conceptual art. Think about that!

JENNY. THURSDAY EVENING

At Exeter, I join a train packed with holidaymakers, and ride standing in the aisle balancing a slopping polystyrene cup of tea and a packet of crisps. As the countryside slams past the window, I try to smile at the wailing kiddies and fraught mums.

And push away the haunting images: Rachel, Alisdair, Nathaniel. Human suffering and human weakness. Max: cool, efficient, in charge of himself and others. Fee, Val, Daze: Secrecy.

Would I be here if Max hadn't proposed?

Late afternoon, the train slows into Penzance and there's the sea, turquoise, indigo, a treat to live beside. I use the payphone to call home. The sight of Mum's Volvo as it arrives is wonderful: after the miserable day, suddenly desperately hungry, I'm eating a pasty as it draws up. Bought from a shop nearby, served by someone I was at school with.

'Didn't expect this but always lovely to see you, sweetie,' Mum says, 'is that all your stuff?'

'Mm.'

Pity I left the Edinburgh pressies in the Capri, but seizing my photocopies and my army surplus bag was all I could do. Relaxing into the squashy passenger seat, I stretch out my legs.

'How's Max?'

'Easier to untangle the Daze and Persephone mystery on my own.'

'Oh ...' Mum says, in her surprised voice.

'Max can't stay focused on a project, off to take his exam in London. Typical male, interested in his own career. He's settled on becoming a GP. When we met, he was talking about research. Same as me.'

'So that spoils everything?' Mum says. 'Life is full of the unexpected.'

My mind scrolls through the amount of the unexpected that life's presented in the past few weeks. 'His family is too different.'

'Every family is different.'

'His father had a relapse ...'

'Remind me what he suffers from?'

'MS. Max had to fetch his mum from a conference so he *only* left me in charge ...' I can't go on.

'Darling, is this what brought you home so suddenly, then?'

'What else? Max is taking up space in Cambridge. I had to get away.'

As we wind through narrow lanes, past turnings to places with magical names, *Sancreed*, *St Buryan*, the sun's a great orange ball dropping towards earth. Approaching Sennen, Chapel House is mysterious and inviting, its tall two-storey windows catching the golden sunset.

What irony: where've I been staying? With a pastor's family! In a Manse! *'He's all theirs, when he's at home,'* I think. And please, let Mum not mention *the fragile male ego* or there being *more fish in the sea*.

But as she turns the car into the drive, she changes the subject. 'Val's go okay?'

'Yeah ... Daisy at home?'

'What a toughie. She's busy working on a project ... I'd not expect many girls to work long days at anything, a couple of weeks after giving birth.'

'Gypsy ancestry,' I mumble. I'm about to say 'Val talked about the Commune,' but something stops me.

'Well, anyway, it's lovely to have everyone back home. And how about a barbecue, or a beach party, before you all disappear again? Hat'd like that.'

Why've I sidestepped the Commune issue?

Indoors, on the side are my letters: my *one* letter and a postcard from Maeve. And as Daze chooses that moment to pass by, making for the studio, I shove them in my pocket, saying 'Oh—Mum says you're already busy working on something. That's good.'

'Yeah? Why'd that be?'

'Well, 'cos busy is good for getting over ... Actually Daze, we need to talk some time ... about your cousin?

'God! You've a one-track mind haven't you!' Daze slams the studio door, and through it comes the rest of her response, 'Hard luck: I'm busy!'

I turn, with an ironic grin, 'Lovely that we're all here together, Mum?'

'Well, it's all very familiar, sweetie, just how I remember you two girls. You want anything, love?'

'A hot shower. And hit the sack. Thanks for the lift.' And I think how since Val's, Des has changed in my mind. Complicated issue. 'Where's Des? He's okay?'

'Yes, he's okay. Bit quiet. Taken on a portrait and teaching a few weekend courses for wannabe landscape watercolourists during the holidays.'

I let Mum hug me. Then, upstairs, to tear my letter open.

Dear Miss Guthrie ...

Scan the first lines. Then wish I hadn't.

The words get all muddled up. *Blah, blah ... We Regret ...*

Oh we do, do we?

Roslin rejected me? I can't believe it. But it's true.

197

Maeve's card bubbles on about the children's club she's helping with, and how her postgraduate study plans have fallen into place. Like Max saying things are 'meant' by God.

I let Maeve's card fall on the floor, and head for the shower. Well doesn't my life just fit together, huh?

It's then I realise I must've left Val's ring on the basin at the service station. Or did I even have it there?

Lost it forever. Another bum thing.

*

Cambridge over, like it never happened, I'm in bed surrounded by my now-too-small homework desk, pink sprigged wallpaper, creamy-white furniture, and dog-eared posters. An idealistic teenager—me—once lived here.

Could failing to be accepted for research at Roslin be 'meant' (by God)? It's about Dad's being too cutting-edge. Because he's working for a private lab, for profit, and academics kid themselves they work ever so ethically, purely to further knowledge.

Or the unthinkable: it's about me. (A Max-type thought.) My determination to pursue the Persephone project, and Professor Nicholson's knowing who I am, and who Daze is. Which took him two seconds once he knew (from the obs team?) I'd been there when she gave birth. Dad was hinting when he mentioned he sometimes saw Nicholson.

It's about the stupidity of grabbing an opportunity to work with Max. Of course, us meeting up a second time could look *meant*. Then at the manse my background made a dog's breakfast of our relationship.

And, what'll Mum have to say when I tell her Val filled in facts I, and Daze, never knew?

I curl up tight. Trip was a disaster. Allowing myself to feel at all is too painful. Max: that cord that holds us together. Is it broken? Is that really what I want, and what's best?

Someone pushes my door open. Our lovely tabby cat leaps softly on top of me. Miaow ... I reach out one hand, rest it on her furry back. She purrs, kneads and settles to sleep. Animals lead simple lives.

And if Daisy isn't working on something related to Persephone, I'd be astounded. She's welcome. My efforts about Persephone led me away from what I meant do.

Meant!

MAX. THURSDAY, CAMBRIDGE

Arriving back alone, late afternoon, I go straight to Addenbrooke's children's ward. Sarah, Nicholson's senior registrar, comes bouncing up, 'Max: good holiday? Splendid. Serafina. The Prof mentioned he'd suggested you might join us?'

On cue, the patient appears, catching her wheeled frame walking-aid between our feet and the legs of a cot. Screaming with frustration. Almost as if Serafina isn't there, Sarah rattles off the reasons for the op, while I squat down to help. 'Right. You'll be familiar with the problems. Anophthalmia of the left eye: microphthalmia of the right, which is underdeveloped, lacking a retina, and the optic nerve is incomplete.' Serafina and I communicate silently, through the subtleties of nerve-endings in our skin, as we touch hands. 'Because of the absence or very small size of the globe of the eye ... Max? You're looking thoughtful. You've got a question?'

Shake my head. 'No.'

'Okay, there have been some concerns about her heart in the past.' Yes, like the time when Serafina was a tiny scrap having heart surgery. I recall her Mum spent the whole five hours of the op praying over an awful picture of the exposed sacred heart of Jesus, clasped to her chest. 'But Serafina's a survivor. She should come through ... I'll see you in theatre, then? First thing, tomorrow?'

Serafina moves on, battling her way through life in this home from home, Addenbrooke's paediatric ward. If I let myself, I'd feel Jenny's presence, the day she came up to the ward. So impressed meeting real dysmorphic children. I was impressed by her bright and open innocence about how much we could already do, and how genetic research would conquer all the problems. And, not stopping myself in time, I now let a wave of regret at the whole debacle of our trip North break over my head.

'No—no problems,' I tell Sarah, as the wave breaks, 'No questions—see you tomorrow.' And she hurries away, reading the next patient's notes as she goes.

*

To get rid of an unpleasant task, I drive to Jenny's place. Unpack her gear, hump it to the front door. Most of these houses are let to undergraduates. It's the vac, the street's deserted. Fishing out my key, I let myself in.

The door squeaks as I close it. The house dreams in the warm afternoon, motes spiralling downwards in a beam of sunlight that shines from the landing window.

Up in the bedroom where we *made love*, such a stupid phrase, the bed's untidily pulled over. A typical Mullins, I begin straightening it out. And stop myself: not a way to go.

I don't ask to re-run the scene at the service station, but my brain does it anyway. I was inept and I've managed to hurt the same person twice. Whether we share a faith is irrelevant. This has nothing to do with *don't be unequally yoked with unbelievers*! What goes on at home isn't a faith, it's a culture. Without God, Dad would find some other reason to be a control-freak.

With Dad's attitudes burned into my communication style, instead of asking her to share my future, I came out with something like, *I've adapted myself to your needs, I'll live in the south, away from my family. How about marriage? You become dependent on me, and I'll protect you from life's vicissitudes.*

And she responded: *I can't be Mrs Pastor's-Son*, and *Something's come up.* Touché.

I pile Jen's overnight case and carrier bags from the Edinburgh shops, bulging with tartan scarves and tins of shortbread, neatly against the wardrobe. Her shoes in pairs beside them. And hang her interview suit on its hanger on the back of the door.

Then look around for the last time: leave the key on her desk, or on the kitchen table? Which?

It's then I notice the jeans, thrown over the back of the desk chair, one leg smeared with something. With Daze's blood, from when Jenny, led by her insatiable curiosity, took Persephone out of the cot where I'd laid her, still bloody and still warm. Suppose a sample of Daze's blood would answer at least part of Jenny's questions? Seeing the Addenbrooke's lab won't tell her, or me, its findings ... If there's enough DNA there, if I could get these small stains analysed elsewhere ... Maybe not ...

*

Finally, I'm home: my room at Wil's more a home than the Manse. Sam Skull, perched midway on the shelf between the two piles of Dad's sermons on my desk, stares, despite the total absence of ocular globes, from under his panama hat. 'Hi, Buddy.' *Memento mori*: a strange way to put the creeps into that student Bible study which used to meet in my room! Sam and I are friends: I cast myself on the bed, pushing away regrets, and fall asleep.

Waking from a doze, I make my way to the bathroom. Tampax, and contact lens solution, on the windowsill? Diaphanous underwear drying over the shower curtain rail?

In the kitchen: a portable TV. And strawberry yoghurts in the fridge? A pink fluffy slipper half under the living room sofa, a lipstick, and *Hello!* magazine?

Patty. Turn my head, he's moved her in!

'Man, view her as an asset: she's hoovered all through twice since she's been here! And the telly's great for the rugby,' Wil argues.

'Could you take your mind off your new-found asset a few minutes and listen? The new DNA tests, from very small samples on, say, clothing, are they available here?'

'You've committed a crime and you don't want to be detected, huh?'

'Right. I murdered a heartsink patient ... Seriously, I have a debt to pay someone.'

Wil's grin slowly expands and becomes a guffaw and a friendly punch. 'The beautiful micromanipulator! Is this about that screwed-up kid you two were using as an excuse to spend time together?'

'It might help to uncover a mystery. The labs have samples I sent them. Nicholson's told me I can't access them myself: conflict of interest. What would you do?'

He laughs. 'Guthrie? He's got the private, or government, lab contacts. And I believe there's a research paper on extracting DNA from various surfaces.'

'Thanks, Wil.'

'Did I say anything?'

Waking, I go down straight away, put the kettle on, hunt for the coffee. They've changed where they keep things ...

'Looks like you drink too much coffee. You know, you're peaky: go and have some more shut-eye.'

'Daze! I'm okay ... shall I do breakfast? Muesli or bacon?—Oh, you're vegan, aren't you.'

For answer, Daze shakes muesli into a bowl, and rattles about in the drawer finding a spoon.

'Looks like Mum's into fruit tea. Daze, rose-hip suit you?'

'Today, I fancy coffee—seeing I'm working.'

Hat bounces in, wearing her swimmers and cut-offs. 'I was at the beach. Anyone want to come to a hen party? Mindy, from school—you two know her?'

This is too much: anger, and misery I can suppress, but bounce I can't take today. 'Hat, too early! Daze, I've got photos, including the Wake: could I use the darkroom? You're not, are you?'

'Not while I'm using the studio, you can't.'

'Oh. Why not? I mean, I only have to, like, walk through the studio.'

'D'you have to pick an argument?' Hat entreats. 'C'mon Daze, Jenny?'

'It's no big deal, Hat, okay?'

'Was your trip shit or what?' Daze asks.

'No. Why'd you think that? Listen, I was at my Aunt Val's: Val showed me her loom.'

'So?'

'So nothing. Thought you'd be interested, she's a traditional weaver. She uses veggie-dyed wools. She also talked about a Commune where she'd lived. And told me stuff.'

'Like what?'

'Like she'd known your mum and Des way back, and your aunt Loose. Mum of that cousin you met, maybe?'

'If you know, why d'you ask?' snaps Daze. 'Can you never stop interferin'?'

'I thought we might ask Mum and Des. Look, it's just useful, interesting, to know about family.'

Daze frowns. 'Is that so?'

God, I'm blundering about. Where's my brain gone?

Hat saves the situation, more by luck than planning. 'So *what about the party?* Remember Mindy? Her dad has a mysterious business, and they live in that big house looking over that bay?'

'Sorry, sorry?' Daze responds.

'Not just a few drinks in a pub. A females-only rave in costume round their swimming pool. With,' Hat lowers her voice, 'a male stripper?'

'Did you say a *male stripper?* In West Cornwall?'

'She works in London. Her dad's arranged the guy to come down, from a club there? Dress to kill, Mindy said—be cool to go into Penzance, the three of us, and buy some crazy outfits?'

'Maybe.' Daze picks up her mug of coffee. 'Though since when was Penzance cool? Or selling crazy outfits?'

'Let's … do that …' I say, grateful Hat's moved us from a dodgy subject to an inane one. But Daze tips her remaining muesli into the bin, and sweeps out. 'Jenny, sometimes a creative person needs to be alone! And, he wasn't like my *boyfriend*. I've no reason to ask them *anything*!'

She's rattled. That is sus. But I've screwed up again: I phrased it all wrong. So she's humped off to wrap herself in her invisible Byronic drama cape. An aura of darkness, romance, angst. The Daze recovery vehicle.

Suppose eventually, sometime, I'll have to face Cambridge again: consult Dr Woods about what work to apply for, seeing as Roslin's rejected me. Retrieve the stuff I left with Max. For now, I let Hat haul me off to the beach. And try to relax and read a brainless magazine. Hat pokes into the Max situation. 'Trouble in Paradise, Jen?'

'Hattie, maybe it's over. I don't know.'

'But he's lovely: whatever's wrong?'

'Just everything?'

'Oh Jen. I'm so sorry …' The story comes out. Hat listens thoughtfully. I should've listened to Max like that. About his home and his faith and his options. Regret is awful, especially on a beautiful bright beach before the tourist season really hits. By lunchtime, I'm determined to make things up with Daze, if not with Max, and head off home, leaving Hat with her mates and the surf.

Maybe, being very careful, I could try again, and then together we could ask Mum and Des about the Commune? We do have a right to know. Daze certainly has a right.

Home's quiet with the total stillness of a perfect summer day. Bees buzzing in the foxgloves up the drive, scent of cut grass from a nearby hayfield, droning of a microlight overhead. Cat snoozing on the back porch. Dog panting on a shady patch of lawn.

'Daze? Daisy!'

Silence. She said she was working. I try the studio door: empty.

On the easel, the ghostly beginning of a portrait, some elderly guy—obviously Des's commission. And something bulky under a cloth. Curiosity demands I lift one corner.

A plaster mould, female torso? Hey, that dressmaker's dummy in Daze's bus! Her project, the one she's so secretive about, begun before Persephone's arrival? Could they be linked?

Her sketchbook, with the little mouse and mouse embryo drawings, is lying on a shelf. She's added drawings of Persephone, carefully observed. Courageous, to draw that baby with such accuracy and detail, the poor little scrawny malformed limbs and that face, the expression governed by the deformities. What a memory: like when she coolly drew that rabbit I put out of its misery at Botallack. Then showed it around at school.

Daze with her cool detachment and apparent interest in physiology could as easily be my father's daughter as I am. She nicked and kept my cut-up chrysalis. For her Nature Table! We were ten maybe?

Hmm. Daze's work's always dark. The crucified child, the beating heart project. Why does serious art tend towards the dark ironic? On trips to galleries with Des, the contemporary exhibitions disturbed me in a way that science never could. But I like the studio: I like its scent, oil paint, fresh wood, varnish. And I like *some* contemporary art: I like David Hockney. Those swimming pool pictures. The colours.

Well, no Daisy, but here I am with time, after all the stress of final exams, and the Manse, and stuff. I begin browsing Des's art books.

Here's contemporary art. *The Shock of the New.* Flip through it. Marcel Du Champ exhibited a mass-produced urinal, Paris, 1917! *Conceptual art. Art in which the concept or idea involved in the work takes precedence over traditional aesthetic and material concerns.* Why the hell imagine the concept's more important that the execution? If we did that as scientists we'd never achieve—Hockney doesn't just have an idea, he paints it. Sensible guy.

Then that phrase hits me between the eyes. *Conceptual Art.* How about *Conception Art?*

Surely not? Would anyone? Would Daze? Get pregnant in order to make a shocking, witty, philosophical point? Playing with a phrase is permissible. Playing with human life is not, simply for art!

I'm crazy. Too much sun! Too much stress at the Manse!

But, a sensational idea.

*

Later, Hat finds me in the garden, reading another art book. I've found this: *many of the early video artists were involved with experimental film, performance, and conceptual art.* And this: *currently video art is connected with installations and multi media.* Daze kept my film to use it?

'Hey, since when did you—That belongs to Daze!'

'Where is Daze? She told me she was using the studio.'

'Gone to Bryn's. Down St Just. Back for dinner? Your photos—you could still nick an hour or two in the darkroom.'

'Hang about. Bryn? As in Bryn Williams?'

'As in Bryn Williams. Your school ex.'

'God, what a combination! What's she seeing him for?'

'Art school stuff. Bryn's helping her brush up her video technique.'

'I thought Daze wasn't into technology.' Hat shrugs. 'Actually, yes, I'll do my photos.'

*

Video art connected with *installations* and *multi media*: lifting that cloth again, what's that beside the woman's body thing? Our video player? In a carefully-constructed wooden box, with a small TV monitor, fitted above it? The kind Bryn's dad would often have in his repair shop. And somehow it's no surprise to find cassettes. At least, cases. Daze must have the videos with her. One box is labelled: *Daddy's Girl*, 12-6-87. The other: 17/06/88.

Seventeenth June: what happened that day? *Push! Now pant, pant gently, Daisy, like a dog—the head's crowning!* The malformed face appears, and I drop my camcorder onto the delivery bed … Boing! The door opens and there's Max … Definitely, my film.

'Jenny!'

Yikes! Dropping the cloth back, I pin on a smile for Daisy, framed in the doorway. 'Daze! I was going to develop my holiday pics.' My voice shakes with the guilt of the discovered, I plough on. 'You don't mind really if I use the darkroom? It was meant for all of us …' Did she see me snooping, or did I jump up quick enough?

'Go ahead,' Daze says, 'though you'd need to have your camera with you—or at least your used film.'

'Just needed to know you weren't busy here before I fetched it.'

*

Daddy's Girl? I think, preparing to develop my film. Puzzling over conceptual art, conception art, and that title.

Daddy's Girl? Gradually my pictures appear in the bath of developer: Persephone's wake, with all Daze's traveller crowd comforting their adopted sister. Max, asleep at Black Sheet Cottage, relaxed and beautiful, pale against the black of the sheets, his hair all tousled. John Knox glaring down on Edinburgh. Val, and my island-named cousins, grin broadly from their chemical setting. Max, at the service station. The last one blurry with movement.

Fighting down grief with the presenting task, I peg up my pictures. Still speculating about those dates. After her graduation, June '87, Daze went straight to Colombia. Where, at Dad's clinic, she was surrounded by … *Conception Art*. If 17/06/88 is my cassette, what can 12-06-87 be? Twelfth June wasn't her graduation, or the day she travelled.

Suddenly, the key turns in the lock.

Alisdair couldn't do that, I think guiltily. Daze can.

DAZE

Locked her in so's I know where she is.

Daze picks up both video cases, replacing the videos in each. She takes her sketchbook from the shelf and stuffs everything into her funky black velvet shoulder bag.

Bugger Jen snooping around. What's alerted her? What'd get rid of her? Touching the mould, satisfied it's dry, she wonders if she could relocate. Where, with all my stuff?

What was it Jenny said, at the market? No good for cousins? Yeah. Sneaky Shane's taunt wasn't a lie ... Suppose Shane does have some weird problem, a genetic flaw, an abnormality, like Dr Guthrie explained would happen if the Hox genes went wrong. We're cousins: that's what Jen's getting at. We might *both* have this flaw. *He was my friend and he deceived me. Let me down. Ruined my life.* Like Mum at Glastonbury: *Daisy, stay right there, and I'll get you an ice cream!* And she never came back!

Whatever it was: duff genes we might share, or duff work he did, Shane's responsible.

So, a quiet exit to East Anglia when nobody expects? Shane's people's farm might well have a nice big barn they're not using. Shane owes me more than one, she thinks. Check the address (Lily would have it, his parents are among the café's suppliers). At the (theoretical, but they must have one?) barn, hitch up a cable for electricity? Private space, electricity, a place where the mould can be cast professionally.

JENNY

Daze, you *bitch*!

A sisterly trick, a Daisyish piece of annoying behaviour? Or a knowing act to keep me here while she removes the evidence?

Shouting and banging doesn't make any difference. Daze's sense of fun, which could be all this is, doesn't impress me. And then, as I lean on the sink, furious, being stuck here begins to focus my thoughts.

Daze's underlined my interest in the art project by turning the key. *Daddy's Girl* is dated 17/06/88, Persephone's birthday. Daze didn't conceive her child by mistake.

Thinking about that second cassette, and what Daze said, *he wasn't, like, my boyfriend*, I have an idea. 12/06/87. Second half of 1987, Daze was in Colombia.

So, how about using American dating, as they probably would out there? Read American-style: 6/12/87—Persephone was born at, Max's reckoning, about 27–28 weeks. Reversing the month and day, 12/06/87 means the twelfth month, December, the sixth day ... which would neatly fit conception!

So what's the art of conception? A pun on a phrase. Dad's work is on fertility. Daze admires Dad. Her desire for fame got caught up with how she views him: powerful, charismatic, outrageously certain that he's right to push the boundaries of knowledge about conception. He's the Creator. Father of human life.

But she wouldn't, couldn't ...

Daze must've filmed herself having intercourse. With Shane. Bizarre. Voyeuristic. Believable. Once pregnant, she returned.

I can't stay stuck in here. When this room was the cloakroom for the chapel, there was just enough window to air it (if ever they did). Climbing up onto the bench, kneeling on the draining board, I open the blackout blind. Then I have to bash and bang at the window, until it suddenly gives, and swings wide. I can just squeeze through, and drop the five feet or so to the ground. Landing in the flowerbed under Daze's window.

There's something pink caught amongst the leaves. Persephone's footprints that the hospital did for Daze to keep, torn into pieces. Why?

I don't know, now. Maybe I'm wrong about the baby being an art object? Maybe Daze is normal, under all the bluster. Suppose we're similar, falling apart underneath, pretending we're not miserable?

DAZE

'Sorry about that, but if you were a creative artist you'd understand—' Daze declares, unlocking and flinging wide the darkroom door ...

Shit! The room's empty.

Jen appears at supper, cool as a cucumber. 'Well, ain't it Miss Houdini herself,' Daze hisses across the table. 'Amazing!'

Jenny raises an eyebrow. Caro shakes her head.

'Can't hack anyone eyeballing my stuff till it's ready. If you were a creative artist you'd understand,' Daze says, piling her plate with salad.

'Yeah, I guess we understand each other, don't we Daze?' says Jenny. With a smile.

As the meal proceeds, plans continue taking shape in Daze's mind. Jenny'll obviously want to play the shining but innocent scientist and spill about the project: how clever she was to guess, blah, blah ... Rather than appreciating the social comment and irony life dealt through a chain of deceptions.

Always hide your finer feelings! A lesson I learned at Dad's knee. The world's dark and unforgiving, stealth is necessary. Daze offers sweetly to pack the dishwasher, and then, everyone happy that Daze's happy, and helpful, she hurries to her room, puts on a Depeche Mode album, and turns the volume up high. Oh wow, I have a plan ... Bryn's taught me all he can and I'm ready for the next stage. Now, when was that party?

Later, she goes to the kitchen, and makes two mugs of cocoa. Apologises properly to Jenny. 'There's a lovely sunset: come and see, on the terrace? I made hot choc, there's one for you if you want it. Look, I don't know what got into me but—sorry? And, friends? And when's the hen party?'

'Tomorrow. I'm so glad you want to go. So do I.'

MAX. FRIDAY, CAMBRIDGE

Nicholson left me to sign off another patient. It's good to be kept busy. The grateful, still anxious, parents ask, 'Are we really out of the woods, Doctor?'

'Looking good but some way to go yet. Don't forget to make another appointment with the cardiologist.'

From there to the ward, to see Serafina. Am sorry she's already had her pre-med, and so drowsy the eyes we're attempting to improve are tight shut. 'Well He,' says her mother, showing me the picture she brought along before, stabbing at it with her index finger, and looking me in the eye, 'took our burdens which we laid upon his sacred heart, last time.'

I squeeze her hand. And Serafina's, though she's not conscious enough to notice.

*

Later, hours later, a sombre mood grips us all. Weary, I sit on a bench in my scrubs, Serafina's blood on my front, staring into my soul. Has God put his answer there?

Nicholson pokes his head in the doorway: 'Max? Max Mullins in here?' I emerge from around the lockers, pulling off my head covering. 'Max, do you have a moment?' (As in, *drop everything, you do have as long as it takes.*)

'Of course.'

'You took a special interest in Serafina. You've talked a bit with her parents. I think it would be appropriate if—'

'Of course,' I say.

Thank you, Professor, for handing me the experience I need: giving the parents of a disabled child the news that she didn't make it through, and they have a disabled child no longer.

And without time to think further, once the deed is done, and the sorrowing parents are handed over to one of our paediatric nurses to go and see the poor little body all cleaned and tidied up, I must plunge back into the hustling, bustling world. Tomorrow, my interview for the GP one-year training post. Monday evening, the trip to London for the few days given over to the Diploma in Child Health exam.

*

Certainly good to be too busy to think. Saturday—despite everything, and ironically—my interview at the practice goes well, they offer me the position and they show me around the flat that's suitable for a married couple. It has its own staircase—a fire escape—and its own front door, and it's painted throughout in pale grey like a First Truly Deacon's Sunday suit.

Later, my sister Erin phones. 'What do you think about Dad?'

I report as far as I know. "Spose I'll give them another call for an update,' I add, 'and let them know the sad news that I've got work that'll keep me down here.'

'How was the trip then? Dire?'

'Mum'll have told you enough about what happened there: not the fine details, of course.'

'Fine enough. Didn't go well, did it? She said a few things ...'

I'll not be drawn. So Erin carries on about having fixed up a trip to visit an old art college friend. 'This friend I'm staying with has been designing posters for an exhibition, SixPack: Six Young Artists to Watch. It's at a gallery near you, as they say—actually out in the Fens a bit, converted barn, other half's a gastronomic dream according to the blurb, named Sappho's Orchard! Anyway, I'm gonna be coming over ...'

'And?'

'The short version is we've some furniture we had from family, we can afford to buy our own now. Your new place isn't furnished, QED? I'll hire a van, shall I?'

She lists the items: I accept.

'When's your exam?'

'Tuesday to Saturday.'

'Great. I'll see you Monday. And then, for London, you can stay at our place, keep an eye on Gary while I'm in Cambridge!'

Life is a rollercoaster. As a break from exam revision, I begin a desultory packing of my possessions to move out of Wil's place, and discover a pile of photocopies about the effects of recreational drugs on germ line DNA—belonging to Jenny.

Hell. I'll take the jeans over to Guthrie, and see if he can get Daisy's DNA profile from those stains.

DAZE. SATURDAY, SENNEN

At daybreak the Peninsula is wrapped in a dank, fine, drenching, Cornish drizzle. Daze however is bouncy with ideas, and she gets Hat to sell one to Jenny. 'Daze has a great idea, we all go to the party as Goths!' Daze enjoys the drive into Penzance, where she helps her stepsisters kit themselves out with dark eye shadow, purple lipstick, and pale foundation to transform their sun-tanned faces.

Hat finds hair dye: 'Oh why not!' Jenny seizes the packet from the shelf and reads out the instructions: 'Wait exactly ten minutes ...'

'It's always better for your hair to dry it naturally anyway,' says Hat.

Amuses Daze to think of the two blondes raven-haired! They buy black tights, then she leads the way to her favourite charity shops and to the Saturday second-hand clothes stall, run by a pair of her friends, where anything and everything black is looked over for its potential as a Goth-style outfit.

Finally, coffee and flapjacks in a touristy café: all three very hysterical and over the top, vying to make up little stories about the holiday people with their dripping macs and umbrellas and squalling children.

'Maybe you should've got a piercing each,' Daze jokes on the drive home.

'D'you think this is okay—I mean—a hen-night's supposed to be happy,' Hat remarks.

'She's getting married, for God's sake—becoming a guy's property!' Daze retorts. 'How happy is that? Ball and chain—hey, I should have thought of wearing one ...' *Woops*, Daze thinks, remembering Max ... but Jenny even laughs, though maybe it's bitterly. Hat isn't so sure it's funny.

*

Finding them later busy with the hair dye in the bathroom, 'Hey—how about we go in my bus!' Daze suggests. 'Cool entrance?'

'Your bus stinks,' Hat declares from under the plastic shower hat supplied to wear for twenty minutes. 'Look: I found bat-earrings!' She holds them up, laughing. 'From the joke shop?'

'You can't wear those, we're serious Goths, not Halloween witches.'

'Sorry. Shame, though.'

'Humour her,' Jenny says. 'We'll go in the bus, Daze.'

*

A couple of hours later, three black-haired, black-clad, white-faced Goths with purple lipstick and plenty of mascara climb into the painted bus. Rattling with chain belts, Maltese crosses, wearing studded dog collars, and each with a real red rose behind one ear. Daze has even tied up her hair with fluorescent pink ribbons.

Daze revs the engine. Clouds of black exhaust belch from underneath, and Hat, holding her nose, her little jet-beaded bag swinging from her arm, laughs, 'Great entrance, Daisy, if we survive the journey!'

The party's well underway as they arrive, and the strip-o-gram lad's due to arrive any minute. Clutching drinks and slices of pizza, everyone's moving towards the poolside. Daze doubles back, unnoticed, towards the house.

A few minutes later, she smiles to herself, steering expertly along the winding roads of the Penwith peninsula under a big, almost full moon. What luck they never asked about something bulky wrapped in that old eiderdown Caro had stuffed into the garden shed after the cat had her kittens on it last year, meaning to burn it.

The stripper was so embarrassing. Max has a better body—even Bryn has! I looked around to share that thought with Daze, couldn't see her. We all dissolved into giggles to hide our confusion. After that, some people skinny-dipped in the pool. Several got a bit pissed. I hoped Daze wouldn't, seeing otherwise I'd have to drive that bus. Then when we came to leave, no Daze, and—no bus. Tricked! 'She's left without us! I should've known an upbeat Daze was sus! Now she's bunked and left us in the middle of nowhere!'

All around us, somnolent bodies already snoring unfemininely on sofas. 'I'm flaked: shall we doss down here?' Hat says. I leave Mum an answerphone message. Not mentioning Daze. Yes, I should've known, and even as I played along with her friendliness, kept up a closer surveillance. Suspected when I couldn't see her watching the stripper.

*

Sunday morning, we cadge a ride with some other guests. We're sleepy, but after a strong coffee I grab my opportunity to find those cassettes. Now she knows I've seen them, the logical thing would be hide them in her bedroom. But in there, things don't look quite right. I may be a little hung over, but not that much. Her bed's too neatly made: under the patchwork quilt, no duvet! In her drawers, no underwear. Her wardrobes's half empty. Jewellery, and her favourite albums, the bands she really listened to, all gone.

In the studio, I almost know already what I'm going to find. Like, nothing! The old guy stares from Des's easel but the naked torso's vanished, the cloth lies folded on the windowsill. Every Daze possession gone. Videos, sketchbook ... everything. She's on the road again. And with her conception art.

*

The bell sounds from St Sennen's, calling people to morning service, as I go back upstairs.

'Mum? Mum?' I put my head around her door. Hat's in there using Mum's remover on last night's deep purple nail varnish, and sharing a pot of coffee. Mum, having a lie-in, looks up from her book. 'Jenny. Thanks for the answerphone last night: good party? All of you back now?'

'Not quite: it looks like Daze made a pre-planned exit.'

'Oh Jen,' Mum sighs. 'I wish she wasn't such a gypsy. I thought she was happy to be back here.'

I walk over to the window, wondering whether to tell them the whole of it. You can just see the sea from here, shimmering in the sun. Inviting, if things were different. 'She's taken her work,' I say, 'in fact she's taken everything that, like, means stuff to her.'

'What?' they both gasp. 'Why'd she do that?' Hat adds.

'To, possibly, be left alone to work,' I say. A creeping horror tells me I'm implicated in this: it's like the things which happened at the Manse. In fact worse: that domino effect began with Colin. Did I start this one with my investigations?

Leaning on the sill, I say, 'Did I tell you Daze asked me to video the birth? The cassette disappeared. Then yesterday, I found it, here, in the studio. She locked me in the darkroom to keep me from finding out more. Now she's taken the videos with her. She's taken her work because—because she knows I must know what it's about.'

'You only know she's been working with Bryn, who knows all about video editing' Hat says.

'More than that. It was obvious the birth film was an integral part of what Daze'd call an installation. Actually, she'd begun on the installation before the birth. I saw something in her bus. It's *conceptual* art and *conception* art! Isn't that Daze's kind of humour?'

They gasp, horrified. 'Jenny! How can you be sure?'

I pause: let a beat go. 'I don't want to be right. But it'd be stunning, highly controversial, even if the baby was healthy and normal. What I guess might have happened—and it is only a guess—is that the father is a cousin she met at Dad's place. Remember the visitor she had who upset her? The cleaner who was cleaning up some mess in Daze's room? They'd obviously had a row. Daze chucked stuff at him, I bet. That guy's a technician, a biochemist, and might have— Look, it's all theory. Whatever, despite the deformities, she's pushed on with the idea. I can't yet prove the second video was connected, I don't even know for certain what it is, but it's possibly dated the day of conception.'

Hat is pale and stunned. 'I hope Jen's wrong,' she says.

'So do I. It could do enormous damage.'

'To Daze. To your father's professional standing. I think we should proceed with extreme caution,' Mum advises, 'Des is back tonight: he may know something. Oh Jenny: why've you kept this all to yourself?'

'Maybe because, although I began to suspect on Friday, I played along over the party and hoped to gain Daze's confidence and ask her?'

'Let's be organized,' Mum says then, shooing us towards the door of her room. 'Jenny, Hat, you can't live on black coffee, all day. How about you make brunch while I do a few phone calls—the waffle-maker's on the counter, ingredients—all the usual places.'

'Shouldn't I—'

'Jenny—waffles.'

Dismissed to displacement activity, I recall the secrecy and anxiety in the Mullins household as I beat up batter, while in the laundry room Hat silently feeds our animals. Daze yet again centre of attention and not even here to enjoy the fuss and bother.

'Who's she calling—getting Des back?' Hat has the fork we use to put out the cat food in her hand, she waggles it at me like a teacher with a piece of chalk. 'You didn't need to freak Daisy with stuff about cousins and babies. 'Spose she's gonna do some crazy thing?'

'She isn't. She took her stuff. *That's* the crazy thing she's doing, going public with a—Hat, I had no idea she'd used Dad's clinic for ... I don't even know she has. But I know people do dreadful things to each other because of how they are themselves.'

'So? Daze is unhappy, we failed her.'

'No, she was okay yesterday. Mum's thinking of calling the police, maybe the hospital as well, but I don't think she needs to. She will call Des. Come and eat something.'

When we sit down and eat, Hat takes a big spoonful of maple syrup and leans across my plate. 'Dad', she scrawls in syrup over my waffle.

'What? You mean we should call him?'

'No, Dumbo. I mean you're so like him.'

I remember what I've said to several people about Dad, 'Yes, he lives to help people.' And I think, *like I was only trying to help Daisy.*

'Jenny?' Mum's calling me.

'Yeah?'

'Des for you.'

*

Des' usual laid-back attitude sounds different after what Val has told me about him. 'Let's wait and see: more likely she's gone to a festival, meeting up with people who'd understand that video differently. It's not a frivolous whim, Daze wouldn't do it to scare people. She'll be in touch.'

'Really? Well some people always keep what they do secret.' I want to say *Murky McShanes*, but stop myself. Not a good idea.

'I'll see you this evening—don't worry you've done anything, Princess.'

After that, we agree we can't do more, and when Hat says she'll be hanging out at home anyway, I get the concerned look from Mum and 'How about we go and blow away some cobwebs, sweetie? I could do with a stroll along the cliff path and I've a cell phone now so no need to stay put here.' She gives Hat her number.

*

Time to admit to my own worries. I've avoided the subject of the Roslin rejection long enough: as we walk along the cliff path at Treen, I blurt it out.

'The letter from Edinburgh: the research station don't want me. Possibly the Guthrie name didn't help.'

'Sweetie, I'm sorry. I don't think it was all about Dad: they probably had some picture in their heads of the person they wanted for their team. If you aren't it, then you're better off not working with them. A lab's a small group ... Actually, I'm also, rather selfishly, relieved you won't be so far away from us.'

Yes: how easily I jump to conclusions. Mum's vision of me not fitting into their team somewhat mitigates the disappointment. In myself.

'So, next step?'

We negotiate a steep bit, pausing to look at the view. Almost-white sand shimmers in the sun, curving beside a turquoise and azure sea. Across the bay, the Minack Theatre clings to the cliffs.

Beautiful, isolated Cornwall. 'I'd better scour the sits vac: New Scientist, British Medical Journal.'

'And talk to what's-his-name, Dr Woods?'

'Not yet. I didn't mean to break up. A whole lot of stuff's happened I haven't told you. Basically, Max and I belong to different cultures. It's like—like West Side Story, really. We're ... scientific rationalists, their lives are ruled by texts from the Bible.'

I recount the short version of Colin's vile response to the articles on Dad's work, ending with one sentence on the marital rape. And a brief description of my caring for his father, 'Mum, I'd have done clinical medicine if I was your type of person ... and it was his *father*, how could he make me nurse him, when he's seen him making it oh-so obvious he doesn't want me around?'

The memory of his pathetic need and weakness—that I had to manage—his weight leaning on me, the smell of his sweat, the touch of his skin. Most of all, his physical likeness to Max. My emotional inadequacy is almost unbearable. 'Like I had to help his dad go to the loo!'

'Mm, well ...' Mum says.

I explain how Max just threw me that task.

'Jenny, he's trained to make snap decisions. Faced with a crisis, he'll turn to the nearest competent person and tell them what to do. He didn't think it all through. Your training means you tend to backtrack over what you did, if it didn't work perfectly. You'll consider why, set it up again, with some changes, see if you get a better result.'

'So?'

'Max assigned you a role for that time. He trusted to you to look after his father, he treated you as one of the family.'

'I felt used and incompetent. I hated doing it.'

'Move on, sweetie. Max would.'

I want to spit, I want Mum to be as angry as I am. But she's coolly rational. I think how she and Dad must've fought over this kind of thing. Which reminds me ...

'If that wasn't enough, he pushed an antique ring across the table to me when we had a coffee on the way home.'

Mum gives me a sharp look.

'He could hardly tell me about the rape, as if I'd not be able to cope. And, because they all close ranks against the unbeliever: me. But he hadn't a clue about leaving me with his Dad.'

'Oh darling ...' Her arm goes round me. But I want to move away. She senses it. 'This view always takes my breath away. And I'm bushed if you aren't. Quite a climb. Let's rest here. You can tell me anything you want to, not if you don't. I think you've had a rough time, a sharp learning curve. But I don't think you're defeated.'

Sitting on a rocky outcrop, we pull the rings from cans of ginger beer. The dog lies panting, her tongue lolling from her mouth like a pink flannel.

Re-telling the Manse experience in more detail begins to drain my anger, like pus from a wound. By the end, I feel something else welling up. 'Yes, the view's fantastic, but the rocks down there have broken a hundred little ships in their time. I *feel* defeated, I *feel* a failure. I jumped in with both feet: Max, investigating Persephone. I've lost Roslin, and I've possibly lost Max. I want to kick myself in the butt. Worse than Daisy!'

'How's that?'

'Well, of course not. I just feel … stupid,' I say, my specs misting up. 'Inept's my middle name, same as Max!'

'Darling, you're not. Neither of you.'

'Did you—did you bring the binocs? I'd like to look at—look at the Iron Age Fort?'

Mum, who knows this is really because I'm trying not to cry, rummages in her rucksack and hands them over. 'I'll wait here, shall I?'

By the time I walk slowly back to where my mother and her dog appear to be asleep, I'm facing up to grief. Mum doesn't mention Max again.

'What'll you do while you look for look for work now? Any ideas?'

'Nope. What'll Daze do? Not replace Persephone with another baby!'

Mum is quiet.

'You don't know something that you can't tell me?'

But then the cell phone rings. It's a query from a patient who's had to give up her waitressing job because she's pregnant and her blood pressure's soared. After dealing with the immediate medical questions, Mum tells me, 'Trendy little fish restaurant. They'd be grateful for someone to cover for her, to start this evening. You could try them?'

'Perfect way to revive my bank balance and forget the bad stuff. Yeah. I might. Phone number? I'll say I'm available—thank God for holiday jobs in a tourist town.'

To untangle the Persephone mystery, to get Daze, or anyone, to talk and share stuff, I'll have to be more subtle.

MAX. SUNDAY

We've only met maybe twice, but Guthrie is hearty and personal, grasping my hand, wafting aftershave over me. 'Max! How are you? How's my *bodacious* daughter?'

He claps me on the back, puts his arm around my shoulders. Saying that Daze-style word emphatically preceded by just enough calculated hesitation to tell me he's mocking Valley-type slang here.

A maid in uniform delivers us a tray of coffee.

'Jenny's at home,' I say, 'getting over being with my family.'

'Jeez, the Pastor's not flavour of the month, then? I thought that kid could handle anything.'

'My father's quite hard to take. Even for his own children. Anyhow, I came with a request: a slight medical problem an artist mayn't be aware of?'

Guthrie laughs, immediately identifies who, and asks me to expand my concerns.

'I don't know how much you know about Daze's birth family.'

'Some,' he says. With a wry face. 'My sister's crazy commune.'

'When Jenny was in Edinburgh, she visited her aunt. Val mentioned a few things: evidently, and in a million to one chance, Daze and her boyfriend in Colombia at the time of the conception are closely related. So, what do you think? We don't yet know, but if there were underlying chromosomal abnormalities, it's a possible explanation for the malformations. Obvious to us, though I haven't done the maths. One chance in four? But the point is, Jenny had an idea possibly Daze could be planning to include the baby in some art works.'

I pause. Guthrie merely listens.

'As a prominent researcher in the field of fertility, you won't want the media, were Daze to present this artwork publicly, to connect the artist's malformed baby with your clinics. And, if we can access the new methods to obtain DNA from some very small bloodstains which I know are Daisy's, we might be able to eliminate the possibility that the abnormalities are connected in any way with your technique. So I thought it might be wise to mention it to you.'

'Wise?' He laughs quietly. In that laugh, I hear dismissal of both Daze's intentions, and work, and my rightful concerns. 'I'm flattered if she's interested enough in what we do here to include us in her first major exhibition. But you have a point, Max. Damage limitation may be a tad necessary.'

A pause. 'You should make sure she attends her postnatal, they'll give her any information,' says Guthrie. 'And of course their findings on her DNA.'

So, a hint that he's not willing to get involved with me and Jenny discovering Daze's genetic profile? Fair enough, I suppose. It was a try. It might've even have pleased Jenny.

'Dr Guthrie, I've no idea where Daisy is.'

'Oh. Huh.' Guthrie rubs his chin, looks thoughtful. 'You could ask Jenny.' And then, annoyingly, 'I'm about to go away ...' (standing, looking at his watch) 'I need to be at the airport.' He bashes a button on the intercom, and speaks to his PA about tickets and luggage, then turns back to me. 'She knows Daisy better than I do. You said she's back in Cornwall.'

I jump up, about to reply, when Guthrie gives me a look. Penetratingly, he says, 'But you and she aren't seeing each other, are you? Shame. Religion's very divisive.'

'Women are unpredictable,' I say steadily. 'Religion, ambition, the weather, time of the month. She's thinking things over.'

He moves towards the door, then turns and, hand on my shoulder, says, 'These small bloodstains: where did you say they are?'

'Pair of jeans—Jenny's house.'

'I've an hour—let's go.'

*

At the house, of course, no key. *Left mine in her room.*

'No problem!' John Guthrie grins. Conspirator-like as if we both know more than I do about entering locked houses, and accessing girlfriends' rooms. We go round the back, shifting the dustbins and someone's bike as we squeeze past the overgrown shrubs. A flight of bright butterflies flashes up into the air.

'Now,' Guthrie delves into his pocket, and produces a credit card and a hairpin. It doesn't take him long to break into his daughter's house—although it's me who has to slide sideways through the kitchen window and step carefully into the sink, avoiding three mugs and a saucepan.

'Government laboratory,' he grins, folding Jenny's jeans into a neat square and tucking them into his briefcase. Off he goes to the airport, suave as always. 'I'll be in touch.'

JENNY. MONDAY MORNING

No news from or about Daisy. Hat says, 'Send Max a good luck card for his exams—you know you want too!' Yes, I do. And, trying to remember the me who was decent to Rachel, I buy and send her a card as well. To say I hope things are working out for her and Nat.

Waitressing is hectic. Maybe it's even going to be healing. I do the lunchtime slot at the expensive fish place, and have a couple of hours off before the evening diners. Decide to go home—maybe Max has written, or Daze has turned up? Hardly!

MAX. MONDAY LUNCHTIME, THE VEGETARIAN CAFÉ

'Okay: so you're over the foul mood now, are you? Or should I watch out for sparks to fly?'

Erin and I are settled in a window seat at Lily's place. We have slices of veggie quiche and mugs of milky coffee. 'I think the sparks are over for now,' I say.

'Well the shades make your becoming-ex-housemate very sexy, what-ever. Wil, you said? A biotech wizard? When he, Wil, opened the door to me, I was impressed.'

'Och, it was an accident: and after all, he could've had a worse partner—I knew what to do until we went to casualty.'

Erin raises an eyebrow at me, then thoughtfully takes another forkful of quiche. Cameron, my gorgeous nephew, wriggles on her lap and nuzzles for her breast. Across the shop, Lily and another woman behind the counter diss each other as they bustle about.

'Ironically, you know who I almost played a game with, when I was up North? Col. Rache's Colin. I'd no' mind bashing the hell out of him some time ... though that's the wrong approach.'

'Mum said, you'd hardly been in touch since you came back.'

'I am always hardly in touch, according to Mum! I've noticed you and she are closer than you were,' and I nod at Cameron, 'is he *the ties that bind*?'

'Stop it, Max. I know what you're doing.'

'You do, do you?'

'You're having a go because I left home for good, and now in your eyes I'm crawling back to the family, settled down with a good man and a legitimate child to my name. It's not like you, and it's not like that.'

'No?'

'Are you sorry you didn't make it with Rache?'

'Rache! I'm angry at Dad's teaching that led to her pairing off with that rat. I'm incandescent—when I think about it—with the whole First Truly screwed-up lifestyle. I'm no' regretting Rachel, but I may, I just may, be kicking myself about for an idiot whenever I think of Jenny! From Dad giving me the wee talk, to us finding Rachel, and my stupidly giving Jenny the task of caring for Dad while I collected Mum from Carlisle, that trip was a disaster! The game with Wil was probably the first time my emotions got the better of me. Consider that week: Rachel was attacked, Dad got ill, Jenny walked away, then I assisted at a very delicate operation, and we lost the patient. A child I'd known several years on and off. So then, Friday evening, I'd an outburst of negative energy, bashed a squash ball a bit too hard and directionless. Wil's eye is perfectly okay, and I'm sorry.'

'This isn't about that. Actually, it's about me.'

'You're okay aren't you? I mean, you and Gary, you are—okay?'

'Yeah, yeah we're fine.' Erin looks about, 'Do they allow breastfeeding here? They ought to.'

And whether they do or not (I suspect they do, seeing they employ Lily and display a whole rack of leaflets on every possible alternative subject), she shifts Cameron about, and opens her shirt. By now the café's crowded with lunch customers. Cam latches on greedily, nobody objects.

'Only, after all the feminist stuff and the independence, as you said, you've trammelled yourself with a legalised relationship, first the white dress, then—him—he's lovely but ...'

She takes a long look at me. 'People change. No, they don't change, they find something which makes sense. We felt marriage was right for us. It's more than just living under the same roof and having a sexual relationship! It exists as itself, like Gary and I were two halves who've become one whole, and not only and primarily by the act of sex. I never liked the way Dad puts it: every mature male should find a suitable good woman to housekeep and bear children. That's antediluvian. What about what the good woman wants? Define *good*!'

She looks down at Cameron, and then, at the tabletop, not at me. 'Max, I should've said this before: I should've said ... that I'm desperately sorry I messed up your relationship.'

'Mine? How?'

'With Jenny: when Dad was taken ill the first time. Because I'd spent so long at school waiting to escape the manse, once I was in London, at college, I knew if I came back ... I'd have to be the dutiful daughter. So I just disappeared myself, didn't answer the phone, didn't call home: let you take the brunt of the caring and the sorting out of everybody. Didn't think it'd do any harm, seeing you're ...'

'His blue-eyed boy? Well I'm not now! Nor Jenny's: it was she who got hurt, it's she you should—. Och, can we move on from this? Now I've got the job and the flat, you want to pass me some of the furniture Gary's Gran gave you, and I'm grateful you drove up here with it, and I don't want us to spoil everything with a row.'

Erin sorts Cam and reaches into her bag, out comes one of those dreaded cassettes recorded by our father. 'Mum sent me this. You ought to listen to it. It's not his usual leading-edge fundamentalist ranting.'

'Hi guys!'

Before I can react to what Erin's said with a reply dripping with cynical realism, someone's by our table with a tray of soup and salad. I'm astounded: it's *Daisy*.

'OK if I join you?'

DAZE

Max's sister is wearing a white shirt over a black bra: this, Daze decides, isn't a mistake, it's a fashion statement. Seeing she has on denim overalls with the bib supported by only one strap.

And, oh *shit*, a sucking baby.

Max sits back, after the introductions. 'Hi,' Daze says again, pinning on a smile, addressing Cameron. He looks at her very seriously, then sicks up some milk.

Erin wipes his front, 'Oops! Sorry!'

Max says, 'Daze ...' and Daze thinks, *He's embarrassed by me coming over when they had the baby with them. Or maybe he was going to ask about Jenny, and changed his mind.*

'Daze,' Max says, 'we were going to finish with some of their home made ice cream: can I get you one?'

'Uh uh, nah, thank you,' Daze tells him, and dips her roll into her soup.

Max goes to the counter and comes back with two untidily heaped bowls of chocolate ice cream, topped with crushed hazel nuts. 'Ooh, yum!' says his sister. The baby waves his arms, joining in the excitement, and up comes a gobbet more milk.

'You not busy then, Max?' Daze asks, ignoring her own thoughts which tell her that yes, in reality it probably would've been impossibly difficult to develop her project and care for someone who hiccupped up their meals so readily.

'I am busy, I'm about to go to London for an exam. And Erin's come over with some furniture for my new home.'

'Unfurnished: a step up, hey?' Erin says, teasingly.

'You want any help shifting your stuff then?' Daze offers. 'I've got the bus with me.'

'It's a kind thought, but you shouldn't be heaving stuff around yet, Daze.'

'God,' Daze says. 'I'm tougher than that, you know.' To demonstrate, wickedly, she pulls up her sleeve and offers Max her hand, elbow on the table, 'arm wrestle?'

'Really, I'm grateful you offered ...' he says, declining, eyes on her slender, but muscular, arm and the broad studded leather dog collar round her wrist.

'Aw, go on!'

At several nudges from Erin, Max submits. The tussle is long, swaying first this way, then that. Finally Max grounds Daze's fist to the tabletop, and Erin, putting down her spoon, claps Cameron's hands.

'There, the baby wants to learn!'

'So, what's your daytime job?'

Glancing at her man-size watch, 'Daytime now, innit?' Daze says. 'I'm an artist. Professional boho. Scrounger.'

'Specialist in some quite dark subjects,' Max adds.

*

As they enter Max's new flat, Erin exclaims, 'Oh my God: battleship grey! This place's like a manse.'

'Isn't the usual phrase, *a morgue*?'

'A manse: cheerless, serious-minded, and uninviting. A porch to the Last Judgment. What it needs is some serious transformation. I'm okay for a couple of extra days up here. You, Daisy?'

'Yeah, yeah ...'

'Right, kid bro: you've got yourself a team. We'll wield the brushes while you wield the pen and scalpel, or however you doctors do five-day exam stints. Incidentally, where's it you know Daze from?'

'Jenny's stepsister.'

'Right.'

'A porch to the Last Judgment? Awesome. Wicked. Got possibilities: what did you say you do?' Daze asks.

Erin laughs. 'Graphic artist, school textbooks! I'd like to get into comic books. Know my last judgment? I think the old Max is somewhere in there, deep down. I think Jenny was a step on the way to curing his soul of the insidious doctrines of long-faced preachers, which don't suit his fun-loving nature.'

Daze warms to this woman. 'I've got some casting to do, but I can give you a day.'

'Casting?'

'Fibreglass.'

'Wow: I've never done that. Don't you need goggles and masks and stuff?'

'Borrowed from my old college.'

'Right, well, today or ...'

'Couple of days' time?'

When I'm not out, running about between tables with platters of exquisite seafood for the tourists, I'm either sleeping or paging through the possible research posts at other universities than Cambridge. Oxford? Imperial College, London? Or even Monash, Australia or Wisconsin, USA?

Really, applying from West Cornwall isn't practical: I ought to be nearer a proper centre with a decent library packed with relevant journals, and easy travelling to interviews. Really, I ought to think about returning to Cambridge, and facing walking into Max in the street.

When I go home, there's a packet from Edinburgh on the mat. Big italic handwriting—Val's. Inside, a whole pile of photos and a note: *Jenny, I found these, and if you want, when you've looked, give me a call. XX Val.*

Found? Interesting. How come I didn't see them when she had the album out? Val was turning the pages, she didn't let me browse, and she kept pointing at irrelevant people like Old Jock the boatman or whoever, and yattering about raising sheep. These photos are clearer than those 'core group' ones. Several are individual families, and Val's put names on the backs. Here's the one of her with Harris and Lewis, and their Dad. Bunny McGregor. And here's the Potters, Des, Jewels, Daze. And this is Daze's Aunt Loose, with her slim rangy guy and a little boy, about three years old.

'Loose, Sunshine, and *smudge*.' Wouldn't you just know—the only name I can't read. Dropped something on it, all smudgy. 'Sunshine.' I remember Harris and Lewis laughing, as I look again, carefully, at the photos. That man's so like Shane. Sunshine'd be that age now.

Here they are again, swinging that child between them as they walk. The child's even got a pony tail like his father. Must be his father, they are so alike. *He must be Shane*, who Lily's convinced is father to Daze's baby (and so am I). Two families with one child, several families with at least two or several. Sunshine's Mum is Loose, who Val said is Jewels's sister. This is Daze's cousin ... Thinking back to my theory at the manse, I wonder: any significance? Daze is an only—what if Sunshine was as well?

Heading for the fridge, taking out a Diet Coke, picking an apple from the fruit bowl, tossing thoughts around. My head spins. I am a geneticist, after all. I want to call Max, share ideas with him, see how the exam went. But, hell, his crazy family's beliefs have screwed everything up.

I'll call Val. She offered. Chuck apple core into the bin with decisive gesture! Say no to dog asking for a walk. Dial Val's number. Can check part of my theory.

'Your photos—yeah, great. Thanks. I was looking at the one of—Loose, is it? Daze's Mum's sister—Daze's aunt—Who's the guy?

Val laughs, 'Jack the Lad McShane.'

McShane. *Sunshine's family.* Yay! Keep calm!

Sunshine changed his name, to Shane McShane?

'Was Jack a lad? Didn't you hint that Jack had two girlfriends with him when he arrived? And weren't they Loose and her sister, Daze's mum?'

'I think Jack settled for Loose soon enough.'

'You'd still say the McShanes weren't murky?'

'No more than the rest of us hairy hippies,' Val laughs.

'Daisy has no siblings. How many McShane children? There's only one in your photos.'

'Just Sunshine. You know, Jenny, it was kind of sad: both sisters suffered several miscarriages. Probably the lifestyle: tough for women, heavy lifting—logs for fires, communal cooking pots, hauling boats ashore and stores from boats, even the sheep if they got caught in a dangerous place. And we ate a subsistence diet. Still, they both had one healthy child, and I had two. I felt sick as a dog all the way, which is supposed to be a good sign—I guess I naturally produce oodles of the right hormones ... they—little slight creatures—unfortunately weren't that type.'

My mouth opens, and shuts. Something says to me, don't go blagging to Val about Persephone. Same as I didn't want to ask Daze about the video.

'That's so sad. Anyhow, thanks for the photos and letting me know a bit more.'

We say goodbye. I stand there holding the receiver, thinking ...

How about this? Research is beginning to show that trisomy 16, for example, is the probable cause of many miscarriages. Embryos with three sets of chromosome 16 pretty much never survive.

Sisters Jewels and Loose have one live child each, and suffered several miscarriages. Both sisters arrived with Jack. More spin if Jewels and Jack never really severed sexual connections despite Val's protests, as well as the girls carrying some faulty gene ... I'd need to somehow test Daisy, and Shane as well, to prove if they're half-siblings. Addenbrooke's wouldn't let me near her blood test from the day of the birth.

Whatever, I'm thinking there could be a genetic problem in the Jewels and Loose family. Then the sisters' only surviving offspring make a baby together. Cousins would have a one in four chance of a malformed fetus, and what if they're more than that—half-siblings?

I put the phone back. And think about the conception tape. Daze said, 'He wasn't like, my boyfriend!' But, *he was a technician.* Would she—would they? *'Daddy's Girl.'*

Can't think about it now. It's time to go back to work.

I get home late, but Mum's still up. 'Sweetie! I was doing some paper-work and having a cup of tea, join me?'

'Please. We didn't talk about my visit, but now Val's sent me some photos of Daze's birth family.' Mum gives me a look. 'In Edinburgh, Val told me stuff you've never said: like Des's family lived on her commune. Daze was a baby there.'

'Darling, I never kept anything from you!' Mum exclaims.

'Really? Was that nothing?'

'Well I thought—Maybe I didn't.'

'Val told me how she introduced you to Des.'

'She wrote cards to each of us saying the other was a single parent moving to Cornwall. It's a sizeable county, Jen. And it never crossed my mind one of Val's contacts …'

'Did you know much about their commune life?'

'Of course Val told me Des had lived there with his family. He felt he'd moved on and wasn't that person any more. I think that's true.'

'But you don't believe in secrecy. Or Dad's crablike explanations. What about Daze's birth certificate: has he kept her from seeing it?'

'She was actually born in a Glasgow hospital. And the subject of the commune's never been discussed because it never came up. If Daze wants to know more, it's for Des to tell her.'

'Didn't he even tell you about how Jewels and Loose both had repeated miscarriages? The research is new but possibly relevant to Persephone. If you'd known about Jewels and her sister, you could've warned Daze: Des can't've not realised Daze's been having sex for years. Probably unprotected sometimes.'

'Some people, well, they feel a genetic problem's a kind of slur, what used to be called bad blood,' Mum says.

'That is so dated. Nobody'd think that today.'

'Jenny, they do.'

'I guess. You're more understanding than me.'

'I'm just older, sweetie! The idealism's worn through!'

'You're a doctor. Dad's a fertility expert. What was Des thinking, when he first heard about Persephone: when he saw Daze at Addenbrooke's?'

'We were both upset, Persephone was his first grandchild, he was dev-astated. Looking back, maybe I should've—'

'Yeah, if you could've. Des not sharing stuff with you, it's not secrecy, it's deception. He took a risk. Suppose you'd had a screwed-up baby?'

'Darling, that's a strange way to put it. Besides, we'd agreed not to have a child together.'

Mum pauses: I've been too brutally honest. Then she says evenly, 'Des and I'll work it through, sweetie. So will you.'

And so to bed, as the old diarist we learned about in history, Mr Pepys, used to say. I don't sleep. My mind whirrs into action. Daze called that video *Daddy's Girl*, she knew it was a female. To screen embryos they must be created outside the womb.

WEDNESDAY

I wake to a silent house: have overslept, it's mid-morning.

I'm ready to take the next step: I call Mum.

'Can I ask you something? On our walk, your silence implied Daze'd have trouble conceiving. Was it because she's had a brush with a love bug?'

'A PID? Well, you know Daze's selection of boyfriends, when doing the festival circuits, wasn't that good to begin with.'

'Did she or did she not? Or aren't you allowed to do more than heavy hints?'

'Sweetie, I'm in the middle of a busy surgery: is this discussion important?'

'Sorry: oh sorry, sorry. You see, I need to know if Daze was likely to have needed IVF to conceive: that is to have a reason to give someone in order to get the treatment? Not Dad, but one of his staff? To talk them around?'

'Daze came panicking home from college, running a fever. The college doctor who diagnosed her mentioned she'd probably picked up an infection several years previously. Now it was showing itself. She was frantic about long term effects—'

'And that'd maybe mean—'

'Chlamydia can be asymptomatic in many women and thus remain untreated, can spread through the reproductive organs and ultimately … pain, fever, etc. They seek help too late. That can be a scenario.'

'Thanks Mum.'

I'm beginning to think I know what that other tape is: Dad gave me a clue when he took me to his office at the Drey and showed me on a TV monitor three little human embryos he'd created! I've a hunch where and how Daze obtained it. I feel certain now about the art of conception.

But if she succeeds with her exhibition, and if she's chosen to be considered for the Turner, what about Dad's reputation as a fertility expert? When the media trace the story to its roots? Dad firmly believes all embryos should be screened, to eliminate misery and suffering. Shane evidently looked at one aspect of that embryo, but why not the other, which was more vital?

Scientists don't display these babies. If Daze thinks she can use Dad's work to tell her story, imagining she's coolly, objectively, displaying to public view what the humane scientist keeps under wraps, she's in a dangerous place. She's displaying what shouldn't be put in a gallery to scare, and titillate, and entertain. Dad's work, and mine, are focused on helping sort the problems. We keep the knowledge to ourselves for a good reason: taste, decency, compassion. And people don't understand how real science proceeds. It's a frustratingly slow process. They don't know about the failures and the tiny steps. Like Colin, and that media article, Daze will destroy the good because she doesn't understand!

Should I call Dad?

His PA says coolly, 'Dr Guthrie's away until next weekend. Would you like to leave a message?'

No point yet: would sound too bizarre. Who could talk Daze out of this? Max ... she admires him, he helped her when she was in Addenbrooke's. Max is the only person who might dissuade her. But I've no idea where she is. And Max didn't even acknowledge the card I sent to wish him luck.

*

Val's already shown me another side of my stepfather: I've seen Daisy in Des, and now before I leave for work I confront him. 'Listen, Des, Val told me about the commune. I think you should've told Daisy at least that her mum had fertility problems. When the chromosomes break, or mis-attach, the signals are jammed, mixed, distorted, everything goes horribly awry. The biochemistry is wrong. So the mum's body usually— not always—rejects the embryo. Sometimes, when they should, they don't. It's mega unfair to dump ignorance of something so significant on a person.'

'Not everyone shares your attitude to disability and diversity,' Des says coldly.

'You could've let her keep in touch with her other relatives.'

I turn away, and go to change into my waitressing clothes. I know I didn't speak to him the right way: it was unkind, and unnecessary. But I'm worried about my Dad's reputation. As I leave, Des and Mum are in the garden, sharing a bottle of wine: Mum is talking earnestly, Des is studying her face. He looks grim.

Is he sorry I know so much that Daze doesn't? That I have a theory about Persephone's deformities?

Later, I imagine what Des said as a possibility: suppose when the bio-chemistry went wrong, Daze decided to accept that as a dark spin on the process of conception?

It doesn't add up. Why'd she do that? And put Dad's reputation in danger? Makes no sense.

Get home and decide to call Max. A woman answers. 'Oh, Max doesn't live here any more. Hey, is that Jenny? He left this number, where he's gone.'

Relieved to hear she's nothing to do with him. But my heart turns over. 'Gone?'

'Flat that goes with the job.' She gives me the number, I write it on my hand. ·

'Thanks.' I leave a message.

Erin phones. 'Your friend Daisy: is she a bit unstable or what?'

'What's she done?'

'Walked out on me. We're midway through painting your bedroom wall when she downs tools and says she's remembered something she has to do!'

'Did you, maybe, say something?'

'Nothing heavy. I showed an interest in her work.'

'You asked her what she's doing, and she took exception?'

'Daze's a Goth, right? Jude, my friend, who's designing the SixPack exhibition poster, remember? She mentioned one of the young artists is a bat-caver who's working on some theme involving the developing human embryo. Daze had told me she'd been casting a female body in fibreglass, which had to accommodate a video player in order to replay a video of a developing embryo, and a birth ...'

'She told you she's got a film of the embryo—?

'I said, ace idea, that'll be totally controversial. A birth video's what everyone does now, but the spin on it here's—oh you know, I wittered about how topical, with that government committee deciding on what fertility research's permitted. I asked Daze whether she'd been able to get inside a clinic for her research. Jenny's dad's a fertility doctor, isn't he?'

Holding back fury at Erin's inadvertent and less than tactful clod-hopping all over Daze's sensibilities, I say, 'You know why I told her she shouldn't help with the move, don't you?'

'Should I?'

'Daze just had a baby. A dysmorphic, malformed baby! Which died.'

'Damn: I couldn't know that, could I? Nobody told me! And I've had Cam with me all this time! She wasn't upset before, she didn't seem upset. By him. That he's normal.'

'Yes, but that's not the point: the point is that Daze's been working on this mysterious project and—You couldn't have known, but Jenny was there at the birth and so was I, you get the picture?'

'No. Something about your relationship?'

'Erin, since when were you a total airhead? Daze doesn't want any more members of our family interfering in her life. I'd imagine she's trying to forget?'

Awkward pause. 'Well, sorry I stepped on her memories.'

'Yes. I'm sorry. Should've warned you.'

What Erin's described sounds harmless enough as a weird, contemporary artistic statement. But harmless would end if it includes Jenny's tape of Persephone's birth. And where else could Daze have obtained footage of the developing embryo, but at Guthrie's Colombian place?

'Did Daisy tell you anything else?'

'She was explaining some special effects, but I didn't get to learn much more because I asked my dumb question, and she found an excuse to scarper. I'm really sorry. If only you'd told me.'

With an effort, 'It's not your fault,' I say.

'She hinted Jenny's still locked into the childhood competition between the two of them. Obsessive. Needs to chill out, should take up Yoga.'

'That so?' I respond.

'Isn't Jenny the oldest girl? The appointed protector of the others by busy Mum, and the responsible heir apparent. Do something nice to show you still care about her: at least try being cheesy and sending some flowers. Oldests have become used to not being spoilt.'

*

Since that time we talked at Lily's café, Erin's definition of marriage has been working on my brain. Things fall into place. Gary and Erin have this idea of marriage as a unity of souls. By contrast Dad's definition, the unity of bodies, is ironically earthbound despite his emphasis on God.

My assumption after Jenny and I slept together was Dad's definition: we are committed because we do this thing. I even found it was like coming out of the chrysalis, becoming the butterfly, making my own choices. Saw our sleeping together as symbolic. Told myself it was a sort of marriage!

The worst realisation is, Jenny doesn't believe that. To her, we did some physical act, but that didn't make us united in a permanent way. While I assumed because we were almost married she'd cooperate in caring for Rachel, in helping with Dad. That it was part of the deal, that it was the service part of love.

The irony there is that she's the girl in this situation.

While I assumed we'd committed ourselves to each other, and were just waiting now for the public bit, the wedding service, Jenny was bouncing along having fun, being free, living for the moment.

The irony is she's the girl!

Is it that which drives me mad with a renewed emotional pain? *Fool, fool, fool.* Headbanger. Idiot.

She never understood your culture!

JENNY. THURSDAY MID-AFTERNOON, SENNEN

I arrive home mid-afternoon to a small parcel forwarded from my college. A letter, addressed in Dad's confident black scrawl. And a small, cellphane-windowed box delivered by the florist in Penzance.

Oh my God, a yellow rose, just one. There's a note: '*If I cause you pain, who is there to make me glad but the one I have pained?* All apologies, and love, Max. PS. I did listen to what you learned from Val: and realised D's *genes* may've stained *yours?*'

Is this his response to my card?

The weird quote's awful, makes me feel responsible for his emotional state, whatever that is. I can't be. I shouldn't be. And the postscript: he's elliptical as always. But, he's right. About the *jeans*. After Val's information, if I could access a lab away from Addenbrooke's and conflict of interest, we could have any spots of Daze's blood on my old jeans analysed. Maybe Dad would help? Then if I could get Max and Daze together—if we could find Daze—Max might dissuade Daze from her stupid, dangerous art project.

I hardly dare touch the rose. Does it have a scent? A faint sweetness. It's delicate: it's whatever Max and I have now. Fragile, but maybe ...? I don't know. I don't want to be put in a trap like Fee and Rachel!

What's Dad written about?

'... *a great opportunity to demonstrate your skills on the very edge of emerging areas of biotech, both at micromanipulation and as my PR officer ... Eat your heart out, Roslin! We can also take in all the Colombian sites you quite rightly envied Daisy last year, as I'm planning to spend more time at that clinic.*'

He's offering me work. It's a thought. Though would I do his public relations for him better than he does it for himself? Hardly.

Why is he planning to spend more time out of the country now? Because I'm no longer at Cambridge? Because he's anticipating that the new Human Fertilisation and Embryology Authority, once formed, might restrict the research potential too much? Would being part of his empire be only another kind of trap?

What's in the parcel, and who sent it? No 'sender' label. As I open it, out falls a notelet and a tiny object wrapped in tissue paper.

'*I found this in the bathroom, and think it must be yours.*'

Val's ring! Thought I'd left that at the service station where I was so awful to Max. But no. Fee found it in the kids' bathroom. The way Alisdair stared, I'd have expected that if any of the Mullins family got hold of it, they'd chuck it away.

Makes me think how I cared so much about Max, then junked everything because he wanted me to wear another sort of ring. I don't exactly want to read the rest of Fee's message. But having put Val's ring on again, kind of fast and sideways, I do.

Jenny, I did enjoy our talk and all you said about your work: you have a true talent for explaining complicated science in understandable, and appealing, terms.

We are all well here. Alisdair continues to make a good recovery from his attack and preached his first, wonderful, sermon on Sunday morning. I have sent you a copy ...

Yes, as I tip it out of the parcel, a cassette with last Sunday's date!

... hoping that you can use your powers of persuasion on Max, who I know perfectly well does not play the cassettes we send him week by week. Please, Jenny, even if Max will not listen, listen yourself to what Alisdair says. Your visit was not a disaster for First Truly and the Manse family: it was an example of God's blessing.

Fee is a lovely person. You can't hate her. But God's blessing? How?

Something I forgot I had with me at the Manse was the tiny leather-bound book, inscribed *James Maxwell Mullins from Grandad, Thy Word is a Lamp unto my Feet*. I reach for it now: it falls open at a Psalm. And there's the quote Val and Fee both know, the developing fetus being *woven together*! Lovely poetry for a remarkable process. *Search me, O God, and know my heart; test me and know my anxious thoughts*. If the book falls open at this page, then Max must've—must—find a lot of meaning there. And I've got anxious thoughts too.

The cassette's another ballgame. And I have to rush to do my evening shift at the restaurant.

Later, as home settles into silence, curiosity overcomes distaste. I just have to insert Pastor Mullins's tape into my player, and press play.

The familiar, Scottish voice. *'My passage today is from Matthew* 22: 14–22.'

A woman reads that same Bible passage I heard at First Truly. A horrible experience, that service. *'God demands everything.'* Under the Pastor's eye. With Max all distant-moody. Put me right off God, whatever sentimental thoughts about his possible existence Minister Melanie's ceremony for Persephone had suggested.

So, what's Max's father got to say, since Rachel was raped? He kicks off by telling everyone there's more to learn on what we owe Caesar and what we owe God. Reaching over to switch off the tape, I stop myself. Do I need to be afraid of him? After Max's apology ... I have to put all this Mullins stuff together and make it mean something.

Did you hear the story of the man whose home was threatened by a flood? As he stands on the steps someone comes by in a tall truck and offers him help to escape. He says, 'thank you, but no, God will save me'.

As the waters rise and the man is looking out of an upstairs window, someone comes by in a motor boat and offers to rescue him. He again says, 'thank you, but no, God will save me'.

The waters continue to rise, the man is on his rooftop. A helicopter comes by and drops a ladder down. But the man calls up, 'thank you, but no, God will save me'. The waters rise even higher and the man drowns.

What's his point?

By now in heaven, he asks God why he did not rescue him. God replies, 'I sent you a tall truck, a motor boat, and a helicopter. What more did you want?'

Alistair pauses: the congregation shifts about and laughs. I take off my black waitress skirt and white shirt, and reach for my pyjamas.

Now, suppose the man had not even realised that he needed help? Suppose in his arrogance he had shut his eyes to the rising floodwaters? From this pulpit today, I confess to you that I am that man.

The congregation gasps. As I do; would my father admit he's done wrong? What do I do about Fee's request? Go to Cambridge and try to see Max?

*

Friday, I decide yes, I shall. And talk to Dr Woods about work.

Where *is* Max? Maybe he never got my card? If only we all had cellphones!

MAX. SATURDAY EVENING

Home at last, my own place: the flat is brill—I have an ace sister, both of us trained by Dad and Mum of course to service and perfectionism! Canary coloured bedroom walls, a tasteful off white in the living room, none of that iron grey left. On my new-old sofa, slightly the worse for wear, lies a small blue teddy—Cameron's. This gives me a strange pang— if Jenny had agreed to marriage, what about babies? Set up by my religion, I'd have assumed we'd have several, and soon. The cold realisation is probably not. Back to the present moment: clasping teddy in one hand, pressing the answerphone button with the other, Jenny's is the first voice I hear.

Message one, left Tuesday evening: *'Max? Daze has disappeared. I found my lost cassette and she bunked off. I think I was on to her reason for wanting a baby ... she's working on an installation, title is* Daddy's Girl *... call me?'*

Message two: *'Max, where are you? Val sent me photos and I spoke to her! Remember Daze and Shane's mothers are sisters. Both had one live child and several miscarriages: possibly a genetic problem? We must stop Daze display-ing Persephone or being in any way connected to Dad or fertility work!'*

And finally, *'Now even your family's asking me to be their courier to you!'*

So what's my family up to now?

Jenny, where are you? I know where Daisy *was*. Seems we each have half an answer to the problem!

*

Sunday morning, first thing, I set out for where Daze might be, or at least where I might find somebody who knows: Sappho's Garden Restaurant and the Mill Gallery. I'd kick myself forever if publicity and grief made that poor girl do something stupid. Daisy doesn't realise how putting her grief in the public domain might rebound nastily on herself, when the critics write it up, and the public has its say.

And I'd be as sorry as anyone to see good, ongoing work on human reproduction becoming wrongly discredited, even if I don't think all of what people like Guthrie do is ethical. Even if I knew what I suspect: that he uses the ova of aborted fetuses in his research, or sells them on to other labs.

Turning into the gravel drive of the trendy gallery-cum-foodie's-delight, I see a creamy yellow Mercedes leaving. I slow, give him space. Notice the driver: John Guthrie! He waves, grins, and accelerates away.

The Gallery's marked *Closed*: outside on a bench is Daisy. 'What the hell?' she says.

'Daze—Daze, was that who I think it was?'

'Who did you think it was?'

'Jenny's father? Dr Guthrie? Your employer in Colombia?'

'Good eyesight, Max.'

Ignoring her attitude. 'Can I join you a second?'

'Go ahead. Though it looks like rain to me.'

'We doctors have a saying, it goes back a long way, to when medicine had far less in its range of clinical tricks than we have now. *First do no harm.* That sound familiar?'

'No. You came to say?'

'I could say, your family's worried about you. Disappearing without leaving an address. But it's me who's worried, that the Daze I met and knew when you were in hospital has run off somewhere. D'you know where that Daze went?'

'I was in shock, wasn't I? Freaked out?'

'What I noticed was, while your parents were a bit freaked, how beautifully *you* managed to cope. It's a huge trauma giving birth your first time—I'm told—a major life experience for a woman—then, you discovered Persephone wasn't quite right, and she wasn't going to live—'

'Cut it out, the soapy stuff, Max! What're you here for? You aren't an artist, why hang about a gallery in the back of nowhere?'

'But you're an artist. First time we met, remember the picture you were working on? A mother and child?'

'A child crucified on a mother, yeah. So what?'

A cloud drifts over the sun. We sit silent in the chill it brings. Then 'Quite close to home, that picture, maybe?'

'What?'

'Your Mum walked out. There's other ways a child can feel crucified by the parent though.' Here, I am thinking of Dad, but I don't say, and I wait for Daze. She hesitates, chewing a few strands of her black, wavy hair. Her nails are bitten to the quick: did I notice that before?

'Okay, you're here like John was, to stop me. I had this really cool idea, and first Shane deceives me and uses his own filthy spunk, and then … the rest is history.'

'Shane?'

'A technician guy I asked to do one simple thing: he screwed up. Bugger him.'

'He screwed up. He was involved with your work how, Daze?'

'He's got weird genes, hasn't he? John—John told me he'd been to Colombia to check Shane's files, and Shane's got defective DNA of some kind. He'd sworn he was giving me superior stuff, couldn't get it, so he just jerks off in the toilet and brings me his filthy muck, doesn't he? And my baby's born screwed.'

'You'll have to help me here, Daze: you're talking about a medical procedure? And damaged DNA?'

'Okay: I'm mad as hell with one of John Guthrie's technicians who spun me a story about how he had access to the sperm bank, where they keep the—raw materials for making babies, yeah? I ask him then, Could you do what it takes to get me one, a baby? Explained I'd need to overcome a bit of a blocked tube problem, and I wanted the embryo to be a girl.

An' when Persephone's born all weird, Shane comes knocking on my door, we have one hell of a barney when I tell him how he must've done it all wrong in his laboratory, doesn't know as much as he claimed. An' he throws back at me, well I'd insisted, he'd blagged about having access but he doesn't have, he'd lied, he'd had to use his own stuff!'

Daddy's Girl: a public accusation of Shane? Sounds like Guthrie's been and uncovered Shane's carrying some damaged DNA: he made the same guesses as Jen. And, according to her, Daze and Shane are cousins.

Meanwhile, tears stream down Daze's face and she whips her hand across to wipe mucus from her nose. She doesn't sob, she bends over silently, and shakes.

'Daze!' I put my hand on her back, hoping to reassure.

'Don't!' She springs upright again. 'Don't be kind. I'm all made of shit—Mum knew that back when—'

'Well at least have this, and clean yourself up a bit. I hand her my clean handkerchief (brought in case this happened). 'So Daze, what I remember isn't that you're shit but you're a loving mother, I remember the naming ceremony and it was the most moving thing I've ever seen. In my clinical work so far. It was amazing. Your acceptance of Persephone, your gentleness with her.'

'Oh, I can do it when it's needed.'

'Maybe that is the real Daisy?'

'Wanna bet? I was gonna show her off in her Moses basket as part of the exhibit, you know. *Conception Art*, hey, different, eh?'

Shocked, amazed, I just manage to assume a cool exterior. 'Yeah, different. Maybe not quite the best beginning for a baby, but you have a certain flair, inspiration, ingenuity ...'

She grins. 'An artist has to push the boundaries.'

'Was that what you said to Dr Guthrie back before I arrived?'

'Nah. I told him to bugger off, didn't I?'

'Perhaps—shall we go over to the Drey, and see if you and he can ...'

Rain begins to fall from the purple sky, a soft, persistent, misty rain. Standing, 'Do a deal?' Daisy suggests.

'A deal?'

'Over Shane, and my loss of earnings—well, my having lost my exhibit if I agree to pull out, to save his clinic's reputation? Seeing it wasn't actually his clinic's fault, but his employee's?'

Incorrigible, I think. Caroline certainly raises them, her own and other people's. Determined, focused young women. The kind Dad dislikes!

'I can't believe I was so naïve, that Shane got away with a thing so obvious,' Daisy says, as I start the car.

'What's worse is, we're cousins and I thought that was kinda cute. Then Jenny kept going on about cousins—having babies together was unwise, blah, blah—but we didn't know we were at the time, did we? Only after we talked about our Mums' daft nicknames, and then it was too late. "Let your legs hang a bit loose," he said, and he laughed—my legs were up in those stirrup things! He was putting that straw thing in me, to feed the embryo up inside—and he said "My Mum's nickname, Loose for Lucy, you see," and we got talking ... about the places he grew up, about having shit parents like his, and my mum, about meeting John Guthrie ... about John being his inspiration, as well as mine, about chance in a million, and stuff.'

'D'you miss him, despite what he did?'

'Miss him? The screwed-up pothead? No. You miss my bossy sister?'

'Yep. I do. So Shane used, did he?'

But Daze goes silent on me. After a while I glance sideways, see her pert plum-lipsticked mouth pursed shut, and recall driving Mum home from Carlisle. My dismayed astonishment at what she'd planned—suppressed for the moments we talked earlier—surfaces.

'Daze, how and why did you ever imagine you could present a live baby as an art object?'

'Conception art, innit? Max, you're a scientist, don't even try to understand.'

'I'm a human being, and I think I know where the boundaries lie. You've definitely transgressed them in terms of more than public taste.'

'God,' she says, 'the minister's son speaks. Or the paediatrician. Leave it? Like what am I doing in your car?'

'We're going to the Drey clinic, and you are planning your apology to John Guthrie for taking advantage ... I thought better of you, Daisy.' Suddenly I hear Dad's voice in mine, and how this lecture's veering towards his style. 'Let's agree to differ, and you and Guthrie sort it? Just, think of other people. Your parents, your sisters, Persephone herself? That's all I'm going to say. We're nearly there: you want me to come in with you?' I ask, trying my best to resist the impulse to march her inside and keep an eye on her until she's delivered into Guthrie's office.

'No way: all that stuff I did, the service an' that, Lily's funeral, Melanie's ministry, I didn't believe it, I did it all for them.'

'And the naming: for them? For you? For me?'

'Public relations!'

'I didn't hear that. Here we are, off you go ...'

She gets out, slams the car door and doesn't look back. But she does go inside.

*

Midday, climbing my fire-escape private staircase, first thing I see's a bundle of clothing piled against my front door. Someone's dumped something? Or some one: shoes, legs, black skirt, a denim jacket, long black hair across her face and shoulders. Jenny? Yes, despite the dark hair. Sleeping on the doorstep, her head resting on her backpack!

JENNY

My eyes fly open: a guy in a well-known rugby shirt. 'Max! You're back!'

He grins that grin which can mean many things: here's amusement, and real pleasure, unthinkable kindness after my last remark on our journey away from the Manse. 'Baby, you came to see me?' He kind of twinkles with delight, knowing I did just that (although if I'd not rushed without thought I might've remembered my key and been able to get into my own house!) 'Home last night: I got your calls.'

'I got your rose,' I say, stretching my cramped limbs. Then reaching into my backpack, 'and I brought something your mum sent, and, can we talk?'

'Do we need to? Except, maybe about the hair? An evil disguise?'

We both laugh. 'A Goth disaster. Costume party. Don't ask! It'll grow out.'

'Jenny,' Max says.

We embrace for a long time, wordlessly recalling how good we are at this. So different to our last re-meeting, after a big, huge, break-up! Coming up for air, Max finally moves away to unlock the door, and we make it through to the flat. He makes me coffee and toast: moving a tiny blue teddy, I sit on the sofa. So tired, and relieved to know things are okay between us, I can't begin to talk about Daisy, or the sermon.

'Drove here overnight: Mum worried and told me not to. Better just— you know, if I could use your phone?'

When I tell her where I am, 'Crossed fingers for you, precious,' says Mum.

'You're not on call or anything?' I ask Max, once home's been satisfactorily dealt with.

'Job starts tomorrow. Prescribing a bath and sleep for you, now, though.'

'Show me the flat first—who's Teddy belong to?'

'Oh—haven't introduced you—he's my flatmate!'

'Hi, Teddy, I hope Max doesn't make you do all the shopping?'

'Of course I don't! Just most of it.'

The bedroom's en route to the bathroom. 'Same colour as the nursery at your sister Erin's place!'

'Welcoming.'

We lie on the bed: after a while, 'I'm all travel stained,' I say.

'No problem: when we first met, you'd just travelled all the way from Cornwall!'

*

Waking a second time, some church bell chiming the hour—six—I don't know where I am. Max is ending a call on the bedside phone, 'No worries,' he says, and I think: *no bath*. 'Did I fall asleep? In the middle of something?'

'Pretty much: you turned over when you'd had enough of me! Possibly a good idea?'

'Okay: but I drove all across southern England with a purpose, and all we've done is fool around.'

'I've seen Daisy: you can tell your family.'

'What? That's amazing, she came here? To find you? She always seemed to think you were—you know, empathetic.'

Max laughs, the old cynical kind of laugh. 'Our meeting was accidental.' But he tells me the whole chain of events. And I don't mockingly ask, 'meant?'

'So I let you know and you followed it up. And the jeans. That pun you made, awful.'

'Added two and two.'

'God.'

'That's what Daze said.'

'She's not going to—?'

'We'll have to wait and see: she knows what I think, and ... let's wait?'

'But ...'

'Give her a chance, Jen, leave her some self respect. Why else did you come over, what's my family been up to?'

'To see you, dumbo! And bring you this thing your mum sent. I respect your mum, you know. Whatever her religious views. Where's my stuff?'

MAX

I could almost have guessed, as she pulls it out: Mum's sent Jenny a copy of the tape she mailed to Erin.

'Listen, Max, I've heard it. Listen, and don't comment: it's almost Max-friendly.'

Cynically, I laugh.

'Can't you cut him some slack like you did me? Your dad's done the sort of U-turn mine never would. He's said sorry to a whole bunch of people in public.'

'A designer confession? The Congregation will deselect him!'

'Just listen to it? I did! D'you need to graze? I've got tortilla chips left from my journey!' She rustles about in her bag, and produces them. 'A bit broken, but eatable.'

Meanwhile, I'm puzzled: something's convinced her about my father's sermon. So, we get dressed, we make cocoa (Jenny's request), we put the tape in the player.

*

The intro's painful enough: Dad in recovered, *I have this message from God* mode, and Jenny across the kitchen table from me, hands clutched around her mug. '*From this pulpit today, I confess to you that I am that man.*'

Instinctively, my hands cover my face, shame on his behalf. 'Max?' She snaps the player off. 'Max: I couldn't do this but, somehow, he can?'

'Och, it's awful!'

'But in a positive way. I've heard it all, and you have to.' She clicks it back on.

> *God sent me a high truck, a motor boat, and a helicopter and still I refused to be rescued.*

Yes.

He pauses.

> *You have heard about Rachel Eccles. I failed her because I did not give to God what belongs to God, as we learned from this passage before. I made my own judgments, I failed to depend upon God.*
>
> *Let's elaborate. First that truck: my own dear Fiona. Many of you are already aware of her gifts and ministry in caring for and teaching special needs children. Fiona asked me about taking a degree in special educa-tion. I have steadfastly said no, believing I needed her in the home to help with my ministry.*
>
> *I listened to my own needs—I did not listen to Fiona and I did not listen to God.*

Yes: I see Mum's slaving in the house, her eternal baking, her toiling to be a perfect Pastor's Wife: her gentle submission to Dad's iron will. Which was what Jenny saw, when I proffered Gran's ring? Mrs Pastor's Son?

I know now that this stubbornness on my part has been sin and selfishness. I believe now that God does, indeed, want Fiona to proceed with developing her ministry and should have the preparation to do it.

I learned this even more acutely as my MS has suddenly worsened and Fiona has taken charge of my life. I have had to depend upon her completely—and in the process I have learned how incompletely I had been depending upon God.

I recall him wrestling in prayer alone in his study, that dreadful afternoon. Only God himself could wrestle with Dad, and win. Remember Euan mentioning I should try?

Now the motorboat. My son Max and I have been at odds for some time now over his choice of career path, which has hurt our relationship. I dug in my heels and insisted that I knew what he should and should not do. I have not truly listened to Max or seen how God might be leading him. Usurping God's own authority, I tried to lead him myself.

Dad pauses. Jenny grasps my hand, as I'm about to speak. 'Hang on—he's not finished!'

What's more, many years ago, and Max will remember this, I destroyed something precious to him. On an impulse. Thinking I was obeying scripture. For that, I am very sorry.

'See: the microscope!'

Finally, Max brought a fine young woman, Jenny, home to meet us. They are engaged.

Jenny doesn't loosen her grasp. Our eyes meet. I want to look away. She nods. Oh, hell: what's Dad up to?

Contrary to Scripture's expectations of us, I was inhospitable to Jenny. I did not give her a chance, because I discovered, not who Jenny is, but who her father is. I disobeyed God in failing to offer her both true Christian hospitality and true Christian love.

If ever anything was toe-curling. 'Is he serious? Aren't you ready to crawl away?' I say.

'But he means it. My Dad would never, ever, admit he'd done anything wrong. In public! Totally a no-go area!'

'It's not unknown in the denomination: we're all supposed to keep each other in check. He's acting before they throw him out.'

'You really think?'

'How can I know? He's a performer.'

'Isn't that a bit cynical?'

'Yes. Because I don't want it to be a performance.'

'I think your Mum was impressed: she'd know.'

'Aye.'

... The helicopter. Rachel came to me desperate, in despair. I didn't listen or acknowledge the danger she was facing. I refused to believe Colin was other than a good Christian husband, and would never hurt his wife. Even though I had experience of domestic incidents, outside of the faith.

Scripture teaches us that 'if we confess our sins, God is faithful and just to forgive us our sins and to cleanse us from all unrighteousness'. Today, in God's presence and among my brothers and sisters in Christ I confess that I have sinned, I have failed.

I know that if in contrition and penitence I confess my sins and turn away from them God does forgive. I have failed you, the congregation that God has given me, and I need your forgiveness as well as my family's.

I can't speak.

If you can forgive me, I ask that your response be that you go home and ask God to help you see the areas in your own lives that you have withheld from him, and ask him to help you amend your ways.

'Give to God the things that are God's.' What we owe to God is the whole of our lives.

May I now and always give to God that which is God's—completely. And may the God of all mercy, grace and love forgive me and make of me a better husband, father, friend, and pastor. And may God grant you a similar grace.

Thanks be to God.

Silence falls, except for the faint hissing of the tape.

What'm I supposed to do? I see them all, faces tilted up towards him, in that cool, green light of First Truly on a summer morning.

'Max?' Jenny squeezes my hand. 'You see? He's asking *you* to forgive *him*: aren't you pleased?'

'*... please stand and sing the final hymn, Be Thou My Vision,*' says Dad's voice, and they do, but I'm torn between quietly disposing of the awesome thing and praising God that he's shown my arrogant preacher father the light.

And catch myself there: me, his arrogant son.

'Well?'

'He's abdicated. I need time to think it through.'

I struggle with a response to my father's awful soul-bearing. Turn away from it by re-focusing on Jenny's life. 'I never asked: what did Roslin say?'

'That they didn't want me.'

'I'm sorry. Bummer.'

'I'll talk to Dr Woods. Dad offered me work. Yours apologized about the microscope. It's not only your dad who can say sorry. I was horrible ... I hadn't considered what all that stuff would do to you: Rachel being attacked, and the MS, and the whole visit to your family. I only saw how efficiently you dealt with it. Like a doctor. I'm just sorry I didn't trust you.'

'I'm sorry I sprung a quite inappropriate question on you.'

'I could've handled it better. It was daft to run away. The rose was beautiful. Your note: I didn't know what to say.'

'Serafina: she didn't make it. Through the op.'

'I am so, so sorry. It doesn't have to be ... it wasn't, you know, symbolic?'

JENNY

Max stands and moves away from the table, puts our mugs in the sink. We're poised in a fine-tuned balance. I'll be really careful this time.

But then, he looks so bereft, my arms kind of fling themselves around him. And we stand silently close, and Max buries his face in my horrible dyed hair.

We stay like that for several quiet minutes. Then, break apart, agreeing to go out and find a nice quiet place to have a meal.

Where we put together our two ends of Daze's story, her intentions, the probable reasons Persephone was so flawed. We're still interested in how flawed, and the details. And, how she brought us back together.

'Did you really forget to bring your key?' Max asks.

'Yes, I really did! Left straight from work—at a fish restaurant, would you believe. I didn't have a moment. Hence the black and white waitress gear? And I have to be back for work on Wednesday: they hardly gave me time off!'

Max says, 'I know how we can break into your house. And retrieve a key. Your father taught me.'

'Figures. You broke in to ... collect my jeans?'

'Guilty. I nicked them from your room. I wanted to—'

'I think I know. I'm the elephant's child with the insatiable curiosity. It was sweet of you. He's arranged to have Daze's DNA analysed?'

'Yep. So, if you want to?'

'I don't know. Did you keep—you know—what you offered me before in the little box? That I was so awful about?'

'I may have it somewhere. Back at the flat.'

FEE. THE MANSE

Late that night, the phone rings. And Fee, lest Alisdair's disturbed, hastens to answer it. 'Max?'

'I heard his tape. With Jenny.'

This is all Fee needs to hear. She discerns from his tone that Max has accepted Alisdair's attempts at reconciliation over the microscope. 'Of course, your father's used that story about the rising waters before, the Congregation's heard it. But to admit that he had not perceived his own need for rescue, that's new. He'll not admit it again, of course. All in the past now! But I perceive he's learned a wee bit. There's a difference in him.'

'He's going the right way, is he?'

'Going the right way? He's stronger every day now. Euan's well pleased. And the specialist. You'll be going to Cameron's baptism? It's not First Truly of course but ...'

'We'll see. I'll consult the rotas at work.'

Ever hopeful, Fee smiles with her voice, accepting Max's gentle refusal. 'That's good. We'll see you when we do, then. You'll pass my best wishes to Jenny?'

Ending the call, Fee sets the receiver in its cradle, and picks up, from the telephone table, the brochure for her diploma course. Can hardly wait for September.

JENNY. THURSDAY, CHAPEL HOUSE

Hat's gone to a festival with her friends. I'm here alone with Mum and Des.

'We thought you'd gone to Cambridge to stop Daisy doing something destructive. But you've not seen her. And you've come back having decided to tie yourself legally to a preacher's family—I know, a very successful evangelist, but a preacher all the same. Sweetie, have you lost the power of rational thought?'

'God,' I say.

'Yes, exactly—God. Not someone we expected you to ...' I give Mum a look, and she changes the subject. 'What about Dr Woods, what did he say?'

'About my future? About when I've got five babies under five, like you keep insisting will happen to me? And an ex who won't acknowledge divorce because of his religion?'

'About—your career, funding, research, precious.'

'Could you get off my case? We've had this conversation twice already, in twenty four hours! Seems there's no middle way we can agree about.'

'If I could understand, why ever are you doing this to us?' Mum says, pouring herself a glass of wine and virulently stirring the roux that's to become a sauce for cauliflower cheese.

'Hormones?' I try. Disappointed by their minds, as closed as Alisdair Mullins's. 'Do you ever stop to think you're religious too?'

'Religious?'

'I think it's called secular humanism, isn't it?'

'Oh!' Mum laughs, relieved. 'I've made a joke!'

'You were so supportive before. When I thought we'd broken up. You explained how Max's training makes him act, over the caring for his father bit. You treated me as an equal, you've spent years emphasising I've a mind of my own I can make up how I choose, and you'll respect my choice.'

'Sweetie,' (she slops wine into the now-creamy sauce, along with pile of Mature Farmhouse Cheddar), 'I thought—'

'You thought, but didn't say, *good, she'll be thoroughly put off by her visit to the Manse. She'll see hypocrisy for herself!* Actually, it's not only evangelicals who keep secrets, and play mind games.' Yes, Mum takes my point: her face drops its confident smile. 'You hoped it'd all burn out. In fact, that's it, you wrote me a prescription for the Pill. Wear out your passions together, you thought. Have sex. Just don't take it anywhere long-term. Well, maybe I'm marrying into a family very like this one. He's kind and intelligent, he loves me, he's great at the work he does, I've seen him at it. He even cared about Daisy. He loves his family: that's why—oh, forget it! His mum's brilliant even if his father's weird.

'And I have to go to work now: four more evenings serving fish dinners.'

'Jenny?' She says something about why she married Des. But I'm already out of the door.

*

It's sad to be leaving home on a sour note, a week later. But I'm not sticking around to be pulled in two directions like Max was. Under pressure to give the ring back and betray Max the way he once betrayed me. And go to work with Dad. Hattie told me when she got back, 'Dad was here while you were gone.'

'Really? Nobody said.'

'He was going to fly the company plane up to Scotland.'

'What? Why? How come you know and they don't?'

''Cos I wanted to go with him, meet Val. He said no go, he had somebody with him and stuff to do, confidential. He's gone to Edinburgh, I saw his flight plans. I thought you knew.'

'That'd be Karen, who was with him. At least he didn't bring her here. Why would I know?'

'He was talking to Max. While you must've been together.'

No worries. Sunday late afternoon. 'They're plotting something. They've left me out of the loop!'

'What?'

'Daisy. Max found her.'

'Max found her how?'

I explain the story he told me. 'So he took her by the scruff and marched her to Dad's office. Before I even arrived in Cambridge. They'll have—actually, they'll have dealt with her better than I could.'

'So were you right, about her art project?'

'Nobody's confirmed that to me. But would Dad have taken steps otherwise?'

Mum comes back from the surgery, especially to see me off. Well, almost. She did have a home visit nearby. 'Don't totally disappear,' she says.

'I love Cornwall too much. Now. After all the years we've lived here.'

'I suppose you have to follow your heart. But don't give up your career before it's begun.'

'If you think that, you don't know me. Why was it you married Des, Mum?'

'Because he was kind, he loved me, and he cared about Daisy.'

'Oh. Okay. Like Max really.' At least we hug goodbye.

Epilogue

'So here's your property, kiddo,' says my dad, handing me a parcel.

'My old jeans! Thanks, Dad!'

We're at the smart Sappho's Garden café, half of a converted barn—the other half's the Mill Gallery, where Daze will be hosting a private view in an hour or so's time. On the table, spread out between the remains of our cream tea, is a computer printout.

'So, Daze Potter, Shane McShane, dysmorphic child: we have karyotypes and DNA profiles linking them as a family. We've got the whole thing pulled together.'

Clearly Dad gathered most of the facts right away, soon as he knew about Persephone. 'Could've saved us lots of hassle,' I comment.

'I've always respected your desire for independence, seeing we're in the same field.'

Yes. But he also chatted to Nicholson! That is Dad. No point in hoping he'll change.

'We each had a piece of the picture,' he says. 'Okay, I knew she found it exciting that all living things share the ancient genes that organise embryonic development. But I couldn't have guessed she'd think up this 'conception art' from that chat we had in the Sculpture Garden. And, you know? I like that pun. Wicked.'

'Yeah, but …' I admonish him. 'And you never wondered why she asked you for work in Colombia?'

Dad spreads his hands in that characteristic gesture. 'She talked about pre-Hispanic art, and archaeology. How could I guess it was a ruse?'

'You didn't share her growing up! Daze is full of stories. Always has been, I could list examples. Even to get herself back to Sennen, she spun me a tale about her bus being impounded—she doesn't need to do this, she just does it.'

'So—was she never abandoned at Glastonbury?' Max asks.

'Oh, that's true. Val read it in the national press—unless Daze made it up and sold it to the newspaper, age five!' We laugh.

243

Then, 'But it's quite clear what she did once she got to Colombia. She'd been told that summer she'd need IVF if she was ever to have a child. She decided to access a clinic, yours, in a country she was fairly certain wasn't regulated. She seduced a technician with her stories. Someone who'd shared her kind of early childhood. And had something to hide: a drug habit. Like you said, Dad, drugs not allowed on site. But in Colombia, hardly difficult to obtain. Shane had revealed something, probably one of their rainforest trips, which she could blab to his employer about if he refused her.'

'And was an ambitious bastard wanting to run before he could walk, push boundaries I wasn't ready to contemplate. It was Daze's appalling million-to-one luck he's a relative. I was amazed when Jenny told me. The stats on that…. But I guess it is nonetheless possible that one day we'd give someone treatment from an anonymous donor and discover that they were a relative. Though their stuff would one hopes have been screened.'

As we think about this one, Max adds, 'But the whole irony of the situation is that this wouldn't have been an issue as far as her original plan was concerned. Daze thought Shane had access to the bank and was going to use screened donor sperm. He was probably so scared of her he didn't dare admit that he was too junior to have the door code. It never crossed her mind he'd pop outside and donate his own! She was spitting with fury when she told me about finding out.'

I can imagine that scene. 'I wouldn't be him! Incidentally, where's Shane now?'

'What happens to employees who mess with the product?' Dad says.

'Okay: you've dealt with him. What happens when Daisy catches up with him is the more scary bit.'

'We see here that they both carry a balanced chromosomal abnormality which, if it becomes unbalanced during meiosis, would lead to a fetus with a known syndrome. Even if Shane hadn't had a drug habit, they'd a four in one chance of a malformed infant. Add into the mix recreational drug use damaging his sperm.' Dad jabs at one of the chromosomes on the printout with his finger. Recalling aunt Val's gesture, showing me the pictures of Old Tam, the boatman. (Or shepherd.) 'Shane's DNA, as we see, also has this unbalanced translocation—'

'—And we have an inviable infant born with a spectrum of abnormalities not seen before,' continues Max. 'As a paediatrician, I was of course fascinated, incredibly tempted to discover all I could. Then torn in two because I knew the patient. Why do we think Daze decided to continue with her project?'

Max and Dad both look to me for answers.

'I think, really, because she thought it was democratic to continue. You know, Persephone, if she was human, should be counted as of as much worth as any other baby?'

Dad snorts. 'Unthinkable. There are limits!'

Max says, thoughtfully, 'No, John, I respect her view. What I don't think she should have done is decide to display Persephone to public view. The two decisions are separable.'

Dad laughs, not unkindly. 'The pastor's son—pro-life, Max?'

And it's Max's turn to shrug. 'Just my opinion.'

The waitress comes by with our bill. We all reach together for our credit cards, cash, whatever, and laughing, Dad pays. 'Last time, Kiddo— you're his responsibility now!'

And I say, 'No. Whatever gave you that idea?' Glancing at the price of our cream tea, knowing Penzance prices from a host of holiday jobs, I calculate how much profit they must make here.

'Half an hour's break and then: we see what she's made of it.'

'She found a beautiful perfect girl embryo at the Drey—whose?' I ask. 'Like, just anyone's? Did they give consent?'

'Does that matter?'

Dad's secretive look alerts me. 'Dad? An artist has to push the boundaries—so does a fertility expert—whose baby?'

'You know nothing about this, Kiddo. Or Max. Karen's had a bit of trouble conceiving …'

'So Hat and I can expect an announcement within the next year. A step-sister. Figures.'

'See you in half an hour,' Dad says, wending towards the exit, stuffing the bill for our meal into his wallet as he goes. Max and I go for a walk outside, along the reed beds, under the wide, cool Fenland sky.

*

The Mill Gallery's packed with champagne-drinking, cigar-smoking women. Fewer men. And some humps under sheets. 'Where's the art?' Max asks me, sotto voce.

'Hmm: I think we're in for a performance, and the rest's under those?'

Lights are dimmed, a red glow illuminates the gallery. We guests form a wide semicircle. *Performance art, to introduce and enhance static displays.* SixPack appear, Daze and her fellow exhibitors, difficult to tell whether their bodies are naked or enclosed in very tight, very diaphanous suits. To loud, persistent, mechanical noise, and with mechanical movement, in perfect time with one another, they mime a factory production line. Followed by cartwheels, arabesques, fire-eating.

Max looks to me, bemused. 'What is this?'

'A feminist statement,' I whisper in his ear. 'Possibly the formation of the embryo?' Though I didn't know Daze could eat fire, I'm not surprised.

The room darkens further. One woman crawls across the otherwise empty floor. Groaning.

A placard appears, inviting us to '*Groan!*' I can't help it: I rather enjoy the lunacy of participating. But Max needs a nudge. 'Hey, you've been there: do it!'

A few feeble groans escape as we watch, to the sound of whales communicating under water, a second woman emerging between the legs of the first. Then arms around each other, we disguise that we're shaking with mirth with our joint groaning, as on stage the birthing repeats until all six women are visible again. It's incredibly athletic and clever. A ripple of applause.

They bow. Daze steps forward. One of the others drapes a shimmering full-length cape around her. 'My working title was *Daddy's Girl*,' she says. 'And my concept was Conception Art. I'd like to hugely thank my Sponsor, Dr John Guthrie of the Drey Clinic,' (she gestures, Dad appears, cigar in one hand, champagne glass in the other), 'for his help in so precisely clarifying my remit.'

Oh, Daze, so ironic a barb! And I hiss in Max's ear, 'That's practically a quote from him, about his Colombian clinic. He so loves giving people what they want most. And then basking in their undying gratitude!'

'Your dad needs to make people happy. He admires her chutzpah. And wants to help her.' Max holds me close against his side, adding, 'They need each other.'

'He's got Karen, remember?'

'And my sister Jenny,' Daze adds, picking me out of the crowd (a spotlight rests momentarily on me like a halo), 'for making certain I pushed that envelope. Without her, this project would've lacked drama and suspense.'

And how!

'My Installation, *From Here to Perfection*.' Daze steps back and whips off the cover of a lumpy object revealing that female torso, the legs apart. A video screen inset within the abdomen. As we watch, suddenly, out from between the legs flies a real bird!

Enormous applause.

Daze's smile, in our direction, is huge. Her bowing exaggerated. 'Thank you very much.'

Then the video begins: soft seductive music, a perfectly filmed *in vitro* fertilization. I can hardly listen to Daze for watching my new stepsister becoming ... or maybe this isn't my step sister, it's someone who could've been her twin, but isn't. And Dad's voice has taken over from Daze's.

'... will be positioned in the foyer of the Drey for the next six months: where clients can watch the process of the cells of a perfect embryo multiplying: to become the perfect flawless baby.'

And then, 'It can't be! That's Addenbrooke's—'

'That's the delivery suite!'

'That's Daze!'

'What's she thinking ... has she tricked him? Us? Where's Dad?'

The camera—mine—featuring the place where the baby should emerge, leaves off once we see the head crowning, and pans the room.

It's bouncing all over the place ... my hand grips onto Max's, and sweat prickles between my breasts. 'She can't have, can she?'

'I hope not, I don't think—'

I expect any moment the paediatrician's voice, '*What do we have?*'

A black second, and … a panorama of my photos, and her photos: flipping through in quick succession, Hat and me, when we were small, the Commune families, Lily, her kids and her friends, the Greenham women … even my grandmother Ianthe, who campaigned for contraceptives for unmarried women, is there!

And Daze is bowing and accepting everyone's praises. And Dad is grinning. And how come Daze got hold of these photos of my childhood?

*

Max and I are slipping away from the limelight. The moon is rising. My hand fits into Max's as we walk to the car park. 'I liked your comment on Persephone. I liked it that you didn't think she ought to be just chucked away like rubbish.'

'Daze … when I took the baby in, something happened, like the veil was turned back. Just for a few moments, and I saw the real Daisy. And … the real Persephone. I suppose.'

'Special.' I put my arm around him. Laughter comes from the gallery.

Don't belong to a book group? If you give a copy of this book to a friend, you then have an excuse to share your reactions to this story over a cup of coffee, a glass of wine or a lunch hour. You two might even invite a wider circle to join in, and that would be … a book group, ready to share thoughts on this and other books.

1. Jenny is moved by the use of weaving and spinning imagery to describe meiosis, the sorting and uniting of the strands of DNA from each parent at fertilisation. Will this bring her closer to Max's philosophy of life? Do you think she is losing objectivity or gaining insight?

2. Jenny says she and her mother Caroline are 'moving on to a more adult mother/daughter relationship'. What is your assessment of Caro's relationship with Jenny? Does it progress in the book? What does Hattie add to our picture of the family?

3. Jenny appears to have a good relationship with her stepfather, Des. But which father is more worthy of respect by the end of the story: Des, or Jenny's biological father, Dr Guthrie?

4. How does each of them perceive being a dad?

5. 'Cross stitch, how apt,' Fee thinks. Daze painted a child crucified on a woman. What do these images say about the lives of women and children, and/or how they see themselves? Does the image of crucifixion (the way Christ was killed) speak to us today? What image would you choose?

5. Daze's story is told in the third person. Why do you think that might be? Do we ever get a real understanding of her motivations? What do you think they might be?

6. Do you think Max simply gave into family pressure on him to become a GP, or is it his own considered decision? Suppose he had followed his earlier school ambitions and pursued a career in music?

7. Max is obviously drawn to research into genetic malformations and their prevention. Why does he capitulate to Nicholson's hints about the ethical side of the research? Should he have? What motivates Max's practice of medicine?

8. Max observes that 'what goes on at home isn't a faith, it's a culture.' Has he only just gained this insight? If not, at what stage in his life do you think he began to see it? What is the difference between a faith and a culture?

9. Max's father, Alisdair, believes he has a vocation. How much do you trust his confession near the end of the story?

10. Jenny decides to marry Max after all. How do you envisage their future together?